MissMusketeer

BY THE SAME AUTHOR

Around the World on Five Sous (with H. Chabrillat) – translated by by Brian Stableford

Miss Musketeer

by
Paul d'Ivoi

Translated from the French by
Stuart Gelzer

A Black Coat Press Book

ISBN 978-1-64932-108-4. First Printing: January 2022. Published by Black
Coat Press, an imprint of Hollywood Comics.com, LLC, P.O. Box 17270, Enci-
no, CA 91416.

TABLE OF CONTENTS

VOYAGES EXCENTRIQUES

PAUL D'IVOI

Miss
Mousqueterr

ANCIENNE LIBRAIRIE FURNE

Introduction

Miss Mousqueterr [Miss Musketeer] was first serialized in the weekly magazine *Le Journal des Voyages et des Aventures de Terre et Mer* (a.k.a. the *Journal des Voyages*) from 7 October 1906 to 21 July 1907. It was then collected in book form the same year by publisher Boivin & Cie.

Paul Deleutre (1856-1915), who signed all his published works with the nom-de-plume of Paul d'Ivoi, wrote a series of 21 volumes, collectively entitled *"Les Voyages Excentriques"* [The Eccentric Voyages], clearly inspired by Jules Verne's *Voyages Extraordinaires*, most of which were first published as feuilleton serials before being republished as books. The series started with the classic *Les Cinq Sous de Lavarède* (1894), translated by Brian Stableford as *Around the World on Five Sous*, available from Black Coat Press (ISBN 978-1-61227-369-3).

Paul Deleutre began his writing career as a reporter for *Le Figaro*. His name crops up, amongst other places, on the preface of a work published in 1860 by Antoine Gandon, *Récits du Brigadier Flageolet* [Tales of Brigadier Flageolet]. However, it is possible that the same pseudonym was being used by his father, Charles Deleutre, who also published two books under his own name, or by his uncle, Édouard Deleutre. The overlap in usage causes some confusion in the catalogue of the Bibliothèque Nationale, because it is also attached to four dramatic works produced in the 1880s: *Jeu de Dame* [Checkers] (1881), *Le Marabout d'Aïn Sebka* [The Marabout of Aïn Sebka] (1884), *Le Tigre de la Rue Tronchet* [The Tiger of Rue Tronchet] (1887), *Le Mari de ma Femme* [My Wife's Husband] (1888) and *Une Infusion de Fidélité* [An Infusion of Fidelity] (1888). The only major works that predate *Around the World on Five Sous* are four otherwise unrelated novels: *Les Juifs à travers les Âges* [The Jews Throughout the Ages] (1890), *Le Capitaine Jean* [Captain Jean] (1890), *La Femme au Diadème Rouge* [The Woman with a Red Diadem] (1892) and *Olympia et Cie.* [Olympia & Co.] (1894).

In his heyday, Paul d'Ivoi's feuilletons were published in *Le Petit Journal* and its rival, *Le Matin*, but also in the weekly *Le Journal des Voyages*. D'Ivoi also wrote two science fiction novels in collaboration with "Colonel Royet," a man who went on to write other novels after Deleutre's death, but about whom little seems to be known:[1] These are *La Patrie en Danger* [Our Homeland in Peril] (1904), a Future War story, and *Un, la Mystérieuse* [The Mysterious

---

[1] He may be Maximin Léonce Royet, who cited his rank as Capitaine and Commandant in various books about the scouting movement.

Number One] (1905), as well as a three-part series featuring Special Agent X-323,[2] a.k.a. The Faceless Man (1909-10).

Paul d'Ivoi's bread and butter nevertheless remained his *Voyages Excentriques*, a series which he continued until his death, producing one book a year. It was the most successful French series of its kind after Verne's.

In some ways, Paul d'Ivoi's works exhibit all the worst features of popular fiction of its times. They are derivative, slapdash, uneven, full of outrageous co-incidences and, if the pattern of its events is considered with a clinical eye, rather silly, but none of that seemed to have mattered to its readers who loved the books.

Most of them—if not all—have enjoyed an enormous and enduring popularity, including many adaptations into film and television. The balance between comedy and melodrama, the extraordinary perseverance against all odds of its heroes, the charm of its virginal heroines, the Machiavellian, mustache-twirling schemes of its dastardly villains, and his exuberant plots featuring exotic means of travel by land, sea and air, all made for an entertaining, easy and relaxing read.

Paul d'Ivoi never matched Verne for ingenuity, verve or invention, but then very few of his imitators did. However, he contrived to reproduce adequately the essence of Vernian appeal for a new generation of readers, updating many of Verne's concepts as opposed to creating original ones himself.

Cousin de Lavarède [Lavarède's Cousin] (1897) features an airship with mobile wings; *Jean Fanfare* (1897) employs an amphibious mobile fortress; the eponymous *Corsaire Triplex* (1898) uses a super-submarine; *Le Docteur Mystère* [Doctor Mystery] (1900) displays an array of novel mechanical devices; *Millionnaire Malgré Lui* [Millionaire Despite Himself] (1905) features a radiation projector; and even more fantastic weaponry is employed in *L'Aéroplane Fantôme* [The Phantom Airplane] (1910).

One aspect of Paul d'Ivoi's oeuvre that has aged badly is its blatant, outrageous xenophobia. Some of it is, of course, par for the course for the times and present in many 19th century/early 20th century works: looking down upon Africans, treated as children if not worse; mistrusting fiendish Asians and their ever-present Yellow Peril... But d'Ivoi was über-chauvinistic in his outlook towards the world outside his beloved France. In fact, he often mistrusted the British and the Germans (admittedly with good reasons at that time) more than he did the sympathetic natives, and in his books he sometimes sided with Asians over their Colonial Overlords because of this.

There are, of course, historical reasons and context for such feelings, especially in works written just before World War I, and Paul d'Ivoi is hardly the

---

[2] For some reason, X-323 was renamed Z-212 when the series was reprinted in 1914.

worst offender! Nevertheless, we have thought it best to soften such language, especially when it is totally gratuitous and not relevant in terms of plot, in order to not offend our readers needlessly. In fact, except for one expensive archival facsimile edition, there hasn't been an unexpurgated edition of his books in France since World War II.

Finally, Black Coat Press does not intend to translate and publish all of Paul d'Ivoi's works. In addition to the seminal *Around the World on Five Sous*, we intend to limit ourselves to three novels: *Le Docteur Mystère*, *Miss Mousqueterr* and *Les Dompteurs de l'Or*, which, for a variety of perhaps subjective reasons, seem to us to be the most interesting from the perspective of the evolution of the *roman scientifique*.

Jean-Marc Lofficier

Bibliography of "*Les Voyages Excentriques*"

(only first serialization and first book publication are listed.)

1. Les Cinq Sous de Lavarède (co-written with Henri Chabrillat) [*Around the World on Five Sous*]
* First serialization in *Le Petit Journal*, 24 August-27 December 1893.
* First book publication: Furne, Jouvet et Cie., 1894.
Characters: First appearance of Lavarède.

2. Le Sergent Simplet à travers les Colonies Françaises [*Sgt. Simpleton Across the French Colonies*]
* First serialization in *Le Petit Journal*, 26 May-8 August 1895.
* First book publication: Furne, Jouvet et Cie., 1895.
Characters: Even though some characters are identified as Lavarède's "cousins," this book is only marginally part of the Lavarède series.

3. Cousin de Lavarède! a.k.a. **Le Bolide de Lavarède** [*Lavarede's Cousin / Lavarède's Bolide*]
* First book publication: Furne, Jouvet et Cie., 1897.
Characters: Second appearance of Lavarède. The hero is a genuine cousin of Lavarède and the two are reunited at the end of the novel.

4. Jean Fanfare [*Jean Fanfare*]
* First book publication: Société d'Édition et de Librairie, 1897.

5. Corsaire Triplex
* First book publication: Société d'Édition et de Librairie, 1898.
Characters: Third appearance of Lavarède.

6. La Capitaine Nilia
* First book publication: Société d'Édition et de Librairie, 1899.
Characters: Fourth and final appearance of Lavarède.

7. Le Docteur Mystère
* First book publication: Combet et Cie., 1900.
Characters: First appearance of Cigale.

8. Cigale en Chine [*Cigale in China*]
* First serialization in *Le Français*, from 3 December 1900 to 8 March 1901.
* First book publication: Combet et Cie., 1901.

Characters: Second appearance of Cigale.

9. Massiliague de Marseille
* First book publication: Combet et Cie., 1902.
Characters: Third appearance of Cigale.

10. Les Semeurs de Glace [*The Sowers of Ice*]
* First serialization in *Le Journal des Voyages*, from 7 December 1902 to 28 June 1903.
* First book publication: Combet et Cie., 1903.
Characters: Fourth and final appearance of Cigale.

11. Le Serment de Daalia [*Daalia's Oath*]
* First book publication: Combet et Cie., 1904.

12. Millionnaire Malgré Lui a.k.a. **Le Prince Virgule** [*Millionaire Despite Himself / Prince Comma*]
* First serialization in *Le Journal des Voyages*, from 6 November 1904 to 25 June 1905 under the title *Le Prince Virgule*.
* First book publication: Combet et Cie., 1905, under the title: *Millionnaire Malgré Lui*.
Characters: First appearance of Dodekhan.

13. Le Maître du Drapeau Bleu [*The Master of the Blue Flag*]
* First serialization in *Le Matin*, from 25 July to 2 November 1906.
* First book publication: Société d'Édition Contemporaine, 1907.
Characters: Second appearance of Dodekhan.

14. Miss Mousqueterr
* First serialization in *Le Journal des Voyages*, from 7 October 1906 to 21 July 1907.
* First book publication: Boivin et Cie., 1907.
Characters: Third and final appearance of Dodekhan.

15. Jud Allan, Roi des « Lads » a.k.a. **La Fiancée du Diable** [*Jud Allan. King of the Lads / The Devil's Fiancée*].
* First serialization in *Le Matin*, from 21 July to 19 November 1908, under the title: *La Fiancée du Diable*.
* First book publication: Boivin et Cie., 1908, under the title: *Judd Allan (Roi des Lads)*.

16. Le Roi du Radium a.k.a. **La Course au Radium** [*The King of Radium / The Radium Rush*]

* First serialization in *Le Journal des Voyages*, from 18 October 1908 to 11 July 1909, under the title: *Le Roi du Radium*.
* First book publication: Boivin et Cie., 1909, under the title: *La Course au Radium*.

17. L'Aéroplane Fantôme [*The Phantom Airplane*]
* First serialization in *Le Petit Journal*, from 24 February to 21 June 1910.
* First book publication: Boivin et Cie., 1910.

18. Les Voleurs de Foudre [*The Thieves of Lightning*]
* First serialization in *Le Journal des Voyages*, from 20 October 1907 to 21 Lune 1908, under the title: *L'Automobile de Verre*; then from 17 October 1909 to 15 May 1910, under the title: *Les Trois Demoiselles Pickpocket*.
* First book publication: Boivin et Cie., 1911.

19. Message du Mikado [*Message from the Mikado*]
* First serialization in *Le Journal des Voyages*, from 5 November 1911 to 12 May 1912, under the title: *L'Ambassadeur Extraordinaire*.
* First book publication: Boivin et Cie., 1912

20. Les Dompteurs de l'Or a.k.a. **Le Chevalier Illusion** [*The Gold Tamers / The Knight of Illusions*]
* First serialization in *Le Journal des Voyages*, from 15 December 1912 to 8 June 1913, under the title: *Le Chevalier Illusion*.
* First book publication: Boivin et Cie., 1913, under the title: *Les Dompteurs de l'Or*.

21. Match de Milliardaire [*The Billionaires' Match*]
* First serialization in *Le Journal des Voyages*, from 9 November 1913 to 31 May 1914, under the title: *L'Évadé Malgré Lui*.
* First book publication: Boivin et Cie., 1917, under the title: *Match de Milliardaire*.

The Story So Far...

Much of what happens in *Le Maître du Drapeau Bleu* [The Master of the Blue Flag], the preceding volume in Paul d'Ivoi's *Voyages Excentriques*, is recapped in fragments sprinkled throughout *Miss Musketeer*, but the emphasis is different: in *Miss Musketeer*, more sci-fi, in *Blue Flag*, more geopolitics.

Nevertheless, here is a quick plot summary of *The Master of the Blue Flag*.

Newlyweds Sara and Lucien de La Roche-Sonnaille, honeymooning in Holland, overhear two Tibetans, Log and his sidekick San, plotting to attack a Turkic[3] man named Dodekhan, so that Log can replace him as Master of the Blue Flag, a pan-Asian secret society.

Sara and Lucien try to warn Dodekhan, but all three are captured and held prisoner on an unusual, electric-powered ship, the *Maharatsu*.

With Lucien as his hostage, Log sends Sara to the Peace Conference at The Hague[4] to trick two girls into getting on the ship: Mona Labianov and Lotus Pearl Asaki, whose fathers are respectively the Russian and Japanese delegates at the conference. Both fathers have instructions to obey orders from Dodekhan—but they don't know the Blue Flag has been taken over by Log, who now sends them orders to torpedo a generous peace deal. Both daughters are after Dodekhan: Mona, because she fell in love with him when he saved her father during the Russo-Japanese War;[5] Lotus Pearl only because the Japanese Empress told her to marry Dodekhan to secure a Blue Flag-Japan alliance.

---

[3] From Turkestan, a historical region in Central Asia corresponding to the regions of Transoxiana and Xinjiang.

[4] The First Hague Conference came from a proposal on 24 August 1898 by Russian Tsar Nicholas II. Nicholas and Count Mikhail Nikolayevich Muravyov, his foreign minister, were instrumental in initiating the conference. The conference opened on 18 May 1899, the Tsar's birthday. The treaties, declarations, and final act of the conference were signed on 29 July of that year, and they entered into force on 4 September 1900.

[5] The Russo-Japanese War was fought between the Empire of Japan and the Russian Empire during 1904 and 1905 over rival imperial ambitions in Manchuria and Korea. The major theatres of military operations were the Liaodong Pen-

The trick works, and—with five prisoners (Dodekhan, the newlyweds, and the two girls)—the *Maharatsu* sails to the Far East.

Now for some geopolitical backstory: Dodekhan's late father created the Blue Flag to liberate Asia peacefully from European colonial domination. He recruited Log, the leader of a Tibetan tribe, the Prayer Engravers. That was a bad move, because Log secretly aims to turn the European powers against each other and produce a bloodbath that will leave Asia not just free, but world-conquering.

Dodekhan (who shares his late father's peaceful vision) was chosen over Log to be the next Master of the Blue Flag... but Log is now fixing that.

He offers an exclusive Blue Flag alliance to both Russia and Japan (both countries expect dominance in Asia), to be sealed by the secret marriage of Dodekhan with both girls—performed while all three are sedated, so no one knows whose marriage license was first and therefore legitimate.

(Log tells each girl, and her father, that she's the real bride.)

At Kiautschou Bay, the German colonial concession on China's Shandong Peninsula, Log controls a secret society of Chinese factory workers, the Amber Masks. He means to set Germany and France at war over their Asian colonies. But his plans are overheard by two Chinese orphans, Merry and Twinkle, who were rescued long ago by Dodekhan—and who have a pair of tame black panthers.

Though they're devoted to their savior, Dodekhan, the children pretend to be loyal to Log. Log orders the Amber Masks to rise up and murder their German overlords—but Dodekhan (now held captive in a cave with Lucien) gets Merry and Twinkle to post a signal that reduces the order to mere looting.

Now follows a long sequence in which Dodekhan and Log, each claiming to be the Master of the Blue Flag, countermand each other's orders, Log always aiming to incite bloodshed, Dodekhan always working to make peace. Log has to keep Dodekhan alive because he possesses certain secret Blue Flag codes that Log needs; he uses threats against his hostage Mona (with whom Dodekhan is in love) as leverage.

Dodekhan tries to contact his mysterious Central Exchange, using wireless video and audio telecommunication (almost the only sci-fi element included), but Log has changed the access codes.

After convincing the Germans at Kiautschou Bay that the French provoked the looting, Log heads south with his Amber Masks, and with his hostages, Sara and Mona and Lotus Pearl, to attack French Tonkin,[6] so the French will blame the Germans and start an inter-European war.

---

insula and Mukden in Southern Manchuria, and the seas around Korea, Japan, and the Yellow Sea.

[6] Tonkin was a French protectorate encompassing modern-day Northern Vietnam.

Merry and Twinkle (still posing as Log loyalists) rescue Sara and Mona from a monastery Log burned down, but now Dodekhan, Lucien and Lotus Pearl have fallen back into the villain's clutches.

Sara and Mona reach Tonkin and warn the French troops, who have mined the border at the Kilua Pass and can blow up the invaders. But Dodekhan, Lucien and Lotus Pearl are still prisoners, and are now used as human shields. Will Sara and Mona give the signal to blow up the Kilua Pass and kill their beloved? They do—out of patriotic duty.

The pass and the enemy blow up... but not before Merry and Twinkle lead the prisoners to a cave, where all survive—except for Lotus Pearl, who is crushed by a falling boulder.

(That ends the dispute over who's really married to Dodekhan.)

After many more adventures (tigers, etc.), Dodekhan and the four Europeans are reunited in Haiphong. Log's electric ship *Maharatsu* is in the harbor, un-manned and unguarded. Dodekhan hijacks it, and they all sail around into the Bay of Bengal, where they're stopped by the British fleet, because they've been reported as pirates.

The British admiral scoffs at the Blue Flag global-conquest conspiracy story. While they're on the British flagship arguing, Log blows up the *Maharatsu* by radio; he actually meant for them to steal the ship in Haiphong. The British take all the alleged "pirates" to prison in Calcutta.

Log can't get at our heroes in a British prison, so he tricks them into escaping, and scoops them up later. Now we discover that Log was mangled in the Kilua Pass explosion: he's a legless stump with only one arm and almost no face, and has to ride around on his flunky San's shoulders.

To get the secret codes, he begins to crucify Dodekhan and Mona in tandem. Dodekhan cracks and says he'll tell—but only when he has proof that Mona and Sara are safely back in France. Lucien says he'll stay here too, to guarantee that Sara will send the signal to free him. But secretly, he has Merry and Twinkle (still secure as Log's favorites) get him a revolver.

At this point events begin to overlap the opening of *Miss Musketeer*: Sara and Mona sail to Marseilles and go directly to the country villa of Dr. Rodel, a trusted friend of Dodekhan's. He sends the telegram that they're safe. In response, the women are told to watch the wireless audio-video setup at Rodel's house. On the screen, they see Dodekhan explain the Central Exchange in the Celestial Mountains to Log (still riding San)—but before he can reveal any more, Lucien shoots Log dead. San's henchmen overpower Dodekhan and Lucien, and the screen goes blank.

A week later, Sara and Mona turn up in Marseilles: Mona is truly mad from the trauma, and Sara—though sane—is considered equally mad because of her wild story. Plus, Dr. Rodel has been dead for a year and his house is empty!

So they're sent to an insane asylum, where Sara vows vengeance for the murder of Lucien and Dodekhan.

As you'll soon see, that story continues seamlessly in the volume you're holding—but d'Ivoi moves those characters to the background, and gives the foreground to a new set of people: Max Soleil, Sir John Lobster, and Miss Violet Musketeer herself.

Now, read on…

Stuart Gelzer
Santa Fe, 2021

MISS MUSKETEER

PART ONE
THIRSTING FOR THE LIGHT

CHAPTER I
What You Find in an Old Newspaper

"Of course, Sir John, I'm grateful for your kindness. But between that and making my heart flutter sweetly like a fiancée's there's a wide gap, wider than the Thames."

"Won't you at least give me some hope?"

"I think I've given you…"

"You've asked for the impossible."

"I don't agree. I said, 'My wealth, my pile of banknotes, bores me.' Your wealth does too. When I exclaim, 'I want this, or maybe I want that,' all it takes is opening a checkbook to buy it. I can't spend even a tiny moment wishing for anything—and I'm angry that I can't wish for anything. So I suggested that, using your imagination, you find something I'll consider interesting and that my pounds or guineas couldn't buy. I repeat, find a way to interest me, and then I'll be your fiancée."

This odd conversation was taking place in a murmur on the terrace of the Hôtel Mirific in Nice, between Miss Violet Musketeer and Sir John Lobster. Both of them had been born in England, but any resemblance ended there.

Violet was of medium height, but her aristocratic slenderness made her look taller. She had the slightly loose-hipped charm of athletic Englishwomen. She was very pretty—tawny blonde hair, a bright complexion, large gray-blue eyes that looked innocent and bold at the same time—and she had all of the somewhat stiff gracefulness from across the Channel that was so different from French grace, though it was no less captivating. Her white wristwatch, her matching blouse, and her tennis shoes suggested that she'd just come from the arena of British lawn sports. She might've been twenty years old.

Sir John, ten years older, crammed his short, prematurely plump body into a white flannel vest with wide pink stripes; trousers of the same fabric impris-

17

oned his thick legs but let escape two long feet shod in yellow calfskin. In one hand he held a lightweight straw boater decorated with a green ribbon, thus exposing his red hair and scarlet face—so red, so scarlet, that the select company gathered on the Côte d'Azur had to wonder whether Lobster was his real name or his nickname. This fat man, in any case, was a Member of Parliament and was listed in the London and County directory as one of the richest landowners in the United Kingdom.

On her side, Violet was the sole heiress of the late John Musketeer, who when he was alive had been a prominent manufacturer of tinned meats in Brisbane, Australia. We all remember the origins of that bold speculator's wealth. Leaving England with a small fortune of twenty-five thousand pounds, he'd gone to Australia—where at first he'd been taken for a madman. Indeed, how else to describe a man who used most of his capital to build enormous sheds filled with strange and expensive machinery? The most amazing thing was that, when people inquired, he answered with a smile, "I'm not yet sure what business I'll settle on... But so as to be ready I've built the factory anyway."

Surely he was a madman to talk that way. But a madman who noticed that the whole of Australia suffered from a terrible scourge—the proliferation of rabbits. Those countless rodents devastated farms and harvests. Farmers howled, legislatures were moved. One fine day it was decided by law to destroy the four-footed foe. An enormous beat was organized. Over five hundred thousand hunters rushed to join the slaughter. In six days they wiped out more than a hundred million rabbits.

That was all John Musketeer was waiting for. Brokers he'd hired long since scoured the country, buying at wholesale—skin and meat—all the rabbits, which because of their abundance had dropped to a ridiculously low price. In a month, Musketeer's factory turned thirty million of those fascinating rodents into rabbit pâté, with a net profit of about sixpence apiece, and the manufacturer's fortune rose by six hundred and twenty-five thousand francs, to eighteen million.

His former detractors now wore themselves out in cries of enthusiasm. The "John" brand competed successfully against the best-known American tinned meats; and when Sir John Musketeer, Privy Councilor of New South Wales, recipient of forty-three decorations from both England and abroad, baronet, etcetera, etcetera, rendered his admirable soul to the Lord, he left to his heiress—educated at the finest schools in England—the trifling sum of two hundred and seventy-five million.

The "Rabbit King" had done very well. A number of gentlemen hoped to do even better, by redirecting that honorably acquired fortune to their own profit. Violet's hand was asked for by three lords, a hereditary German duke, a pretender to one of the Balkan thrones... Even a Russian grand duke, frightened by the approach of revolution in Muscovy, didn't hesitate to get in line.

Violet refused all aspirants to her lovely, long, slender, pink-nailed hand. Did she think she deserved better than those self-serving sighs? No. All those gentlemen bored her, that's all. She dreamt of wanting something money couldn't buy. What? She had no idea. And not knowing what it was that would guarantee her happiness, she'd decided irrevocably that she'd marry only a man who could make her feel something novel, unknown, sought in vain until that moment—a man gifted with a mind original enough to reveal to her eyes some joy, some pleasure, that gold couldn't provide.

She traveled a great deal. Only Sir John Lobster had been determined enough to follow her. The Member of Parliament had sworn to himself that Violet would be his wife and the charming keeper of his hearth. And as a man who'd managed to win the votes of his fellow citizens, he had no doubt that one day he'd win the lovely heiress's vote too. He strove therefore to satisfy her slightest whim. Even now, on the terrace of the Hôtel Mirific, overlooking the garden—in bloom in spite of it being winter—and the palm trees along the promenade bordering the blue sea glittering under the bright sun, he seemed to be laden with a multitude of small parcels.

He enumerated them as he set them down on a small garden table. "I say! Your words bring sorrow to the ears of a lover and a suitor, Violet, but I believe my attentions will make you change your mind. Here's the silver and tortoiseshell lorgnette you looked at yesterday... and the new tennis balls invented by the brilliant Strible... and the tickets for the box at the theater... Plus which, here's your missing tennis racket. It was Prince Nielsa, you know—who's staying at the Buckingham Palace in Monte Carlo with that charming, witty Madame Norès—who sent a bellboy to bring the racket back with his apologies and this bouquet."

Violet murmured distractedly, "All of this is just a matter of money. Is there really nothing that can't be bought?"

"Poor Violet. Still dreaming that dream?"

"Always."

"You're seeking the impossible."

"That's all that attracts me."

"Well then—an unfulfillable desire already exists, by Jove! Ask for the moon, and you won't get it."

Her lovely eyebrows gathered in a frown. "An Englishwoman isn't mad. She wouldn't express a wish like that."

"That's honest, anyway. But if you reject follies, I really don't see a way to satisfy you."

Sadly, she shook her charming head. "Me neither, alas! Hence my boredom. Oh, for something difficult, yet feasible... something to bring a little crumb of interest, a hint of excitement, to my monotonous existence!"

She rested her elbows on the terrace balustrade, turning her back to the packages piled on the table—and also to Sir John, who was redder than ever.

That stubborn suitor studied her with an indulgent smile, exposing long teeth: a patch of yellow in the middle of his purple face, that brought to mind unbidden the multicolored gewgaws of a Spanish medal.

Suddenly he stopped smiling and listened. Violet too had lifted her head and was looking down into the garden. At the low gate leading to the promenade had just appeared a man of twenty-seven or twenty-eight—neither tall nor short, neither fat nor thin, neither handsome nor ugly, and dressed in white flannels with a yachtsman's cap—who was humming while he read with great attention a crumpled newspaper wrapped around a large bunch of pale violets.

It was the newcomer's voice that had drawn the notice of the two English people.

"Monsieur Max Soleil," whispered Violet.

"Pff. That French writer—an insignificant person. His writing brings in barely twenty thousand francs a year…"

Violet firmly cut short Sir John's thought. "Yes, but a happy man, always smiling. He's alone and he's singing. He's interested in so many things. Shh! Don't answer; he doesn't need to hear that we're talking about him."

Her suggestion was to the point. Max Soleil, since that was his name, had stopped reading, and with a brisk, lively stride he was following the sandy path leading to the hotel terrace, still humming as he went. He took the twelve steps in three bounds and stopped short at the top.

A lovely voice had just said, "Good morning. You've already been for a walk?" Violet came toward him, her hand outstretched.

Max cordially shook the multi-millionairess's hand, followed by Sir John's much heavier hand. Then, tossing his cap onto the side table, he said, "Yes, I went out, because I'm melancholy."

"Melancholy—you who are always so cheerful?"

"Oh, I'm in despair! I've been forced to kill Marthe Lussan."

Violet and Sir John started. "You killed someone?" they stammered.

"Oh, rest assured—only in my imagination. Marthe Lussan is the heroine of the novel the *Morning News* is publishing right now. But I worked so hard on that character, took such care over details, that I developed a little crush on Marthe. It took a huge effort for me to decide to follow the dictates of logic that led her to the grave."

Sir John let out a loud guffaw. Violet didn't even smile. She was observing the writer, noticing the wide, well-shaped brow that rose to his short brown hair; the clear, limpid, gray-green eyes that expressed both sincerity and firmness—as well as an indefinable something else that clouded them when he looked at her. Then she felt that the bright spark they threw out went straight into her, penetrating all the way to the secret places where her true thoughts were hidden.

Max Soleil was in fact no ordinary person. At eighteen he'd managed to get into the École Polytechnique. He'd graduated ninth in his class, giving him the choice of a career in either civil or military engineering. With a peace of mind that stunned his friends and acquaintances, he'd chosen... literature. Abandoning the engineering career open to him, he'd thrown himself into journalism, publishing news articles, human-interest stories, pieces on science—whatever turned up. Two years later a light comedy he wrote was a huge hit at the Théâtre des Variétés. Six months after that, he published a pitch-perfect tragic serial novel, then a four-act comedy that had all Paris rushing to the Théâtre du Gymnase. By the age of twenty-seven Max Soleil was famous. Publishers, theater producers, magazine editors all wanted to work with him, and—as Sir John had observed so disdainfully—he was earning at least twenty thousand francs a year.

Perhaps Violet was thinking about all that.

"So I wanted to shake off my sorrows," Max went on cheerfully. "I watched Miss Ladscheff and Miss Hurtington play golf on the links, then—a little restored by the sight of other people exercising—I was strolling back, when I met a flower seller laden with violets. The flowers naturally made me think of you. I bought some to give to you—which made me the happiest of men."

She interrupted him with a shake of her finger. "Oh, you Frenchman, you composer of gallantries, you're going to court me too."

"Like everybody, here and elsewhere," muttered Sir John.

Max paid no attention to him. He gestured with vexation at her words. "Mademoiselle, we've been acquaintances at this hotel for two weeks now, and I hope I've come across to you as neither conceited nor greedy."

"Conceited? Greedy?" echoed Violet in surprise. "I don't understand."

"No doubt. To court you would be to assume that I could inspire love in you: conceit! Or else that I'd have designs on your fortune—which is far too great for me: greed!"

"Or else that you're just a flirt," exclaimed Sir John, still smiling.

"I never flirt," replied Max curtly. "Flirtation is a parody of real feeling—something done by heartless, witless people."

He stopped short. Sweet Violet was holding out her hand to him. "Shake hands, I beg you. I spoke without thinking, and I apologize."

He ungrudgingly pressed her hand in his. "Thank you. Now I'll be able to go away with the memory of a dear companion, almost a friend."

"What? You're going away?"

"This evening. That's the happiness I mentioned."

"Happiness! But you were to stay here another two weeks!"

"True."

"And the way you described your life the other evening: eleven months of work, of simple and methodical existence, then a month of vacation in Nice, living like a millionaire... I'll admit, I don't understand what kind of happiness could cut short your month of reward."

"You mean what could increase it?"

"You're speaking in riddles."

"The most interesting thing possible!"

She threw up her hands. "Have you really found something interesting?" She had a worried look in her gentle eyes.

"At least to me. It's the premise for an extraordinary novel—a mystery that the police of France, England, and Russia have been powerless to solve—a mystery that I want to unravel."

"But you said you were made happy by buying those violets!"

"Exactly. Here, Mademoiselle, take them."

And as he put the bouquet into her hands, he showed her the sheet of newspaper in which they were wrapped. "Here's my happiness… given to me as a bonus by the flower seller."

"That newspaper?"

"A *Petit Marseillais* from four months ago."

"I still don't get it."

"This newspaper is from last October," he continued. "My flower seller no doubt bought it as part of a bundle meant to wrap bouquets. How it came into her possession doesn't matter. The lucky thing—as good old Capus[7] says—the lucky thing is that my attention was drawn to this evocative subhead." Then, chanting the words as if to magnify their effect, he read, "*Strange case of 'folie à deux': the Marseilles mystery. Are they nihilists? The conundrum deepens.*"

"*Folie à deux?*"—"Nihilists?"—exclaimed his two listeners.

Max bowed slightly, motioned for silence, then went on reading. "*Yesterday*—meaning last October 23rd—"*Officers Peyral and Barbon, making their rounds on the Corniche promenade…*"

"In Marseilles?"

"Yes… *Officers Peyral and Barbon found two young women, dressed alike, sunk in a deep sleep. They tried calling to them, even shaking them, but in vain: the unresponsive sleepers didn't open their eyes.*"

"Oh, pooh!" exclaimed Violet, but her rosy cheeks and shining eyes expressed her interest.

"Wait, wait. That's nothing yet. Going on: *Tiring of their pointless efforts, the officers concluded that the unknown women's sleep was unnatural. Thereupon Barbon went to requisition stretcher-bearers and stretchers, and the mysterious sleeping beauties were carried to nearest police station.*"

"Oh!" murmured Violet. "To the police station! Shocking!"

"*There,*" went on Max, talking right through the interruption, "*it took more than three hours to bring those mysterious women back to consciousness. Captain Bellugga, the kind-hearted police chief, therefore concluded that the ladies were under the influence of a powerful sedative.*"

---

[7] Alfred Capus (1858-1922), French journalist, playwright, and novelist; member of the Académie française.

"Oh! A sedative!"

"It's like an Ann Radcliffe[8] novel!"

"All that's still nothing," said Max with a smile. "Listen to the next part: *When the unknown women had come to, Captain Bellugga questioned them. One, a pretty blonde barely twenty years old, answered only with incoherent phrases: 'Night is the accomplice... Toward the light... Over there... The Orient... Brightness...' The other woman said she was the Duchess of La Roche-Sonnaille and the wife of a well-known member of Parisian society. She said her companion was named Mona Labianov and was the daughter of the general who had the honor to represent the Russian government at the last Peace Conference. Then the young woman told a strange story—so strange that Monsieur Bellugga immediately notified the magistrates.*

"It concerned a vast pan-Asian conspiracy against Europe, involving kidnapping Monsieur and Madame de la Roche-Sonnaille on their honeymoon and dragging them into an astonishing plot against all the European governments maintaining a presence in the Far East. It was like an episode of recent history brought to life, because certain facts about which we've informed our readers when necessary, such as those concerning the German concession at Shandong or the Kilua Pass in French Tonkin, surfaced in her gripping account.

"With admirable clarity and precision, the duchess added that she and her companion had arrived from Calcutta on the steamer Oxus, of the Messageries Maritimes shipping line; and that as soon as they disembarked they'd gone to see Dr. Rodel at his villa, called Loursinade, on the road to Aubagne. She claimed that there they'd witnessed a terrible scene, which had caused her companion to lose her mind. But an investigation immediately set in motion revealed that Dr. Rodel had been dead for more than a year—and that since then the Loursinade villa had stood vacant. Our reporter got into the house and confirmed the report: the loose floorboards covered in dust and the damp walls oozing saltpeter left no doubt: like her young friend, Madame de la Roche-Sonnaille has been struck by madness. Though she seems to be fully in her senses when she speaks on any other subject, she falls back into her distressing hallucination whenever the Loursinade villa is mentioned in her presence.

"In any case, telegrams were soon dispatched to the Roche-Sonnaille and Lillois families in Paris, and to His Excellency General Labianov in St. Petersburg. All of the telegrams produced the same astonishing reply: 'Vanished without leaving an address.'

"What is the heartrending mystery that has robbed two young women of their reason—women who certainly appear to be, as they claim, one the Duch-

---

[8] (née Ward) (1764-1823) English author and a pioneer of Gothic fiction who was hugely popular in France. Her technique of explaining apparently supernatural elements in her novels has been credited with gaining Gothic fiction respectability in the 1790s.

ess of La Roche-Sonnaille, who disappeared about eighteen months ago, along with her husband, during their honeymoon along the Rhine, and the other the only daughter of General Labianov?

"The connection to the Russian envoy raises the concern that Russian revolutionaries, nihilists, have a hand in all this. It's high time the government took steps against that violent faction, to which this country has been too hospitable. If nihilists wreak havoc in Russia, that's their business and doesn't concern us; but for them to come here and attack French citizens is unacceptable."

Max fell silent for a moment. His shining eyes fell on Violet. She hadn't moved. Her eyes wide with surprise, her rosy mouth open, she seemed to be waiting for more. For once she seemed to feel the interest that half an hour earlier she'd been complaining that she never experienced.

"Well?" he asked finally.

She seemed to come out of a dream. In a hesitant voice she said, "It's extraordinary."

"Don't you think it'd be fascinating to solve the case?"

She nodded.

"Besides presumably finding the plot of a true-life novel, I'm sure I'd be carrying out a good deed."

"A good deed?"

Max raised his arms eloquently. "I was forgetting…" He turned the page of the newspaper. "Here, in the late-breaking news. Listen: *Given their mental state, Madame de La Roche-Sonnaille and Mademoiselle Mona Labianov have been taken to Dr. Elleviousse's asylum. We're all familiar with that eminent psychiatric practitioner's miraculous cures and with his books that have revolutionized the theory of madness. We've all, if not read, then at least heard of his 'Essays on the Loss of Reason and its Causes.'*

"We visited his asylum and had the good fortune to meet the scientist in his laboratory, where he is pursuing his research into 'the effect of beams of colored light on the progress of insanity.' Dr. Elleviousse, like all superior beings, is a saint. His exposure to the insane has not jaded him to their suffering. It was with deep sadness that he confirmed the genuine madness of his new residents, and his faint hope of curing them.

"We were allowed to see those unfortunate victims of a mystery that seems likely never to be solved. Mademoiselle Mona Labianov, as lovely as a tormented angel, as blonde as wheat, continues to utter meaningless phrases: 'The Orient… The light…' In the asylum garden, it's as if a secret attraction forces her always to look east.

"As for the Duchess of La Roche-Sonnaille, one of the most charming representatives of the French nobility, she conversed with us at first with great good sense. Unfortunately our professional duty and our wish to keep our readers informed led us to bring up the subject of the Loursinade villa—which we regretted immediately, because the poor woman gave way to delusion babbling,

repeating the far-fetched story that investigation has shown to be impossible. It was with an aching heart that we departed Dr. Elleviousse's asylum, leaving those poor women the victims of an inexplicable fate."

Max added calmly, "Now you understand why I used that expression: a good deed. Either a terrible shock unbalanced those women's wits—in which case tracing the matter back to the culprit is an act of justice—or that duchess, who's so sane in all other respects, is perhaps just as sane when she talks about the Loursinade villa."

"What? You don't think she's mad?"

"No, I don't. I'm in search of the truth. I therefore have to consider both hypotheses."

"You don't favor either one?"

"Honestly, I do. My intuition is to lean toward believing that she's perfectly in her right mind."

"But then how awful to be locked up in a madhouse!" Kind-hearted Violet clasped her hands, and her whole attitude expressed her horror.

"Well, don't get too upset. It's not a certainty. I'd even like to begin my investigation by letting go of that idea. Logic alone must guide me."

"When will you begin your investigation?"

"I already have."

"How?"

"A little while ago I sent a telegram to Dr. Elleviousse, asking him to see me tomorrow. My pretext is that I'm writing a thriller. As soon as I hear from him I'm off to Marseilles."

With unaccustomed energy, Violet cried, "Oh, I hope you succeed! I make wishes, you know. I can't tell you how interested I am in those poor dear madwomen."

A loud guffaw made her jump. Sir John was bent over in spasms of noisy laughter. "Come on now. Pull up! Here you are—interested! Not for long, because with a little cash…"

"Cash?"

"Yes! I'll send a telegram to the chief of police in Marseilles. I'll offer a reward of two thousand pounds sterling to whatever officer brings in the solution to the mystery. And I'll soon get results—without inconveniencing myself in the least." And he concluded mockingly, "This still isn't something money can't buy."

Violet's face fell, but Max protested, "I think you're mistaken."

"No, I'm not."

"I beg your pardon. The Russian government generously offered a reward of a hundred thousand rubles, and still nothing's been learned."

Those words reassured Violet—but Sir John, stung, cried, "If that reward produced nothing, why do you think you'll have better luck?"

"Because I'm diving into this case, not to earn a certain sum of money, but to bring satisfaction to two things I value a hundred times more."

"And what might they be, if you please?"

"My heart and my mind."

The Member of Parliament didn't have time to answer: Violet clapped her hands together with delight. "That's exactly right! Will you set off today, Monsieur Max?"

"As soon as I hear from Dr. Elleviousse."

"Why so soon, since you're not meeting him until tomorrow?"

"I want to try a few experiments that'll show me whether Madame de La Roche-Sonnaille is insane."

"I say!" grumbled Sir John. "Since the most eminent doctors have decided she is…"

But Violet cut him off. "It's just that… Monsieur Max… if you wait until tomorrow… I'd so much like to see those ladies too…" She coaxed and pleaded. This young woman, so bored not long ago, had truly become captivated by the Marseilles mystery.

Max gently shook his head. "It'd be a pleasure to accompany you tomorrow, but I'm leaving today."

"Why?"

"I'll explain it to you at the Hotel Cosmopolitan, where I'll be staying."

"Well then, tomorrow at what time?"

"Dr. Elleviousse will let me know by telegram."

"All right!" And with a charming smile Violet concluded, "It's very odd: for the last half hour I've felt alive. Oh, those dear ladies, those sweet dear things! I hope it'll be very challenging to work on their behalf—so I don't fall too quickly back into boredom."

Sir John, redder than ever, growled with irritation, "Oh, you'll fall back!"

"You're unbearable!"

"No, I'm being logical too—just as much as Mr. Soleil." With a sweep of his hand he settled his green-ribboned boater back onto his flaming red hair and headed briskly toward the stairs to the garden. "I'm off to draft that telegram to the chief of police in Marseilles. I'm offering a reward of ten thousand pounds: I'm buying you the investigation you want."

Wheezing, muttering under his breath, Sir John went down the steps as fast as his short legs could carry him—leaving Violet Musketeer perfectly furious at his insistence on preventing her from being interested in something for once in her life.

CHAPTER II
Ariadne's Thread

The clock pointed to six as Max emerged from the train station in Marseilles. Dr. Elleviousse had telegraphed promptly, confirming the presence in his asylum of those two unfortunate madwomen, Mona Labianov and Sara de La Roche-Sonnaille, and saying he'd be happy to receive Monsieur Max Soleil—with whose admirable gifts he was familiar—the next day at two o'clock. Upon which the young man, after cordially shaking Violet's hand, and shaking Sir John's, had left Nice carrying only a small suitcase, leaving his trunks in care of the Hôtel Mirific, to be shipped back to his home in Paris.

In the station courtyard he found the Hotel Cosmopolitan omnibus. He put his suitcase on it, and tasked the porter with reserving him a room. Thus unburdened, he hopped into a taxi and called to the driver, "To the offices of the Messageries Maritimes!"

The cab set off. Oblivious to the activity in the busy city, Max reflected. "The newspaper is silent on one question: did those two ladies really arrive from Calcutta on the steamer *Oxus*? If so, I have a series of events that seem like they should hang together. The duchess and her husband disappear while traveling along the Rhine on their honeymoon... Eighteen months go by... She reemerges in Calcutta, embarks on the *Oxus*, and sails to Marseilles. She explains that she was taken, against her will, from the Netherlands to India... That involuntary journey between two voluntary journeys is not at all illogical. Madame de La Roche-Sonnaille was therefore telling the truth about all that part of her adventures. But if that's so, chances are good she went on speaking sense about the rest."

He shook his head. "Let's not get ahead of ourselves. Let's confirm the matter of the *Oxus*. That'll decide for me whether that young woman is in her right mind or not." He smacked his forehead. "Fool! If that were true, the magistrates and police detectives wouldn't have concluded it was madness! I'm an idiot to be going to the Messageries Maritimes!"

He was already opening his mouth to ask the driver to take him straight to the Cosmopolitan—when he suddenly changed his mind: "No, that doesn't follow. They declared her mad simply because they didn't carry out their inquiry logically." He added with a smile, "Those good people don't know how to construct a novel. They don't know that to give the plot a solid structure you have start from the first event and build on it as you go. Of course they rushed to the house on the road to Aubagne to arrest the mysterious person the duchess blamed for her friend's madness. There they learned he'd been dead for year, and the Loursinade villa was vacant. Dust, damp, cobwebs—all was clear. And if that was false, the whole story was false. Once they got that preconceived notion fixed in their heads, the detectives were on the wrong track. And if you add Dr. Elleviousse's opinion... Those psychiatrists see madmen everywhere—I bet when they look in the mirror they're ready to prescribe themselves cold showers and a straitjacket. Anyway, the source of the mistake is, they started from the wrong place, which skewed their judgment." Here he couldn't help laughing. "Easy for me to criticize others. I'm doing my best to prove them wrong, when I don't even know whether the women were aboard the *Oxus*." He looked around. "In any case, I won't remain in doubt for long."

Indeed the cab was stopping in front of the offices of the Messageries Maritimes, whose large signboards announcing departures struck the eye. Having paid his driver, Max entered the office.

"Can I help you sir?" asked a bellboy. "Tickets? Freight? Information?"

Max put fifty centimes in the boy's hand. "May I speak to the director?"

"Monsieur Ponchel... I'll go see... What name?"

Max's only answer was to pull a card from his wallet; under his name, *MAX SOLEIL*, he wrote one line in pencil: *In the midst of researching a future novel. Would like one piece of information.*

Ten minutes later the bellboy came back and—with a little more deference, prompted by his boss's obvious eagerness to welcome his visitor—he said, "Monsieur Ponchel expects you, sir." He led Max to a closed door, opened it, and stepped gravely aside to let him go by.

The director came to meet Max with his hand outstretched. "Come in, come in. Delighted to meet you. Thrilled if I can be of any help."

"Too kind, really."

"What's it about?"

"As I said in my note, it's a novel I've been working on since this morning."

Monsieur Ponchel's eyes widened in surprise. "This morning?"

"Yes. A newspaper from last October came to my attention. A wonderful mystery—unique, original. In short, a daily paper is too concise for a case like this, and I'm carrying out a little research to expand my notes."

"If I can be of any help..."

"I hope you can. It's about Madame de La Roche-Sonnaille and..."

"The two poor madwomen. You're quite right. With your gifts... But you'd like to know..."

"If they really did take the steamer *Oxus*..."

"From Calcutta —but of course they did. You can imagine, I've been questioned about it."

Max rubbed his hands together. "I assumed so, and I thought you might agree to tell me what you know about them. For example, did they show any signs of insanity while they were on board?"

"Well... hell!" The director remained uncertain for a moment—then he suddenly made up his mind. "Wait... I'll share with you the report written up by

Captain Alice, who was in command of the *Oxus*. It's a confidential report, but if it'll give us the pleasure of leading to a new novel from your hand..." He rummaged in a box. "Ah! Here it is... *The two lady travelers caused no trouble on board. However, they seemed strange. At the start of the journey they seemed very melancholy. They appeared to be impatient to arrive. Several times a day they expressed concern about our speed, about our course. They consulted the charts.*"

"Surely lots of passengers act the same way."

"Of course. But when the ship reached Marseilles they gave unmistakable proof of outlandish eccentricity."

"Can I take unfair advantage of your willingness to help?"

"It would never be unfair. Imagine this: once the ship docked, they disembarked, leaving their luggage on board. They went straight to the streetcar that runs out the road to Aubagne."

"Where the Loursinade villa is?"

"Exactly. The conductor of the streetcar they took came forward on his own at the investigation. According to his statement, Mademoiselle Labianov seemed fairly calm, whereas the duchess by contrast appeared to be very agitated. They asked about the Loursinade villa."

"Oh ho!"

"Yes, the conductor even thought they were going to see the villa with the intention of renting it."

"And they got off?..."

"At the streetcar terminus, eight or nine hundred meters from the mysterious house. After that everything gets confused. The duchess claims they spent only twenty-four hours at the villa. And yet when they were found, on the Corniche promenade, a week had gone by since the *Oxus* arrived."

"But the women knew the house?"

"As I warned you, here everything gets confused. According to the unfortunate madwomen, they were supposed to meet the doctor there—the one who'd died a year before they reached Marseilles. He was a friend of theirs, who'd sent directions to them in India. There's some story about a telegram. Who knows. We're deep in the fog of madness."

Clearly, to the director, the madness of the ladies now living at the Elleviousse Asylum was axiomatic. Max understood that he shouldn't express any doubt about it. So instead he resumed carelessly, "And the poor women's luggage? The trunks left on board the *Oxus*?"

"They were delivered to Dr. Elleviousse."

"Good. But did the magistrates examine them?"

"Of course. That's how they found papers confirming the travelers' identity."

"But nothing besides those papers—nothing to corroborate their claims?"

"No. Fine Indian and Chinese fabric, a few valuable jewels. Basically, the same souvenirs any wealthy tourist brings back from Asia."

Monsieur Ponchel had clearly told everything he knew. Max rose. After many thanks to the good man he took his leave. At a stroller's slow pace he headed toward the Hotel Cosmopolitan. "That little duchess told the truth," he mused. "She's not the least bit mad." Then he went on thoughtfully, "Yes, yes… She knew of the existence of Dr. Rodel, and of the Loursinade villa. She expected to meet him there. Who sent her to him? Her husband… or Mona's fiancé… those two vanished men… But why?"

For a moment he stood still, frowning, his brow furrowed in a way that suggested the intensity of his train of thought. Finally he resumed walking. "All right! I'll see her tomorrow. She'll tell me… and then… I usually write my novels; this one I'm going to act out. It really fascinates me." He shook his head cheerfully. "And now it's time to think about dinner. You have to fuel the machine if you want it to run right."

Something like a slight hesitation flitted across his lively features, but soon gave way to a smile. "Between now and tomorrow, I'll make use of my time by visiting that house on the road to Aubagne. Who knows!"

On that mysterious note Max reached the Hotel Cosmopolitan. At the front desk he found out what room the omnibus porter had reserved for him, as instructed, and he was already heading up the stairs when a voice made him start.

"Excuse me, Madame or Mademoiselle, has Sir John Lobster not arrived yet?"

Lobster! Max spun around. A stout man stood in the vestibule, hat in one hand, the other pushing on the knob of the glass door to the office. No doubt someone answered him, but too quietly for Max to hear.

The man closed the door, saying, "Many thanks! I'll come back tomorrow." But then he broke off: "Huh? What? What do you want?"

Having leaped down four steps, Max had just dropped beside him like a meteorite and had put his hand on his arm. "Sir John's a friend of mine. He's joining me here tomorrow. I saw him this morning in Nice."

"Ah! Then that fellow's not a mythical creature?"

"Not at all. So you were asking for him, and yet you don't seem convinced that he exists?"

"Since you were in Nice, perhaps you know about it. Monsieur Lobster sent a wire to police headquarters…"

"Offering a reward to whoever unravels the mystery of the road to Aubagne."

"Exactly."

"And you're a police detective…"

"Undercover, sir. Landré, at your service. In the department they call me Dodo, on account of my theory about police work: to see what the crooks are up to, you have to close your eyes. When the cat's asleep, you know… the mice aren't so careful."[9]

"And you're in charge of the case?"

Landré, known as Dodo, began to laugh. "Oh, come on, sir, it's completely solved. The poor women Dr. Elleviousse is caring for are mad, mad beyond a doubt."

Max showed no surprise. "Ah! You think so?"

"By God! I had no trouble putting the case together. Long experience with detective work, you know. You're acquainted with the details, I assume?"

"Yes, Sir John told me all about it."

"Good. Well, then. The Duchess of La Roche-Sonnaille and Mona Labianov met up at The Hague."

"But weren't the duke and the Russian girl's fiancé there too?"

"Exactly! The ladies hadn't yet gone mad. Then, I don't know why, but it doesn't matter, they really did go to Asia, just as the madwoman says."

Max gave an imperceptible start. "You think so?"

"It's indisputable. They came back on the *Oxus*. To return from Calcutta, you certainly have to have gone there."

"True enough. But what about the two men?"

"Oh, well, they stayed there. Some kind of mishap. Tortured by tribes in Tibet… eaten by tigers… bitten by poisonous snakes! Thousands of people vanish in Asia every year. The two ladies wanted to return to Europe, to seek consolation with their families."

"So, in your opinion, when they embarked, they were still in their right minds?"

The detective gestured broadly. "Perfectly. And they were still sane when they reached Marseilles."

"Ah!" murmured Max. It troubled him to see that the detective's hypothesis was the same as his own. The investigation hadn't gone so completely wrong as he'd thought up to a moment ago. And that realization caused his own certainty to weaken. Still, he made an effort to keep going. "You're inclined to think they fell into…"

"Into lunacy… at the Loursinade villa, sir." And then with great authority, articulating each syllable so as to drive it deeper into his listener's mind, Landré went on, "They arrived exhausted, their nerves shaken by whatever disaster had separated them from their loved ones. They went to see Dr. Rodel, who'd been dead for a year—which they didn't know, since they'd been gone eighteen months. He was a friend, no doubt, a friend from before. They were counting on him for help, maybe just to prepare their parents to see them again. They found the villa empty. That's nothing, but in certain circumstances a single speck of

---

[9] The nickname "Dodo" doesn't refer to the helpless bird, but means "Sleepy" in French.

31

dust can jam a four-thousand-horsepower engine. The break occurred. As of that moment, their wits wandered, and they couldn't distinguish reality from their hallucinations."

"Are you sure?"

"And I can prove it, sir. Starting from two of their claims that I could test, I was led to conclude that all the rest were false."

Max felt heartsick. The detective was demolishing his dream. He'd reduced to a mere banality an adventure Max had considered mysterious and strange. "What claims?" he said dully.

"This: the duchess said the house was fully furnished, with expensive curtains and with the floors covered in carpets. She claimed Dr. Rodel received her and her companion. That's very amiable of a man dead for months, but quite unbelievable."

"A criminal could've taken his place."

"Very unlikely, sir. Yet I proceeded as if that were so. Still according to the poor woman, Dr. Rodel went to Marseilles that same day and sent a cable on her behalf, using a prearranged code, to a certain Mr. Dodekhan in Calcutta. The answer was delivered that very evening by a telegraph agent... Well, sir, no trace of the telegram sent to Calcutta... No trace of the agent who brought the answer... And you'll admit that a telegraph agent coming out to the Loursinade villa—where, since the real Rodel's death, of course no messages would've been delivered—wouldn't have forgotten such a thing, and would've come forward."

"It's true," agreed Max sadly.

"Likewise," went on the detective, "a wire in a special code, being something odd, would've attracted the attention of the clerk who received it. Even if the original had been lost."

"Yes, yes."

"Therefore those poor little ladies are absolutely bonkers. Your friend Monsieur Lobster has promised a large reward that won't cost him much. I just hope he'll give me a little gratuity if he agrees that my information correctly sums up the business on the road to Aubagne. On that note, sir, until tomorrow."

"Come around eleven. He'll arrive at the latest on the ten-thirty train."

"Thanks for the tip, sir. Your servant." Landré bowed and departed.

In the vestibule, Max remained deep in thought. "Oh, sure," he muttered. "That worthy fellow's deductions have all the earmarks of logic. Everything could've happened that way. And yet..." He stamped his foot on the marble floor. "Why would the duke and duchess, newlyweds, starting from Paris on their honeymoon along the Rhine, make such an enormous detour by way of Asia? That idea came from Mona Labianov, or her fiancé. Dodekhan, the detective said. Dodekhan, that's a foreign-sounding name! The 'khan' ending suggests someone from Turkestan: Turkestan, a vast region four or five times larger than France, divided between the Russian Empire and the Chinese Empire. Dodekhan! That's the connection between the Rhine and Calcutta..."

The dinner bell interrupted him. Still lost in thought, he made his way to the grand dining room of the Hotel Cosmopolitan. But—though he'd promised himself he'd dine well—he absentmindedly put away the skillfully prepared courses on the gourmet menu.

Dinner over, Max finally went up to his room, tidied his disheveled appearance, and went back down. As he handed in his key at the desk he said he was going to the theater, where a friend of his expected him. He finished by advising, "Don't look for me to return later—I may not come back until tomorrow morning."

Thereupon Max arbitrarily went to the first theater he ran across, sat through the show without hearing a word, and when it was done, found himself back outside. He looked at his watch. "Twenty to twelve. The last streetcar out the road to Aubagne leaves at five till. After that the road'll be deserted. Without being spotted, I could visit the mysterious villa at my leisure."

CHAPTER III
An Uninhabited Villa

At thirteen minutes past midnight the streetcar dropped Max at its terminus on the road to Aubagne. He lost a few seconds rolling a cigarette—a slow job, because by the time he was done all the other passengers had disappeared. He saw with a smile that he was alone. Without hurrying, he set off along the dusty road, which, in spite of the darkness, traced a white line past enclosed yards and gardens and fields bathed in shadow.

"Almost a kilometer to cover," he said to himself. "A grove of olive trees, then the garden walls of Loursinade, topped with blue Vallauris tile. Oh, that hotel clerk sure gave me careful directions."

After five hundred meters he saw the predicted olive grove. He walked by very close to it, as if he wanted to merge with its deep shadows. And at one point he dove into the trees: a lightweight carriage was passing at the speedy pace of a strong horse. Max noticed that the carriage lanterns weren't lit. "People heading to town. They'll earn themselves a fine." He'd barely formed the thought when the carriage turned onto a side trail that seemed to follow the edge of the olive grove perpendicular to the road. "No, they're not headed to town. Not as careless as I thought."

Why was he paying attention to those passing strangers? For the same reason that a man alone in the countryside feels the need to fix his gaze on some random object. The complete idleness of the sense of sight is in fact an affliction we struggle against unconsciously.

He'd resumed walking. He left the olive grove behind him. A short way ahead of him he could vaguely make out the smooth outline of a garden wall. "That must be it."

As he drew near he could tell he wasn't mistaken: the glazed tiles along the top of the walls were exactly as the hotel clerk had described them. The wall wasn't too high, barely two meters: easy to climb for anyone with basic athletic skills.

"All right, let's reconnoiter the area." Max walked slowly all the way around the property. He estimated the walled garden to be a rectangle, nearly a square: fifty meters by about forty-five. Within, the wall was bordered by trimmed trees with very thick foliage, making it impossible to see the house. Only from the entrance gates on the road side could one get a vague view, across a lawn encircled by beds of shrubs, of the roof of the house. It was a house for people who wanted to avoid the curious eyes of their neighbors, he reflected.

Then he looked around. "Not a particularly worrisome neighborhood, however. The olive grove that way. That orchard across the road. Over there some kind of factory building. Together they isolate the villa from the rest of the world. My word, if you were looking for a quiet spot on the edge of town, you couldn't do better."

It was true. No matter which way he looked, his view was blocked not far away by natural or manmade barriers. You had to lean against the gates even to see where the house was—and then, only because the roof rose above the foliage that hid the house.

"If necessary," thought Max, "you could certainly move in and move out without anyone noticing. A truck full of furniture shows up, say around this time of night. They open the gates. The truck enters the garden and disappears behind the flowerbeds. And a hundred people could walk by on the road without suspecting that furniture, pictures, anything, was being loaded or unloaded. A week went by between the arrival of the *Oxus* and those two young women being found on the Corniche promenade. The person or persons who conned them had plenty of time to rig up the villa at their leisure."

He nodded firmly, with the rising sense of satisfaction that comes from the happy feeling of making progress across solid ground. His entire train of reasoning, with all of his reckoning of probabilities, was unfolding methodically, without contradicting the hypothesis that the Duchess of La Roche-Sonnaille might've been telling the truth.

"Now," he thought, "it's time to get inside." He smiled. "Climbing the wall might be seen as breaking and entering—a serious charge. Luckily the Loursinade villa is vacant and unfurnished. Therefore…"

Still, out of caution, he decided to climb the wall at the point furthest from the road. That way he could be almost completely sure no one would notice his bizarre venture. "Bizarre" wasn't overstating it: certainly, when the book Max Soleil was working on came out, when its preface revealed to the public how the young author had researched and acted out his novel, those clever people who— never having done a bit of conscientious work in their lives—dismissed the possibility of conscientiousness in others, would complain that it was implausible, and would try to call his bluff. That thought crossed Max's mind without affecting his decision in the least.

Slipping around the perimeter to the point he'd chosen, he leapt high enough for his hands to grasp the top of the wall. One pull-up, one pushup, and he sat astride the line of blue Vallauris tiles. Swinging his leg over, slipping down, and dropping to the ground with his legs bent took him only a moment. He stood up. He was in the garden of the mysterious house. He felt a certain emotion: up till now he'd been advancing toward a secret he sensed was tragic, but now he'd entered the play himself, coming on stage in the setting that had witnessed the scene unfolding.

But—as is inevitably the case with any true writer—Max was above all a man of action. Producing a work of literature wasn't, as people generally and mistakenly thought, done by dreaming. Creation required action. A dreamer produced nothing. A real author was a kind of living machine for transforming thought into action.

So he reached into his pocket to find his small electric flashlight, checked that his revolver was easily accessible in its tailor-made pocket in his jacket, and set out resolutely along the narrow path that wound through the flowerbeds. Clearly he'd come well prepared for his expedition.

Two minutes later he reached the back of the villa. Two steps led up to a small service door on the right, almost at the corner of the building. He went closer, switched on his flashlight, and aimed its beam at the keyhole. It was thickly coated in rust, the kind of reddish fur that showed the metal was "rotten," to use the technical term—meaning the iron had oxidized to the point where it couldn't be restored no matter how it was cleaned. All the evidence suggested the door hadn't been opened in a very long time.

Max slid the blade of his pocketknife into the keyhole and felt around for a moment, and the bolt slid back without clicking, making only a soft rustle. The lack of any tension in the lock confirmed his initial impression. The door swung open stiffly on its hinges. He could see a narrow corridor, at the end of which four steps led up to a second door. It opened by means of a tarnished copper doorknob, and he found himself in a tiled room, which he knew from the sink of worn black stone and the oven faced with dirty tiles to be the kitchen.

On the floor the slowly accumulated dust of time had preserved footprints. He examined them, but almost immediately stood up with a shrug. "The footprints of the police detectives who came here four months ago to check on the duchess's story. Hell, the people who took away the furniture weren't stupid—they would certainly have gotten rid of such obvious marks."

He took a careful look around. "No, nothing. Let's go further in. That glazed door must lead to the living quarters." He meant a door whose top half consisted of two panes of glass that were thick with grime. "Very clever," he said to himself. "If the duchess was telling the truth, her enemies took a lot of trouble to dirty the place up again when their job was done." The door panes were in fact so filthy they were completely opaque. "Dust sure seems to build up fast around Marseilles!" he joked. "That Marseilles dust is thriving!" Then he nodded. "Of course the idea was to make it look like the villa had been vacant for a year."

Opening the door partway, he reached through to hold his flashlight on the other side and examine the light coming through the glass. "As I thought: they dampened the glass with a slightly viscous liquid—probably water mixed with a little flour—and then they blew fine dust onto that. They let it dry, then they rubbed it with a rag, or a piece of paper, whatever, to brush off the lumps."

He laughed silently. "But that wasn't enough to get rid of the water streaks made by the sponge they used to 'glue' the windows. The police noticed nothing—because you have to look at a light through the glass—and they didn't bother, because as soon as they'd heard Dr. Rodel had died they concluded, *ipso facto*, that the villa had been vacant since then. Well, well, duchess: the doctors and the police think you're mad, while a mere novelist considers you perfectly sane. It doesn't seem like much, but at least it's something."

Beyond the glass door stretched a hallway with a flooring of tattered, mildewed linoleum in numerous mismatched patterns. Max didn't even pause. In the middle of the right-hand wall, a door covered in peeling paint led him into a fairly large room that he knew by its furniture to be a dining room. Suddenly he stopped still, as if nailed in place. The beam of his flashlight made a bright circle on the dusty floor, revealing a single footprint.

Ah! A foot that couldn't be confused with those whose prints he'd seen in the kitchen. This one, no doubt shod in a felt slipper, looked small, high-arched, elegant. The neatness of the print made clear that this foot had been set down lightly but decisively, in a way that seemed alert, even mischievous. Only a small woman or a young boy could've made it. Max studied the print. Oh, it was clearly more recent than the others, because the dust that marked its contour had kept its sharp edge. The rim hadn't been rounded off by the slow fall of particles down the slope into the hollow of the impression.

"Someone came here, after the police were here. Who the devil would do that?"

Looking more carefully, he saw that the print was preceded and followed by other similar prints. Their maker had come in by a door across from the one through which Max had entered the room. He or she had walked to the center of the room and stopped there for a moment—as shown by the deeper, more distinct prints there—then had turned around and left the same way.

Stirred by a sudden rising curiosity, Max followed the trail. A surprise awaited him: he found the door ajar. The visitor hadn't bothered to reclose it, but had simply pulled it shut behind him or her. "Who can it be?" he wondered as he pushed open the door. He found himself in the vestibule. To his right stood the main front entrance, whose glazed double doors faced the road. But those doors weren't closed: one of the doors was open to the outside, swung flat back on its hinges against the wall.

And the tile floor preserved more of those mysterious footprints: they ran straight across the vestibule and disappeared through a doorway directly opposite the door to the dining room. Max could see the villa had been built on the classic plan for small country houses on the outskirts of town: vestibule in the center, dining room on one side, sitting room on the other. The unknown person had therefore gone into the sitting room. To do what? Well, his prints would speak for him: the best course was to follow them.

But sometimes the hardest things were those that looked easy. No sooner had he put his hand on the knob of the door to the sitting room than it opened abruptly. A person—that from its silhouette Max took for a boy—leapt into the vestibule, knocked his flashlight into the air, making the light go out, and fled through the main doors, which shut behind him with a loud slam that echoed through the empty house.

Taken by surprise for a moment, Max dashed off in pursuit of the mysterious figure, but the garden gate was locked. His pocketknife easily defeated the lock, but at the cost of a few seconds. By the time he emerged, the visitor had vanished. Still, listening carefully, he thought he could make out a faint sound of running, coming from the rear of the garden, the side furthest from the road. Without hesitating, he dashed that way.

He'd gone barely twenty meters when he heard a crash, like a stone falling and shattering on the ground. "He's climbing the wall. He knocked one of the glazed tiles off the top." And Max ran even faster. He reached the wall. But there was no one. On the ground he could see the fragment of one of those blue Vallauris tiles. He leapt at the wall. His fingers gripped the top. But he didn't finish pulling himself up. Not far away, the sound of a carriage rang out in the night. A burst of mocking laughter went by in the darkness.

Max let himself drop back into the garden. He understood: the fugitive was safe. A carriage was taking him away too fast for him to be caught. Max suddenly remembered that carriage with its lamps unlit that he'd noticed on the road to Aubagne. "Is there some connection between the two?" But then he shrugged. "Let's go back inside. That odd pedestrian's footprints might show me what he was after in that empty house."

Max recrossed the garden and entered the vestibule. He lit a match to find his flashlight, which had rolled to the far end of the room. Unexpected luck: the bulb wasn't broken. The flashlight must've landed on its metal case. The switch still worked, the light came on, and he could pursue his investigation.

He went to the sitting room. The mysterious person seemed not to have stopped there. Obviously whatever he was looking for wasn't in that room. He'd gone directly across the floor, without the least hesitation… Yes, but in the next room that wasn't the case. Here he'd lingered, his prints crossing and recrossing.

"What room is this?" A library—no doubt the late Dr. Rodel's library.

The wallpaper, as decayed as everything else in the house, still held traces of bookshelves. Yes, Dr. Rodel must've been a hardworking man. He didn't own glassed-in bookcases, the costly furniture of people who didn't treat books with affection. No, all around the walls ran lines like yellowed cuts, where shelves had been. They stopped on either side of the window, whose heavy solid shutters were sealed tight.

Across from the window, two cast-iron columns, standing no more than thirty centimeters from the wall, interrupted the line of the shelves, no doubt reinforcing columns. There must once have been a subsidence in the structure, which they cured with these "iron crutches" to protect the stability of the villa. It was obvious. And yet that simple explanation didn't seem to have occurred to the stranger whose trail Max was following. The footprints crossed and recrossed around the pillars: the visitor had circled around the cast-iron columns.

The position of the feet, revealed on the dusty floor, suggested that the boy had been feeling the iron posts, examining them in some way. Why?

Max could understand nothing of the stranger's behavior. Idly, he rapped on the barrel of the columns. "They ring hollow," he thought to himself. "Of course. For lightweight construction like this, there'd be no point in using solid posts." With a hint of annoyance he went on, "What was that person looking for here?"

He didn't have time to answer his own question. His flashlight was taken from his hand and went out. In the now total darkness, many hands seized him. He tried to struggle—in vain. The sides were too unequal. He felt himself being pulled, pushed, dragged. He could tell that his attackers had pushed him up against one of the cast-iron pillars. With the dexterity of professionals they wrapped him in a complicated web of ropes.

"What do you want with me?" His voice was calm. Max wasn't one of those nervous people terrified by the least surprise. His logical mind had provided an explanation for what was happening. He was in a vacant house. There was nothing to steal here. So it couldn't be burglars surrounding him. Then, who? Well, hell—tramps, poor homeless fellows, who must've thought his own unexpected presence here was a threat to their shelter, which they might've been using for a long time. When they didn't answer, he said, "Who are you? If you think I'm with the police, you're mistaken."

Still silence. And yet they were there—the brushing sounds of clothing and shoes proved it.

"All right, you've tied me up. Why?"

This time, an obviously disguised voice answered him. "To give you a warning."

"A warning? About what?"

"Do you admit you're absolutely in our power?"

"Without a doubt."

"Well! If we wanted to eliminate you, nothing would be easier."

And Max bowed his head, submitting to the logic of the invisible voice in the darkness.

The voice insisted, "Is it true?"

"Yes, damn it, it's true! It's pointless to make me say so."

After a short pause, the voice spoke again. "By sparing you, we're being merciful."

"Merciful? Damn!"

"Yes, merciful—because you've started down a path that leads only to death."

The tone of voice was so fierce that Max couldn't help shivering a little. Still, he wanted to appear calm, so he asked sarcastically, "What path might you be referring to?"

But the mockery died on his lips. A harsher voice replied, "The road to Aubagne, leading to the Loursinade villa."

"Where we are now?" he stammered in surprise.

"Where we are now," echoed the harsh voice. "Anyway, no more beating around the bush. You're on the trail of a secret that cannot be revealed."

"But I'm just curious…"

"It doesn't concern you. You didn't know our will, which is why we're sparing your life. If you persevere after this, we'll have no further reason to spare you."

"But who are you?" Disoriented by the unexpected turn in his investigation, Max had spoken idly, just to say something. His thoughts collided chaotically. This villa stunned him. Everyone thought it was vacant, uninhabited—but damn, this empty house seemed to be as crowded as the Canebière district. At every turn he ran into mysterious people, whose presence furthered complicated the knot he'd flattered himself he was unraveling.

So he was shocked to hear the voice say, "You want to know who we are—all right. But remember, we can only be seen once. The second encounter brings death."

Death! Oh, he wasn't worried about that now: he almost shouted with triumph. These people, at least, he'd see. They wouldn't vanish into the night, like the nimble boy he'd barely glimpsed earlier.

But then he shivered from head to toe. Light filled the room: he recognized his own flashlight in the hands of one of the strangers, who obligingly aimed the beam of light at himself and at his companions. And with haunted eyes, feeling like he was living out a nightmare, Max stared.

His enemies faced him. Who were they? Impossible to tell. Their race, their profession, even their gender remained in doubt. He could see three human figures, their shapes indistinct under loose-fitting burnooses. Large turbans hid the backs of their heads. As for their faces, they were of a yellow-amber complexion, unmoving, as if frozen. In that frightening rigidity, only the eyes seemed alive. "Masks," he said to himself.

Darkness fell again. From out of the dark, the first voice he'd heard said slowly, "You've seen us. Wait patiently to be freed. But once you're out of here, remember that to see us again is to die."

A strange noise accompanied his words, like silk fabric being dragged across the floor. Then there was the soft click of the door closing, then nothing. Max sensed he was alone, bound by ropes to the cast-iron pillar. What did it all mean? Why had his unknown adversaries left him like this? They didn't mean him any harm—they'd said so, and Max had sensed undeniable sincerity in their voices. Then why had they tied him up? Why had they left him here in the dark, unable to make the slightest movement?

Indeed he couldn't move at all. With his back pressed against the iron pillar, and his arms pulled around behind and secured against the post, and the rope tightly wrapped around his neck, shoulders, body, and legs, he felt as if he'd been merged with the column. Ah, those strangers must've had practice tying up prisoners. The ropes were expertly wound. They didn't hurt him, but they kept him absolutely still.

Who could these people be? Enemies of the Duchess of La Roche-Sonnaille and Mona Labianov—they'd admitted it, when they threatened with death anyone who tried to solve the mystery. Why that animosity? No point in looking for the answer. Max would see the duchess at the Elleviousse Asylum, he'd tell her what he'd done, what he'd seen, he'd offer her his help, and the pseudo-madwoman would explain the whole business.

If he went on wondering who they were, it was because of their expertise at tying him up, and because of their peculiar disguise: the amber-colored masks. Didn't the precautions they'd taken to conceal their identity suggest that they expected to meet him—meet Max Soleil himself, who that very morning hadn't known that by evening he'd be breathing the air of Marseilles? How could they have—he was too logical to use the word "divined"—but how could they have been warned in advance of his movements and his intentions?

A painful feeling led his thoughts in another direction. His wrists were secured behind the pillar. Several loops of rope bound them together, keeping them from separating, but his hands were free—if you could call hands in that position "free." But it meant his fingers could move, and they instinctively took advantage of that freedom to drum on the curved surface of the pillar.

Any man left alone inevitably ended up drumming his fingers while he waited for something—anything—to happen: through a window, behind a door, across a table. Max realized with a smile that cast-iron pillars were especially inviting for fingers to drum on unconsciously. But he realized it in a painful fashion: one of his fingernails got caught in a crack, no doubt a flaw in the iron cylinder; his hand, finding itself stuck, instinctively jerked free, and the nail broke off cleanly at the tip of the flesh of the finger. That hurt. And from the main question of what he was doing here, his thoughts turned to that detail, that small new fact. "That's odd. The surface of a column is curved, but smooth. How could I have caught a nail in it?"

Shallow minds couldn't understand that kind of thinking in those circumstances, but more observant people would realize that the process of reasoning considered no question too trivial. It was certainly true that a perfectly smooth surface shouldn't catch a fingernail the way a rough surface would. And yet it had. That anomaly led naturally to a why?—which Max immediately felt a great desire to answer.

Stubborn effort—whose first result was to make the ropes dig into his wrists—finally enabled him to move his fingers along the pillar that held him still. After a few seconds he finally found, just under the damaged nail, a slight bump in the metal. "All right," he thought. "There it is." But then he bit his lip

41

to keep from crying out. Beneath the unintended pressure of his hand, the bump was sinking into the column, like a call button.

For a minute he stood stunned. "What's that?" And then he made the connection. "Maybe that's what those little feet were looking for around the iron columns!" With rising confidence he thought, "It must've been that!" But then, applying deduction, he went on, "Those little feet didn't know it existed, but they presumed something of the kind might exist. Yes, yes, the footprints show it. They were looking without being sure. If they were sure, they'd have gone straight to that button, that spring. Their hesitation shows they were just following a hypothesis. But in that case, in that case... those little feet were carrying out an investigation—just like me. Could it be the same one?"

Forgetting he was bound, he tried to nod, but the rope bit into his neck, and he quickly pressed his head back against the pillar. "I don't have enough data to solve for that 'X' factor. Let's leave that for now. Immediately at hand—pun intended—I have another 'X.' Let's solve for that."

He remained thoughtful a while, concentrating all the powers of his intellect. "Oh, but," he realized suddenly, "this proves the house has been occupied since Dr. Rodel's death!" He clenched his fingers—the only movement his ropes would allow; at any other time he would've rubbed his hands together in the universal gesture of great satisfaction. "I don't know exactly what this moving button does, but a push button always serves to communicate between someone in the room and one or more people outside. In my present circumstances I can't see, but I can assert with confidence that this button is at the very least connected to some signal buzzer. Now, a signal buzzer has to be practical. You don't install one unless you're going to use it often. And you don't put it where no one can reach it. That said, this apparatus couldn't have been here when Dr. Rodel was alive, because my examination of the walls clearly showed that the cast-iron pillars were built into the bookshelves. A buzzer requiring you to move aside several books—a buzzer oriented not toward the center of the room but toward the wall—no one would think of such a thing. Since it wouldn't be thought of, it wasn't."

He smiled in the darkness. His logic satisfied him on every point. "All right," he said to himself after searching in vain for an objection, "now let's consider the case in which—for reasons unknown to me—mysterious people secretly furnished the villa with the intention, formed in advance, of luring the duchess and her young friend here. I saw those people's representatives here earlier. They tied me up, so I know they're real. They could've had a reason to communicate between themselves, unbeknownst to their victims: to have an undisclosed, invisible signal. To wit, that call button, facing the wall, hidden by the thickness of the pillar. What would've been absurd for Rodel becomes logical for them. Therefore they must've installed it after his death."

He followed that train of thought a long time. The more he considered the elements of the problem, the more convinced he became. Meanwhile the hours went by. How long had he been tied up? He didn't have the slightest idea, but the beginnings of painful stiffness led him to suppose that his involuntary vigil had passed the limits of human endurance... when a strange feeling suddenly shocked him. It seemed as if his bonds held him less tightly—that they were loosening.

Before he could be sure of that, the rope across his chest tightened violently, slamming him hard against the cast-iron pillar; then the rope slid rapidly around him, like a snake unwinding. There was a whistling sound, and something whipping against the wall, then nothing. And Max stretched out his arms, felt his body, and realized he was free. The rope had vanished. He bent down, running his hands along his legs, feeling the ground around his feet. Nothing—no rope. How had it disappeared? No one had come into the room. Max would've heard even the softest footstep of a visitor. Anyway, he would've noticed someone untying the ropes. Hell! There were certainly knots: you couldn't tie someone up securely without a few knots.

The first priority was to be able to see. He pulled out his box of matches and struck one. "Bravo!" he cried. His electric flashlight lay on the floor a few steps away. Luckily he hadn't walked anywhere, because he would've crushed it underfoot. He picked it up happily: it was still in good shape. No doubt his adversaries had left it there, not wanting to take away anything of his.

With the light on, he looked around. Two things struck him simultaneously: first, the total absence of any footprints of the three people who'd shown themselves to him in such a fantastical way. But then some kind of smooth trail in the dust, leading to the door, gave him the solution to the problem: he remembered the sound of silk fabric he'd heard when they left. His assailants had dragged a strip of cloth behind them to erase their tracks.

That question settled, he noticed that in the space between the pillar to which he'd been tied and the wall—a distance of thirty centimeters—the floorboards had been severely lashed. Examining the marks more closely, he recognized the pattern of a rope pulled violently. And in the wall dividing the library from the sitting room a circular hole the size of a silver five-franc coin showed him how his rope had disappeared. Obviously the men in amber masks had wound it up in some prearranged way. The ends of the rope must've been threaded through that hole and been secured by some special knot. One of his jailers must've waited in the sitting room and then, at the moment decided on for freeing the captive, had untied the rope and pulled it through to him.

To confirm his deductions, Max opened the door. He found the hole on the other side of the wall. The floorboard just beneath it had been considerably displaced, and another smooth trail ran toward the door to the vestibule. Here again, the man had dragged a strip of cloth behind him to cover his footsteps.

"These fellows are clever," Max said to himself. "Very clever. They think of everything!" Then with a shrug he added, "They must be far by now. But the duchess will put me on their track. For now let's concentrate on that moving button in the pillar."

Not for a moment did he think of giving up the contest. His attackers had threatened him with death if he continued his investigation, and no sooner was he free but he resumed it without seeming to notice that his perseverance was becoming absolutely heroic. But—having been caught by surprise once—he took care not to let it happen a second time: he closed the door, put the rusty key in his pocket, and returned to the cast-iron pillar. He'd been right: a push button stood out against the metal cylinder. He pressed it, gently at first, then harder. What a strange button. It was still sinking deeper. What the devil could it be for? The range of motion of a button like that is always very limited. Why was this one able to go so deep?

He took out his pocketknife and used the narrow awl blade to push on the button. The steel blade sank entirely into the column, and then suddenly there was a kind of click. The knife and the hand holding it were flung back. He gave a cry of shock. In place of the push button a short tube had now appeared, with a disc at its tip made of parchment paper stretched across a jointed steel rim.

"My word, it's like a telephone mouthpiece." He was dumbfounded by his discovery. "Sure, with the telephone wire inside the column, totally hidden. But where does the wire go? Upstairs!"

He ran out of the library, across the sitting room, across the vestibule, up the stairs leading to the second floor, to the room directly above the one he'd just been in. "More cast-iron columns." It was true: two pillars identical to those downstairs rose from the floor to the ceiling. "By God!" he thought. "I was wrong. They aren't support columns. They were installed specifically to enclose the wires." Then he considered. "An expensive, uncommon system. So it was very important to have a means of communication."

But no matter how much he circled around the columns, tapping them, examining their surface, he found no irregularity. They sounded hollow, that was all. "Well, hell! Do they extend up into the attic?"

With that thought, he went on searching. A narrow, steep staircase—really a ladder—led up to a trapdoor: the only access to the attic. He lifted the trapdoor and got up into the attic, a low space that ran the whole length of the villa, the builders having thought it unnecessary to partition it with walls. Even so, he had no trouble finding the spot that corresponded to the rooms he was interested in downstairs.

Here, instead of cast-iron columns, there were pillars of lightweight brickwork that resembled chimney flues. He burst out laughing. "Very ingenious: chimneys on top of columns—that's guaranteed to draw well!" But then he grew more serious. "It's true that if those gentlemen hadn't put me, against my will, in a position that allowed me to find that button, I'd never have suspected anything."

44

He gave the fake chimney flues a quick examination. "No, nothing. The wires must go through to the roof. But outside there's no way to hide them. Well, we'll see. Nothing I can say now will be worth more than having a look."

Two hinged skylights had been set into the attic roof. Though he was spurred on by rising curiosity, he took the time to examine them carefully. One hadn't been opened for many months: its steel frame had lost its paint, rust had attacked it, and it took a violent effort to make it turn on its hinges. The other one, by contrast, though it too was rusty, moved with relative ease. "So it's through this one that the mysterious inhabitants of the villa came and went," he thought. "Let's follow the same route."

He opened the skylight and climbed out onto the roof. It wasn't especially steep, so it was easy for him to get to the fake chimneys that were the extensions of the cast-iron columns inside. But neither on the brick footer nor on the ceramic flue piping could he find the slightest hook to which could be attached wires capable of transmitting into the distance a signal from the telephone in the library. And yet it had to: it just couldn't be that you could only talk to the person on the ground floor by perching on the roof. To build such a complicated, expensive arrangement just for that would be absurd.

Like any proper chimney, the one Max was studying ended in a cylinder of red terra cotta. "Terra cotta is an insulator," he murmured. "The connection point must clearly be below it."

And, unthinkingly, he pressed hard on the cylinder. He felt it move under his hand. He pressed harder, and the pipe pivoted on some invisible base and revealed the opening inside the chimney. He gave a cry of joy. Inside the flue he could see rings attached to the surface of the tube, holding metal plates that vibrated constantly. "An amplifier!"

As we know, that's the word for an apparatus that, by means of the delicate vibration of thin sheets of metal, amplifies sounds the ear couldn't otherwise detect. The amplifier is to hearing what the microscope is to vision. And, serving as a support for the virtual "reeds" that turned the flue into a sound conductor, Max saw a sort of metal console placed like a stopper along the axis of the fixed rings. The very center was shinier than the rest of the surface, suggesting that there'd been rubbing there.

"They slid a rod through the rings," he reasoned, "and it rested on that stopper. What was the rod for?" And then he slapped his forehead. "I'm an idiot! No wires visible—therefore they're making use of telluric current. The rod was an antenna for a wireless telegraph-telephone!"

Ideas raced through his mind. "By God, that's it!—the wireless that was used to send the telegram of which no evidence was found later at the regular Marseilles office. And that accounts for one of the facts checked by that worthy detective Landré, known as Dodo." And then with great joy he went on, "But that gives me a clue to two at least of the Amber Masks who caught me here. Clearly one of them must've impersonated the late Dr. Rodel. Another must've played the telegraph clerk who brought the reply to the telegram. And none of the real telegraph clerks said he'd delivered a message to the Loursinade villa, which was the second point checked by Landré. Bravo! I'm convinced. Back to the hotel."

He was already heading back to the skylight when a strange voice made him stop as if petrified—a voice that seemed to rise from the depths of the garden: "This villa was built on top of an old quarry. It will collapse, along with the busybody who scorned the warning of the Amber Masks!"

"Who's there?"

No one answered. But beneath his feet Max thought he felt a muffled explosion that started deep in the ground. And as he wondered what it could've been, the roof seemed to tremble under him. A strange swaying shook the house, followed by an ominous cracking sound. He felt like the house was collapsing, dragging him down in a sudden fall. He ran to the edge of the roof, instinctively meaning to jump. He had the confused idea that a drop of eight meters, though dangerous, wasn't impossible. But the cracking sounds increased, the collapse sped up. Max felt a violent blow and lost consciousness, not knowing whether he was dying or merely passing out.

CHAPTER IV
In Which Miss Violet is Charmed

Miss Violet Musketeer, accompanied by Sir John Lobster, arrived at the Hotel Cosmopolitan at ten fifty in the morning. She took Room 3, on the second floor—the one known at the hotel as the "princes' suite." Then she asked that Monsieur Max Soleil, who should've checked in the day before, be notified of her arrival. She was informed that indeed the gentleman named had taken a room and had dined in the hotel; but he'd gone out in the evening, telling them not to be concerned if he didn't return that night. As of now he still wasn't back.

She didn't have time to be surprised, because almost immediately Sir John sent her word that a police officer whom he'd summoned was waiting in the hotel parlor, and he invited her to join them if the conversation seemed of interest to her. She sent back the chambermaid with these words: "Very well. I'll be down in a moment."

However, it sometimes happens that woman proposes but God disposes. A bellboy brought her a sheet torn off the pad of stationery at the front desk of the hotel, on which she read, written in pencil:

César Landroun, on behalf of M. S., urgently begs to be seen right away.

"M. S... Max Soleil's initials. Send him up." With a little anxious pout she thought, "I hope Sir John and his detective don't come spoil my happiness. The truth is, since yesterday this mysterious story has distracted me. I haven't been bored. And it's so good not to be bored!"

After a gentle knock, the door opened, and a man entered, whom at a quick glance Violet had to admit she'd never seen. The visitor, of medium height, wearing a suit that looked brand new, had a silk bandage over his left eye. His right eye was hidden behind a pince-nez of darkened glass. His short graying hair and mustache and sideburns suggested he was in his fifties.

"Mademoiselle," he said with a bow, "I beg your pardon for insisting on seeing you. But since Sir John will be busy in the parlor for a good while I thought I'd be able to speak with you without being interrupted by him."

"Ah!" she said, surprised by this odd beginning.

"First of all, here's a note to accredit me." He handed her an unsealed envelope.

As soon as she saw the inscription she murmured, "Max Soleil's handwriting."

"Shh! Shh!" he said quickly. She gestured inquiringly, and he added, "You have to keep your voice down. You never know when someone's listening. Just read the note, then I'll explain."

His tone of voice was so convincing that she obeyed without pressing him further. The letter consisted of these few lines:

Mademoiselle,

    As I must return suddenly to Nice, I'll presume so far as to ask you to settle my bill at the Hotel Cosmopolitan and to take charge of my suitcase on the way back. Enclosed please find the necessary money, with the thanks of your most obedient servant.

                                                  Max Soleil.

"Oh," she said, "of course I'll do as he asks, with the greatest pleasure."

The visitor bowed. "Now I should tell you in person why he's enlisting you to do this."

"Indeed. I don't quite understand…"

"Monsieur Max isn't coming back to the hotel, because he wants to throw off his trail certain people who think he's dead."

"I say! What are you telling me?"

"The truth."

"I can't make any sense of it."

"And that, Mademoiselle, is why I'm going to tell you what happened last night at the Loursinade villa."

"At the duchess's villa?"

"Yes, but let's waste no time. This is meant for you only. Let's be done before Sir John gets back, because he's brought in the police. The police won't find anything. And Monsieur Max even thinks that their involvement is more likely to create danger for the women you're interested in."

"Oh, yes," Violet declared with great feeling. "They interest me extremely, and increasingly so."

In fact, the appearance on the scene of César Landroun had intensified her desire to solve the mystery of the Loursinade villa. But her satisfaction knew no limits when her visitor concisely but clearly recounted the night's events. Violet punctuated the tale with constant enthusiastic exclamations: "Really! Poor man! Tied up! The Amber Masks! Oh, dear me, I think I'd have been terribly afraid." But when he reached the critical moment when the villa collapsed, dragging Max down with it, she cried out in fear. "Poor man! He's done for!"

But there she remained, her mouth wide open, her big blue eyes aghast— because her visitor had replied with a smile, "No, no. Besides a fairly hard knock on the forehead, I'm not doing too badly."

"You!" stammered Violet. "You—in disguise?"

"So as not to be recognized by the Amber Masks."

"Of course! But how were you saved? I'm wild with curiosity. Forgive my incoherence, but the truth is, I've never been struck in such a sensational way." In fact, the heiress had lost her customary propriety. She clasped her hands, shook, muttered. At one point she even squeezed her visitor's hands. "Oh, believe me, I'm so full of happiness… so completely… to see you again. But how is it that I do see you again, after a house fell on your head?"

Max—since it was he—replied with a laugh, "Not on my head."

"I think, I think... that would've crushed... but anyway, the house fell to the ground."

"Even further than that. Its ruins are at the bottom of a pit."

"And you fell into the pit?"

"No. I'd meant to jump off the roof. I must've done so at about the time the roof reached ground level. I must've struck my head against a tree, near which I found myself lying when I came to."

"You say it like it's a natural thing."

"Because it's known about head wounds that if they don't kill you right away, they're the least harmful of injuries."

Violet, truly moved, took his hands again, squeezing them with an emotion she didn't try to hide.

"The proof," he went on calmly, "is that when I opened my eyes I knew right away what I had to do."

"Right away?" she echoed.

"Absolutely."

"So you realized..."

"That if I didn't disguise myself, the fellows in amber masks would cause all kinds of trouble for me, and that they'd keep me from speaking freely with the Duchess of La Roche-Sonnaille."

"That seems clear."

"So I left the villa, keeping a careful eye out. Nothing suspicious. No doubt the rascals assume I'm dead."

"Oh, those bandits!"

"I came back to Marseilles, and a closed car took me to the Nouvelles Galeries. I came out with this suit, this bandage over my eye, this pince-nez of dark glass. I made another stop at the theater hairdresser—passing myself off as an actor heading to Monte Carlo—and I got a wig and sideburns and mustache."

"Why come here? I tremble at the thought that the Amber Masks might be following you."

"No, they've lost track of me for now. I'm sure of it. And besides, I need you."

"Oh, with all my heart!" Then, blushing a little at the fervor of her own exclamation, Violet added, "Because I feel responsible. I should never have encouraged you..."

"Bah! I was so interested in the mystery."

"Just as I am, you know."

"Anyway," Max went on gently, "you're going to introduce me to Sir John as an old friend you ran into."

"A friend he doesn't know."

"Of course."

"That won't be hard. He's only been following me around for the past six months. I knew you before that... where?"

"In Paris?"

"Yes, that's right, in Paris. And then what?"

"And then, you told me about your idea of visiting Dr. Elleviousse's asylum this afternoon."

"I told you... well, well!"

"And I answered, 'I'll go along with you, if I may.'"

She clapped her hands with joy. "Hip, hip, hurrah! I get the idea: you come along with us without it looking planned in advance."

"Exactly."

"And once we're there you arrange to meet secretly with the duchess."

"A meeting that all the Amber Masks can't prevent, because they won't know it's coming."

Before Violet could reply, there was a sharp knock at the door, and a chambermaid's head appeared at the opening.

"What is it?"

"Sir John Lobster asks whether Miss will receive him."

"Of course."

"He warns Miss that he's not alone. A man is with him."

"The detective!" murmured Max and Violet and the same time.

After which she added, "No matter, I'll receive the gentlemen." But then she stopped the servant before she went away. "One moment. Here's a letter from a traveler who will not be returning to the hotel. Please put his bill on mine. And also give orders that his suitcase is to be added to my luggage."

"Very good, Miss." The chambermaid took the letter Max had given Violet earlier, and went away.

"He's going to introduce his detective to us."

"Yes, so it seems. What should I do?"

"Give him a warm welcome. In return you'll introduce me, César Landroun, whom you bumped into here and who's eager to resume a connection of which he has delightful memories."

"Agreed."

Without even realizing it, Violet had just done something that would've shocked not only Sir John but all of her friends: she'd voluntarily put herself under Max's direction, asking him to guide her actions and conforming without resistance to his instructions.

The door opened again to reveal Sir John and Landré the detective, known as Dodo. Sir John seemed to be bursting with great cheer, which split his mouth from ear to ear and gave his red face a vague resemblance to a Dutch cheese overcome by mirth. "I say! Just as I was telling you, dear Violet: the facts at law are only a matter of money. This is Mr. Landré, a detective, who made inquiries about the ladies at the Elleviousse Asylum. He'll tell you they're quite out of their minds, and their whole story is nothing but a romantic fantasy."

He probably expected her to react with annoyance, but not at all: she smiled in Max's direction and didn't answer. But her glance had the effect of drawing Sir John's attention to the visitor.

"I say! I beg your pardon. You're with someone."

Violet smiled again. "Monsieur César Landroun, one of my friends in Paris, whom I'm happy to have run into again here."

"Pleased to meet you." Sir John was sincere. To his eye, the newcomer, with his greying hair, didn't look like much of a concern to a fiancé. "With your permission, I'll continue. So here you are, dear Violet, robbed of the pleasure of the dramatic fantasy planted in your mind by that French lightweight."

"Monsieur Max Soleil," she said gently.

Sir John was momentarily taken aback by her calm. He'd expected more excitability. Nevertheless, he pushed on. "So I thought that the duty of your fiancé…"

"Which you are not," she interrupted quickly.

"No, indeed, in your eyes I'm not; but in my own estimation I am, and when speaking of myself I have the right to describe myself as I please."

"Oh, very well. I understand that right. You're engaged according to your own opinion, not mine. All right. Continue with your story, please."

Her calm irony disconcerted Sir John a bit, and he went on in a less confident tone, "I've had the clever idea of replacing the imaginative experience you were hoping for with another one, equivalent to it."

"You're really too kind."

"And I've been lucky enough to have found…"

"Found what?"

"This: Mr. Landré is leading an investigation, and he suggests that he take us along to observe police procedures, as spectators." An expression of scorn was already forming on Violet's rosy lips, but Sir John added, "And it's about the madwomen we're interested in."

"The duchess and Mona Labianov?"

"Precisely. Following a distraught telephone call from Dr. Elleviousse, Mr. Landré has been assigned to find out how they managed to escape from the asylum last night."

"Escape?" The word burst like a roar, not only from Violet's mouth but from that of the pseudo-Landroun. Sir John cheered right up: this time he'd made an impression.

"Escaped!" repeated Violet.

"Yes, during the night."

"But how—how?"

"They don't know. That's what Mr. Landré is in charge of clearing up. And I've just sent for a landau. He'll allow us to join him."

"Oh, I'd be thrilled to go along," said Max quietly.

"With the greatest pleasure," replied Sir John. "As you say in France, our friends' friends are our friends. You're a friend of Miss Violet's. I'm her fiancé—fiancé in my own mind—and I say, come along."

The detective nodded.

"So, we're leaving immediately. I'm going to my room to get my hat. Violet, get yourself ready to go." And, taking Landré by the arm, Sir John dragged him away.

Max was following them, when Violet held him back by his sleeve. "This is a setback for your own investigation, isn't it?"

"Perhaps. Thanks to the detective, I'll be able to make an examination that Dr. Elleviousse would otherwise have been unlikely to allow."

"Ah!"

"Plus—plus—now it's a fight to the death against those people who tried to murder me last night. I'll pursue it to the end."

"And I will too," she said solemnly, holding out her hand to him.

He drew his hand back. "No, no, not you. Too dangerous."

But she insisted gently. "There'll be two of us. Anyway, I've made up my mind. It's the good deed that'll drive away boredom. Since yesterday I'm no longer bored. You wouldn't want me to die of boredom like before?"

Her blue eyes shone so sweetly, so clearly, so trustingly, that Max was moved, and didn't have the courage to resist the charming Englishwoman's heroic whim. Almost reluctantly his hand met the one she held out. While they shook on it, he murmured—without really being aware what he was saying— "All right then, let's both march off to war."

And, with a suddenly flushed brow and a gentle flutter in his heart, he left the room and went downstairs.

As he reached the vestibule, a landau was stopping across from the main entrance to the hotel. The doorman got out, crossed the sidewalk at a run, and said to someone seated in the office, "The carriage is here, sir."

"Ah, good. Thank you."

Max recognized Landré's voice. The detective soon emerged and went out to the landau, on which a slender, almost gaunt coachman sat, stiff and motionless. Max followed.

"Is it you who's going to drive us out to the Elleviousse Asylum?" asked the detective.

"Yes, Monsieur Landré," replied the coachman.

The detective started. "So you know me?"

"By God, you know me too. You don't remember? During that business on the road to Aubagne, you hired me to run errands."

"You... Wait a moment... You're..."

"Félix. You know me. I was out of work just then. And you helped me earn my living so I'd buy time to look."

"Ah! Well, isn't that something! This concerns the same case—the two ladies..."

"The madwomen?"

"Sure—they escaped last night..."

"And you have to find them. Ah, that's what I call a coincidence."

Max was no longer listening. A strange feeling had come over him. That
coachman's voice was familiar to him. He was positive: he'd heard that thin
voice before, with its working-class Marseilles accent and yet also with something foreign about it. But where? And when? He couldn't pinpoint it.

He was prevented from digging further, because at that moment Sir John
and Violet appeared at the door of the Hotel Cosmopolitan. They all got into the
carriage, which set off at a gallop, the coachman seeming very proud to be carrying Police Inspector Landré, known as Dodo.

CHAPTER V
The Elleviousse Asylum

Nothing could be more delightful than the asylum established by Dr. Elleviousse a few kilometers outside Marseilles. The sprawling house and the grounds full of rare plants had sprung up by the whim of a banking tycoon of Greek origin, whose name was remembered fondly in the capital of the Bouches du Rhône region: Phlorinopoulos, commonly dubbed The Generous, had dazzled Marseilles by his extravagance and his charity.

Why the lucky Greek had wanted a country house, no one could say. But one fine day he'd decided to build, and in six months—thanks to the magic wand of gold—the park and the palace had risen from the ground. On the portico Phlorinopoulos had engraved, in letters of gold, an inscription for which in vain people sought a symbolic sense: Λουλούδι.[10] What—what—could the banker have been thinking of when he chose that name? He explained to no one. Neither did he explain why, when the estate was all ready to move into, he seemed to grow sick of it, nor why he went back to Greece without ever having enjoyed his costly fantasy.

After he left, the lawyer in charge of liquidating his real estate assets had put the Louloudi mansion up for sale at an extremely low price—barely a quarter of its value. Elleviousse had taken advantage of the bargain, and Louloudi had become the well-known asylum. The buildings and the sumptuous halls intended for the parties and ostentatious celebrations of the wealthy were now home to the moans of the outcasts of society, the wretched victims of madness. The dark tragedy of the underside of life was played out on the happiest stage imaginable. From the gilded gates, from the carefully sanded formal driveway lined with flowering hedges, all the way to the house, with its multicolored marble and its bas-reliefs on the façade illustrating the joyful procession of the Heliades, everything smiled, everything was an invitation to pleasure.

Dr. Elleviousse was in his study. He received his visitors immediately. He was a plump little man, who would even have seemed coarse if his face—his entire person—hadn't been lit up by very large black eyes whose piercing look had great charismatic power. His welcome was most courteous. "Oh, I'm not concerned about what happened. My two guests are quite harmless—no danger either to themselves or to the public safety."

"Are you sure?" asked Landré self-importantly.

"Absolutely. The Duchess of La Roche-Sonnaille spent her time reading and taking walks. I even thought she was getting better, because especially in

---

[10] "Louloudi": flower [*Note from the Author*].

the last few days the mention in her hearing of the road to Aubagne didn't trigger her usual ravings."

"And Mademoiselle Mona Labianov?"

"Oh, as for her, I believe her madness is incurable. I'd almost call her spellbound. The Orient has a strange pull on her speech, on her whole way of being. The Orient and light. I'd noticed that double attraction, and I brought her into my laboratory. You know I concentrate my research on the influence of various prismatic light beams on my patients. My experiments seemed to interest her enormously."

"She can't possibly have understood them."

"On the contrary, that very unusual lunatic, whose mind seemed closed to all other things, became lucid, intelligent—startlingly intelligent—as soon as the subject was her own madness. Sometimes she even asked me questions or raised objections that caught me completely off guard, that surprised me."

"Very odd!" murmured the two English people. Pseudo-Landroun nodded without saying a word.

But Landré shrugged carelessly. "Fine. All that's of no concern to me. You think they're harmless, that's the important point. Now, how did they leave the house?"

Dr. Elleviousse lost a little of his calm. He lifted his arms in a gesture of annoyance. "I have no idea."

"What? With madwomen, it should be easy to figure out."'

"Perhaps for you, inspector, but not for me."

"Anyway, they got out. Now, doctor, will you permit me to make inquiries?"

"Please, be my guest! You're in charge. I'll do everything to make the job easy for you."

Max, Violet, and even Sir John had listened to Dr. Elleviousse with evident surprise. That madwomen should escape was understandable. But that they'd arranged their escape in such a way that the staff was subsequently unable to discover how they'd gotten free seemed fairly surprising. Violet exchanged a look with Max, a look that meant, "You alone are in the right—they're not mad."

But her attention was drawn back to Inspector Landré, who was speaking. "When were they last seen?"

"Last night, at ten o'clock."

"Who saw them?"

"Sidonie Lougé and Berthe Marroy, the two wardens specially assigned to their care."

"Good. We'll question those two women later. Where were the patients at that time?"

"In their rooms."

"And those rooms?…"

"On the third floor, adjoining rooms with access between them through a shared bathroom."

"What's the way out?"

"Their two doors open onto a corridor, at the end of which is the glass-walled loge where the night wardens sit. There are two of them, as I just explained. They alternate the day shift and the night shift. At ten at night the two wardens meet, and together they lock the residents' doors, and then the keys are hung up in the observation loge until morning."

"So, according to you, doctor, it's impossible to get out by way of the corridor?"

"Impossible. Besides, you'd have to go down the main stairs, and you'd certainly be seen by the wardens on the second floor or the ground floor. Finally, the door leading to the garden is also locked and reinforced by bars secured with padlocks."

Landré nodded with a knowing air. "So, there's no doubt. The third floor seems a little high for women. But even so, the fugitives must've gotten out through the window."

"Alas, no." The doctor sounded a little annoyed. Clearly he was growing irritated at the detective for offering theories that he'd already dismissed.

"You say no?" cried Landré in astonishment.

"That's what I say. This morning, when the staff entered the madwomen's rooms, the windows were locked. Since they lock from the inside, even if the women had reached the ground by means of a rope or something similar, they couldn't have relocked the windows."

"Who was present?"

"Sidonie Lougé and Berthe Marroy. They follow the same procedure to open the doors that they do for locking up. Berthe, arriving to start the day shift, met Sidonie at the loge and took the key down from the board. They unlocked the doors together; Sidonie couldn't hand over the duty to her partner and go sleep until that was done."

The police inspector suddenly stamped his foot. "It's too much! Yet they could only have gotten out by one of the exits you've mentioned? And to reach the garden, you must absolutely—understand me clearly here—absolutely use the main staircase?"

"There's no other way out. In a little storeroom on the third floor, there used to be a door into the corridor leading to the service stairs that gave access to the wardens' rooms. But I had that door sealed off, and the bolted steel plates that keep it from opening were found intact."

"What the hell!" grumbled Inspector Landré. "They can't have slipped through the keyhole. Let's go take a look at the ladies' rooms. People who aren't trained investigators notice nothing. I'm sure it'll all become as clear as spring water."

No one challenged the inspector's rather presumptuous claim. Dr. Elleviousse rose, and they all followed him to a grand white staircase with a wrought-iron balustrade. Right at the foot of the stairs stood a glass booth, a little like a station master's telegraph booth in the Paris Metro. "The ground floor warden's loge," said Dr. Elleviousse.

On the second floor stood a second, identical loge. The doctor just pointed to it. They all understood: it was physically impossible to go by unnoticed on a staircase guarded like that, especially because the many electric lights showed that it would be even brighter in here by night than by day.

The visitors reached the landing on the third floor: a third glass loge. "This is where Sidonie Lougé was posted last night," said the doctor.

"All right," muttered the inspector. "Where is that individual?"

"Probably in her room. The night wardens have to sleep during the day."

"Perfect. We'll go question her later."

"I could have her notified."

"No need. I'd rather surprise her."

"Do you suspect her? I believe I can trust my staff. I accept only people with first-class recommendations, and because I don't skimp on salaries, both probity and self-interest guarantee the zeal of everyone I hire." Dr. Elleviousse's tone was firm. There was no doubt he had total confidence in his subordinates and was ready to defend them against any accusation.

"What about Berthe Marroy?"

"She must be in one of the rooms on this floor, since she has the day shift today."

As if in answer to the detective's question, the silhouette of a woman appeared at the far end of the corridor. She was tall, slender, almost gaunt. A black wool dress emphasized the austerity of her appearance and her manner. As she drew near they all observed that her dark face looked like the model for one of those profiles of Caesar preserved on Roman medals, and that her expression was one of melancholy seriousness. Her very black hair, marked with a few strands of silver, fell in straight bangs onto her smooth forehead. The warden seemed like a woman of the world who'd been broken by misfortune.

"Madame Marroy," said the doctor, "these people have come to investigate how two of our residents were able to elude surveillance."

"No doubt they'd like to see those ladies' rooms?"

"Of course you understand that this is just a routine inquiry."

"And I hope it succeeds, doctor. You might not believe me, but since this morning I've been racking my brains to figure out how two poor madwomen could've found a way out that we sane people can't discover." With great dignity she opened two doors standing about three meters apart. "Go on in, ma'am, gentlemen. The room on the right was the duchess's, the one on the left was Mademoiselle Mona's. Between them is the shared bathroom, which opens neither onto the corridor nor onto the garden." She spoke in the flat tone of people who've suffered much and who no longer let their emotions be seen. Even her voice, though it was very clear, had something broken about it.

They'd all entered the rooms formerly occupied by the two patients. Violet felt oddly upset. Her eyes were damp. For a moment she hung back, near Max, and murmured, "Poor women!"

"They have two friends now," he replied.

She rewarded him with a smile, then rejoined the group—at the center of which Inspector Landré was holding forth pompously. "Windows locked, so the lunatics didn't get out that way. And even if an accomplice had locked them after they left, either the windowsill or the walls would show some trace of the rope, the ladder, whatever it was by which they climbed down."

"Quite right," said his listeners.

"For the moment I'll proceed by absurdities: I'm proving what couldn't have happened. Whatever's left after that process of elimination is the right answer. All right, the windows are dismissed. Let's see the chimney flue."

"Oh," cried Dr. Elleviousse, "too narrow."

"I believe you, but let's have a look anyway." So saying, the inspector moved aside the fireplace screen. "Well!" he said. "You let your residents have fires. That seems a little risky to me."

There was a general exclamation. "Fires?"

"See for yourselves." So saying, the inspector pointed to a pile of ashes in the firebox. "Papers were burned, a lot of papers—probably newspapers."

Max had drawn close. He bent down, picked up some of the charred dust, and examined it carefully—an action that didn't seem to please Inspector Landré.

"Oh, it's certainly paper," he said curtly. "You can see that at a glance."

"I do believe there's paper here, sir," replied the pseudo-Landroun with such subtle irony that only Violet caught it. "But you forget that I'm not a trained detective like you. Since I'm observing an investigation, I'm trying to learn."

The detective didn't care for Monsieur Landroun; Dodo turned his back and addressed the doctor again. "The windows and the chimneys have been crossed off my list of theories. The lunatics must've gone out the door."

"Impossible, for the reasons I explained earlier."

"Anyway, it doesn't matter. The cold hard fact is, they're gone, and we'll easily nab them again. We just need to send their description out in all directions. By God! Two madwomen left to their own devices won't get far." Then he addressed Madame Marroy. "Can you tell me what they were wearing yesterday?"

Something like a smile passed momentarily across the warden's face. But maybe that was just an illusion, because she replied with the greatest indifference, "That's easy enough, because they only took away one dress each. They left everything else. Therefore..."

Landré rubbed his hands together with excitement. "Just as I was saying. Where are their clothes kept?"

"Next door, in the bathroom closet."

"Let's have a look."

"There's no need, inspector. I've already looked. I beg your pardon, I seem to be giving orders. I'll show you."

"No, no, don't apologize. You were quite right. Since I'm not familiar with those ladies' clothes, I could look all I want at what remains without learning a thing. So, go ahead. They left wearing…"

"A navy blue tailored suit with a jacket."

"Which one wore that?"

"Both of them, inspector. The duchess took charge of their clothes, and she ordered the same dresses for Mademoiselle Mona that she got for herself."

Landré rubbed his hands even more vigorously and said to the doctor, "Dressed identically—even easier to find them." Then he returned to Madame Marroy. "Shoes?"

"Lace-up ankle boots."

"Hats?"

"Pillbox hats with blue feathers."

The detective had pulled out his notebook, and was writing down the descriptions the warden gave. "Don't you worry, doctor," he said. "With a description like that, the fugitives will be back here inside forty-eight hours." He broke off suddenly and put his hand on Madame Marroy's arm. "By the way, did they have any money with them?"

"I don't think so, inspector. but I've been away for a few days: one of my children was sick."

"Far from here?"

"Near Aix. It's my son Louis—a fine fellow, eighteen years old. The doctor gave me permission to take care of him. I was there a week, and I only returned the day before yesterday."

"But I can answer your question," interposed Dr. Elleviousse. "The La Roche-Sonnaille family lawyer usually sent me the payments for their treatment and whatever was needed for their living expenses. I settled the accounts directly."

"So, no money passed through their hands. It won't be forty-eight hours, it'll be twenty-four hours until you retrieve your birds who flew away."

Madame Marroy cut him off. "Well, now, they might have objects of value."

"Objects of value?" echoed Dodo, swinging quickly around to her.

"Yes. I don't see a red leather bag that held gems from India or China. I couldn't tell you if they were worth anything; that's not my line. Anyway, I thought I'd point it out."

"Quite right. But that's more likely to get them caught than help them get away." His listeners protested, and the inspector explained smugly, "The buying and selling of gemstones is highly regulated. If those poor madwomen try to convert their precious stones—assuming they are precious—to convert them to cash, we'll hear about it right away." Then, more and more pleased with himself, he added, "There's nothing more to see here. Shall we go question that Sidonie Lougé, the one who was on duty last night?"

The doctor bustled forward. "Just as you wish. As I explained, we have to take the main stairs down, go outside, and go around behind to the entrance to the service stairs."

They'd all reached the corridor, and Landré already had his thick red hand on the balustrade, when César Landroun said, "Didn't the doctor tell us there's a connecting door between this corridor and the service stairs?"

"Sealed off," said the psychiatrist.

"I remember, but as long as we're here, it seems to me—unless you disagree—that we'd be wise to make sure it's still impossible to use it."

"It is," said Madame Marroy quickly.

"By God," grumbled Landré, "That's the ABCs of investigation. The staff thought of that right away. Anyway, if it'll make Monsieur happy..." He emphasized the words with a scornful glance at the fake Landroun. "To make him happy, let's go see that blocked door."

And as he went down the corridor with the doctor, the detective complained in a loud voice about people who know nothing and want to interfere and lead investigations. Sir John Lobster followed with great interest, questioning Madame Marroy, who answered in her calm, indifferent voice.

That gave Violet a chance to whisper to Max, "Well?"

He glanced around to make sure no one could hear them. "Well, they got help to escape."

"From the warden we're going to go question later?"

"I don't think so. Certainly it would be foolish on her part to choose exactly the night when she was on duty to carry out the operation, since suspicion would inevitably fall on her. I'd go further and say she knew nothing, otherwise she would even have tried to prevent it."

"One more question. What makes you think they had help from outside?"

"The ashes in the fireplace."

"The ashes?"

"Yes. Someone burned a lot of paper—but underneath that, first, they burned cloth."

"You mean?..."

"No doubt the dresses that are missing from the closet. The fugitives no longer match the description given to the police." Then he broke off. "You'll hear the details later. Let's catch up to the others, because I too want to make sure that connecting door is truly blocked."

At the far end of the corridor stood a small cramped room of irregular shape, probably the result of some architect's blunder during construction. It got light only through a narrow window looking out on a wall, so that a sort of twilight prevailed. At the narrow end of the room stood the door described by Dr. Elleviousse. Steel plates bolted to the door and the doorframe clearly showed that the passage was no longer in use.

Landré eyed the pseudo-Landroun up and down ironically. "We've been very obedient, we've seen the door. Now, we've wasted enough time. Let's hurry up and go see Sidonie Lougé." He was gloating, using his superiority to crush the busybody who'd dared give him advice and made him go down a long corridor to admire a doorway sealed with steel plates.

No doubt the doctor and Sir John secretly blamed Violet's friend for having displeased the detective, because they rushed after Landré as he strode confidently back toward the main stairs.

Max, on the other hand, went to the door the detective had given such a cursory glance. "It's too dark in here," he murmured. From his pocket he drew a box of kitchen matches, lit one, and held the flame up to the heads of the screws that held the steel plates to the doorframe.

"What are you doing, sir?" asked the warden, Berthe Marroy, softly. Though her voice was as calm as usual, it seemed to contain a hint of concern.

Landroun reassured her. "Oh, just looking. I've had to seal up several doors this way at my place, and I can see that here the plates were just fastened to the wood, without cutting grooves for them. It causes less damage, and I'll mention it to my locksmith."

"Oh, workmen are all the same," said the warden. But Max was no longer listening: he was hurrying to catch up with the group. Violet kept up with him.

"The sealed door was opened," he whispered. "The slots of the screw heads show fresh scratches. The screwdriver was used last night."

"That would explain why the guards on the main stairs saw no one."

"I assume the fugitives got out by way of the service stairs. But shh! No one must know."

The procession went silently downstairs and reached the front steps facing the formal entranceway to the grounds. Led by Dr. Elleviousse, they all followed the façade around the left wing to the rear of the building, and finally reached a rounded bay, at the back of which they could see the high, narrow steps of the service stairs.

Beneath the first few steps there was a dark space piled untidily with wooden clogs.

"Is this where you sell wooden shoes?" joked Landré, who'd fully recovered his good humor.

"A precaution for rainy days. Our wardens normally wear slippers in their rooms. If they have to go out, they put on clogs."

"Fine, fine. Let's go on up."

"One moment," called Violet, to whom Max had just spoken quietly.

"What is it, Mademoiselle?"

"Where does that garden path lead?" She pointed to a little path running away from the house at an angle and ending—as well as good be judged—at a narrow door set into the outer wall around the property.

"Oh, that's an alleyway reserved for the use of tradesmen and delivery people." And with a smile the psychiatrist added, "You can tell, can't you: the gardeners have neglected to rake it. You can't blame them—they'd have to redo it every day."

"Speaking of gardeners," exclaimed the pseudo-Landroun. "They must've discovered footprints on the paths through the grounds?"

"None, sir."

"Oh ho! That's odd," muttered Landré. "There should've been some, since your patients didn't have wings, that I know of."

"Of course not, but they left no footprints. I myself looked around the house and explored the lawns."

"Your gardeners must've raked before you showed up."

"They say they didn't. Now, in spite of what they say, it's possible. Anyway, they would surely have noticed. As you heard earlier, the ladies were wearing the same shoes: ankle boots for small, elegant feet."

"Their footprints might've gotten mixed up with those of visitors to your other residents."

"Impossible. Visiting hours are over at seven, and all the alleyways around the house get raked. You can see how that would be a useful precaution for just such a case as this. You can't guarantee that a patient won't elude monitoring."

"And no footprints. Bizarre. Your worthy gardeners must've erased them without noticing. Come now, doctor, people who really apply their minds to their work are uncommon. But, please, show us the way to that Sidonie Lougé's room…" The inspector paused a while, then went on with a crafty air, "The one who could've had a… criminal willingness to help madwomen who wanted to escape from your institution."

Dr. Elleviousse opened his mouth. The look on his face suggested he was going to protest—but the detective cut him off: "Up we go, doctor, up we go. All will be explained in the end."

They went up the steep stairs in single file. They climbed one floor, then another. On that landing the warden pointed out the sealed door opening onto the corridor.

The inspector nodded with little interest. "Where's Sidonie Lougé's room?"

Dr. Elleviousse pointed to one of the doors along the corridor serving the part of the building dedicated to the female staff quarters.

"All right. Quiet, everyone. Leave it to me." Landré tiptoed to the door and bent down to listen. "Nothing," he murmured after a moment. "The key's in the lock. He, he! Is the bird trapped?"

They all gathered behind him: the psychiatrist and Sir John breathless, Max and Violet indifferent, Madame Marroy with a look of vague unease. Abruptly the detective turned the key and leapt into the room.

A terrified voice cried out with a strong local accent, "*Té, quésaco*? Robbers?"

A sturdy brunette in her late twenties sat up, pushed aside the covers, and got out of the bed placed in one corner of the room. It was a cozy little room: the iron-framed bed, the table, the pine chairs were clean and cheerful. Small shelves on the whitewashed walls held cheap trinkets from Vallauris and Golfe-Juan—little vases, tiny teacups, artificial flowers... But it was all neat, in bright colors. And the occupant herself, still emerging from sleep, had the round face and the fresh golden complexion of a real Provençale. She pushed back the stray locks of the tousled mop of hair that fell into her eyes, and said in a loud voice, "*Té! Monsou* doctor. Why'd you climb all my stairs?"

But it wasn't the doctor who replied, it was Landré, as calm and stiff and dignified as a trial judge. "The law has entered your room, Mademoiselle."

"What law?" she said, her eyes opening wide with a spark of laughter.

"The law that has come to ask you what you know about the escape of the Duchess of La Roche-Sonnaille and Mademoiselle Mona Labianov."

"What I know about it?"

"Yes. I don't need to remind you that it's in your interest to tell the truth, the whole truth."

She laughed, revealing strong white teeth. "The whole truth, right? You'll hear it, poor man. But if you've been in hopes of learning something, sweetheart, might as well order up the dunce cap for you right away!"

That only magnified Landré's stiffness and solemnity. "The strongest suspicions weigh upon you!"

"Oh, they don't weigh nothing on me!"

"Make sure you're not lying!"

Her black eyebrows gathered in a frown. "And make sure you stay polite, eh, sonny boy!"

"I am Detective Inspector Landré of the Marseilles Police."

"And I'm Sidonie Lougé of the parish of St. Charles, of an honest family, from father to daughter, *monsou* policeman, and if you don't watch it you could be the police commissioner himself and I'd still massage your face with my fists. There, you been warned. Now what do you want to know?"

"You should know, Sidonie," said the doctor, "that I guaranteed your innocence."

"Oh, you, doctor, you're the best of folks!"

"But answer him. Some residents escaped. There's a routine police investigation. Some detail that seems unimportant to you might put us on their track and save me a lot of trouble."

The big brunette clasped her hands. "Ah, good man! He's thinking, 'I've got to cool down Sidonie's temper, else she'll eat that detective and get a tummy ache.'" She began to laugh again. "*Bé, bé.* Sidonie's not so tough as all that. Go on, go on, police fellow, do your investigation thing. If you behave it won't cost you a thing."

Violet and Max couldn't hide their pleasure at hearing the handsome brunette express her thoughts with the whimsical invention so charming in the people of Marseilles.

The inspector, on the other hand, grimaced. But he knew he'd never have the last word with Sidonie, and he went on in a less arrogant tone. "Well, Mademoiselle, what we'd like to know is: what happened during your night shift?"

"What happened... *Té,* at ten o'clock I went to relieve Madame Marroy, and we locked the doors and took away the keys."

"You're quite sure the doors were locked?"

"Course I'm sure. If between the two of us we failed to lock up, that'd mean never again having sea urchins or carpet-shell clams or sea squirts."

"All right. The patients were locked in. What did you do next?"

"We went to our glass 'perch' and hung the keys on their nails on the board. And then I got our bottle of crème de cassis. Every evening we have our little cassis. It helps the one on the night shift stay awake, and it helps the other one sleep well." She burst out laughing. "Then Madame Marroy went away, and I began reading a book the concierge at the gate lent me. I thought, 'This'll last me until morning.' *The Green Pigeons* is so well written. That's the title, *The Green Pigeons*. It means a man and a woman billing and cooing. If you read it, it would just break your heart. *Té*—'cuz even in the police you can still have a heart. I don't reckon the government can forbid it!" And on she went, that talkative Marseillaise.

Annoyed by all the chatter, the inspector was about to cut her off, or at least try to put the brakes on her unwanted eloquence, but Dr. Elleviousse leaned toward him. "Let her go on in her own way—it'll be quicker in the long run."

But Sidonie Lougé was continuing. "Anyway, it's nothing to me. Where was I?... Oh, yes, I expected to read all night. Well, I was wrong—and this proves I'm telling the truth—because it's forbidden to sleep on duty. Well, *bé*, I slept, and slept, and slept—slept like an old beached boat in the Vieux Port!"

"What! You..."

"Fell asleep like a garter snake at high noon."

"And meanwhile someone took the keys?"

She shook her head. "Nope, not possible."

"And why's that, if you please?"

"Because the monitor's loge locks, and I'd turned the lock. You never know, with those crazies. Better to avoid surprises."

They all looked at each other. To the doctor, and the detective, and Sir John, the further the investigation went the murkier the case seemed. Meanwhile Landroun whispered in Violet's ear, "Just as I thought, this Sidonie knew nothing. And they even shut her eyes, with some sedative, probably opium, mixed into the cassis she drank."

"But who added the sedative?"

"Probably her companion. Anyway, I'm going to check." In the midst of the general silence Max asked in a thoughtful voice, "Mademoiselle Sidonie, do you usually fall asleep like that?"

"When I'm on duty? Never."

"And it didn't occur to you that your sleep might've been induced..."

"By what?"

"Hell, a few grains of opium in your cassis..."

But before Sidonie could answer, Berthe Marroy exclaimed, "In that case I'd have slept too, and unfortunately I didn't shut my eyes all night."

"Obviously!" added the detective, happy to contradict this stranger who set his teeth on edge.

With a careless gesture, Max turned back to Violet. "You hear that? It's her."

She gave him a look of agreement.

"I say," grumbled Landré, "this isn't getting us anywhere. In short, two lunatics have escaped, we need to catch them as soon as possible, and to do so we need to send out a description. So, to the telegraph office!"

"Wouldn't the inspector first like to examine my room?" The detective was about to decline Madame Marroy's suggestion, but she turned to the doctor. "It's very important to me, doctor. The incident took place on our watch. Sidonie and I hope to be cleared of suspicion."

"Oh, you're above suspicion. Still, to satisfy you, we'll go take quick look at your room."

While all the others followed Dr. Elleviousse to Berthe Marroy's room, Max slipped downstairs and out to the garden. There he slowly followed the walkway that had been described earlier as reserved for delivery tradesmen. With a look of astonishment he examined the path and the grass borders. "I see nothing. How the devil did they do it?" He slapped his forehead. "The clogs under the stairs. That's it! The prints they left attracted no one's attention. Well, might as well go back."

Still, he kept on going until he reached the door set into the outer wall of the grounds. He even opened it and glanced curiously out at the road. And then suddenly he stifled an exclamation. A little to the right of the road, on the grass at the foot of the wall, was a clear footprint. Max recognized it instantly: it was same small foot whose print he'd seen in the dust at the Loursinade villa. And that small, delicate, elegantly arched foot was so different in all respects from the prints left by other passersby that without hesitation he declared, "It's her!"

Thereupon with the tip of his boot he quickly rubbed out all trace of the print he'd just discovered so unexpectedly. Then, closing the service door again, he returned to the stairwell just as Landré emerged, more self-important than ever, saying in a deep voice, "My vast experience of investigations gives me the feeling that this whole escape, which looks so complicated, was actually child's play. But to solve the case would take valuable time—time better spent pursuing the fugitives."

It was the detective's unsuccessful attempt to hide his annoyance at going away empty-handed. The pseudo-Landroun's smile must've betrayed that he understood, because the inspector grumbled, "Oh, there you are, sir. Might you by chance have found something I missed?"

As if he hadn't caught the sarcasm, Max replied modestly, "Surely not, sir."

That fully satisfied Landré, and amused Sir John, who couldn't help disapproving of this gentleman, a friend of Violet's, who considered himself qualified to give technical advice to a professional detective.

Both of them would've been mightily surprised if they'd overhead the exchange that followed between the amateur sleuth and the pretty Englishwoman.

"I'm not going back to Marseilles with you, Mademoiselle."

"What? You're not?"

"I'll explain this evening. I've solved the escape of our unknown friends."

"Then why stay?"

"Because I don't know where they went. And because the person who helped them escape will probably tell me."

"So that we can go to them," murmured Violet, her cheeks flushing with joy.

"I believe so."

Meanwhile the little group had returned to the front entrance of the asylum. Landré and Sir John were taking leave of Dr. Elleviousse. The latter shook Violet's hand, saying gallantly how sorry he was to have received such an attractive visitor on a day when his duties as director had kept him from expressing his welcome adequately. Then he turned to the last of the tourists. "Mr. Landroun..."

But Max interrupted him. "Don't bid me farewell yet, please, doctor." In answer to the psychiatrist's questioning look he went on, "This is the first time I've been inside this kind of establishment, and I'm dying to stay longer, if you'll allow me."

The inspector's loud voice interjected, "I can't stay. In the interests of the case..."

"The interests of the case will be safe. You'll go back to Marseilles with my friends without worrying about me. With the doctor's permission, I'll explore the house, which seems quite remarkable."

Dr. Elleviousse bowed at the compliment.

"And," continued Max, "to keep my intrusion to a minimum, I'll beg Dr. Elleviousse not to be the least concerned about me. I'm a wanderer, full of curiosity, and I'd just be a nuisance to him in all his preoccupations. I'd be perfectly happy to have Madame Marroy for a guide, since the escape of the third-floor patients has given her some leisure time."

All of that was said in a careless, bantering tone, beneath which even the sharpest observer would've seen only the slightly bothersome curiosity of an idler. But Dr. Elleviousse was proud of the establishment he'd created—and rightly so, in his eyes. He declared himself delighted, and turned the visitor over to the solemn Madame Marroy; and as she took on the role of tour guide, the doctor went back to his office—but not before admiring for a moment the English multi-millionairess heading toward the main gate with the detective.

Playing the part of a man captivated by what he was seeing, Max obediently let himself be led around the facility. With her serene seriousness, Madame Marroy showed him the rooms for the "harmless," the cells for the "frenzied," the wing for the "improved," the common rooms for the "sociables," the sections for the "isolates," the alcoholics, the morphine addicts. She showed him the "curables" and the "incurables," stressing the distinct properties of those two forms of dementia.

Then she led him to the laboratory, where—using special phototherapeutic equipment—the wretched victims of insanity were treated by being bathed in green, red, blue, yellow, violet, indigo, or orange light. In her calm voice she explained the effects produced by each of those colors, the hopes that were inspired by this new science of healing light—a science that was still in its infancy and that already showed astonishing results.

Max had endless questions. You'd never have thought, seeing him so attentive—attentive to the point that his guide, flattered by such deep interest, dropped her somewhat stern reserve and grew almost confiding—you'd never have thought that her questioner's mind was absorbed by thoughts quite distant from madness and its treatment with light. That went on for two hours. The warden was in raptures. She'd never met a stranger who was so quick at getting her explanations.

Now she was leading Monsieur Landroun across the grounds toward the pavilion for the "baths," a still unfinished facility, thought up by Dr. Elleviousse, in which the cold showers and harsh ablutions of old madhouses would be replaced by luxurious methods and the humane use of all the pleasures available to sane people: Turco-Roman baths, hammams, Scottish rain, and other gentle hydro treatments—not forgetting scented ablutions—according to the wishes of the patient.

The walkway they were following crossed a large roundabout shaded by Italian poplars of the hybrid "gray" variety, whose trunks are steel gray, with the scars from their fallen branches looking like giant eyes. A stone bench had been placed at the foot of a fine tree. Seeing it, Max made a slight movement to stop.

Madame Marroy noticed, and, full of consideration for such an agreeable listener, she said, "Would you like to sit?"

"Well, Madame, I'll admit, if it's not an imposition…"

"Not at all. For those who aren't used to it, there's nothing so tiring as walking among crazy people."

"I'm not exactly tired; mostly I just need to put my thoughts in order. It's upsetting to confront the challenges of madness."

"Then rest a moment, sir. As you can see, I don't need to be talked into it. I'm not as young as I used to be."

"You have a grown son, I think you said."

"My Louis. He's eighteen, sir, and a head taller than I am, kindhearted and everything." Once launched, the mother would have gone on and on.

Max cut her off. "And what does he do?"

"He's foreman at the olive oil plant in Toumarenc, near Aix."

"And he knows how to handle a horse."

She looked him in astonishment. His comment seemed to have no apparent connection to the last thing she'd said. "Oh, naturally, he can drive a horse. You can imagine, a well-educated, well-brought-up boy; his bosses trust him, and they often send him out on errands, with Monsieur Lesbanade's carriage—he's one of the owners."

"Oh, yes, a cabriolet!"

"You know the carriage?"

"I saw it last night on the road to Aubagne; but since its lanterns weren't lit I couldn't make it out clearly."

By a spark of intuition, since the moment when, during the earlier questioning, the warden had been led to mention the name of her son Louis, Max had felt sure the young man must've been the driver of the carriage he'd glimpsed near the Loursinade villa. Now he had proof.

Madame Marroy had flung herself back, frozen, staring wildly at her companion. Her handsome smile had vanished. There was terror in her eyes. Still she tried to play it off. "Last night, on the road to Aubagne," she stammered. "I don't know—maybe he was there…"

"He was definitely there. And he was entrusted with an important mission."

"A mission?" she echoed, her voice shaking.

"Yes. He was escorting two victims to freedom: the Duchess of La Roche-Sonnaille and Mademoiselle Mona Labianov."

He'd barely spoken those names when Madame Marroy sat up straight and said with sudden firmness, "Well, sir, I'll lose my job, so be it. But to you—to all the detectives in the world—my answer will be that I know nothing."

Max burst out laughing. "I'm not with the police, my good woman, rest assured." And as she stared at him, incredulous and breathless, he added, "If I were, I'd have told Inspector Landré—who saw nothing—how the escape was carried out."

"So you know?"

"Perfectly. I'll prove it to you. With the pretext that your son was ill, you were away for days. You prepared everything for the escape of those ladies—one of whom, the duchess, you're convinced is not and never has been mad."

"Ah! You think so too?"

"It's because I think so that you see me here. But let me continue. You came back, having secured your son's help. He was to wait at the service door last night with Monsieur Lesbanade's carriage. He has the use of that carriage, with plausible excuses, doesn't he?"

She nodded, held under the influence of this stranger who knew what she thought to be a secret from everyone. Besides, something told her that her questioner would not be an enemy.

Max went on, "That way you avoided the reef on which all escapes founder. They always locate someone who rents carriages—and once there's a detective on the other end of the line… enough said. With the carriage and the driver made sure of, you came back to the asylum, bringing the disguises that would throw pursuers off the trail."

"Disguises?" she echoed, stunned.

"Of course. Those ladies don't look in the least like the description good old Landré is going to telegraph in all directions."

"Why would you think that?"

"Oh, for a conclusive reason."

"Say it!"

"The dresses the police are after are now a pile of ashes in the fireplace of the duchess's room."

"Ashes of paper."

"Oh, you were careful, and you burned a stack of newspapers whose ashes fooled the inspector. But I crouched down. I wasn't distracted, the way he was, by the narrowness of the chimney flue. I knew the fugitives had gone out the door, since that's the only way they could've escaped." Since she was silent, he went on, "You want to be informed, dear Madame. Fine. I'll tell you the story in detail." He continued with an ironic smile, "Around nine in the evening you unscrewed the steel plates that sealed off the door between the third-floor corridor and the service stairs."

"It's demonic!" she murmured, in spite of herself.

"No, it was the screwdriver, whose fresh scratch marks revealed your work. But don't interrupt me anymore. You dropped a little opium into Sidonie's glass."

"Oh!"

"There's no magic to it. If she'd been awake she'd have seen you and the ladies. So she had to fall sleep. You had your usual cassis, then you went quietly to your room. Toward eleven, all was quiet in the house."

"Why eleven?"

"That's when it was. I'll tell you why in a moment. I'll ask you again not to interrupt me."

"All right, I'm listening."

"So, at eleven o'clock you left your room and went silently to the connecting door, no longer blocked. Now you were in the patients' corridor. In her glass loge Sidonie was sleeping like a log. All was well. You reached Madame de La Roche-Sonnaille's door and opened it."

"How could I?"

"You had the key."

"No. Sidonie told you herself: she'd locked herself into the glass loge, and the key was hanging from a nail."

Max laughed and shrugged. "She told the truth. But she didn't know that while you were away, taking care of your son, you gave that sweet boy an impression of the key, and he had a copy made in Aix."

"Why him and not me?"

"Because he could claim to have lost the key to a bedroom, an office, a workroom. He was replacing it to avoid getting reprimanded by his bosses. In case of an investigation, it wouldn't even have been noticed."

Madame Marroy lowered her head. To anyone not accustomed to the marvels of deduction, Max's clairvoyance would've seemed almost magical.

"So, you opened the door. The ladies were ready. They'd put on the disguises you got for them. I don't know about Mademoiselle Mona's, but the duchess was dressed as a boy and wore felt-soled shoes."

The warden let slip a muffled exclamation: it passed the limits of her comprehension.

Without seeming to notice her emotion, Max went on, "They had their suitcase, containing their valuables and precious things. They followed you to the service stairs. You went down. At the bottom, all three of you got clogs out of the cubbyhole under the steps and put them on over your shoes."

"What an idea!" stammered Madame Marroy, still trying to resist.

"A good idea, you mean."

"Good?"

"Sure. The tradesmen's path had been raked that evening as usual. But the deliverymen come first thing in the morning. Clog prints, mixed with their hobnail boots and heavy shoes, wouldn't suggest the fugitives' small feet. Anyway, you got to the exit. Outside on the road your worthy boy was waiting with the carriage. The ladies climbed in. Once they were on the running board they handed you back the clogs and settled in. But the duchess lost her balance and had to hop down and get back up."

"What? So you were there?" stammered Madame Marroy, stunned. That last detail seemed more incredible than all the rest of this incredible reconstruction.

He calmed her with a smile. "The grass preserved a print. I erased it."

"You what?"

"Erased it. There was no need to leave it, was there?"

Suddenly Madame Marroy gave up her denials. "Then why were you investigating? And why did you keep quiet in front of that detective who…"

"I'll tell you later." And he went on calmly, "Once the carriage was gone, vanished into the night, you retraced your steps. You put away the clogs, then climbed to the third floor. You went through the connecting door into the corridor, where Sidonie Lougé was still asleep. You screwed back on the steel plates you'd taken off earlier. So the door was once again sealed, as before."

She confessed it with a nod.

"You went to the duchess's room. You were in no hurry. So you took the time to cut to ribbons the dresses the fugitives had left, and burn them gradually in the fireplace, mixing them with newspapers. Finally you burned a bundle of papers, whose ashes covered everything else. Then you waited for daybreak. When you could tell by the comings and goings of the staff that the ground-floor and second-floor wardens were doing their shift change—and that as a result the monitoring loges would be unoccupied—you decided to wake Sidonie."

"Why did I wait until then?"

"So your partner could see for herself that you were late, which would explain logically why the wardens on the lower floors, busy opening their patients' doors, hadn't seen you go by."

Madame Marroy bowed her head; then, as if with sudden resolve, said, "It would be pointless to lie. Everything happened just as you say. You hold my job here in your hands. So tell me—what do you want?"

"To find out from you what I don't yet know."

"What could that be?"

"To know where they've gone, in what direction they've fled."

"They didn't tell me…" she began.

But he interrupted her. "Before you answer, let me tell you how I came to be here, and what feelings and sympathies have led me to get mixed up in an adventure that, fundamentally, is none of my business."

He told her briefly about the old newspaper he'd seen in Nice, which aroused his curiosity and that of Violet Musketeer, his departure for Marseilles, his night at the Loursinade villa, his encounter with the boy—whom he'd been led by later circumstances to guess must've been the Duchess of La Roche-Sonnaille.

She listened in stunned admiration. She looked terrified when he came to the sudden appearance of the Amber Masks, and the collapse of the villa. "Ah," she cried, "I was sure of it. I didn't need to hear that to know she wasn't mad."

"I've never thought so, and Miss Violet later agreed with me. After what happened last night, you'd have to admit that any doubt would be stupid."

"And the men who tried to kill you?..."

"It occurred to me that I could carry on the investigation undisturbed. In the end the case concerns two women who've been tortured by those wretches. They're alone, and powerless against their enemies. I want to bring them the support of two friends: myself as her champion, Miss Violet as the 'banker.' And so that I can make them that offer, I'll repeat my earlier question: where have the fugitives gone?"

He'd taken her hands in his. When their vanity isn't involved, women have a wonderful intuition for sincerity. Madame Marroy understood her questioner's trustworthiness. She murmured softly, "I'll tell you everything I know. You're right: those poor women—of whom one, alas, is certainly mad—have great need of defenders. I'm not rich. The goat has to browse where it's been tied. Still, I've done my best. But you, and the young Englishwoman, can perhaps be of tremendous help to them." She broke off. "But my opinions don't matter to you. Here's what you need to know." She cautiously lowered her voice, as if she feared that even in this deserted spot invisible spies might overhear her words. "When they left, the little duchess, Madame Sara, wanted to go by way of the Loursinade villa."

"She carried out her plan. She wanted to examine the house, didn't she, in the hope that..."

"That she could solve the awful mystery of which she'd been the victim."

"I interrupted her, poor woman. She must've thought I was an enemy. Bah! At least I found something, and I've even got it in my pocket."

"What is it?"

"A wireless speaker, which'll prove to her that I didn't dream it all up. I tugged on it instinctively, it came loose, and in the midst of all these events I forgot it in my pocket. I've just now remembered it; but please go on, Madame Marroy, go on."

"My son Louis was then to take them to the train. The duchess wanted to avoid the Valance-Lyons line, for two reasons: *Primo*, it's the busiest, and would therefore probably be the most closely watched. *Secundo*, leaving Marseilles, that line heads west, which could've provoked a fit in Mademoiselle Mona."

"A fit?"

"Yes, her madness draws her to the east. When she walked in the grounds with me, she always chose alleyways running west to east. She fell into a fury if anyone tried to make walk another direction."

"A peculiar mania."

"But perfectly understandable: the poor child is following her heart!"

Max studied her. "Did they tell their story in detail?"

"Yes. The duchess trusted me, and she was right to. I may not be as educated as a magistrate, but I sensed she was telling the truth. I was sure she wasn't describing the inventions of a madwoman."

"You can fill me in later. For now, what train line did they take?"

"The Veynes-Grenoble line, with a branch line to Culoz-Modane. They planned to cross Italy, then go by way of Austria to reach Bohemia."

"Why?"

"To get to Stittsheim."

"And what is Stittsheim?"

"The place where Dr. Elleviousse has all his equipment made for his treatment using beams of colored light. It seems that's where they do manufacturing of the greatest precision and quality."

"Ah! The duchess doesn't really intend to..."

"Oh, yes, sir, yes!" Madame Marroy exclaimed quickly, without letting him finish. "With the help of certain devices, and of Mademoiselle Mona's madness, the duchess hopes—it seems that over there crazy people are considered emissaries of the gods—she hopes to reach the place where her husband and her young friend's fiancé died."

"Why doesn't she ask for help from her relatives or her friends?"

"Her relatives have disappeared, as you know. Anyway, she wouldn't turn to them, because no one can know where she is, since legally she's been declared mad. Besides, even if she weren't, her friends or relatives would still try to stop her from carrying out her plan, and she often said, 'We must go there—we must—it can't be for nothing that in her madness my dear Mona says over and over, "Toward the Orient! Toward the light!" It's divine inspiration, it's a call to hope. We must obey that voice. We must go there, no matter what.'"

There was a silence. Above them a gentle breeze moved the leaves in the trees. The rustling of the foliage seemed like an encouragement whispered into the ears of these two people, so different in rank and intellectual culture, but who shared the same pity and the same belief. For a long while they remained quiet, mutually lost in thought.

Finally Max, whose head had been bowed down under the weight of his reflections, looked up and murmured uncertainly, "Now, Madame Marroy, tell me—holding nothing back—all you know about those ladies' story, and the adventure that led them to this madhouse, an adventure that the law, as dim-witted and shortsighted as always, scornfully dismissed as a fairy tale."

"Well, sir, here's what the duchess herself told me."

CHAPTER VI
Which Concerns a Blue Flag and Its Two Masters

"First, you should know, sir," said Madame Marroy, "that Madame de La Roche-Sonnaille, whose maiden name was Lillois, and her husband, Duke Lucien, were on their honeymoon. They were in the Netherlands, peaceful and happy. They'd gone on a little motorboat excursion; they'd landed, and were taking a nap on a thick, fragrant lawn, sheltered by bushes, when they heard the voices of strangers: men who had no idea they were there were planning to attack another person who was going to pass by. Those two men were named Log, the master, and San, his servant."

"Log, San," repeated Max, committing the names to memory.

"Two giants of some kind, wearing amber-colored masks."

"Amber-colored masks?"

"Yes, sir, like the ones who attacked you at the Loursinade villa."

"Go on, go on. This business is growing to dimensions that are…"

"Colossal, sir, you can say that again! The person they were waiting in ambush for was named Dodekhan. Monsieur and Madame de La Roche-Sonnaille didn't know all that until later, but I'm telling you now to make things easier. This Dodekhan, a nice young man, good and honest and with every fine quality, was the son of a worthy man, deceased, who'd spent his life gathering into a single entity all the secret societies of Asia."

"Damn!"

"You're aware that millions and millions of Asians belong to organizations like that."

"Yes, indeed."

"Well, the father had been the paramount leader of the whole thing. His dream was to liberate Asia, to emancipate it, to throw off the yoke of European control—but to do it all merely by the power of logic, without bloodshed."

"Yes, yes, I get it. To avoid war by showing how dangerous it would be."

She looked pleased by his explanation. "I couldn't have put it as well as you, but that's how I took it. So, upon his father's death, young Dodekhan had inherited his power and his title, Master of the Blue Flag. A blue flag, with red-encircled yellow symbols at its center, was the emblem of the united secret societies."

"Curious, curious," murmured Max, very caught up in the story. "So that's the 'pan-Asian conspiracy' those idiotic magistrates turned into a madwoman's fantasy. Fools! Imbeciles!"

"So, Log and San, two fierce and ambitious men, wanted to seize power. Log would become Master of the Blue Flag and would put everything to the torch and the sword. But to do that he had to capture Dodekhan, render him

74

helpless, and above all force him to reveal certain symbols and secrets that had a hidden meaning for initiates."

"Of course."

"Now, Dodekhan had once saved Mademoiselle Mona's life. He loved her and she loved him. Log, who'd disguised his plans under an appearance of loyalty, had gained the young man's trust and had been his lieutenant. That's how he learned his secret, and that's how he found a way to bring down his rival. He was going to kidnap Dodekhan, and he was going to kidnap Mademoiselle Labianov. He would put them on a ship that was waiting off the Dutch coast and take them back to Asia. There he would torture Mademoiselle Mona while Dodekhan watched, if the latter refused to tell him what he wanted to know."

"The wretch!" growled Max with disgust.

"Yes, really. To turn the sweetest feeling to a vile end. To make tenderness into a stepping stone for crime—I too think it's the wickedest thing you can do."

"You're right."

"But you don't need to hear my opinions. As I said, the duke and the duchess didn't make sense of the plot until later. At the time they just thought it was a holdup, and—good people that they were—they wanted to warn its intended victim."

"Right."

"So they slipped away in their boat, landed again a kilometer downstream, hid at the edge of the road Mr. Dodekhan would be taking, and waited to talk to him as he went by."

"But he came by another road!" cried Max.

"No, no, sir. He showed up that night, at the hour the criminals had named. The duchess and the duke ran to meet him, but just as they were starting to explain why they—two strangers—had intercepted him, *pfuit*! There was a whistling sound in the air. Something heavy and flexible fell on all three of them and knocked them down, unconscious. Log and San had uncovered the nice Parisian couple's plan, and had thrown—over them and over Dodekhan—a fishnet soaked in chloroform."

"Fantastic!" exclaimed Max. "The net! The chloroform!"

"Naturally," went on Madame Marroy, "they all fell asleep. When they came to, they were prisoners on Log's ship. Soon Mademoiselle Mona joined them, and then began a life of torture: Dodekhan refusing to reveal the secrets of the enormous organization his father had created—refusing not out of ambition, but out of goodness. His father had built a formidable army, just as a means of persuasion; and the young man wanted to keep it from becoming, in Log and San's hands, an engine of destruction and extermination. The unequal struggle went on for months, taking them to Asia—to the German concession at Shandong, to French Indochina, to the heart of British India... Escapes and stratagems followed one after another, always keeping that cruel giant, Log, from carrying out his plan of torturing Mona."

"Poor child!" said Max sadly. "How could her sanity hold up?"

The warden put her hand on his arm. "It held up, sir. The duchess never tired of praising her young friend's steadfastness and courage. She loves her with all her heart—they've been through so much together! Anyway, I'll skip over some details to get to the final calamity. As you'd expect, one fine day Log got the advantage. His followers made ready to crucify Dodekhan and Mona, facing each other."

Max couldn't suppress a gesture of horror.

"Isn't it vile, sir? Picture this: he had Dodekhan's left hand nailed to the cross, and then he said, 'Now I'll do the same to the woman you love. And I'll go on doing that, to make it easier for you to know what suffering you're causing her.'"

"He's a torturer!"

"And a shrewd rogue. He knew very well what he was doing. When his bandits approached Mona, when the enormous nail was pressed against her hand, Dodekhan didn't have the courage to let the crime go forward."

"By God! I can imagine. You can be brave on your own account, but for someone you love…"

"In short, Dodekhan gave his word that he would reveal all of the organization's secrets to his enemy. But since he didn't trust him…"

"With good reason…"

"He made a condition that the two young women would be sent back to Europe. No doubt to make the deal more attractive, the Duke of La Roche-Sonnaille volunteered to remain with him as a prisoner."

"Very chivalrous."

"Wait, sir. Dodekhan had prevented a massacre of the French at Tonkin—a massacre planned by Log—and the duke had sworn his eternal gratitude. He said to himself, 'Dodekhan is sacrificing his honor for Mona and my dear Sara's sake. It's up to me to save the honor of this gallant man and faithful friend.'"

"Of course, the duchess didn't know that."

"No. She and her companion went to Calcutta and boarded the *Oxus*…"

"Of the Messageries Maritimes line?"

"Yes, and reached Marseilles. It had been arranged that they would go to the Loursinade villa, home to a Dr. Rodel, who'd known the young man before. Rodel would immediately cable Calcutta that the travelers were safe on French territory."

"No doubt that rascal Log already knew of Rodel's death," interrupted Max, "and one of his agents took the late doctor's place."

"That's what Madame de La Roche-Sonnaille assumed. But let me tell you how Mademoiselle Mona went mad."

"Ah! You know?"

"Yes. The false Dr. Rodel invited the travelers to make themselves at home in his house. That way, they'd be able to receive without delay the answer to the cable he'd had taken to Marseilles. They accepted. The answer came that evening, asking the poor women to be in the library at the villa at ten the next morning, to witness the interview between Dodekhan and Log and the release of Duke Lucien."

"What? What are you talking about? I thought they'd stayed in Asia."

"You thought right."

"In that case, how could they be seen in Marseilles?"

"As you can imagine, it made the detectives laugh until they cried. And yet I believed it."

"What, damn it! You believed what?"

"What the duchess told me: in the darkened library, on a kind of screen, like at a cinema…"

"A wireless telephote!" cried Max. "Now I get it! Yes, of course, the hollow columns weren't just for transmitting voices, they transmitted light rays, images!"

Madame Marroy listened to him with increasing satisfaction. "So you believe it's possible?"

"Absolutely."

"All the better. As you can imagine, I believed it because—because I believed it. But I'm happy you do too. You understand, that resolves my last doubts."

"Anyway, what did they see on the screen?"

"What did they see?" She looked distressed, and clasped her hands. She went on in a dull voice, "They saw a room in an Indian palace where they'd been held prisoner. At a distance of three thousand leagues, they could recognize the walls, the decor, the furniture, the window with purple curtains that looked out onto a marvelous garden."

"Where is that palace?"

"They never knew, but it must be approximately a hundred kilometers northeast of Calcutta."

"All right. Then what?"

"Then Log and San appeared on the screen…"

"The two giants in amber masks."

"Then Dodekhan and the Duke of La Roche-Sonnaille. And the young women inside the Loursinade villa could hear their voices, which seemed to come right out of the screen."

"Yes, the wireless telephone. Go on, my dear Madame Marroy. It all makes perfect sense."

"Log was saying, 'I've kept my promise, now you keep yours.' And Dodekhan replied, 'Yes, you really did save the women we love. I'll teach you the signs you don't know, and then I'll die—for I'll have betrayed the secret my father entrusted to my honor.'"

Max coughed a little from emotion. "That announcement of a suicide, three thousand leagues away—with no way to stop it—I understand. Poor little Mona!"

The warden motioned him to silence. "No, you don't have it yet. Suddenly the Duke of La Roche-Sonnaille—who'd said nothing yet—raised his arm. He was holding a revolver. The shot rang out. That monster Log fell to the ground, his skull shattered, and Duke Lucien cried, 'Dodekhan, I'm preserving your honor. You protected my countrymen at Tonkin, and I'm repaying France's debt with my life!'"

"Valiant duke!"

"Then San shouted and called. Bandits burst into the room, knocked down Dodekhan and the duke, raised their daggers…"

"Oh, those poor women—forced to see their loved ones' throats cut!"

"Worse than that, sir. Suddenly the screen went blank. They found themselves in total darkness. They were overwhelmed by drowsiness. When they came to, they were at the police station, and Mademoiselle Mona had gone mad." Madame Marroy now fell silent.

His head in his hands, Max sat motionless, reviewing the strange, unexpected tale he'd just heard. He marveled at the strange turns sometimes taken by chance or fate: Because he'd had the punning whim to give violets to a young woman of the same name, he'd been led to read an old newspaper… And now he found himself in the thick of a labyrinthine adventure, threatened with death by the mysterious Amber Masks, and firmly resolved—in spite of everything— to locate the fugitives, to offer them his assistance, to help them find the graves of the men they loved, struck down far away in India: that majestic, unsettling land of mystery where the voice of humanity first arose.

Suddenly he started. He looked around confusedly, as if he were coming out of a dream. Seeing Madame Marroy sitting motionless, her eyes fixed on him, he said, "My dear woman, I'm going back to Marseilles. No one else must hear what you've told me."

"I swear I won't say a word," she answered with feeling.

"I'm sure of it. You gave me the tour, I wanted to see everything, just like any curious visitor. I asked you two or three times about the fugitives, but since you knew absolutely nothing beyond what the investigation already found, I didn't insist."

"All right, but why dwell on them?"

"Because I fear the Amber Masks are capable of anything. In fact, if someone questions you, and seems interested in what I might've asked you about the missing women, please take a good look at the questioner, and cable a description to Miss Violet Musketeer at the Hotel Cosmopolitan."

"Understood. I'll do it."

"Thank you. Will you walk me to the gate?"

"Of course."

"Let me shake your hand, as a worthy friend met on the path to justice." He pressed her hands; she was very moved. "At the gate I'll make a show of offering you five francs for your services as the guide everyone must go on believing you were."

"And I'll accept it, sir."

Max stood up. Madame Marroy did the same. Walking slowly, seemingly absorbed in a discussion of the phototherapeutic methods applied at the Elleviousse Asylum, the two of them strolled across the grounds to the main driveway and then to the front gate. Max was pleased to see that the doorman was observing them closely. "Please be kind enough, Madame," he said, "to pass on my thanks to Dr. Elleviousse. His establishment is beyond praise."

Madame Marroy bowed gravely, and Max politely held out a five-franc piece. "To repay you for your trouble."

She mimed refusal, he gestured his insistence, and the coin disappeared into the worthy woman's pocket. They'd played out their parting scene.

Once out on the road, Max could see a little village nestled in the trees a few hundred meters away. He headed that way, with the idea of hiring a carriage of some kind to take him back to Marseilles.

CHAPTER VII
Paw in the Trap

"Now you know everything."

"And what do you plan to do?"

"Leave tomorrow for Stittsheim, in Bohemia. Since the fugitives need to order or buy phototherapeutic equipment, it won't be hard to find them."

"I want very much to go with you."

"No, no—don't forget, the Amber Masks must be prowling around us. I beg you, go quietly back to Nice, with the suitcase belonging to Max Soleil, my alter ego. As soon as I've succeeded I'll let you know, and..."

"I'll come join you and those charming ladies."

"Shh! Sir John's coming back."

This conversation had been carried on in whispers in the reading room of the Hotel Cosmopolitan. Taking advantage of the momentary absence of Sir John Lobster, who'd gone to smoke a cigar along the Canebière, Max—still passing as César Landroun—had shared with Violet the results of his inquiry. The conversation was ending when portly Sir John burst back into the room, prompting Max's cautious advice.

The new arrival approached them. "Oh, you don't know," he said, puffing as if he'd been running, "something truly hilarious."

"Tell us."

"I came back on purpose to do so... I saw Landré... the detective."

"And?"

"He's furious."

"Because?"

"Because in spite of the description he sent out everywhere, the madwomen from the Elleviousse Asylum weren't spotted by any police in the entire region."

"Spotted?"

"Yes, exactly. They all say, 'No sign of two ladies in navy blue tailored suits, not at any train station, nor on any streetcar, nor at any carriage hire shop.' And yet they're not traveling on foot, because you can't get very far very fast that way."

The pseudo-Landroun began to laugh. "You're thinking logically. Don't forget, we're dealing with lunatics, who as a result are perfectly capable of setting off on foot."

"You're quite right. I'll see Landré again tomorrow. I'll tell him your idea, without saying it came from you." With a loud laugh, Sir John added, "Because I have to warn you, that worthy detective gets angry just thinking about you."

"Oh, come on!"

"Yes. It seems you annoyed him greatly by interfering in his investigation."

"I didn't mean to."

"I'm sure. But those police officers are so full of themselves and take offense at the slightest suggestion."

"Well, his annoyance won't keep me awake. I'm tired, and I'll bid you good night."

The look in Violet's blue eyes clearly showed that she understood Max's fatigue, but Sir John didn't notice her tender glance, which suggested understanding and shared thinking.

Max withdrew. When he'd returned to Marseilles he'd taken a room under his new name. He went to the one he'd been given. A few minutes later, rid of his false whiskers, he climbed into bed and fell fast asleep. For forty-eight hours his body and his brain had truly been working overtime, so it's no surprise that he gave in to the need for deep restorative sleep. Sweet rest made him smile with bliss.

And perhaps he was having happy dreams. Perhaps in his dreams he saw again Violet's lovely features, her long-limbed charm, her shining azure eyes sparkling with feeling. Or perhaps his thoughts followed the track of those unknown women, Sara de La Roche-Sonnaille and Mona Labianov—those fugitives whose names he hadn't even known a day ago, but for whom, over the course of his arduous investigation, he'd developed feelings of brotherly affection.

But—when the silence in the hotel suggested that the night was well advanced—in the depths of his sleep Max became aware of a gentle tickling. Still asleep, he decided someone was rubbing a feather under his nose. The feeling that produces is well known. Of course he had to be imagining it... but the idea was a nuisance anyway, since it troubled the peace of a well-earned sleep. Without opening his eyes he rolled over and buried his nose in his pillow. Alas! The tickling went on, but now it had moved to his ear.

What could it be? A fly, a mosquito, perhaps. Max moved a hand to the irritated ear. That gave him a moment's peace. He sighed. Still half asleep, he decided he must've chased away the bothersome fly. But then he grumbled: the tickling had begun again. It was becoming intolerable. He opened his eyes, raised himself on one elbow, and reached for the switch of the overhead light. But he quickly pulled his hand back—after meeting another hand, which had immediately drawn away into the darkness of the room. He was suddenly wide awake.

"Who's there?"

No one answered. But the light switch clicked, the ceiling lamp came on, and Max sat stunned. In the light from overhead he saw... no, it wasn't possible... he thought he saw, standing silent and unmoving beside his bed, the men in amber masks he'd met the previous night at the Loursinade villa.

But, yes, it was them, in their large loose robes and their strange masks of translucent yellow amber, molded to their faces like another skin—those rigid masks within which moved piercing, ironic black eyes that gave their peculiar appearance a disconcerting power. It had to be a hallucination. But no sooner had that thought crossed Max's mind than it was driven away by facts.

One of the Amber Masks spoke. "You weren't expecting to see us, dear sir."

Oh! That voice! He knew it well—the harsh voice he'd heard at the Loursinade villa—and at the same time he recognized it as the voice of Félix, the coachman who'd driven the landau when they'd visited the Elleviousse Asylum. And that discovery restored his presence of mind. He examined the one who'd spoken. In spite of the loose robe he could make out the man's narrow shoulders and frail body.

He said calmly, "Not at all, Monsieur Félix. I just thought seeing you when we went to the Elleviousse Asylum was enough for one day."

He regretted those words almost as soon as he'd spoken them. The strangers started. The one he'd addressed turned to his companions as if asking for instructions. But the tallest of the three men lifted his hand and spoke. His voice too was familiar to Max: he was the one who, at the villa, had said, "You want to see us—look at us." This time his words rang like a death-knell: "It's dangerous to recognize us."

It wasn't his tone of voice that was disturbing. No, the Amber Mask had spoken calmly, in a monotone, without feeling, without anger. But under that seeming indifference Max could sense a cold resolve that nothing could resist. Still, being brave by nature, he shrugged. To scoff at danger is practically victory. He answered, "It's also dangerous to be recognized."

The other shook his head. "No."

"Because?"

"Because we have three daggers that will guarantee your silence."

"I only have to give one cry for you to be arrested."

"That's true," said the stranger calmly.

Max stared at him in surprise. "You agree?"

"Completely!"

"Then that should make you think. You have me: fine. You can kill me. But I also have you. At this point it's a bad bargain—to risk three heads for the sake of bringing down only one." Max fell silent.

The mysterious person said quietly, "That doesn't give us pause. When in pursuit of certain goals, you have no idea how little the lives of those involved in attaining them matter."

"Ah, yes, the liberation of Asia," said Max impetuously, a little disconcerted by the unexpected direction of the conversation.

The Amber Masks exchanged a meaningful glance, and the one who seemed to be the leader went on, "Oh, you know that as well."

"Of course." Then, refocused by his adversary's question, Max added, "It was reading an old newspaper that drew me into this business. That's how I learned what Madame de La Roche-Sonnaille claimed was the truth, and what the police thought were the ravings of madness. I'm curious. I saw an interesting novel in it. I wanted to study the case. By tying me up in the Loursinade villa you convinced me that the duchess was perfectly sane."

"Oh, really?"

"The casual way you tried to kill me in the collapse of the house just confirmed that opinion."

"And you're very interested?"

"Very. Think about it: a novel I predict would be a success—because my profession…"

"We know."

"Ah! So you've taken the trouble to find out about me."

"It's always a good idea to find out about an enemy you respect."

Though his position in the bed didn't make it easy to perform elaborate gestures, Max bowed.

The three strangers bowed as one, and the leader went on, "And it was still with a novel in mind that you visited the Elleviousse Asylum?"

"Absolutely. One question: did Monsieur Félix recognize me?"

There was a short silence. The Amber Masks seemed to hesitate before answering. Finally the spokesman for the trio came to a decision. "No. You'd thrown us off the track. Monsieur Félix only guessed the truth when he saw your companions return to Marseilles without you."

"Monsieur Félix is good at deduction."

"Perhaps not as good as you are, Monsieur Soleil. But, anyway, yes, he is. Your prolonged stay at the Elleviousse Asylum, and Landré's anger toward you—you who had, according to him, tried to be clever and meddle in the investigation—put us back on your track."

"Congratulations, gentlemen."

But the speaker in the amber mask said quietly, "We're not flattering you. You're certainly better than we are at deduction."

"It comes of being a writer."

"We were aware of every single move you made at the Loursinade villa. We were filled with admiration when you found the wireless antenna."

Max began to laugh. "You proved it, by trying to… help me get down from the roof the quickest way."

"With sorrow, Monsieur Max."

"Much obliged."

"And to be quite frank, we regretted that violent move almost immediately." Then he went on with a certain recklessness, "Here's the situation, all laid out. We'll only be your enemies if we can't come to an agreement with you. In which case you'd be in danger; you already know we don't hesitate…"

"Indeed."

"But I don't want to make threats. For now let's talk amicably."

The Amber Mask made a sign. His two companions brought three chairs over to the bed, and the strange visitors sat down. Max was thoroughly dazed by the direction the interview was taking.

The leader went on, "You learned a lot at the villa. What did you learn at Dr. Elleviousse's facility?"

"No more than Inspector Landré."

"Oh," chuckled Félix, "Landré's an idiot."

"Since you've worked under him," joked Max, "you know him."

"He's an idiot," agreed the leader. "But you, sir, are not."

"I thank you for your flattering assessment."

The Amber Mask gestured impatiently. "Enough courtesies. As you said, we too can make deductions. You stayed at the asylum, not to get a tour, as you claimed to want, but to pursue your personal investigation."

"So you say," answered Max evasively.

"I'd add," went on the stranger, taking no notice of the interruption, "that you must've uncovered the trail, because otherwise you wouldn't have stayed there three hours after your friends left."

With an ironic smile, Max replied, "Oh, you were timing me?"

"Félix took his carriage back to Marseilles, then returned along the road to the Elleviousse Asylum."

"I get it, it's perfect."

"You'd just come out."

"Believe me, I'm sorry…"

"He was able to question the warden who gave you the tour."

Max's heart pounded: what if Madame Marroy had let herself be manipulated? With a fierce effort he managed not to betray the anxiety that choked him.

The Amber Mask went on, "Unfortunately that woman had noticed nothing. She described your route through the rooms and outbuildings and so on. She remembered that a few times you mentioned the fugitives' names, but without dwelling on it."

Max breathed. The warden had played her part well. So it was in a tone of happy mockery that he asked, "And so you conclude?…"

"That you know which way Madame de La Roche-Sonnaille and Mademoiselle Labianov went when they escaped."

"You're imagining things."

"No."

"No?"

Max was going to emphasize his objection—but the other man stopped him by saying enigmatically, "Don't be in a hurry to deny it. Our respective positions have changed since last night."

"Really?"

"I'll lay my cards on the table. Yesterday we were adversaries. Your curiosity risked compromising the success of plans we'd made to bring about the escape of the two prisoners a couple of weeks from now."

"You wanted them to escape!" exclaimed Max, stunned.

"Yes."

"Why?"

"That's our secret. Or rather a secret that…"

"Wait. I've got it. The Blue Flag the duchess mentioned when she was being questioned. Don't shake your head, I'm sure of it. It was important to…"—he was about to say to Dodekhan's enemies, but he caught himself and said—"to the prisoners' enemies."

The Amber Mask protested, "Oh! Enemies…"

"Yes, yes, that's the right word. I'm a writer, you know. And the way you made me take a high dive at the Loursinade villa…"

"Forget about that. I'm telling you, the situation has changed."

"I'd be happy to. I'd just as soon focus on pleasanter memories."

The good-natured way he said it seemed to satisfy his listeners. "So I'll go on," said the leader. "Your curiosity was a nuisance to us. Now that the two ladies have flown the coop without our permission, that same curiosity can assist us."

Max started slightly. He could guess the purpose of this nocturnal visit. The Amber Masks were here to extract information from him that would enable them to get their hands once again on those poor women. Still, he disguised his thoughts with feigned surprise, and answered innocently, "Well, now I don't understand you at all, sir."

"Then I'll explain. The way you operated at the Loursinade villa left us with the highest opinion of your powers of induction and deduction." Max bowed silently. "We're therefore sure that you now know, after the long time you spent at the Elleviousse Asylum… that you know, as I say, how the women we're looking for got out."

"Once again, you're mistaken."

"No point in denying it—we're convinced. The satisfaction shown by César Landroun—because you were César Landroun at the time—that satisfaction said plainly: I succeeded."

Max shrugged carelessly. "I won't argue. You're sure I know something—suit yourself."

"I'm likewise sure," the Amber Mask went on, "that if you continue your investigation, since you've found one end of the trail, you'll follow it correctly and reach the women who are now on the run."

"I'm so confused."

"And who's to stop you from succeeding? No one, since your adversaries yesterday are now on the contrary ready to help your investigation."

"Oh, pooh!"

"And even to…" The man seemed to hesitate over the word, then resign himself to it: "To subsidize it handsomely."

A spark flashed in Max's eyes, but vanished in a moment. These villains were frankly a little over-bold. They dared suggest that he sell himself out to them, that he become the bloodhound who'd lead them to their victims!

"Well? What do you say?" asked the stranger.

"I say I'm a writer, a novelist—not a detective."

"Didn't you investigate like a novelist?"

"I suppose."

"Then what's stopping you from continuing?"

"Ideas that might seem odd and old-fashioned to you. Up to this point, while trying to uncover a secret, with the sole aim of living out a novel, a book, before writing it, I was acting as an author. I was following my trade conscientiously, and I could take pride in doing so. But now it wouldn't be the same thing: I'd be acting as the accomplice of people—you asked me for the truth, and here it is—of people whose way of doing things doesn't appeal to me enough for me to associate myself with their dealings."

"So you refuse?" The Amber Mask's voice shook with anger.

Max's answer was to stretch out his arm and put one finger on the electric buzzer at the head of the bed. "You're about to pull out your big knife, but at the slightest move I'll ring. You'll kill me, but you'll be caught—which will save your victims once and for all."

He stopped. The leader had raised both hands in the air. His companions did the same. "We're unarmed," the leader explained.

"Happy to hear it."

"Kill you? Of course not! Because the favor you're refusing us… you're going to perform for us anyway. I wasn't sure when we came here, but now I'm sure: you mean to go find the fugitives."

"Never. From the moment I knew you were following me, I abandoned my novel."

"The novel, maybe, but not the deep interest those ladies inspire in you and in Miss Violet Musketeer."

The sweet Englishwoman's name, when spoken by the sinister visitor, made Max shiver.

"You're romantic Occidentals. No matter what you say, you'll try to find the duchess and her companion. And, as of now, we'll be right on your heels. We won't let you out of our sight."

"Well, thanks for the warning. I'll go where I please without worrying about you."

"Wrong."

Max burst out laughing. "You think you can make me a detective against my will?"

"Maybe."

The answer fell on Max's ears like an icecap. "What do you mean, maybe?"

"I'll explain. If, by the end of a certain time of which we'll be the judge, you aren't working for us…"

"Don't stop, I'm listening with pleasure."

"I'll remember that in Asia, the land of psychic sciences, I was famous for my powers of hypnotism."

"Ah, then I know who played the false Dr. Rodel."

"What do I care!"

"So, you have some subject whose thoughts you'll read. If you're counting on that to change my mind, you're wrong! I don't believe in it."

"You'll believe in it when I've named, not the subject, but the subjects I'll question. They're named Monsieur Max Soleil and Miss Violet Musketeer."

Max's heart pounded. What! The charming girl who—with such kindness—had seized on the sweet idea of protecting two weak, abandoned women who'd been pushed around by the fraudulent political schemes of an entire race! Violet in turn would become a victim of those vile Amber Masks! Still, he put on a brave face. "You can only hypnotize people who consent. Either that, or you have to choose anemic or neurotic subjects. And Miss Violet and I are perfectly healthy."

"You won't refuse."

"That's too much!"

"It's too easy. A sleeping subject is unaware of approaching danger. He doesn't resist."

"A sleeping subject?"

"Of course. Some fine night, when you're sleeping like the perfectly healthy people you said you were a moment ago, we'll try the experiment— either on you or on that charming Miss Violet. I'll transport you from sleep to hypnosis, and you'll see that once you're in that state you'll easily tell me your own thoughts. And since you've shared them with the young Englishwoman, she can do me the same favor." And then with biting irony he added, "I've acted fairly, I showed you my hand. I'll leave you to think it over."

The overhead light went out suddenly—no doubt one of the mysterious visitors had flipped the switch. Caught by surprise for a moment, Max felt for the switch. Once again the room was filled with light. But his eyes widened: the Amber Masks had vanished. He got up and ran to the door. The key had been on the inside, but not locked. Only the copper doorknob had secured the latch. The wretches had been able to come and go without trouble.

That realization should've calmed him, but it didn't. Until morning he pondered the strange threat he'd been issued, to force him to reveal the hiding place of those two fugitives—victims he wanted to help.

In the morning he felt some reassurance, especially after he'd reported his nocturnal adventure to Violet.

"Oh," she said with an Anglo-Saxon's practical instincts, "I assume neither of us is going to sleep in a public place. So all we have to do is lock our bedroom doors to keep anyone from disturbing our rest."

"Exactly right."

"And if we think about it—you especially, being a novelist, with a good imagination—we'll surely find a way to throw those unbearable spies off our track." She considered for a moment and added, "Haven't you spotted them in the hotel?"

"No. But, believe me, I've been eyeballing everyone I meet."

"Then I suggest we make them walk plenty."

As a result, the two young people strolled around all day, dragging along Sir John Lobster, who was made miserable by all the forced exercise. The stout gentleman kept on mopping his face, and expressing his surprise at seeing César Landroun—because Max was once again a man of fifty with false grey whiskers—stride along without seeming to tire.

"I say," moaned Sir John, "I don't get you—you're old, much older than I am, and yet you're not perspiring, whereas I'm boiling."

Every fifty feet he stopped and murmured timidly about how badly he wanted a drink. But Violet was amused at the thought that, while she might be annoying the Amber Masks, she was certainly annoying this fiancé who'd appointed himself her bodyguard, and she answered with a laugh, "For the sake of your health, I won't let you drink. You already look like a giant water nymph. What would happen if you drank any more?"

And Sir John rolled his pale eyes in the middle of his scarlet face.

Up to now, though he'd often been a nuisance, Violet had felt pity for him. But now some transformation had taken place in her—she couldn't have said exactly what. The only thing she was sure of was that this red-faced individual displeased her enormously, and watching him pant and gasp and sweat only made her feel what she expressed in words murmured aside, "If he's tired, he can just go back to the hotel."

The result was that in the evening Sir John—exhausted, aching, worn out—went to bed without dinner, leaving his companions free to stay up in the reading room chatting at their leisure. They observed to each other that all day long they hadn't spotted their enemies, the Amber Masks... and they observed it in so many different ways that it was eleven o'clock before they finally decided to part and return to their own rooms.

They spent five minutes holding hands, giving each other sensible advice:

"Don't forget to lock your door."

"Push the bolt."

"Make sure the window's closed, and that no one can come down the chimney."

"And that there's no connecting door."

When they finally stopped holding hands and parted, they turned repeatedly to look back at each other, and they kept up that no doubt pleasant activity until a bend in the corridor put a wall between their glances.

In the morning Max awoke in excellent spirits. He'd slept, as he put it to himself, like an emperor. Fresh, rested, ready, he carried out his morning ablutions, then decided that a little cigarette would give him pleasure. His cigarette case was on the night stand. He went to it, but his hand—already reaching for the case—stopped in mid-movement.

On top of the Morocco leather case lay a sheet of paper folded like a letter, and on the side facing him was written, in large, thick letters: *To Monsieur Max Soleil*. What could it mean? Who'd put it there? For a moment Max thought it might've been there the night before. He could've gone to bed without seeing it. But he rejected that idea immediately. In the evening his cigarette case and his matches had been in his pocket. He'd taken them out and set them on the marble side table. If the mysterious letter had been there already, it would now be under his things and not on top of them. Ergo: no one could've gotten into the room in the night, and yet here was the letter.

He ran to the door. It was locked, the key was in the lock, the bolt was pushed. That door had obviously not been opened since last evening. The window was hermetically sealed. The fireplace was just for show, since the Hotel Cosmopolitan had central heating, so the chimney was a fake and didn't lead to the roof.

Defeated, Max ended where he should've started: he picked up the letter and unfolded it. But no sooner had he glanced at it than he gave a roar of anger. "Them! Oh, they're mocking me!"

On the paper was written:

Dear Monsieur Max,

Nothing can keep us from entering anywhere we feel like entering. We came to watch you sleep. The deadline we set hasn't passed; otherwise we could've carried out the little experiment in hypnosis we mentioned.

Don't worry, it's just being put off to another time. But our warm feelings for you lead us to hope that the thoughtfulness of our behavior will earn us your friendship and your cooperation.

Signed, F of the A.M.

P.S.: You must've worn yourself out yesterday. I beg you, don't overdo it, and don't make that poor Sir John Lobster melt into a puddle!

Words can't express the unease this letter caused Max. He finished dressing in a rush, and went down to the reading room. Violet hadn't yet appeared. He sent a chambermaid up. She returned to report that Miss Musketeer had slept very well, that she was having breakfast in her room, and that when it was done she would hasten to meet Monsieur Landroun in the parlor.

That answer relieved Max quite a lot, since it showed that at least Violet hadn't been bothered by the Amber Masks. With that concern eased, he brought his thoughts back to the mystery of the letter left on his side table in the night. He questioned the housekeepers, showing them the address on the letter: none of them had seen the paper.

"And yet," he said to himself, "it was certainly put there while I was sleeping! But how did they get in? The days when genies got into houses through the keyhole are long gone, and it's not in the power of any man—even if he belonged to all the Blue Flags in the world—to bring them back."

Violet found him deep in those obsessive thoughts. His report made her burst out laughing. "I say! My poor friend, you forgot to lock your door, that's all." No matter how much he denied it, she wouldn't change her mind. She was English, and could countenance only occurrences that were possible and could be explained plausibly.

Max didn't insist. He was sure he'd locked the door. So that was a mystery, and he resolved to keep his eyes open.

After lunch they went out together. This time, though they urged Sir John to join them, he flatly refused. For the sake of his health he chose to rest at the hotel. He wished the fearless walkers a pleasantly tiring day and settled himself comfortably in an armchair with an ample supply of cigars.

They returned at six. Sir John was waiting for them, pacing anxiously up and down the sidewalk in front of the Hotel Cosmopolitan. Oh, he wasn't the friendly, smiling gentleman he'd been when they left! His entire portly self expressed agitation pushed to fever pitch. Seeing the two walkers in happy conversation, he hurried over. "For shame! For shame!" he bellowed. "You've been making fun of me in the most shocking manner!" And, facing Max, he clenched his teeth and growled, "It seems you're in disguise, and that you're Mr. Max Soleil."

"What?" they cried.

"Max Soleil, who's been making fun of me by flirting calmly right under my nose with Violet Musketeer!"

Violet was the first to recover from her surprise. "Who told you that?"

"Oh, a worthy traveler who came to smoke beside me in the parlor."

"How did it come up?"

"I assume he didn't know I was your fiancé. He said, 'Oh, I say, what a nice couple: Miss Violet and that Frenchman, Max Soleil.' I corrected him. 'Not Max, César. Not Soleil, Landroun.' Well, that made him laugh. 'No, no, Max Soleil, with a wig on his head and fake whiskers on his cheeks.'"

The young people now looked at each other with unspoken concern. The same thought had come to both of them: by arousing the fat Englishman's jealousy, one of the Amber Masks had set another spy on them.

Indeed, to leave the matter in no doubt, Sir John went on, "But from now on I won't be leaving the coast clear. I'll fasten myself to your footsteps, and I'll interfere with the flirtation. That's all I have to say. Now come to dinner, because according to the clock it's time."

All three went to the dining room. But it was a sad, silent meal. The cheerfulness Max and Violet had enjoyed all day had suddenly fallen flat. The presence of enemies around them, invisible and untraceable—because Sir John's informant was nowhere to be found—cast a pall over them.

Plus which, the word "flirtation" had prompted a thought that troubled Max's mind. A flirtation between him and Violet could lead to only one thing: marriage. And the idea of marriage between this multi-millionairess and himself—granted, a distinguished writer, but one whose position was precarious by comparison—seemed unworthy of him and unworthy of her. "Clearly," he said to himself, "I'll have to get away as quick as I can."

As the thought sprang to his mind, Violet's big blue eyes were on him. The charming Englishwoman observed him with a concern and a gentleness that pained him. Perhaps she could read his mind! In any case, he was led to think so when she leaned close and whispered in his ear, "Are you engaged to any young lady?"

"Me?" he stammered, surprised by the boldness of the question. "No."

"In that case," she went on, her cheeks growing rosy, "if we enjoy flirting, there's no reason to stop." He gazed at her, his eyes troubled. "I say there's no reason," she went on. "I'll go further: there's even good reason to continue—because I'm afraid, very afraid, of falling back into the boredom I've escaped since leaving Nice."

Just then Sir John asked in a bad-tempered voice, "Why are you whispering in Mr. Soleil's ear?"

She replied curtly, "Probably so you can't hear."

Which raised the gentleman's chronic redness to bonfire level. By the time Sir John had recovered and wanted to get revenge with some devastating comeback, Violet had risen and beckoned Max to follow her. She murmured gently, "Let's go back to our rooms to get away from this insufferable fellow. Tomorrow we'll go out early." She gave his hand the sweetest squeeze. "By the way, sweetheart,"—and she laughed brightly, with a hint of languor and confusion—"by the way, lock up properly tonight, so the nasty Amber Masks can't get in." She broke off suddenly. "Here's Sir John, just like those Amber Masks. Let's run away—I'd rather not even say goodnight to him."

She ran lightly up the steps, and fat Sir John reached the foot of the stairs in time only to see her graceful shape disappear from view onto the second floor.

Max closed the door to his room, and with meticulous care he turned the key, pushed the bolt, checked the latch on the window, and looked under the bed. Convinced that he was alone and absolutely secure, he put on a dressing gown, slid his feet into slippers, and settled comfortably into an armchair. On a small side table nearby he'd set his revolver and a couple of novels he'd bought that day. "There—reading matter to keep me awake, and the revolver for anyone who tries to get in."

Dawn found him still up. Nothing had happened. A bath and a thorough shower washed away any trace of fatigue. A hot chocolate finished the job of restoring him. Dressed and ready to go out, he went to the parlor to wait for Violet.

Sir John Lobster was already in the vestibule, with a big, vulgar-looking man. Sir John seemed surprised to see Max; taking his companion by the arm, he led him out to the street—on the way saying something to the front desk clerk, a vague fragment of which reached Max: "You'll let me know."

Since that didn't concern him, Max sat down, lost in thought. But he'd barely settled in when a rustle of skirts made him look up. Violet stood before him, pale and upset.

"Ah!" she said, her voice shaking a little. "I'm so happy to find you here— it's enough to drive you mad!"

"What's going on?" Max's voice trembled too: he was troubled by seeing her like this.

"What's going on? Look at this note, which was on my dressing table this morning. And yet I swear I locked my room, everything."

He took the paper she held out to him. He shivered when he recognized the handwriting. The letters had been drawn by the same hand as the mysterious message he'd gotten the previous night. This note was brief—just a single line: *Nothing can bar the way of the A. M.*

"Well?" murmured Violet.

"Well!" he said slowly. "You didn't believe me yesterday. But I too had absolutely locked my door."

"I was wrong, I admit it. But I can't live like this. It's intolerable to think that people—villains—can get into my room in spite of locks and bolts."

He shook his head without answering, and she went on, "Besides which, the whole thing is indecent, shocking! And I have to count on my sweetheart to put an end to it."

Oh, the smile that accompanied those mischievous words! For the first time in her life, Violet felt the need to put herself under a gentleman's protection. And though in truth she was a little afraid of the mystery that surrounded her, another very sweet small emotion made her—yes!—almost enjoy her fear.

Max escaped from the impossible embarrassment of answering her, because the string of comical explosions that announce the arrival of a motorcycle rang out, and a moment later Sir John burst into the parlor, looking ridiculous in a leather helmet and enormous driving goggles and a waterproof jacket.

He hastened toward them. "Already together, you two! You're getting ready to go out, thinking I can't walk as far as you can. Mistake! You can stroll around all you want, as long as you please. I'll follow you without getting tired. I've supplemented my body with a motorcycle, and I have enough gas to go two hundred kilometers."

Jealous lovers have a gift for showing up exactly when they're most in the way. Sir John was no exception to the rule. At the very moment when Max and Violet needed privacy and quiet to think and talk and consider what to do next in their odd struggle against the Amber Masks—he'd just flung his importunate self athwart their plans.

"Since that's what you want, let's go," said Max, giving Violet a meaningful look.

"Yes, let's go," echoed Sir John mockingly.

But while he rushed away to get back on his motorcycle, which he'd left at the entrance to the hotel, Max whispered in Violet's ear, "I know Marseilles well. Follow my lead—we'll throw him off our the trail."

"And then?"

"If you don't have any objections, we'll go have lunch in some peaceful spot, and we'll look for a way to defeat the wretches who're bothering us."

She nodded.

The two of them began to follow the sidewalk, while in the road Sir John, with a sardonic smile, kept pace on his motorcycle.

Max's idea was simple, and it had been inspired precisely by the motorcycle Sir John was so delighted to have procured. In every city there are two ways of getting around: One could be called the official way, made up of streets, squares, avenues, and boulevards. That's how visitors get around. The other way, known only to locals, consists of passageways and buildings with two exits. So Max, very familiar with Marseilles, had said to himself, "We'll use the second way. Motorcycles have no access either to the passageways or to the buildings with two exits. Sir John will be forced to choose between letting us escape and abandoning his motorcycle."

Unfortunately Sir John had thought ahead: he'd equipped himself with an excellent map, taken from Bradshaw's guide to the Continent—the guide that's so helpful to pickpockets vacationing in Europe. Indeed, not only were the official streets perfectly drawn in Bradshaw, but the passageways and the buildings with two exits were marked in red. As a result, four different times the young people, having given him the slip by one such way, found Sir John again at the other end: he'd sped around the streets bordering the block through which they'd walked.

Nothing is as tedious as a joke that drags on. The young people felt themselves losing their tempers, while Sir John's rubicund face grew more and more pleased. Two or three more attempts had no better outcome. Max and Violet were about to give up this pointless game—when benevolent luck took pity on them: luck in this case in the form of a streetcar, which emerged from a side road right in front of Sir John's motorcycle as he was going full speed. The motorcycle ran into the streetcar, unseating the fat Englishman, who—after an un-expectedly acrobatic vault—fell into the laps of some tourists, who were left stunned by the intrusion of this human projectile.

Stopped streetcar, outcries, police intervention, gathering crowd... and a chance for Max to lead Violet away without Sir John—tangled up in multiple complaints—being able to follow them.

When they returned at dinnertime, the young people learned that Sir John—worn out and moaning, with a shockingly swollen nose to show the impact he'd suffered—had gotten a ticket for speeding.

The female heart feels pity. Throughout dinner Violet was so gracious and so attentive to the gentleman that he announced, with heavy sighs and amorous looks, that he'd forgotten the pain inflicted on his nose because of the kindness he felt in his heart.

When dinner was over, Violet joined Sir John on his little daily post-prandial stroll—which made him almost faint with joy. Once they were outside she said, "Sir John, dear friend, no doubt you've been thinking that I was paying too flattering a degree of attention to Monsieur Soleil."

Sir John gave her a sidelong look and pursed his lips expressively.

"Oh, don't be afraid to say so," she went on with perfect modesty. "I can see how my behavior gave rise to unfavorable interpretation. That's why I wanted to explain directly to you."

"Explain?" he stammered, taken aback by her new tone. "Explain?"

"A girl's whim."

"A whim, you say?"

"Driven by curiosity. Yes, I want to shine light on the darkness surrounding the adventure of the two ladies who escaped from the famous Dr. Elleviousse's asylum."

"And?"

"That French writer has found out lots of things."

Sir John shook his head.

"I beg your pardon," she said firmly. "And just today we learned positively that the fugitives are hiding either in Paris or in Livorno, Italy."

"And so?"

"And so, if you like, we could part with Monsieur Soleil."

The Member of Parliament's face shone. "Part with him?" he asked, his voice choked with emotion.

"Completely. You to head to Paris, I to go to Livorno."

But Sir John protested. "Oh, you must take me for a numbskull!"

"You really think so?"

"Yes! If I took the train to Paris, that would leave the two of you together in Marseilles."

"Wrong!"

"Wrong how?"

94

Violet summoned all her powers of persuasion. "Here's how. I'll go to Livorno, and if that's not the right trail, I'll go straight back to England."

"What! You really…"

"I'll do as I say."

He clapped his hands with relief. Still, a slight feeling of mistrust lingered. "How about this, my dear sweet thing?" he said gravely. "I'll carry out your instructions obediently—if, before I leave, you allow me to put you on the train to Italy."

Ignoring the mistrust implied in his suggestion, she answered politely, "With the greatest pleasure. I'm taking the train tomorrow at two in the afternoon. Then you could catch the five o'clock train to Paris."

"I'll do it, sweet flower, I'll do it. And in Paris what's my destination?"

"You'll go to Number 5 Rue Palatine, to see Mademoiselle Leonia Caldoveto."

He quickly got out his notebook to write it down.

"On my behalf, of course. You'll ask her to take you to see the ladies from the Elleviousse establishment. And you'll escort them to my manor at Excylon Hill, where I'll join you. But, make note, I'm giving you a confidential mission, and no one must hear of it."

For another quarter of an hour as they strolled they traded questions and answers relating to the trip, then returned to the Hotel Cosmopolitan. And while the triumphant Sir John toasted his joy with a whisky cocktail, the charming Violet had time to whisper to Max—who was sprawled nonchalantly in an armchair and seemed to be absorbed in reading a newspaper—"I leave Marseilles tomorrow at two, and he at five."

Without looking up he answered, "Thank you—you're an angel!"

When Sir John, having drained his glass, turned to face the girl he insisted on thinking of as his fiancée, he found her simpering at her reflection in a mirror, seemingly concerned only with fixing the unruly blonde curls that fell on her brow. She motioned him over to her, and spoke to him at length about the satisfaction it would give her if the facts confirmed her theories, and about how extremely grateful she'd be to him for bowing so willingly to her desires.

This return of her cordiality filled the gentleman with inexpressible enthusiasm. Sir John was a hundred miles from guessing that at the very moment he was tasting this unmixed happiness, Max was engaged in a strange internal monologue:

"Three Amber Masks is too many for one person. They'll split up. One will follow that dear, adorable Violet; another will go with that fat Lobster; so I'll only have one watching me: the leader, the hypnotist. So to begin with, I'm separating him from my dear sweet friend." He smiled. "And to finish with, I'll know how to… lose him."

That was the plan the two young people had thought up on their walk that day.

In the glassed-in courtyard ornamented with potted mandarin trees, the big clock rang eleven. Violet and Max exchanged a reserved "Good night"—they had to keep from arousing their companion's jealousy. Sir John, delighted, shook Max's hand almost cordially. With the arrogance typical in a great cross-section of men, he was convinced he'd driven Max out of Violet's dear little sugar-coated heart. And so before going to bed he ordered three cocktails—cocktails with which to toast to himself, as congratulations for his success.

Meanwhile Max had gone back to his room. He had room service bring him a specially prepared pot of cold coffee. He'd resolved not to sleep. He too would be traveling the next day. He wanted to spend his last night at the hotel awake, so as not to be caught unprepared if the Amber Masks decided to try the experiment in hypnotism with which they'd threatened him.

Perhaps the previous night his light had warned them he was awake. This time he'd turn out the lights. Guard duty would be harder and more challenging in the dark, but—oh, well!—he'd make up the sleep later. He set the coffee pot, glass, and sugar out on the table where he could reach them, rolled his big arm-chair nearby, then—click—he turned out the light. Darkness filled his room. How long did he wait? Hours. A vigil in the dark is the most boring thing in the world. To pass the time he occasionally took another sip of coffee, and counted the strokes of the clock on the hours, the half hours, and the quarter hours. That occupation itself showed how bored he was.

He'd just counted the strokes of three o'clock. "One more hour on duty," he murmured, "and it'll be over. Day will be breaking..."

But suddenly he fell silent. He'd heard a slight brushing noise. He listened. Without a doubt, someone was walking out in the corridor. Whoever was wandering the hotel hallways at this unwarranted hour must be wearing felt-soled slippers: the sound was gentle, unmarked by the tap of hard heels. The sound stopped at his door.

"All right," thought Max playfully. "The key's in the lock, the bolt is pushed..."

With a slight shiver he broke off. He'd heard a rustling noise. No mistake: the latch was turning in its cylinder. Well! These people must have the skills of burglars. To unlock the door with the key still in the keyhole—that was too much! He reached for his revolver, but then changed his mind. "No need: they can't slide the bolt."

A slight click rang out in the silence.

"My word! I'd swear the damned bolt... That would be magic!"

A hand was pushing on the copper doorknob outside. Picking up his re-volver this time, Max moved silently toward his bed and took hold of the light switch. He waited like that for a moment. Perhaps the nocturnal visitor had heard him move, because a long minute went by without anything happening. Then—the silence no doubt having reassured the intruder—the doorknob turned, and Max could hear the slight scraping of the door pivoting on its hinges.

He flipped the switch—the overhead light came on. There was a cry, followed by rapid footsteps. Max had time to glimpse a face hidden by an amber mask before the door closed again. But that wasn't enough to satisfy him: he meant to teach a lesson to whoever presumed to break into his room. He ran toward the door. He was almost there when something inexplicable rooted him to the spot: The key turned by itself, relocking the door; and to top that, the bolt slid slowly back into its cradle. It was becoming supernatural, incomprehensible.

Even someone who wasn't superstitious, who gave no credit to the fantastical fairy tales in Mother Goose, could be forgiven for feeling disconcerted in the face of a phenomenon as abnormal as a latch and a bolt moving without help from human hand.

Even so, it wasn't Max's nature to remain shocked for long, and not to seek an explanation. "Come on!" he muttered to himself. "The joker's robbed me of my wits. He's had time to get away. All I can do now is to try to figure out the ingenious method he uses to manipulate latches—which is nothing—but also bolts, something burglars haven't thought of up to now."

He went to the door. It was perfectly closed, and the bolt was pushed all the way. If Max hadn't seen it—really seen it—he'd have thought he'd hallucinated it. But he knew he hadn't been asleep, and he'd truly heard and seen his enemy. Therefore the Amber Mask had some means of getting past the most complicated locks. Since the key was still in the lock, it couldn't have been done with a lock pick, the faithful tool of all those who covet others' goods. And anyway a lock pick was powerless against a bolt. But then how had it been done?

Max took out the key and examined it. It showed no sign of having been bent or scraped. He set it down on the table next to his revolver, and proceeded to a careful examination of the latch and the bolt shaft. Nothing: not the slightest sign of force.

The thing was growing more and more and disconcerting. Hell and damn! Surely the Amber Masks didn't have the powers of that little green elf of legend, who could open doors and treasure chests just by blowing on them! In fairy tales, inexplicable things are explained by not explaining them—but in real life that's not enough.

"I'll open the door. Maybe on the outer face I'll find signs that will point me in the right direction."

As he said that, he noticed the key was no longer in the keyhole. "The key's disappeared!" He slapped his head. "I'm losing my mind! I took it out earlier. Where did I leave it?"

He looked all around. In his confusion he'd forgotten. But then he spotted it. "On the table, by God! How stupid to have gotten so upset!"

No doubt the reason he hadn't seen the key at first was that it was touching the barrel of his revolver, which cast a shadow over it. He reached out one finger to pull it away. His eyes widened anew in surprise. The key didn't move. He tried again, with the same result. That odd key seemed to be glued to the revolver. He picked up the revolver by its grip: the key remained stuck to the barrel.

"All the devils in hell!" he exclaimed. "It's like I'm putting on a magic show all by myself!"

But like any self-respecting stage magician, he wanted to understand what sudden force now held those two objects together. He gripped the key and pulled hard. It came away from the revolver. He held it under the light bulb and turned it over and over, and examined the revolver barrel the same way.

"No tar, no glue… it's extraordinary!"

As he said that, he unthinkingly brought the two objects close together, and—click—with a metallic snap the key stuck to the barrel. For a moment he remained confused, observing the two reunited objects as if stunned. He rubbed his forehead, then pulled the key off the revolver, then put it back again. Suddenly his face lit up. "This key's been magnetized!" And then, "The bolt is iron too. Has it also been magnetized?"

He grabbed a pen off the writing desk and leapt to the door. He'd guessed right: the bolt attracted the pen—and not just the bolt but the latch and the whole lock plate. "Those Amber Masks are very clever!" he exclaimed. "They unlocked the door using a magnet applied to the outside, moving parallel to the latch and along the direction of movement of the bolt!"[11]

But then he shook his head. "No. There's too great a resistance to overcome—the magnet would have to be enormous. Clearly the rascal wasn't wandering the halls by night carrying something so big it would've been noticed by everyone he met. In a hotel you're always liable to meet someone. So it had to be something easily concealed. Very pretty deduction. Unfortunately there's no such thing as a magnet with large power but small size."

Suddenly he raised his arms toward the ceiling. "Yes, there is—if it's combined with electricity! So, not a magnet, an electromagnet." He grew more convinced as he spoke. "That's it: an electromagnet powered by a battery. A strong enough one could fit in a box ten centimeters on a side."

He put the key back in the lock, pulled the bolt, and opened the door wide, so that the overhead light from his ceiling fell on the outside face. He rubbed his hands with glee. "I was right. There, on the paint, at the level of the latch and the bolt, that small dull mark shows where the magnet was rubbed. Very ingenious, I'll say it again. Unfortunately for them, it magnetizes iron temporarily—and Max Soleil figured out the trick. From now on little Max will carry with him a portable bolt made of copper, which can be attached and detached in minutes, and all the electromagnets in the world won't move that one!"

Then his face clouded. "While I'm gloating like a fool, those wretches, disappointed in their hope to take me by surprise, might be attacking Violet." He

---

[11] Matthew Nicol of Birmingham was inspired to try this by the child's toy known as "The Little Dancers" [*Note from the Author*].

roared, "Poor, generous Violet! I can't let her fall victim—she who opened her heart so kindly to those suffering ladies."

He grabbed the key, locked his door behind him, and ran through the maze of corridors, his heart pounding under the strain of frantic anxiety.

CHAPTER VIII
Rope and "Tailing"

A few strides brought Max to the second floor, where Violet's suite was located—she for whom he felt such strong concern.

Electric night lights lit the hallway, and it seemed to him that, at the moment he reached the far end of the long corridor, a human form moved hastily away from the door to Violet's suite and vanished through an opening a few feet away on the opposite side.

In his present state of mind Max didn't hesitate. Obviously an Amber Mask had been busy trying to force open her door. Interrupted by Max's arrival, he'd hidden in a neighboring room, waiting for him to go by before resuming his break-in.

"If that joker thinks I'm going to let him calmly go on with his job, he's quite mistaken."

His eyes hadn't left the spot where the mysterious person had vanished through the wall. He approached the place. There was indeed a door there, closed at this time of night. But it wasn't the entrance to a guest's room. The door led, not to a private room, but to a place shared by all. Perfect! There are times when even the most private people become collectivists, as everyone would agree before this door painted a soft white, with marked on it in sky blue the initials W.C. The door was closed, but a transom window showed that a light was on inside. To make sure, Max turned the knob: the door resisted. "All right! The rascal's hiding in there—I'll wait for him."

But a second thought drove away the first. "Yes, but if I nab him when he comes out, I'll rouse the whole hotel. And any explanation would lead to sweet Violet being compromised. I don't want that. I'll have to think of something else..." He stood in thought for twenty seconds, then murmured, "Well, well! Why not?"

No doubt his imagination had given him an idea, because he went quickly to the far end of the corridor. There, filling one corner, stood a kind of closet, in which the staff stored brooms and feather dusters and the ropes the maids used to tie up the tubes of vacuum cleaners. As usual, the closet door stood ajar. Max looked around for a moment, then straightened up. "This'll do the job."

Almost running, he went back to the white door with the sky-blue capital letters, carrying a roll of rope as thick as a pinky finger. "With this," he said to himself, his happy face now lit with intense joy, "with this I challenge you get out without waking the whole hotel—which will put a stop to your plans, at least for tonight."

Having unwound the rope, he tied one end securely to the doorknob of the W.C. Then, stretching the rope across the corridor, he wound the other end around the knob of a door more or less facing the one he'd seen the person enter. That way, the man would be trapped, since the taut rope would keep the door from opening. He'd have to call, raise a racket, throw the hotel into a hubbub... after which he could only withdraw quietly.

Having checked the solidity of his trap with one last pull on the rope, Max calmly went back to his room with a smile on his lips. But he left the door to the corridor ajar: he wanted to hear, and to enjoy what was about to happen.

A few minutes went by. The hotel was silent. Suddenly a frightened voice called out, "You can't come in! You can't come in!"

"It's a woman's voice," muttered Max. "What's up?"

And indeed the hoarse, harsh, disagreeable voice belonged to someone of the gentler sex.

It was followed immediately by a deeper voice, reinforced by an odd reverberation, answering, "I'm not trying to get in, I'm trying to get out."

And then the replies—frightened or angry—crisscrossed:

"Then stop shaking my door!"

"You stop holding it!"

"You dare claim I'm holding the door?"

"Obviously!"

The voices rose and grew more combative.

"Have you no shame, frightening a poor woman in her bed?"

"In her bed? In the corridor! This joke's gone on long enough!"

The doors were shaken violently, while the speakers yelped:

"Let go of the door or I'll call for help!"

"Let go of it yourself, villain!"

"Boor!"

"Scoundrel!"

"Stupid cow!"

"Burglar!"

Another furious shaking of the doors was followed by a cry: "Stop thief! Murderer!"

And that was enough to rouse everyone in the hotel, staff as well as guests.

Max thought the time had come to show himself. He ran into the corridor. Doors were opening. Guests were coming out, dressed carelessly in bathrobes, barefoot or in slippers. They questioned each other, worried and a little afraid.

"Someone cried thief!"

"No, murderer."

"No, both."

"So something's going on?"

"Where? Where?"

"The noise has stopped!"

As if to add to the general confusion, the clamor had ceased. But it was only a lull, because almost immediately a great drum roll made everyone jump.

Someone was beating on a door with both fists. The man's voice shouted curses and threats. "By the devil! May Satan wring your neck like a corkscrew!"

"Help!" cried the female voice.

"Let go of the door, you stupid goose, and you wouldn't need to call for help."

"You won't get in!"

"I'll get out!"

A duet of oaths and pitiful cries followed.

It was too much for the fragile nerves of the other guests. Encouraging each other, they all rushed as one toward the source of the cries. Max followed the crowd. In fact he was as curious as anyone, even though he thought of himself as the anonymous creator of all this tumult. But he'd been anticipating a solo of curses, when the Amber Mask realized he was trapped in a space not intended for a prolonged stay... and he'd been treated to a duet.

The heroic, trembling crowd advanced down the second-floor corridor. The noise got louder. On the left side of the corridor a man's voice roared; on the right side, a woman called for help. Max realized that the rope he'd tied had created two victims: when his prisoner tried to get out, he'd pulled on his door, and the motion had been transmitted along the taut rope to the door across the hall—which Max had only thought of as an attachment point. You can imagine the rest: the captive was tugging on two doors at the same time.

The woman in the room across the hall had been awakened by the shaking of her door, which she'd thought secure. Naturally she assumed some burglar was trying to get it, while the prisoner took the resistance to his own efforts to be due to some practical joker in the corridor who was holding onto the door he himself was pulling on. That led to their shouting: one in anger, the other in fear.

It can easily be understood that Max was careful not to enlighten the onlookers, who spent a long time staring at the two shaking doors, behind which the invisible opponents, like soldiers under cover of fortifications, bombarded each other with disparaging remarks.

Finally some citizen more intrepid than the rest hurried bravely forward—and tripped over the rope, falling flat on his face with a terrible cry. The duet had become a trio. But the impetus had been given, and the pack of guests and bellboys and chambermaids rushed forward in a heroic stampede. When the weight of twenty people was suddenly arrested by the taut rope, the weakened doorknob of the W.C. popped out of its rosette.

The door opened suddenly. The prisoner, who'd been pulling frantically on the inside handle, lost his balance, and Max—who'd stayed modestly at the back of the crowd—burst into wild unstoppable laughter. He'd recognized the man sprawled on his back, flailing his arms and legs in the air: Sir John Lobster!

Max had mistaken this unlucky gentleman—who'd been wandering the corridors by night for a perfectly legitimate reason—for an Amber Mask, and had trapped him in that improvised dungeon.

The rope proved the gentleman's innocence. People reassured the woman across the hall, and cursed the bold, ill-bred practical jokers who disturbed the sleep of guests at a quiet hotel, renowned for its modern comforts. Then, having exhausted the subject, everyone went back to bed.

Max noticed it was almost dawn. Daylight: the guarantee that his enemies had to suspend action. Relieved for his own sake as well as for Violet's, he felt perfectly satisfied, and had not one word of sympathy for poor Sir John, for whose recent unpleasant experience he was responsible.

The railway station clock said one forty-five. The train to Nice and Ventimiglia would leave in fifteen minutes. Nervous, preoccupied travelers hurried along, a few steps ahead of the friends or family come to see them off and to call out a final friendly farewell when the train started.

Violet, as charming as possible in a simple alpaca dress, was escorted by Sir John, redder than ever, and by Max, whose expression reflected the understandable sadness he felt at the coming separation. Ah, a compartment with an empty corner seat. The young lady got in. Sir John followed her, to stow her various bags in the luggage rack himself. Meanwhile Max stayed on the platform, carefully examining the other travelers and the staff. He was trying to guess who was the spy, the Amber Mask, who'd follow Violet.

For he was sure the plan he'd thought of was a good one: three Amber Masks, and three travelers going different directions—each of whom would therefore inevitably drag a watching satellite into his or her orbit. And yet, to prove to himself that he'd reasoned correctly, he wanted to figure out who his enemy was. But guessing is difficult, and he was reduced to that, because in fact he'd only seen the face of one of them, that Félix, who'd no doubt been posing as a coachman and had disguised himself for the occasion.

Still, he broke off his fruitless search for a moment. While Sir John was kneeling on the seat with his arms in the air, carefully arranging Violet's luggage, Max whispered to her, "You do have the copper bolt I gave you this morning?"

"The automatic one? Yes, and I thank you."

"Don't forget to attach it every night to the door of whatever room you're in."

"Don't worry, I won't forget."

When Sir John was done with his task and turned around, the young people were no longer conversing.

A crew member ran alongside the train, calling, "The train to Ventimiglia! All aboard!"

Sir John stepped out onto the platform. Over the buzzing of farewells and the impact of slamming doors, a shrill whistle echoed through the station hall. The train was leaving. Slowly it began to move.

Leaning out the door, Violet waved at the two men.

"Now my mind's at ease," said Sir John happily. "I'm going back to the hotel to arrange my own departure—and you'll be left all by yourself in Marseilles, poor Mr. Soleil!"

Max didn't answer. Moodily he left the station with his companion. Back at the hotel, Sir John gave instructions to settle his bill, pack his bags, and arrange a ride to the Paris-bound station for the five o'clock train, after which he withdrew to his room.

A little disoriented—as can happen after a loved one's departure—Max, responding to a wish for solitude, went to his own room. But he'd no sooner entered it than he felt a rush of emotion. On the bedside table, in full view, he spotted a little parcel, neatly tied up in green ribbon. What now? He rang, and when the bellboy appeared he pointed to the object.

"Oh," replied the bellboy, "that was left at the front desk, with a request to bring it up here as soon as you went out. I carried out my instructions, that's all."

"Oh, so it's you who?..."

"Am I at fault, sir?"

"No, no, it's fine, my friend. You can go."

Now that he knew the thing had gotten here by natural means, Max was no longer worried. Once he'd sent away the bellboy and was alone, he unwrapped the parcel. Inside he found a small pouch of soft leather, which enclosed a hard-sided box. He drew it out, and exclaimed tenderly. It held a locket with a photograph of Violet. On the back she'd written:

King Charles 1st, before he left on a journey, no matter how long, would say to the queen and his children—the dearest things in the world to him—only the word "Remember." That word seems very beautiful to me: "Remember." And I would ask you to be fond of it.

Max's vague sadness dissolved immediately. He need no longer regret their separation. With ingenious and sensitive fondness, Violet had left him a little of herself.

Max went back downstairs around four o'clock. Sir John was bustling about the vestibule, supervising the loading of all his many bags onto the omnibus. He greeted the Frenchman politely. By God, it wouldn't do to act surly toward a defeated rival—especially if you harbor the hope that you're seeing him for the last time. He allowed Max to shake his hand—and was not only a little surprised but touched by that sudden cordiality. "At bottom," he said to himself, "he's a jolly good fellow. He's taking his defeat very well."

And not to be behindhand in behaving "very well," he asked Mr. Soleil to have a cocktail with him, to clink their glasses and toast to their meeting and to hopes of future meetings. Once the intoxicating drink had heightened his sociable feelings still further, he swore he'd be truly sorry if that jolly good fellow Max didn't accompany him to the station.

As a result, at one minute past five, Max was standing on the platform, waving back at the fat Englishman, who was waving to him leaning halfway out the window of the train carrying him toward Paris.

But when the train was gone Max pulled himself together. "My turn now. The last train to Veynes leaves at twelve fifty A.M.! At Aix it meets the train going the opposite way. Return here, get across town. By four ten in the morning I can be at the station for the train to Ventimiglia. Then across Italy, Austria, Bohemia... to the little town of Stittsheim, where the poor women tormented by those vile Amber Masks have taken refuge."

He returned to the hotel, stopping for a moment on the way at a telegraph office. He dined well, then moved to the parlor, where he immersed himself in the newspapers.

About eight ten he was handed a telegram that had just arrived for him. He opened it gravely—and immediately asked for his bill and a vehicle. He'd been summoned, without delay, to Veynes, on the Marseilles-Grenoble line... Of course, he'd sent himself the telegram, to provide a pretext for his sudden departure.

At nine o'clock, carrying a light suitcase purchased by César Landroun, he had himself driven to the station serving Veynes, where he made a show of depositing his small bag at the left-luggage office before going back into town. He killed two hours at a music hall, then returned to the station and boarded the twelve-fifty train to Aix and Veynes.

While picking up his ticket, and crossing the waiting rooms, and walking along the platform, he kept a sharp lookout. The important part of his escape plan was about to begin. He needed to find the spy sent on his trail—the spy he had to rid himself of. He studied the few travelers with an eagle eye, looking for signs of a disguise or false hair that would betray a hidden observer. His efforts were in vain. Neither the passengers nor the crew looked suspicious. Would his intuition—on which he'd founded the whole plan—fail him at the very moment he needed it most? Nothing could be more annoying.

But the minutes passed. The heavy black hands moved slowly around the enormous dial that stared out at the far end of the station hall like the eye of time. Another minute, another thirty seconds. The train was about to leave, and still Max hadn't fastened his suspicions on anyone. Hell! There's always a way to throw a spy who's following you off the track; but it's helpful to have identified him. To lose a tail you haven't spotted turns into an impractical conjuring trick—because you have to be suspicious of everyone.

But one last passenger was running down the platform. He had a traveling cap pulled down over his eyes, and wore a long gray duster that flapped around him. Max felt a jolt: the man's figure resembled that of the leader of the Amber Masks in his long white smock—and he thought the latecomer shot him a sly glance. All of that happened in a flash.

The man disappeared into a compartment, two cars behind the one Max was in. The locomotive whistle split the air, and with a clash of steel the train slowly began to move. They were leaving... they'd left; and Max fell back against the seat cushions, thinking, "He waited until the last moment to show himself, but I recognized him. Now I know who I'm dealing with."

The train hurried through the night, filling the countryside with its panting, passing big round red lights that looked like the eyes of giants watching it go by. Then, a stop. At a dismal sleeping station, the crew ran the length of the train. Max rushed to his door. Perfect! He hadn't been mistaken: the man in the gray duster was also leaning out the door of his compartment, looking up and down the platform. It wasn't hard to guess why: he was watching Max to make sure he didn't leave the train.

A jerk—they were setting off again.

Another station. Once again the gray duster appeared at the door.

"Aix! Aix!"

With a sound of rolling thunder the train entered the station in that elegant Provençal city. No sooner had it stopped than a new clatter rang out: it was the train bound the other way arriving, on its way to Marseilles. The two trains stopped on adjoining tracks.

The time had come for Max to put his plan into action. He glanced out at the platform crowded with passengers returning from Marseilles. The gray duster was at his door, obviously eyeing everyone getting off the train.

"And... now!" With those words of encouragement, Max crossed his compartment and opened the door on the opposite side—first checking that no one from the crew was walking between the two stationary trains. He stepped from his running board to the one across from it, opened the door facing his, and vanished into the neighboring train. Now he'd be heading back to Marseilles, while the spy, still on the train he'd just left, would keep going toward Veynes.

Shouts and signals announced their departure. The two trains going opposite directions jerked into motion at almost the same time. Max hunched down to make sure he wouldn't be seen in passing by the man he'd just thrown off his trail, then sat up and stretched out on the seat cushions with obvious satisfaction. The train taking him back to Marseilles had left the Aix station buildings behind.

Since he'd bought a return ticket, he had no trouble when he reached Marseilles. He went to the station serving Ventimiglia and Liguria, and at four ten the "night special" carried him along the beautiful line that follows the Côte d'Azur. Then he stretched out at full length along the seat, and said to himself with a yawn, "At last I'll be able to sleep peacefully for a few hours."

It wasn't an idle remark. Five minutes later, he was deep in dreamland. The train, rushing along under full steam, carried with it a novelist completely free of earthly concerns.

CHAPTER IX
The Rainbow Players

The population of the village of Stittsheim consisted of three thousand people—two thirds of whom worked for the Herbelar and Starem medical and precision glass company. It was one of those industrial towns that spring into being around factories. In the Middle Ages the castle gave birth to the village, which came there seeking its protection. Nowadays the smoking factory chimney serves as the rallying point.

The only place where travelers could find room and board was an inn and hotel—clean, cheerful, its walls covered in ivy—whose signboard carried the proud motto, "The Old Czechs." The name expressed a nation's aspirations: The native Czechs of Bohemia, bowing under the yoke of the Austro-Hungarian monarchy, threatened by German greed, want their freedom. They've worked tirelessly toward that goal, founded associations, revived Czech, their supple, melodious old national language. May that small nation succeed in freeing itself from its overlords! Every Frenchman ought to hope so, if only out of gratitude, for during the calamities of the terrible year of 1870-71—when France, beaten and bloodied, groaned under the heavy boot of the victorious Germans—in terrorized Central Europe the Czech people alone dared raise their voices in support of the French. And it was no timid protest but an outraged clamor that rose to heaven from the ring of mountains that surrounds Bohemia.

Max—having glimpsed in passing the plains of Italy and the Danube, and nodded at Vienna between trains—disembarked at Stittsheim fifty-two hours after he'd left Marseilles.

Before anything else, he went straight to the Herbelar and Starem factory. The director received him cordially. In answer to Max's questions, he said he'd seen no madwomen, but a young tourist—whom he'd suspected of being a woman disguised as a man—had come to buy a set of phototherapeutic tubes, meaning an array of tubes that would produce the seven colors of a prism or a rainbow. That person had even asked for a few unusual modifications, among them the attachment of powerful lenses to the light-emitting surfaces, lenses that would focus the light rays the way a magnifying glass focuses sunlight, thereby infinitely increasing the power of the rays of colored light—to the point of making them almost lethal.

"To whom was the order to be delivered?"

"To a Monsieur Laroche."

"Good. And to what address, please?"

The director hesitated for a moment. Max hastened to show him both his business card and the photo ID proving his membership in the Society of People of Letters of France. "You can see who I am. I would add that your customer is... a relative of mine."

"Oh, sir, no need to explain—Monsieur Max Soleil is well known in Bohemia. We're familiar with everything that comes out of Paris. Your relative is staying at The Old Czechs, the only hotel in town."

With thanks and a cordial handshake, Max took his leave. He had no trouble finding the hotel. When he stated his nationality, the servant—a pretty girl with rosy cheeks and with her hair in thick braids down her back—left him standing at the door and ran inside, calling happily, "Dáma Cvrček! Dáma Cvrček! Another Frenchman!"

Another voice replied just as happily, "Is that true, Jos?"

"Yes, Dáma, yes!"

A large, regal woman of about forty appeared. That introduction suggests in what way Max was welcomed. He was given the best room, with two low windows surrounded by flowering wisteria. It was available: it could've been given to a young Englishwoman who'd arrived the previous evening—but that room wasn't for strangers. It was reserved for distinguished Czechs, or for French people.

That gracious announcement allowed Max to respond quite naturally, "Oh, but not for just any French person?"

"Yes, yes, sir, for any. We love France."

"Then what accounts for the exception I observe?"

"What exception?"

"The best room should already be occupied, since one of your guests is my fellow countryman Monsieur Laroche."

Dáma Cvrček winked slyly. "The little brunette."

Max couldn't help starting, and the charming landlady cried, "Don't worry, I won't gossip! My guests' secrets are safe. I only mention it to prove to you that we Czechs understand your subtle French ways."

"Anyway," went on Max, who was delighted by the good humor of Dáma Cvrček—a name that means "cricket" in Czech—"anyway, that person didn't get the best room."

"He did get it, sir."

"But I don't want to deprive him of it."

"Don't worry, sir, he vacated it himself."

"What?"

"He left yesterday, with that poor sweet innocent creature who was with him."

"Left..."

"Yes, for a town in Italy called Brindisi. Ships sail from there to India."

Max had stopped listening. To have crossed Europe to meet those strangers, Sara and Mona, and to reach where they were staying only to learn that he'd most likely passed them along the way—that could fairly be called serious bad luck.

"On the other hand," went on the landlady, softened by his pitiful appearance, "maybe I'm talking nonsense. You could ask Pavel, the valet, who took their luggage to the train station."

"And this Pavel lives?..."

"Next door, sir. As you can imagine, a hotel and a valet often have need of each other."

"You're right, Madame. I'll go there."

"Breakfast is in an hour. I'm letting you know, sir, because I intend to give you an appreciation for Czech cuisine."

He bowed to the excellent woman and left.

At the house pointed out to him he soon found Pavel, a hearty fellow with lively eyes, who received him with a smile and the hospitable words, "How can I help you?"

When Max explained his disappointment at having arrived too late to join his young relative Laroche, Pavel said without hesitating, "I took a chest to the station, with a tag marked Brindisi, Italy—but it's my opinion those people weren't going that way."

"Not to Brindisi... Then why that tag?"

"So it would be read, and would misinform whoever was interested in where they were headed." Seeing Max's surprised reaction, the good man went on, "Look, sir, the lady—because between you and me, it was a lady, even if she was dressed as a man—so, the lady, and the poor girl she's escorting, must have enemies. She seemed worried, in a hurry to go—afraid of everyone who looked at them."

Max nodded.

"As a result," went on Pavel, "to any random person I would just have repeated what the luggage tag said! But with you it's not the same thing: you mean her no harm, I'm sure of it. How do I know? I couldn't say, but all the same I'm sure. Well, the little brunette had a pocket dictionary. She consulted it at the ticket window, and asked for 'two tickets to Lemberg.' The ticket agent made her repeat it, because her pronunciation was bad."

"Lemberg?"

"Yes, in the province of Galicia. And since at Lemberg the line intersects another line that crosses Bukovina and Moldavia to reach the Black Sea, I believe they could easily catch a ship at Odessa rather than at Brindisi."

A vigorous handshake thanked the worthy valet for his trust. Max had just made a momentous decision: he'd check the train timetable for Central Europe, and leave for Lemberg that same day. He was reaching the state of mind of a veteran reporter with a story to unravel. It was becoming essential to him to find the fugitives from the Elleviousse Asylum, to see them, to speak to them, and to offer them his and Violet's help.

He returned to the Old Czechs Hotel. Dáma Cvrček was waiting for him at the door with a questioning look. "They did indeed leave for Brindisi," was how Max felt he should satisfy her abundant, if benevolent, curiosity.

"Well then, Mr. Frenchman," she said cheerfully, "go straight into the dining room. Dinner is being served right now. And you'll be impressed!"

Mac obediently went to the dining room, where he found an array of small tables spread with blinding white place mats, each of them bearing in one corner a coat of arms in the Czech national colors. He was alone. But it wasn't surprising that this small town didn't host many visitors.

Jos, the delighted servant girl, hastened to set out glasses, plates, and cutlery enough for fifty guests. Max noticed that one chair at a table near his was leaning with its back against the edge of the table: the universal signal for a reserved seat. "Are you expecting a regular customer?" he asked in the casual tone of someone waiting to eat.

Jos shook her head with a laugh. "An English lady who checked into the hotel yesterday."

"Ah!" His sudden exclamation made the girl jump, and Jos thought she might drop the stack of plates she was holding. A choked cry of astonishment had burst from Max's lips. The door had just opened, and on the threshold stood... Violet in person.

She was at Stittsheim—while Max thought she was on her way to England! And the topper was that she didn't seem the least bit surprised to find herself in his presence. The topper was that she came toward him, held out her hand, and said, "As you can see, as soon as I got your telegram I rushed here."

"My telegram?"

He stared at her with such obvious surprise that she murmured, "But you don't seem like you understand!"

"Indeed, that's because I don't."

"Come now, let's be serious."

"I am. I sent you no wire."

"None... Then what's this?"

She withdrew a telegram from her card case and handed it to him. He read it, dumbstruck:

To Marseille, forward to Livorno. Come to Stittsheim immediately. Everything has changed. Signed: Max.

Bursting with anger, he said, "I didn't send this."

"Then who did?"

He gave her a strangely troubled look, then said, with a mix of annoyance and concern, "It must have come from *them*!"

Them! Her cheeks turned pale. That pronoun upset her. *Them* meant the Amber Masks, those mysterious, elusive enemies against whom she'd been struggling for days now. Why had they drawn her to this small Bohemian town? What was the purpose of that trick? It seemed to Violet that some calamity hung over her, and over Max—the Frenchman whose very existence she'd been unaware of a month ago, but who now, as she admitted to herself privately, held such an important place in her life.

Unconsciously her delicate hand squeezed his arm. "Well, I thank them—they've reunited us."

"Alas!" sighed Max.

"And from now on," she continued, paying no attention to his regretful interjection, "from now on I won't agree to splitting up anymore."

He shivered. "What are you trying to say?"

"That from now I won't leave your side. I'll be your companion." She stopped for a moment, blushed, then went on in a rush, "Your traveling companion—because I assume you're not giving up?"

"On my own account I wouldn't give up. But to drag you into a dangerous undertaking..."

She interrupted him. "Oh, hold your tongue instead of talking nonsense."

"I'm stating the unpleasant truth."

"No, not at all. The most dangerous thing is boredom. I've been cured of that since this business began. By keeping on, I'm warding off a relapse. And besides... and besides..." She paused. Her big bright eyes looked away.

"And besides?" he asked.

"And besides, at the end of the road I feel like I'm going to find happiness."

Violet's voice suddenly cracked, as if it had been shaken by the thumping of her heart. She shut her eyes and stood still, while Max enveloped her in a caressing look. Then she raised her rosy eyelids, revealing the gleaming azure of her irises, and in a flustered, uncertain voice she said, "I suppose we should eat."

"As you wish."

"And then?"

"Then?"

"Then we'll hold council and come to a decision."

She gave him a lovely, tender, bright smile. Max pointed out the table where he'd been sitting before, and she responded by taking a seat there. Cheerful Jos, delighted to see the hotel guests sitting together, which made serving them simpler, hurried to set a second place, and brought out a pitcher of foaming Pilsen and the appetizers. The young people, as if dizzied by their reunion, nibbled in absentminded silence. From time to time one of them looked up and—meeting the other's eyes—smiled with a slight charming awkwardness.

Suddenly the door flew open violently. A loud, hoarse voice bellowed, "By Satan's cloven foot, here they are, right in front of me!" And Sir John Lobster, redder than ever, burst into the dining room.

This time they were left speechless. The presence of the Member of Parliament here—when they thought he was in Paris—seemed unbelievable.

Having completed his outburst, Sir John collected himself. He came solemnly to their table and stood squarely before them. "Violet Musketeer, I thank you for my journey. I thank you even more because you sent me to see a person who doesn't exist at the address you gave me."

Since she didn't answer, he went on, "You've toyed with a gentleman's good faith. But I'm not angry, because I'm getting even." He pulled a crumpled piece of paper from his pocket. "Here's what my 'well-wishers' sent me in Paris, at Cambon's Hotel, where I always stay. I'll read you this document, so that you understand how uncivil and risky your behavior has been toward me and toward my good name." Since his stunned listeners still said nothing, he began to read slowly:

"To Sir John Lobster, Cambon's Hotel, Paris.

Violet and Soleil are on their way, separately, to meet at Stittsheim (Bohemia). Those two lunatics..."

"Lunatics!" they protested.

But he ignored the interruption and went on:

"Those two lunatics have carelessly involved themselves in a matter that in no way concerns them. It was the flighty Frenchman who dragged poor charming Violet along in his wake, and who is leading her into the abyss. She'll find out too late what it costs to lend an ear to the muddled imaginings of a descendant of the crackpot race that inhabits France."

"Thanks on behalf of France, thanks on my behalf," said Max, recovering his good humor.

"We want to protect the young lady in spite of herself. Being true friends of the great nation of England, we assert that a young Englishwoman ought not fall victim to a Frenchman. We believe you, a perfectly proper Englishman, would be happy to help us save her, and to thwart the person—Max Soleil—who has exposed her to danger.

"If we're not mistaken about your honorable nature, leave immediately for Stittsheim. You'll find the travelers at the Old Czechs Hotel. Once you're with them, don't leave them again. Watch their every move. You'll inform us every day of their actions and movements, which we don't have time to keep track of."

"Every day!" murmured Violet.

"So you'll be seeing them every day, Sir John?" asked Max, who was truly quite interested in the way this peculiar adventure grew ever more complicated.

"I don't need to see them," Sir John replied self-importantly.

"But how will you report to them?"

"Not with my eyes, but with my mouth, and the little speaker."

"What are you saying?"

"I'm saying that if you wouldn't interrupt, the letter I'm holding would already have answered your question." And he went on reading: *"In the small box enclosed..."* He looked up and explained, "There was a small box that came with the letter." Then he went on with the letter:

"In the small box you'll find a wireless speaker, whose special receiver is in our possession. All you have to do is push the tip of it gently into a telegraph pole or a tree, or fasten it to a gutter downspout or a lightning rod, and then speak into the vibrating disc, for our receiver to transmit your words to us, and for us to answer. Help us save Miss Violet Musketeer, in spite of herself—and three cheers for old England!"

The young people stared at each other, stunned. The Amber Masks had given them a watchman. They only had to look at Sir John to know that any debate, any attempt to explain, would be pointless. That gentleman—fundamentally a decent man—was nevertheless of rather limited intelligence. And his slow wits and moral obtuseness were infinitely reinforced by his wounded vanity. He knew they'd tricked him. His lover's jealousy and the collapse of his matrimonial calculations—because the joining of two fortunes always contains, no matter what, an element of calculation—had turned him inevitably into their enemy.

Almost vehemently, Sir John went on reading:

"One observation: Even if Miss Musketeer agrees to part ways with the Frenchman, she'll remain exposed to great danger, since that madman has shared a deadly secret with her. In that case, your orders will be to stick to him and proceed as explained above. We entrust the young lady's safety to your courage and to your British honor. But above all, lose not a moment. Otherwise they'll have left Stittsheim, and nothing more can be done to stop them."

Sir John spoke those last words in a lugubrious voice. Then with a look of triumph he stood facing his companions—now become his enemies—in the avenging posture of St. George laying low the dragon. He searched for some dreadful, crushing final word. One must not have come to him, because after a silence he concluded prosaically, "And there it is!"

Already Violet, her eyes gleaming with scorn, was opening her mouth, about to reproach her rejected "fiancé" for agreeing to act as a spy for people he didn't know, criminals by all appearance. But at a sign from Max she stopped. She looked at him, and saw him smile. In his eyes she read an idea, a hope, and she said nothing.

He, meanwhile, spun his chair around so he could face Sir John. "All right," he said, "that's pretty funny."

"Funny," growled the Englishman, furious that his message had produced so little effect, "we'll see how funny you find it from now on."

Max held up his hand to stop him. "Sir John," he said slowly, "I could challenge you to a duel, which would leave you in bed for two weeks and keep you from following us. But you're basically a decent man. There's no need to add another to the number of victims of the rascals who've enlisted you to serve them."

"I serve the interests of my threatened heart."

"Let's not quibble over words. Later you'll see I was right. For the moment I only want to make sure your... gullibility doesn't put your life in danger."

"My life?"

"Yes. With the help of science, you can kill a man in quite unexpected ways. Would you show me the speaker you were given?"

Sir John hesitated. Apparently Max's argument had upset him. Even so, he protested, "Yes—and then of course you'll keep it from me, or you'll destroy it."

Max's smile grew more persuasive. "You wrong me. Just show it to me from a distance."

"Ah! Like this." Sir John backed up three steps and took shelter behind a table. Then from his pocket he drew a cardboard box, from which he removed an object that resembled a small umbrella inverted by the wind. He activated a spring, and the umbrella opened to reveal a whitish disc with a metal stem, like a central axis. The whole thing was barely five centimeters high.

Max couldn't contain a gesture of glee.

"What is it?" asked Violet, not taking her eyes off him.

In a barely audible murmur he replied, "Identical to the one I picked up in the Loursinade villa. Sir John has just taught me how to use it. We'll give it a try."

"What's that you're saying?" called Sir John, angry that he couldn't hear.

"I'm saying," replied Max calmly, "that, as far as we're concerned, I'd ask you to allow us to go on with our dinner." Then—with sarcasm that made Sir John's cheeks turn crimson—he added, "There's a gutter downspout just outside, my dear sir. You could try out your speaker—and inform your distinguished correspondents that Miss Violet and I are dining heartily."

Violet was laughing at the Member of Parliament's furious face, when Jos the servant reappeared. She was holding a letter, which she handed to Max. "This just arrived."

"And now a letter!" He tore open the envelope—and gave a cry of rage. The letter contained these brief lines:

Copper door bolts can protect you in a hotel... They're useless on a train. On the way from Marseilles to Livorno, the lovely Miss Violet fell asleep. She talked. That's why there was no one left at Stittsheim. Sorry not to have let you know sooner. We could have saved you the trip to Aix. You gave yourself unnecessary trouble trying to throw us off your track, because no one was following you. Knowing your destination, it didn't matter to us how you got there. But be careful not to wear out our patience. Signed: A.M.

"Well, what the... We're not at a hotel anymore! This is a shack, a cottage."

The boy who'd spoken those words looked around him, stunned. He was seated on a cot, no more than a piece of heavy canvas stretched over a short-legged iron frame. The walls seemed to be made of logs grouted with clay, and daylight entered feebly through a single square window, shaded outside by the overhanging roof.

"What can it mean?" he went on. "There, on a cot like mine, she sleeps—my dear little 'lover of light.'"

Indeed, on a second cot, against the wall, slept a girl fully dressed. She was golden blonde; her clear skin and regular features were typical of the purest Slav. She looked as beautiful and serene as a Madonna in an icon, a Virgin in a painting of a Russian saint. Her body, relaxed in the instinctive posture of sleep, showed her to be slender and strong.

For a moment her young companion observed her; then, with a gesture of resolve, he rose. He made a striking contrast with the sleeper. He was short, with brown hair, an irregular but charming face, and black eyes that, though too small, were so lively and sparkling that their mobility made them seem much larger. He moved freely in a hunter's smock with a loose belt; around his legs fluttered billowing trousers tied at the ankles. But two oddities were noticeable: his adorable, high-arched, aristocratic feet—too pretty to be a boy's feet—and the way the tight beret he wore covered him from nape to crown, leaving only a few brown curls visible on his forehead... curls that also seemed, in some way difficult to put into words, peculiar in a member of the strong sex, even one so young.

He went to the window, rubbed the dust off the glass, and glanced outside. "What can it mean?" he said again. And, speaking unconsciously, as if he were thinking aloud, he went on, "It's fantastical! I'm not the one who's gone mad"—he shot a glance at the sleeper—"not like my sweet Mona. I remember perfectly well falling asleep at the Independence Hotel in Lemberg, in the middle of town, right across from the cathedral... and here I wake up in a cottage deep in the country!"

It was true: outside, a flat gray plain blanketed in a blueish haze stretched to the horizon. Only a few clumps of trees scattered here and there broke the monotony of the scene. There was a certain melancholy, even a kind of indifference, in a landscape the same in all directions.

The boy stood still a moment, his white brow creased, his black eyes expressing the intensity of his thinking.

"It's incomprehensible!" he said to himself at last. Then with a shrug he added, "Anyway, where there's a house there must be people living. They'll tell me how we got here."

He strode decisively toward the door. But in his hurry he didn't notice a rope stretched across the room, which was no doubt used to hang laundry when the room was unoccupied. His beret caught on the rope and fell to the floor—followed by a surprising unraveling: a mantle of dark hair cascaded around the boy's shoulders, a rich head of hair that had been hidden up to now under the beret and that took advantage of the mishap to run free.

"Whoosh!" cried the boy. "That's all that was missing! Oh, this hair! I should've cut it! I didn't have the strength to. Lucien, my dear Lucien, loved it so. And the truth is, it would be too hard to sacrifice it."

As he spoke he repaired the damage, trapping the rebellious hair once more under the beret, which he pulled down tight.

"It won't do to let my own side betray me," he concluded. "And there's a risk of that, as long as—like me—you've got some hair to deal with. All right, all right, let's not dwell on that. The Duchess of La Roche-Sonnaille is dead, at least until new orders—and the student Laroche wants to know how he got here."

Those words explained the pretty foot and the curls on the forehead. The duchess—whom Max had glimpsed that night at the Loursinade villa—the patient at Dr. Elleviousse's asylum, who'd left and taken along Mona Labianov, the poor mad child who now slept nearby—was just as decisive and courageous as Max had guessed. In spite of the hardships she'd been through, Sara even retained the jaunty cheer of a charming Parisian girl.

As Max had learned, she'd left Stittsheim and headed to the Austrian town of Lemberg, where one railway line ran south to the great Black Sea port of Odessa, and the other line went straight east, crossed the Russian border between Brody and Radivilov, and ran eleven hundred kilometers further, passing through Kiev, to end at Kharkov.

At Lemberg she'd found out she'd have to wait until the next day to catch the train to Odessa. She'd then had her chest—the one whose luggage tag the valet Pavel had remarked on—taken to the Independence Hotel, with its ornate façade, on Cathedral Square. She'd settled Mona—whose gentle madness made her docile—in the room next to hers, with a connecting door open between them. Then, leaving the girl to lose herself in her quiet, endless, incoherent chanting, Sara had begun to read...

Up to there she recalled everything clearly. But at that point she was aware of a break in her memory. She'd certainly opened her book. She'd read—again, certainly... What had she done next? Had she lain down?... Probably—but she wasn't sure. And if she'd gone to bed, why had she awoken fully dressed, and above all why had Lemberg Cathedral vanished?

The door was held closed only by a wooden peg. She opened it and went outside. A faint path ran in front of the cottage, showing the way to go. Dogs with shaggy yellow fur lay in the dust. At the sight of the traveler they raised their heads, barked briefly, then stretched out once more on the ground without paying her any further attention.

Heavy boots shook the ground. Sara turned toward the sound. Ah! She saw another house in that direction, bigger than the cottage she'd come out of, but also made of wood. A man was striding toward her. He wore the loose shirt, wide trousers tucked into boots, and cap of a Russian peasant. What could it mean?

He was a *moujik* of some kind. And the house resembled an *izba*, just as the broad plain stretching to the horizon resembled the endless steppes of central and southern Russia—the steppes that the sweet, sad verses of Slavic poets liken to a terrestrial ocean, in the midst of which you travel ceaselessly for days and days, with the numbing feeling that movement is pointless, that you're just walking in place, with no way to vary the landscape, to relieve—with a hill or a dip in the terrain—the unchanging circle that bounds your view.

Sara passed a hand across her brow. Truly it was enough to make her mind spin: to fall asleep in Lemberg, Austria, and to wake with the feeling of having been transported deep into Russian territory.

But the man, the *moujik*, had reached her. He stopped three paces away, crossed his arms on his chest, and said devoutly—in terrible singsong French— "The blessings of the holy angels upon you, Excellency!"

The duchess examined him. He had blue eyes, a very long yellow beard, short hair: everything about him expressed both the deference and the gentle slyness typical of Russian peasants.

"Who are you, *chelovek*?" she asked, on the off-chance using the Russian word for "man."

"I'm Nicolas Petrovich, at your service, Excellency. Your *tarantass*[12] has been put away in the *izba*."

"My *tarantass*?" she stammered, stunned. "I have a *tarantass*?"

"Oh, Excellency, you're joking!"

"I'm not joking in the least. Where did this *tarantass* you speak of come from?"

"From the stagecoach stop at Ostrov, I think, or from some stagecoach stop further away. You must know better than I do, Excellency, because if you have a carriage you must've bought one, or hired one."

Sara listened. The more the man talked, the more amazed she grew. There was no doubt that Nicolas Petrovich was saying what he believed to be the truth.

"Unless *They* gave it to you," he concluded, pulling off his cap and putting it back on.

They: she was struck by the respect with which he'd spoken the pronoun. "Who is this *They* you refer to?"

The man lowered his voice. "I'm just the *smotritel*[13] and I don't like to talk about them. I obey them because punishment would be swift. But the Russian government doesn't want its employees discussing them."

Sara stamped her foot with impatience. "Well, I want to know! Who are they?"

A look of fear crossed the *smotritel*'s face. He looked around suspiciously, then murmured, "The Reds."

---

[12] A four-wheeled covered carriage [*Note from the Author*].

[13] Caretaker [*Note from the Author*].

"And by that you mean?"

"The revolutionaries." Then he lowered his voice again, until he was almost inaudible. "They told me to obey you, to accept no payment from you, and to provide you with good horses and a skilled *yamshchik*[14] to drive you to the next stagecoach stop to the east."

"To the east! And where am I now?"

Her question was met with a great laugh. "Oh, Excellency, you're making fun of me again."

"No. Answer me. Where am I?"

She frowned—and he quickly made up his mind. "At the Boslav stagecoach stop, twenty *versts*[15] beyond the town of Berdichev."

"In Russia?"

The man burst out laughing again. Still, he replied, "Yes, in Russia."

"And I arrived?"

"Last night. You were asleep, Excellency, as was the young blonde woman. They'd given orders not to wake you. So we carried you into the *izba* reserved for traveling officials. Your chest was locked up with your carriage, in a shed"—and here he added with a touch of pride—" that locks with a key! Not just anyone could've taken that precaution, because for fifty *versts* around I'm the only person who has a key. Everyone else closes their doors with pegs."

But Sara was no longer listening. She was wondering anxiously what this strange adventure meant. Russian revolutionaries had seized her. She'd been taken to Boslav in her sleep, while she was sure she was in Lemberg. What did it mean? But getting hold of herself, and managing to drive away her worried expression, she said indifferently, "That all sounds good. When my companion wakes up, you can harness the horses."

"Very good, Excellency."

"But my business is not to the east, it's to the south. So I need a coachman who's familiar with that direction."

But Nicolas shook his head.

"You won't do it?"

"Impossible. The Reds gave their orders. You'd be wise to do as I do, and obey in silence." To convince her he went on, "Maybe you haven't heard: The whole of the south, the Black Earth Region and Crimea, have rebelled. They're looting, killing, burning... Come on, the Reds are doing you a favor by sending you east toward the Caspian. Otherwise... Travelers arrive in a village where there's fighting. They're hit during the battle. Who gets the blame? *Nichevo, nichevo*, as we say—it's nothing to me!"

---

[14] Coachman [*Note from the Author*].

[15] A *verst* is one thousand sixty-seven meters [*Note from the Author*]. (2/3 of a mile; 3,500 feet).

Sara remained silent. Like a rapid series of movie frames, in her mind's eye she saw the bloody saga of the Russian Revolution.[16] The war against Japan, the defeats of the Tsar's troops, the populace calling for peace, then the great movement to elect an assembly charged with drawing up a constitution. And the autocratic regime, harried by the progressive parties, terrified by the massacres bloodying Poland, Finland, Moscow, Odessa, and the shores of the Black Sea, agreed to the creation of that assembly, the Duma.

But the fate of violent revolutions is that they cannot be contained. They exhaust themselves in atrocities and fall inevitably into reaction. Gradual evolution, following natural law, would lead men faster and more surely toward progress. Unfortunately gradualism requires two qualities that remain rare on this earth: goodwill and intelligence.

The Duma was established. Conflict immediately broke between its members and the Tsar's party. And the massacres resumed and even grew worse.

It was at that troubled moment that the duchess, escorting Mona, who'd lost her mind, found herself—without knowing how—deep in Russian territory... and protected by the revolutionaries. Why were they protecting her? She couldn't understand. She scoured her memory, but neither by way of her family—wealthy merchants from Lille—nor by way of her marriage to Lucien, Duke of La Roche-Sonnaille, did she have the slightest connection to the revolutionaries. But if that point remained in question, another point stood out clearly in her mind: the caretaker Nicolas had spoken the truth—any resistance would be futile, and even dangerous.

She showed her true nature; she was a decisive person, and she didn't insist. "You're right, Nicolas Petrovich. Have the carriage and the coachman stand by. I'll go invite my companion to set off."

The man's face lit up, as if that decision pleased him personally, and he hurried away to the main building of the stagecoach stop.

Full of energy, the duchess went back to the cottage. Mona was still asleep. Sara leaned over her cot and covered the sleeper's brow with gentle kisses. That tender, quiet touch had the desired effect: Mona's eyelids opened, revealing eyes as deep blue and unstable as lake water. She smiled at her companion.

"Darling," murmured the duchess gently. "We're about to leave for the east, the direction you love so much."

Delight lit up the mad girl's face. "The east," she echoed. "The Orient... Brightness... Yes, yes... There, the light... The shadow will be driven away."

"Yes it will," said Sara lovingly, putting her arms around the poor child and gently making her sit up. "But along the way we'll have to defeat an enemy."

"An enemy?" murmured the girl indifferently.

---

[16] The 1905 Revolution, not the 1917 Revolution, still in the future at the time d'Ivoi was writing (1907).

"Yes." Then, to reinforce the idea, Sara seemed to give way to Mona's insanity: "He wants to put a screen in front of the light."

At those words Mona's expression hardened, and her azure eyes shone like steel. "Well, I don't want that!"

"We'll stop him, thanks to the tubes in which the good genies trapped the rainbow."

The girl's face lit up immediately. "Yes, yes, we'll compel him. But there's no time to lose. Take me there, sister—you who are following me toward the light."

Lovingly, with maternal care, the duchess put her companion's hat on and straightened her clothes. The mad girl didn't resist, and let it be done with a mysterious smile, like one of those strange gods that the ancient Hindus or Khmers carved in marble or porphyry. She went on smiling, but her lips moved, whispering phrases that were comprehensible only to the reasoning of her madness: "Day... Goodness... Spirits of night, dark bats... Your downy wings hide the stars only for a moment..."

Soon she was ready.

"Off we go!" said the duchess.

And the girl repeated obediently, "Off we go!" But then she stopped, with a worried look.

Madame de La Roche-Sonnaille—or Jean Laroche, as she called herself in masculine disguise—guessed what was bothering her. She said quietly, "The rainbow is in the carriage."

That odd statement calmed the mad girl, and she let herself be led outside. The two travelers went to the main building, before which stood a *tarantass* hitched to three splendid Ukrainian horses, with the coachman already up on his seat. The *smotritel* Nicolas Petrovich and several *yamshchiks* stood by the door, and they greeted the young women with obvious respect. Clearly, people protected by the Revolution seemed to them worthy of first-class treatment.

While the travelers took their seats in the carriage—with the chest Pavel had described to Max at their feet—the onlookers remained bareheaded. Sara wanted to tip them, since tipping plays such an important role in Russian interactions, but they all refused: "The Revolution will reward us."

Then the coachman gave the cry of departure. "Giddy-up, my doves!"

And the *tarantass* set off, while the *moujiks* all said as one, "May the holy angels watch over you!"

"Another twenty-seven *versts*, Excellency, and we'll reach Kiev." Having turned on his seat to call out that answer to the pseudo-student Laroche, the coachman turned back again. "Heeyah, sweethearts!" The horses seemed to pick up the pace. The carriage had been rolling across the steppe like this for hours...

"Twenty-seven *versts*, between eighteen and nineteen kilometers. It's time to act!" murmured Sara. She leaned close to the mad girl—who was letting herself be bounced around by the swaying of the carriage, her blue eyes fixed on nothing—and said in her ear, "Mona, I told you about the wicked man who's making a screen to block the light."

The girl started. "Yes... Yes... Where is he?"

Sara pointed to the coachman.

"We must punish him."

"Yes," said the duchess, "but without doing him too much harm, because he's only a servant obeying his master."

It was truly strange: the mad girl's face was transformed. As Dr. Elleviousse had observed earlier, she became lucid, with exceptional acuity of understanding, as soon as anyone mentioned light.

"Not too much harm," she echoed, sounding like someone perfectly sane. "Not too much harm, so then tube 11-B. Yellow: fermentation. Beneficial light through plain glass, exacerbating light through lenses that concentrate the rays."

She leaned over the chest and opened it. The interior was divided into compartments lined with white velvet. Each compartment was numbered, and each held a tube about a dozen centimeters long, one end reddish wood, the other end glass. The tip of the glass end was rounded and armed with a lens. Where they met was a band of pleated cloth.

Mona drew the tube out of compartment 11-B. She tugged on the pleating, and the cloth band expanded to cover all but the tip of the crystal tube; only the lens still showed. She laughed silently, her eyes sparkling. "You know, sister," she explained in a slightly pedantic tone, "the processes of digestion are just fermentation. Well! You're going to laugh. I'm going to disturb the digestion of the man with the screen. Watch!"

She pressed a little button on the wooden end of the tube. There was a slight sizzling sound. The lens seemed to throw out a beam of bright golden yellow. And the tube disappeared up Mona's sleeve, while she stretched out her arm toward the coachman.

Sara watched with interest. It was the first time she'd witnessed a "demonstration." And yet it was entirely on the basis of the mad girl's claims that she'd carried out their escape from the Elleviousse Asylum. Yes: this young woman—in full possession of her sanity, but always thinking about returning to Asia to find her husband's grave and to kneel on the earth where his heart was buried—had listened to the ravings of her companion, who was obsessed with the idea of walking to the East. She'd listened to the girl explain, with her mysterious lucidity, the actions of light and the effect of colored light on living creatures.[17] The mad girl's enthusiastic description of its results gradually led her companion to think of light as a kind of power, a terrible weapon. And little by little, inspired

---

[17] Numerous applications of that theory have now been carried out, demonstrating the indubitable future of phototherapy [*Note from the Author*].

by her own wishes, Sara had come to believe—to hope. The result was her journey to Stittsheim and her purchase at the Herbelar factory.

Now she was unable to contain her powerful emotions: Would the experiment the mad girl was describing succeed? Or would Sara be forced to conclude that the chest full of tubes, those projectors of colored light, was nothing more than cumbersome luggage? She watched with a worried expression.

A minute went by. The coachman continued to encourage his team with words and gestures. "Giddy-up, my lambs! The stable will be full of feed. Come on, sweethearts, put your hearts into it."

The minutes of waiting seemed endless. Sara felt her heart pounding, and her gasping breath whistled through her lips. And the *yamshchik* still called out, "Stretch out, my darling turtledoves!"

Suddenly he jerked, and put his hand on his stomach, then on his abdomen. "By St. Vladimir!" he groaned quietly.

Sara turned to look at Mona. The girl was smiling mischievously, with her arm still pointed at the coachman—who was unaware of her gesture, since his back was turned. And even if he'd noticed it, he wouldn't have understood it.

The discomfort he was feeling now grew by the minute. He wriggled on his seat, drops of sweat beaded his temples, frantic cries burst from his lips. "St. Mitrofan of Voronezh, have mercy on me! Sacred icons of Holy Moscow, rid this poor coachman of the pain that wracks him!"

St. Mitrofan and the sacred icons must've remained deaf to his Orthodox appeals, because the poor man was more and more contorted.

At the edges of big cities, the steppe loses a little of its monotony. The princely estates are surrounded by hedges, parkland, and hunting cabins. The road now wound through many woods alternating with cultivated fields.

Suddenly, as they were following an alley of beeches, the coachman pulled up the horses, who sank to their knees. He jumped down from his seat, calling out in a pitiful voice, "Forgive me, Excellency, a devil is gnawing at my guts!" And he ran headlong into the underbrush.

Mona calmly slid the yellow-ray tube out of her sleeve, put it back in compartment 11-B, and closed the chest. "There he goes, running away," she said. "That should please you, sister."

Sara—radiant with the success of the demonstration—was no longer listening to her. She'd leaped up onto the driver's seat, gathered the reins, and summoned the team with the aplomb of a veteran coachman. "It comes in handy to have driven in the country a few times," she thought. When the horses were well under way, she said to herself, "South is to my right. We'll turn that way when we reach the first side road."

Decisions like that are easy to arrive at in theory, but complications arise as soon as you try to put them into practice—as she soon realized. A road branched off to the right from the one they were on. But she hesitated to take it, hesitated to the point of halting the *tarantass*. Why? Simply because that road didn't run directly south, but left the main artery on an angle headed east-southeast. And since it ran in a straight line, so that obviously it would keep to that course for a great distance, the pseudo-student found herself quite perplexed.

While Sara was considering, a *telezhka*,[18] carried along at a gallop by its charging horses, passed the *tarantass*. As it went by, she got a confused glimpse of three travelers: two men—one of whom had an unusually ruddy complexion—and a charming blonde girl.

But what astonished her was a projectile, launched from the unknown cart, that landed at her feet. She wanted to call out, to question them. No use: the *telezhka* was speeding away in a cloud of dust. She looked down at the object; it was a tight ball of paper, about the size of a tennis ball.

A thought crossed her mind: it might be a message from the revolutionaries. After all, it seemed plausible. Since the "politicals" were protecting her, since they took it upon themselves to guide her course, it wasn't impossible that some party agent had been assigned to give her instructions. Though she was resolved not to follow such instructions, it was still important for her to know what they were. Thwarting your adversary is easier if you know what he wants.

The outcome of those quick reflections was that she picked up the ball of paper and carefully smoothed it out. She hadn't been mistaken: she was indeed looking at a message. But the contents of the letter were not at all what she expected. Here was what she read: *Madame, I have the same enemies as you—the Amber Masks.*

"The Amber Masks!" she murmured with a shudder, pronouncing the name of one of the most terrible secret societies in Asia. "The Amber Masks!" Then she went on with the strange letter:

Go to Kiev. Check into the Hotel Dimitri on Gregory Avenue. I'll be watching for your arrival. Leave the door to your room open, so I can get in to see you without being noticed. I have to be careful, because I'm accompanied by one devoted friend and one bitter enemy. I think I can help you, and I beg you to consider me—Yours truly, Violet Musketeer.

Violet Musketeer! How had the sweet Englishwoman and her companions managed to recognize the duchess and Mona in passing? It was the easiest thing in the world.

Since Sir John Lobster didn't understand a word of Czech, Max and Violet—now in complete agreement—had taken him by rail to Lemberg, without telling him why. That precaution was understandable, since Sir John had announced that from now on he'd be keeping the Amber Masks informed, using the wireless speaker he'd been given for that purpose.

At Lemberg a crowd gathered outside the Independence Hotel had drawn their attention. They'd mingled, and learned that the police were carrying out a search. Two travelers, registered under the name of Laroche—a student and his

---

[18] Cart [*Note from the Author*].

123

sister—had taken rooms at the hotel. During the night after they checked in, both of them had disappeared without a trace, along with the chest that constituted their only luggage. No one had seen or heard anything. The night clerk at the hotel said nothing unusual had happened. The man had excellent testimonials, and the owners said he was perfectly honest. The police therefore eliminated him as a suspect—which did nothing to clear up the case.

Max, however, didn't hesitate. "That fellow's an accomplice of the Amber Masks," he said to Violet.

"The Amber Masks!" she echoed with surprise.

"Without a doubt. The poor women were probably heading to Odessa. They're trying to return to where they were separated from those they loved, and still love. Who has reason to stop them? I don't know the reason, but I know who has it."

"Oh, I too am well informed about those villains."

"So, we know who the perpetrators are. If you agree, I'll run to the station. They must've been taken in some direction other than the one they wanted."

Max returned half an hour later. During the night several people had brought in two young travelers who were fast asleep in wheelchairs. They were described as the children of some Russian nobleman, stricken with sleeping sickness brought back to Europe from Africa by colonialists. They were being taken home, because few survive the disease, and no one wanted the responsibility of caring for them. In short, the people had bought tickets to the Russian border.

That same day Max and his companions had gone the same way. Violet suggested ditching Sir John, but Max said, "No. If he contacts our enemies, he'll tell them he was left behind, and they'll send spies after us—spies the more dangerous because we won't know who they are."

"Then let's try to take away his speaker."

"Not that either: if he doesn't call them the rascals will wonder again."

"Then what can we do?"

"Try to keep him confused. He'll contact the Amber Masks, but he won't be able to tell them anything definite."

At dinner, taking advantage of the red-faced gentleman's gluttony, Max had plied him with food and drink to such a point that the worthy Englishman, in a condition close to drunkenness, had let himself be taken to the station and put on a train without knowing it. He fell asleep almost immediately. It wasn't far to the border; Max took care of all the customs formalities, and Sir John rolled on into Russian territory without noticing he'd left Austria. At Berdichev they stretched him out on a bench in the waiting room while Max picked up the trail at the stagecoach stop.

Then, shaken and jarred, Sir John woke to find himself on a wild ride with his companions in a *telezhka*. At the relays posts they stopped just long enough to change horses and coachmen—but since at every stop the Englishman was offered a few glasses of vodka, he stayed drunk enough to make the whole journey seem like some kind of waking dream. Up to that point the *moujiks'* clothing hadn't given away to him that he was riding along a post road across the Russian steppes.

At the last stop he'd certainly noticed that the Frenchman, after going away for a moment, had come back to the cart—which was ready to proceed—looking troubled. But even that Sir John couldn't swear to, though he was right: Max had in fact just tried an experiment, whose result had made him shiver with fear.

Since he still had the speaker he'd picked up at the Loursinade villa, he'd thought of something childish: Assuming that his speaker was a twin of the one his enemies had given Sir John, it had occurred to Max that it would be amusing to use it to contact the elusive Amber Masks, and make them think they'd baffled all pursuit. Going around behind the *izba*, he'd walked up to one of the telegraph poles that carry a single wire across the empty steppes. He opened out his speaker and stuck the metal point into the wood. Then—his voice shaking anxiously—he spoke into the vibrating membrane. "Hello? Hello?"

He waited a moment. Was his device damaged, defective, no longer functioning? A little annoyed by the setback, he said louder, "Hello?"

Then his heart beat wildly as a muffled voice replied, "Calling from where?"

"From Kiev," he said on the off-chance.

"Ah, Felly, it's you!"

"Felly," he said to himself. "One of those bandits is named Felly. But who the devil am I talking to?" Then he boldly said aloud, "It's me."

"So the two women are with you?"

That question was like a light going on for him. "By God, I've got it." he thought. "Their speakers only connect to certain receivers. I'm calling the leader of the Amber Masks in Marseilles."

With his appetite for understanding whetted by that discovery, he said into the vibrating membrane, "Of course."

"And what about those crazies who tried to figure out our plans in Marseilles?"

"They've been thrown off the track."

"Nobody suspected you of being the fake Dr. Rodel?"

"Nobody."

"Just as well. No one in Europe should get a clear idea of our organization. As for you, pick up the pace. Go straight across the Russian plains, and the Caspian, and Turkestan. Our agents everywhere have been notified and are preparing the way for you. You must've seen that at Kiev those three Orthodox priests just had to speak up."

"Yes," agreed Max.

"Above all, keep heading south. I need them here, at the underground temple in the Celestial Mountains, so that I can have revenge on them for the death of Log. Go like the blazes to the east—always east."

The voice fell silent. Max waited a moment longer. Then, since the vibrating membrane was still, he removed the device and folded it carefully back into his wallet.

"Log..." he said to himself. "Log was Dodekhan's rival, the one brave Duke Lucien killed, while his wife watched on the screen at the villa, three thousand leagues away. The one I just spoke to must be the other giant I was told about, his servant San. And now I know that the fake Rodel is someone named Felly, a European by his name. So there are bandits in Europe, and at Kiev there are three priests, exactly the number of those rascals. That's a disguise, three priests. I'll be on my guard against churchmen."

But making so many discoveries at one time had disturbed Max's composure a little, and produced the noticeable look on his face when he returned to the *telezhka*.

And now the cart had passed Sara's *tarantass*, a few kilometers from Kiev, where Max was going to wait for the fugitives, with the firm intention of changing their course toward the south. Safety must lie that way—since the leader of the Amber Masks had urged him so strongly to cut off that direction.

CHAPTER X
Through the Russian Revolution

Peter Kunin, First Counselor at Kiev, shook his head as pushed the samovar back toward his wife, Nadia, who sat across from him. "Fundamentally—just between us, my darling Nadia, I can admit—it's rather a good thing." Since his wife, whose straw-blonde hair was streaked with gray, didn't answer, he went on, "It won't displease the government. I protect some travelers by stopping them from going south and falling into the hands of the revolutionaries."

"That's a lie, my dear Peter, because you're doing it to please that society of the Blue Flag, which sends subsidies and... instructions... to our revolutionaries."

The First Counselor laughed condescendingly. "Yes, my purple fox, but the government can't read my thoughts—that's the first principle of politics—and I've been paid five hundred rubles, with which I can buy the darling fairy of my hearth a fine new *kokoshnik* decorated with gemstones from the Volga."

The *kokoshnik*—the national headdress, a diadem studded with precious stones, which is worn on holidays—arouses at least as much desire among Russian beauties as the latest creation of Parisian milliners does among fashionable Frenchwomen. Nadia gave her lord and master a benevolent look.

"You'll be even happier to wear it," he went on, "knowing that it was given to you by your dear husband, and that it was paid for by the friends of the revolution you can't abide."

"A woman worthy of the name," declared his wife in a serious voice, "cannot approve of persons who, under the pretext of making the people happy, begin by massacring everybody."

"Shush! Shush! Those lords have long ears."

"Like donkeys."

The worthy Counselor put his nose in his teacup, which saved him from the awkwardness of replying. It is indeed a delicate trick for an official to praise revolutionaries without condemning the government. Silence is one way around the difficulty.

His cup now empty, Peter stood up. "Anyway, sweet lamb, you'll have your *kokoshnik* in time for the Feast of St. Peter and St. Paul, when my colleagues from the municipal assembly will come offer us their good wishes. But shh—I hear my secretary Gelov's footsteps. There's no need for that snake to know. To get him to hold his damned tongue I'd have to give him a share of the perquisite from the three priests."

There was a soft knock, and the door opened to reveal on the threshold a thin bilious little flaxen-haired man with glasses perched on his nose and an obsequious, hypocritical manner. "First Counselor," he said in a sour voice, "three honorable priests of our holy Orthodox church beg an audience with you."

"Three priests, eh, eh?" muttered Peter, doing his best to feign surprise. "Three priests, you say, son?"

"Yes, First Counselor. I believe they attended the city council deliberations at which you suggested so… charitably… that all travelers heading east should be rerouted toward Kharkov, so as to keep them from falling into the hands of the revolutionaries who are causing unrest along the Black Sea coast."

Peter eyed his secretary with concern. He felt that he sensed some irony in the little man's tone. But the secretary remained impassive. So in a hesitant voice the Counselor murmured, "In your opinion, Gelov, would it be a mistake to close my door to representatives of the church?"

"I have no opinion besides that of my employer."

Peter couldn't suppress a grimace. In that suspicious country, where officials tremble before governmental thunderbolts on one side and revolutionary fury on the other, a secretary can at any moment change from a spy—his natural role—to an accuser; and the worthy Counselor wouldn't have minded being sure that Gelov approved of his receiving the priests. But since he couldn't press the man, he had to make a decision on his own. "Of course, son, of course. But I know your devotion to the holy icons, and I believe I've put your thoughts into words. Therefore be so kind as to bring in those venerable persons."

When his secretary had hastened away to do his bidding, Peter murmured, "Nadia, my dove, wait in the next room, to keep that rascal from hiding there to eavesdrop on me."

Madame Kunin nodded; as she went to the door it reopened, and Gelov announced, "Their Holinesses Volod, Strepan, and Yolev, of the Tsarskoye Chapter."

The priests entered, looking dignified in their long robes and flat-topped conical silk hats. They bowed solemnly with their arms folded across their chests, and waited in silence until both the Counselor's wife and his secretary had left. Then their demeanor changed slightly. In a voice that Max Soleil—if he could've heard it—would've recognized as that of the wretch who'd once posed as the late Dr. Rodel, the tallest of them asked, "Well, Peter Kunin, what did the city council decide?"

"What I predicted when I accepted your generosity. It voted to agree to my proposal."

"So all travelers arriving in Kiev?…"

"Will be sent east."

"No matter what they say, no matter how much they protest?"

"They'll be ignored."

"Even if they ask to go back west."

Peter laughed loudly. "Oh, that would've been the chief objection, but I didn't raise it. Now the council has ruled: it's been decided that all movement must be to the east. Whether they want to or not, travelers will go east."

"Good! We're pleased with your zeal. As a token of our goodwill, the Blue Flag will double your reward. Add these five hundred rubles to those you already received."

The First Counselor suddenly turned crimson, and with a submissive, grateful gesture he grabbed at the roll of gold coins the priest held out to him. "Masters, masters," he stammered. "I'm your humble servant…"

The priest who'd spoken interrupted him. "Enough idle talk. The women travelers our Leader is interested in arrived yesterday. They're staying at the Hotel Dimitri on Gregory Avenue. One hour from now, the municipal *gorodovoi*[19] must be there to witness their departure, and to force them to go if necessary."

"The *gorodovoi* will receive my orders. As First Counselor, I have authority over the municipal police."

"We know. That's why we came to you." Then the priest lowered his voice. "The *gorodovoi* must be deaf."

"Deaf!" cried Peter, clearly astonished. "But there are no deaf men on the force. Deafness would certainly be cause for dismissal."

The priest cut him off with a gesture. "By 'deaf' I just mean that they must not hear whatever the women might say."

"Ah! Good, good: not hearing is easy. If I need to, I'll help them—yes, that's it—I'll give orders that for this job the officers must plug their ears with floor wax."

The priests exchanged a look, one that didn't suggest unalloyed admiration for their host's intelligence.

But Peter saw nothing. He was rubbing his hands with pride at the practical and novel solution he'd found. If he'd been better read he'd have remembered that the wily Odysseus, King of Ithaca of Homeric fame, had used the same trick to keep his sailors from succumbing to the attractions of the Sirens' song. But Peter had no education; the bliss of ignoramuses is that every day they discover America—without suspecting that quite a long time ago Christopher Columbus was so good as to spare them the trouble.

But he had no time to congratulate himself: repeated blows shook the door. "Who is it?"

Madame Kunin appeared, looking agitated.

"What does this mean? I don't like to be disturbed when I'm busy."

But—in spite of Peter's frowning eyebrows, which in his fatuity he imagined could be described as Jovian—Nadia was not at all dissuaded. "Peter," she panted, "odd things are happening in town."

---

[19] Police officers [*Note from the Author*].

"Odd things!" he echoed with sudden anxiety. "What kind of odd things could happen in Kiev under my governance?"

"Come close and I'll whisper it to you. I don't want to give away municipal secrets. Their Holinesses will excuse me." Beneath her tone of apparent respect seemed to run a current of sarcasm.

Peter hurried to her and whispered, "Tell me."

"There are three priests outside who wish very much to see you."

"How about that—three more."

"The number isn't the only interesting thing."

"What do you mean?"

"Their names are even more remarkable."

"Their names?"

"They claim their names are Volod, Strepan, and Yolev."

The First Counselor stared at her in amazement. Then even more quietly he whispered, "The ones who are here were announced with those names."

"Exactly. So there must be impostors."

"Good lord! Now that you mention it... Oh, governing is getting difficult! And no one to give me advice."

Nadia shrugged, with the superior power of women's intuition to solve problems the simplest way. "To foil the liars, bring them face to face."

With a grunt of delight, Peter struck his head a blow that would've stunned a bull, but the worthy man had a skull thick enough to take it. "You're right, my turtledove, you're right. Well then, bring them in, bring them in. You'll stay here to help me get through this ordeal." Then he caught her by the arm. "But if you stay here, that rascal of a spy, Gelov, might hide in the next room. No, you'll bolt the door. Go, my dove, go—I tremble as I wait."

Nadia hurried away. The priests had paid no attention to the domestic conference; they were talking animatedly together. But suddenly they too were surprised. Madame Kunin reopened the door and announced, "Their Holinesses Volod, Strepan, and Yolev, of the Tsarskoye Chapter!"

And from behind her three priests in long robes and flat-topped conical silk hats came in.

The first set of priests cried out as one, "What is this asinine joke? They dare use our names! The Holy Orthodox Synod will appreciate hearing about this!"

But one of the newcomers retorted, "The Holy Synod will appreciate nothing at all, seeing as those names don't belong to you and you stole them from us."

"Stole?"

"That's right. Your real names are... you, the tall one, Rodel and Felly; you, the little skinny one, Félix; and as for the third one, I don't know yet."

The Amber Masks, transformed into priests, had started. For a moment the name Felly—which they thought no one knew—had disconcerted them. Still, they quickly recovered, and shouted, "That's a lie!"

But their accuser just responded cuttingly, "You're impostors, bandits. Having robbed us, now you're trying to compromise Peter Kunin, that distinguished official, by saddling him with the Blue Flag and the revolutionaries!"

"O Holy Icons," sighed the despairing Counselor.

"And," went on their accuser, "the voice of truth has power—I dare you to deny it."

With a theatrical gesture he stretched out his arms toward one of his interlocutors. His companions did the same. Peter and Nadia shook as they saw the first three priests tremble before the accusing fingers pointed at them. Yes, they trembled. They moved like leaves shaken by the wind. Their arms twisted, their knees knocked, their faces expressed torment and terror. Then their eyes stared rigidly, a deathly pallor filled their faces, and they stood still, as if frozen, with an imbecilic smile on their lips.

The priest who'd accused them turned to the Counselor and his wife. "As you can see, these men are fakes."

"Yes, yes. Just as you said, reverend father, the truth speaks powerfully in their silence."

"I'm going to search those jokers and take back what's mine. But before that, worthy Peter Kunin, I want to save you."

"Me?"

"And your partner, with her noble beauty."

Nadia smiled at the graceful compliment.

"Father," pressed the First Counselor, "am I in danger?"

"Serious danger. In carrying out the orders of those wretches, you would've been signing your own death warrant."

"My death warrant! Oh, that would be a regrettable mistake—depriving the city of my services! But why, but how?"

"Because the Blue Flag and the Reds want the travelers staying at the Hotel Dimitri..."

"To be sent east?"

"Not at all. South."

"South? They told me..."

"The lie that would've doomed you if we'd shown up too late."

Peter clutched at his hair in despair. "And that'll still doom me."

"No."

"Yes! I had the city council vote to make travel to the east obligatory."

"Bah! You'll just give special orders concerning the people in question."

"Can I countermand a municipal ruling?"

"Maybe you can't, but the district governor can."

"He could. But, reverend father, you understand why I can't tell him that I—an official—colluded with the enemies of the government!"

"You won't tell him."

"Then how will I explain the matter to him?"

"No need to trouble him for that. You just need to give the necessary orders while attributing them to the governor."

Husband and wife groaned in fear. "If he ever finds out?"

"You'll deny it: a verbal order leaves no trail."

Peter Kunin roared with delight. He seized the priest's hand and kissed it. "Oh, you Orthodox saint—you honest man who urges a lie if it leads to salvation—may the blessings of the Elect be upon you!" Then affectionately, almost lovingly, he added, "So, those guests at the Dimitri?"

"Will leave in an hour."

"Very well."

"But they'll be heading..."

"South instead of east."

"Exactly. I'll spread word of your rectitude and your intelligence, Peter Kunin, and after saving your life I'll make it illustrious."

Hearts are conquered by promises. Cutting short the delighted couple's expressions of gratitude, the priest—in a manner rather more cavalier than priest-like—calmly searched through his immobilized enemies' pockets, taking whatever papers and objects he found. Then, addressing the First Counselor, who was bowing with respect as he watched the act of "restitution," he said, "Worthy and honorable Peter, I leave these jokers to your justice."

"I'll send them to prison."

"As you wish."

"Charged with illegal wearing of holy garments, and with vagrancy." He smiled. "They're vagrants, since now they have no papers."

"They had ours."

"That's what I'm saying, reverend father. Oh, one more thing—look how honest I am!—they gave me a few rubles for the favors they were asking..."

"Keep it, Kunin, keep it," said the priest loftily. "And remember, in forty-five minutes the ladies at the Hotel Dimitri..."

"Will be sent south."

Bowing deferentially, almost worshipfully, Peter and Nadia followed the priests as far the front door. Then the First Counselor brusquely ordered his secretary, Gelov—who was standing there watching as if by chance—to run to the police station and bring back the chief of the *gorodovoi*.

By now the priests had reached the street. They walked along unassumingly, greeting passersby as they went, and sometimes being stopped by a child, a little blonde girl or a solemn-face boy, who said timidly, "Good afternoon, father," and asked to be blessed, before running off at full speed like chickens with a stolen grain of wheat.

Kiev isn't a big city. In a few minutes the priests had reached the outskirts, and farmland spread out before them. A small copse of aspens stood amid plowed fields about three hundred meters away. Those holy men, no doubt drawn by that verdant spot, went slowly toward the patch of emerald green on the barren plains. When they were under the trees, and surrounded by their trunks, they could no longer be seen.

Ten minutes went by. Then three people came out of the woods: a young man and two charming young women. We say "charming," because they were Sara de La Roche-Sonnaille and Miss Violet Musketeer. Their companion, Max Soleil, was carrying a bulky package.

At ease in the country solitude, and sure that what they said wouldn't be overheard by prying ears, they chatted happily.

"What a strange thing madness is," said Sara. "As soon as it's a question of light, poor Mona's mind becomes perfectly clear."

"It's quite surprising," agreed Violet.

Max nodded. "Luckily—because I admit that without her I don't see how we would've gotten rid of those troublesome Amber Masks."

"Ah, yes! Those light-ray tubes."

"Numbers 27 and 29, if I'm not mistaken."

"That's right, 27 and 29, in the blue series."

"But how did you know that the blue rays would produce such extreme torpor and numbness?" asked Violet.

Sara replied, "Surgeons have long known the anesthetic power of blue light. Dr. Elleviousse tested its effect on the mental state of the insane. Thanks to dear Mona, I was kept up to date on those experiments. I knew the rays—like everything on earth—were beneficial in tiny quantities and dangerous when concentrated. Since she and I were alone and facing all-powerful enemies, we needed weapons. I thought perhaps light might be such a weapon—the more formidable because it's almost unknown to most people."

"Formidable is the word," murmured Max. "Did you see those jokers? Frozen, turned to stone! I'm afraid they'll never recover…"

"Their wits," said the duchess seriously. "With our lenses focusing the blue light on specific points, we must have caused burns, which will act like lesions and leave gaps in their memory and their reason."

The three supposed priests, having just overcome the Amber Masks who'd been trying to defeat them since Marseilles, went back to town and returned to the Hotel Dimitri—where Max and Violet had finally joined the unknown young women to whose welfare they'd been dedicated for so long.

The three Amber Masks—those mysterious agents of a man to whom the Blue Flag had granted terrible powers—had been reduced to helplessness. The way south was now open: to Odessa, the duchess's actual goal. There they'd take passage for Calcutta, and strive to find their way back to the sumptuous house where Sara de La Roche-Sonnaille and Mona Labianov had made their final farewell to those they loved.

As they were about to enter the hotel they noticed Sir John Lobster hunched over his wireless speaker, which he'd attached to the lightning rod.

The fat Englishman was talking, out of breath from his own scolding rant. "Hello? Answer me, by Astaroth's big toe!… No—nothing. They've gone deaf. Or they're all laughing at me. No, they're not laughing. Because they've recovered Violet, my fiancée. Hello? Hello?… Thunder and lightning turn me to mincemeat if I understand what's going on."

He turned, stunned, at the sound of three bursts of laughter behind him. Violet, Sara, and Max stood there, looking so delighted that it made the Member of Parliament livid. "I'd ask you not to laugh at me," he fumed.

"We're not laughing at you," replied Max with exquisite tact, "but at the fact that you don't understand the silence of your friends, the Amber Masks."

"And I suppose you understand? Then explain."

"Oh, no, Sir John. The reason is so straightforward that you might think I was treating you like a simpleton."

"Treat me like a simpleton, but explain."

"I won't, because I have too much respect for you to insult you like that. But if in six months you haven't figured it out, I give you my word of honor that I'll provide you with the solution to the mystery."

While his answer prompted his companions to a new fit of laughter, Max spun around and led the young ladies into the hotel, leaving Sir John red-faced, furious—and baffled by his speaker that didn't speak.

"Halt or I fire!" The click of a rifle being cocked rang out in the pre-dawn half-light. On the road, voices called out, "Halt, *yamshchiks*! Halt!"

The horses sank to their knees. The *telezhka* and the *tarantass* stood still. Twenty paces away a soldier in a long green greatcoat stood in the middle of the road with his rifle raised. Resistance was clearly impossible. The road was flanked on the right by the deep, wide Dnieper, and on the left by a steep embankment.

Since the day before, the fugitives had been racing along this road that followed the river. They'd left Kiev: Violet, Sara, and Mona in the *telezhka*, and Max in the *tarantass*, where he could keep an eye on Sir John. They'd headed south, happier with every *verst* they covered. In a few hours they expected to reach the railroad line from Kishinev to Rostov at the point where it crossed the Dnieper, and to catch the train to get to Odessa fast.

Violet and Sara had become friends. Who wouldn't adore the charming Englishwoman who'd given up a worry-free life of luxury to throw herself into an adventure where danger lurked at every turn in the road? And now, in the midst of their enchantment, everything came to a stop.

"Advance, and give the password!" cried the sentry. "No, not the carriages. One traveler, alone!"

They had to obey. Max jumped down and approached. When he was three meters away, the soldier ordered him to stop, then said, "Do you have the passports, little father?"

The question worried Max. He, Violet, and Sir John were furnished with the documents indispensable for travel in Russia. But Sara and Mona had nothing comparable. As for the papers they'd taken from the Amber Masks—since they were countersigned by the revolutionary authorities they couldn't safely be presented to the Tsar's soldiers.

Noticing his hesitation, the sentry brought a whistle to his lips and blew a piercing signal. Two minutes later a lieutenant came down from the top of the embankment by a kind of rough staircase cut into the rock. Two men followed him.

While the lieutenant was conferring with the sentry, Max had gone back to the *telezhka*. He explained the situation to the duchess. "We've got papers. You don't. But I feel like it would be enough to mention your name and that of Mona Labianov..."

She protested vehemently, "No, no!"

"Why not?"

"The followers of the Blue Flag have lost our trail. The procedures involved in checking our claims might put them back on our track. Anything rather than that!"

"Then we'll be arrested."

"Let's let ourselves be arrested. If all else fails, we'll still be able to resort to the extreme measure you propose."

"I think we should do what she says," said Violet calmly. "It'll be very amusing. I never dreamt of such entertainment."

The upshot of that decision was that the lieutenant asked the travelers to step down and follow him, while the soldiers took the carriages along the road to the encampment. They all obeyed. Mona, indifferent, followed Sara. Wherever the duchess went, she went.

They soon reached the tent of Colonel Markoff, commanding officer of the regiment stationed here. He received them with the smiling politeness typical of the Russian Army—but on hearing them say they wished to remain incognito, his face darkened. "I must warn you that my orders forbid me to accept that."

"Your orders!" cried Sara. "Were you warned of our arrival?"

"No, Madame. But we're stationed here as a line of defense. I can't let you pass."

They all looked at each other in surprise.

The colonel lowered his voice, "I can see that my prisoners are people of quality. I even recognize French and English people among you. But the entire Black Sea coast is in the hands of the revolutionaries. They're looting and massacring everywhere. Sailors and soldiers have mutinied and joined the rebels. A political plague has broken out, and my task is to keep it from spreading north, by... quarantining the disease. I'm explaining all this to show you why it would be ill-advised for me to let you go."

They all looked at the duchess. The face of the brave little brunette expressed uncertainty; then suddenly she seemed to reach a decision. "Colonel," she said, "I'm grateful for your courtesy. My reasons must therefore be compelling if they keep me in turn from confiding fully in you. I'd rather remain your prisoner than reveal my name." The officer started in surprise, and she went on, "Keep us. Soon, I hope, peace will be restored. You'll then be released from your orders, and you can allow us to go on our way—knowing who we are. At that point you won't be required to file a report, and I'll be happy to trust your honor as a gentleman with the secret that I don't want to share now with an officer under orders."

"Excuse me, excuse me, I don't agree to being locked up!!" objected Sir John.

But his words ended in a whimper: Max had just kicked him in the shins and whispered in his ear, "The Amber Masks are in league with the revolutionaries. If you talk, this officer of the Tsar will just have you shot."

That left the Member of Parliament with a most comical look of indecision.

Colonel Markoff said, "I'm listening, sir."

"But I have nothing to say," stammered Sir John.

That made his companions smile, but it seemed to astonish the Russian, who shrugged as he examined this red-faced person who insisted on speaking— only to announce that he had nothing to say. "Ladies, gentlemen," he continued, "strictly speaking it would be my duty to have you searched. I won't do it. I'll limit myself to keeping you here in camp, until such time as you feel free to talk."

They all thanked him for his courtesy. The colonel having given orders, they were escorted to a shed, open at both ends, that had probably been built to shelter sheep. Their carriages had already been put there, and their horses were at the manger. Guards had been posted around the building. The travelers were certainly prisoners; but the soldiers who brought them their meal treated them less like captives than like... involuntary guests: the colonel must've given orders. The soldiers talked willingly, and answered the travelers' questions. But their answers were far from reassuring.

The Revolution was victorious on the Black Sea coast. The legal authorities had been driven out, after a chaotic bloodbath. A Revolutionary Committee governed Odessa, Sevastopol, and other cities. Battleship crews had taken up the rebel cause. Naval vessels still loyal to the government had been forced to go out to sea to avoid battle. And since all Russia was in ferment, waiting for the birth of a constitution that would transform an autocracy into a constitutional monarchy, it seemed likely that peace wouldn't be restored for a long time.

Left to themselves, the prisoners remained silent. Here was an unexpected complication, whose inconvenience Sir John put into words, lamenting, "Poor me! This means a long captivity! And who'll fill my seat in the House of Commons? I'll be declared dead, and there'll be a by-election!" His manner was ludicrous, but his meaning rang true.

The duchess appealed to the others, "My new friends, please agree to wait a few days. I won't abuse your patience. You've caught only a glimpse of the formidable organization that controls the Amber Masks, whereas I've lived for months in the midst of those wretches. They have millions upon millions of members, they're everywhere, all around. If we reveal our names, you can be sure they'll be onto us immediately: we'll have to suspect everyone—the porter who carries our luggage, the servant who brings us our meals, the gentleman who bows to us, the sailor who runs into us... I beg you, give me a few days."

As before, Violet immediately agreed with Sara. "You can have many days, dear sweet thing. I'm grateful to you. I was dying of boredom, and thanks to you I've been dragged into the most wonderful, sensational adventures." Then she turned her soft blue eyes on Max. "I lack nothing to make me happy. I'd be sorry if you didn't feel the same way."

Max answered only with an eloquent smile.

Violet went on, "So we're all agreed."

"By the devil—no! I'm not! By the horns of the moon, I find this shed we're not allowed to leave to be... an impediment!" Since no one paid any attention to his ill humor, Sir John moved away from the group and sat down by one of the posts that held up the roof of the shed.

With the passing hours the midday sun beat its oppressive heat down on the plains. Most of the soldiers had taken shelter from its rays in their tents. The sentries snoozed, leaning on their rifles. Every creature and every object lay prostrate, torpid. Tired from their night in the carriages, the travelers sat against one of the closed walls of the shed. Conversation had been halting at first, and soon came to an end. Mona had sung them a monotone lullaby, and then the mad girl had fallen silent. Her eyes had closed. One by one the prisoners were overtaken by sleep, passing unaware from wakefulness to the oblivion of a siesta.

Only Sir John remained awake. The heat lent his ruddiness an extra radiance. He expressed his discontent unceasingly. "Poor me! Those ladies are certainly both fools, if they're not utterly mad. And Violet too, and the Frenchman as well! It's quite unacceptable to force me to share their captivity. I'm an Englishman, and England will not allow her children to be abused." He glanced over at his companions. "I say! They've all fallen asleep! This would be a propitious time—if my speaker still worked—to consult my friends the Amber Masks." But then he said sadly, "But my speaker doesn't work." He pulled it out of his pocket and examined it sorrowfully. "Still, it doesn't look broken, or damaged in any way. Why was it silent the other day? Maybe it's not to blame…"

Sir John couldn't have guessed that his speaker had remained silent for the very good reason that the people who usually spoke to him, having been paralyzed by the blue rays, were in no condition to speak. But out of his wish to escape from the bad spot he was in, he formed a hypothesis. "Perhaps that lightning rod was to blame. It would be easy enough to check."

Upon which he unfolded the vibrating membrane and stuck the spike into the post next to him, and then with feeling he murmured, "Hello? Hello?" He waited a moment, then gestured with discouragement. But just to make sure he repeated, "Hello?"

This time he jumped like a man who just sat on an anthill. His face lit up with joy. An unknown voice had answered, "Who's there?"

"Sir John Lobster."

"Never heard of him."

"Friend and ally of the Amber Masks."

"Oh! That's different. What's your position?"

"Poor."

"No—where are you?"

"In a shed, in Colonel Markoff's encampment, along the Dnieper River."

"In the camp? Be quiet, and I'll come talk to you."

Sir John looked at his companions again. They were obviously deep in dreamland, and had seen nothing. He skillfully hid the speaker back in his pocket. Then he muttered, "That was a perfectly correct exchange—but I didn't think to ask the name of the gentleman who spoke to me." He looked around a little anxiously. "He said he'll come. As long as he gets here before the others wake up! I'd be able to explain more freely. Otherwise that fool of a blockhead, Max Soleil, will kick me in the shins again. Oh, those excitable French! Reasonable people should stay away from them—at least two leg lengths away. Yes, indeed, at least two leg lengths…"

He broke off. "Well, an officer; another colonel—no, a lieutenant colonel. Ah, he's coming this way. I say! He'll be awfully much in the way—my fellow won't come near if he sees him. I'll be a Salvation Army bonnet![20]—he's headed for the shed!"

There could be no mistake: the officer was coming straight toward him. He paused for a moment to exchange a few words with one of the sentries, of which Sir John caught only an indistinct murmur. Then he approached, and greeted him with, "Prisoner? Sir."

"Yes."

"Your name, please?"

---

[20] An informal, comical oath, referring to Salvation Army women's headgear [*Note from the Author*].

"Sir John Lobster."

The lieutenant colonel lowered his voice. "Can you show it to me?"

Sir John showed him the speaker. The officer drew an identical speaker from his own pocket. The two men shook hands.

"I was supposed to contact the Amber Masks," murmured the officer, "fine people to whom I'm fully committed, because they paid my debts—which saved me from having to leave the army."

"Same for me, except for the debts and the army, since I'm a civilian and very wealthy. But how is it that our speakers connected?"

"They're made to do the same job, so they probably have similar properties. But let's get to the point. What do you want?"

"To be set free."

"Your papers?"

"Official papers? Not the slightest. And it seems that the ones signed by the revolutionaries…"

"Be sure to keep those hidden. Where do you want to go?"

"South. Those are our carriages and horses, and my companions."

The lieutenant colonel pondered; then he came close and whispered, "When you see them, tell them that Lieutenant Colonel Polsky has kept his promises. The battalion that'll be stationed on this part of the line tonight is completely loyal to me. You'll be escorted out of the zone of military control."

"Oh! I thank you."

"Don't bother. Those fighting against autocracy saved me. Even if they hadn't, my heart would be with them: I'm Polish." Then, wrapping up the conversation, he said, "Tonight, settle down to sleep in your carriages, and don't move no matter what happens. And no need to remind you to keep silent, right?"

The officer walked away, leaving Sir John delighted but deeply mystified. How had the Amber Masks—whom he'd assumed cared only about catching the fugitives from the Elleviousse Asylum—gotten mixed up in the Russian Revolution, to the point where they had whole battalions on their side? If he'd known more about the power of the Blue Flag, he'd have understood that that secret society's goal was fomenting unrest in the Tsar's empire. Whatever weakened Europe must strengthen Asia. But his antagonism toward his companions had kept him from being told anything, and he puzzled away at the question in vain—producing nothing but even higher blood pressure than his usual.

However, when his traveling companions woke up he told them about the surprising outcome of his call on the speaker. They were surprised and a little worried. But—confident that they'd reduced their three personal enemies to helplessness—they ended up celebrating, and even congratulating Sir John, who was puffed up by his success.

When night fell, Sara and Mona and Violet settled themselves inside the *telezhka*, along with the chest full of luminous tubes. Sir John and Max huddled in the *tarantass*. The silence in the shed suggested they were all asleep—but it only seemed that way: in the dark their eyes were open.

So they heard the battalion marching out to replace the one that had been on duty during the day. And they heard the changing of the sentries' shift. Then once again the silence of the night fell on the camp.

Midnight!... What was that? Shadows slipped into the shed; the horses were led to the shafts and put in harness. The coachmen—who hadn't been seen all day—climbed onto their seats. Slowly the carriages began to move.

Men walked alongside the horses. They reached the first line of sentries. By God!—the order must've been given, because the soldiers turned a blind eye. They went another hundred meters. At the advance outpost, again, everyone seemed to have lost their eyesight voluntarily. Further on they reached the pickets—and again they passed just as easily.

Max, amused, muttered, "Well, if all the Russian defense lines work the same way, you might call them a pointless precaution!"

A corresponding series of guard posts lay ahead, since the military "cordon" had to face both ways. They approached the last line of sentries: in another hundred meters they'd be free. By daybreak, when their escape was noticed, they'd have reached the railroad line, from where a train would carry them to Odessa under full steam.

But whoever was escorting the *tarantass* came back to the carriage and hopped onto the step. Max had a good look at him; from his insignia he knew this must be the lieutenant colonel Sir John had described.

The officer leaned in the window. "Your carriage is going to take off at a gallop."

"But what about the sentries?"

"I'm not sure about these. That's why I put them at the very end of the line. They probably won't stop you. You're coming from camp; if your departure wasn't authorized you'd have been stopped earlier. That's most likely what they'll think. But you'll have to go at a gallop. If anyone hails you, don't answer. At that speed you'll soon be out of reach."

Max's heart ached: he wanted to be with Violet, to protect her on this possibly dangerous crossing.

But the lieutenant colonel hopped down, crying, "Go!"

The coachman whipped up his horses, who went suddenly from a walk to a gallop. The die was cast. They were off. They crossed the hundred meters in a few seconds. Max saw the outline of a sentry standing on a knoll, and it seemed to him the man was looking toward the road. No doubt he was wondering what the galloping meant. But he did nothing to order the carriages to stop. The *tarantass* reached him and passed him. So—the lieutenant colonel's fears were groundless. The prisoners were saved... No!

A voice rang out dismally in the night: "Halt!"

Max turned to look back. The *telezhka* was following them. The coachmen raised their whips, and a rain of blows fell on the backs of the horses, who bolted and charged.

"Halt!" cried the voice again, but it was already distant.

The mad ride went on. A short distance ahead the road entered a cutting; once they were there they'd be safe.

Max cried out, "Faster! Faster!"

A bang punctuated his words: the sentry had fired. The coachmen plied their whips even harder. The carriages plunged into the cutting. *Versts* followed *versts*. They slowed down and listened. There was no sound of pursuit.

But just then Sara called out, her voice sounding choked, bewildered, unnatural.

"What's wrong?"

The *tarantass* stopped. Max ran back to the other carriage. He cried out in grief and despair: lying in the duchess's arms, Violet—covered in blood, deathly pale—looked at him, her big blue eyes seemingly made even bigger by her suffering.

"The shot," stammered Sara, overcome with emotion. "The bullet pierced her shoulder. I didn't know. She said nothing. But then just now she almost passed out, and I saw the blood."

As Max hurried closer, Violet whispered, "If I'd cried out, you'd have stopped. You'd have been recaptured." Her head fell back. She'd fainted—having reached the end of her strength and her courage.

A single sob shook Max. But a soft hand pushed him gently back. "Let me," said a voice in his ear.

Looking up, he saw Mona standing before him. Had the mad girl caught a few words? No doubt—and right away that special lucidity in her madness had manifested itself. She opened the chest of luminous tubes and chose Number 3. She began unscrewing the magnifying lens at the tip of the transparent cylinder, which right now looked just like an ordinary test tube. While she worked she gave orders. "Uncover the wound and wash it carefully."

And Sara, full of trust in her poor friend as soon as it was a question of light, obeyed meekly. Violet's shoulder was bared. On her satin-smooth skin, just above the clavicle, was a bleeding exit hole. The bullet had struck poor Violet in the middle of the shoulder blade and gone right through her shoulder. Mona solemnly brought the instrument close to the wound. The tube emitted a violet light, giving a fantastical look to the whole scene surrounded by night.

The *yamshchiks* watched in amazement, and every now and then they crossed themselves. No doubt it looked like magic to them, and they prayed to the Six Hundred Icons of Moscow to protect their souls from the devil.

"What are you doing, Mademoiselle?" asked Max, no longer able to contain himself.

Mona seemed not to have heard him. Sara repeated the question, and the mad girl smiled at her gently, and—to Sara—she explained her thoughts. "Out here in the country it's impossible to treat her. She might die from blood loss before reaching a house."

"Die!" echoed Max with a moan.

But the duchess motioned to him to be silent, and the mad girl went on, "I'm stopping the blood loss."

"How?"

"The violet rays cause burns. Since I took off the lens, I'm just cauterizing the wound—otherwise I'd be charring it."

As the tube poured its violet light onto the wound, the cells began to change: they seemed to contract. No one spoke. All of them—filled with an inexpressible emotion—reflected on this young woman who'd lost her mind, but whose intuitive intervention might save the life of another young woman.

Finally Mona withdrew the device, reattached its lens, and put it away in the chest. "Bandage the wound, and then let's be off. This is only temporary. We need to find a doctor in the first town we reach."

She closed the chest, got back into her seat in the *telezhka*, and sat unmoving. She seemed to have forgotten the other travelers. At any other time they would've been amazed at the odd and lucky spell of lucidity that interrupted the madness. But at the moment there was too much else to think about. At all costs they had to save the heroic Violet—who'd stoically endured the pain so as not to slow down her friends' escape by a cry or a complaint.

Sara and Max both thought, "It would be awful if she died because she saved us."

With Violet more or less dressed again and arranged as comfortably as possible in the *telezhka*, they all regained their own seats, and the carriages went on—no longer at a gallop as before, but at a walk to avoid bumps.

It was day by the time they reached Berna, a small stop on the Rostov-Odessa-Kishinev line. It had an odd look: a red flag flew from the station roof. In place of railroad employees in regulation uniforms, men in peasant smocks or colorful shirts, wearing ordinary headgear, were doing the work. The line had been taken over by revolutionaries.

However, they gave the travelers a warm welcome, and when they heard the wounded girl had been shot by a soldier, using an army-issue rifle, they suddenly became very interested in the victim. Some ran to get a doctor, others fetched the station first-aid kit, and still others helped Sara and Max carry Violet to the station master's office—he having fled.

The man who was now doing his job roused his entire staff to assist the station's unexpected guests. He interspersed his orders with happy exclamations: "Of course we have to heal her! Maldanov, go get beer and vodka from the restaurant. Shot by a soldier—a pretty girl, holy angels, very pretty, and English to boot! Ah, now the Tsarists are shooting Englishwomen! Makhlov, in the former station master's bedroom, a quilted blanket—it'll be lighter for this poor child. Oh, England will make a fuss, she'll teach the Autocrat's slaves that you can't massacre the English the way you can the Russians!"

Max was filled with such painful emotion that he paid no attention to the flood of words, which just sounded to him like a vague buzzing. He let his hand be shaken by thickly bearded men, whose hard, vigorous faces lit up in his presence.

"Where were you taking this young lady?" asked the station master finally.

"To Odessa."

"Odessa! Did I hear right? Well, you'll be made welcome there, I guarantee it, welcome the way the governor never will be again! Wounded and English—what a welcome!" Then he slapped his brow. "I'll notify the ruling Committee; it's the least I can do."

Max didn't try to stop him. For one thing, he wasn't listening to the terrible chatterbox. But the endless talk, the sentences all tangled up together, annoyed him: his mind spun, his heart pounded as if it was trapped in his rib cage. What mattered Odessa and the Committee's welcome to him? He cared only about the doctor coming.

At last an uproar filled the station. The men who'd been sent to fetch him returned with the local doctor—a distinguished white-haired old man whose soft eyes studied the people around him with a notable authority.

"Doctor, doctor, will she live?" Max's irrepressible feelings surfaced in his anxious blurted question.

With a fatherly smile of understanding for the quivering sufferer before him, the doctor murmured, "We must hope so—always—always."

He was led to the patient, who'd now opened her eyes and was looking around calmly. Max's outburst made her smile too—a smile that the doctor noticed. "Yes, yes," he said. "We'll live."

With a gentle, light touch that would've been the envy of many a female sickroom nurse, he unwrapped the temporary bandage. He examined the wound, taking great care to spare the patient any pain beyond what was unavoidable. Finally he straightened up and turned to Max. "A pretty wound, sir. No vital organ hit. And luckily the shot was fired at close range, so the bullet was moving fast. It went right through the scapula like a grain of buckshot through a window. A round hole, no fracture, and then a dressing. What was used to dress the wound?"

"We were out in the country, far from any town..." began Sara, giving Max a look to stop him explaining.

"Oh," said the doctor, "far from any town. Just as well for the patient. She wouldn't have received better treatment in any big city. The wound is slightly cauterized; how the devil was that done? It's simply perfect—I've never seen the like."

The doctor was through. He left quietly, followed by the duchess.

143

Max forgot the world, and why he was in Berna, and the looming future. Watching over the one who'd become his only preoccupation, relieved by her condition, he thought of nothing but the sweetness of the present moment.

Violet slept. From time to time the station master appointed by the Revolution came to check on the patient's condition. Max was surprised at the solicitude shown by this fierce man—the agent of a bloodstained movement—but he was touched, and he felt a kind of liking for someone who appeared to share his own anxiety.

Sara also came in periodically, her usually smiling face now marked by the concern she'd felt when she first thought Violet was in danger—Violet, the sweet Englishwoman she'd known only a few days but for whom she now felt an ever-increasing affection.

Whenever Violet shut her eyes, Max moved to the window. From there he could see Mona strolling along the platform, unconscious of the respectful group of revolutionaries who followed her. With the naive ideas of *moujiks*, these rough fellows considered the mad girl to be divinely inspired. They eavesdropped on her incoherent babble and tried to interpret her words in a way that would shed light on the outcome of current events.

In short, all of the travelers seemed at ease—except Sir John Lobster: his face on fire, he never stopped pacing around and muttering. Were they going to be stuck in Berna a long time? That stupid Violet—getting wounded over something that was none of her business. He'd never seen such foolishness!

In that way the day passed. Night came, covering the station buildings and the track and the countryside with its darkness. Looking out the window, Max could see only one light: a red lantern a short distance outside the station that resembled a bloodshot eye staring into the night. It was the headlight of a train, made up and ready to go. In about twenty minutes it would be sent off toward Odessa.

Just then the duchess returned to the room, and Max pointed out the lantern and said only, "To Odessa."

She gently shook her brunette head.

"You'd be there tomorrow morning," pressed Max. "You could think again about those who are no more, those from whose memory we've sidetracked you."

She sighed deeply, and said slowly, "I've accepted your dedication to us simply, without explanations. But when I accepted it, I promised myself to give your dear sweet companion a sister's love."

"A sister would understand the need to hurry..."

She interrupted him. "A sister must not be abandoned." Then she went on in a different tone, "Let's drop it. I saw the doctor just now. On his way back from his rounds he detoured by the station."

"Well, what did he say?" cried Max.

"When I told him she was sleeping he rubbed his hands, saying, 'Perfect, perfect! All's well.' When I urged him to come up and see the patient, he declined, saying, 'No, no, I might wake her. Why interrupt Nature's benevolent action?'" Sara paused briefly, then concluded, "I'm telling you this to persuade you to stop worrying."

He found nothing to say. But he grasped the hands of this woman who'd suffered so much, and who showed such tender compassion for the sufferings of others. He pressed her hands a long time, murmuring, "Ah, duchess, you're right: let's wait until she can be moved... And you—who think of giving consolation when you yourself are inconsolable—I swear that we'll find a way to give you the supreme consolation you seek."

She thanked him with a gesture, too moved by the memory of the past to speak.

Suddenly they both jumped: an ominous bang had just shaken the station buildings, followed by a loud explosion.

"What's that noise?" Violet had risen partway from her bed. She asked not in fear but in surprise: she'd been roused from sleep by a sound whose source she didn't know.

Before her friends could answer, a distinctive rumbling went by. Then, on the tracks just beneath the window, a crater seemed to yawn open in the dirt, followed by a burst of flame and a deafening explosion. The windowpanes shattered.

"My God!" cried Max, "that's a mortar shell!"

"A shell?" echoed the two women, stunned.

"Yes—they're shelling the station."

Now they could hear shouting, and voices overlapping. People were running along the platform and into the night. Then came a stampede of heavy boots up the stairs leading to the sickroom. Max leapt to the door, revolver in hand.

The door opened. The station master came in, carrying a lantern, followed by several of his subordinates. "We're under attack by the tyrant's troops!" he panted.

"The troops?"

"Yes: I assume the ones who wounded the young lady got reinforcements. They're attacking—but they'll soon see what we're made of!" He turned to the bed. "Don't be afraid, *matushka*.[21] These fellows will carry you on your mattress to the train readying for Odessa. It'd be better not to shake you around, but a few shakes are still better than meeting up with a shell!" Another explosion punctuated the revolutionary's next words, "Quick! Quick!"

His men hurried forward, and in a moment the mattress and the patient were picked up and carried away.

---

[21] Little mother—a common term of affection [*Note from the Author*].

Max nodded his approval. "I'll get her clothes. You, duchess, bring Mademoiselle Mona."

"And the chest of luminous tubes." Sara had lost none of her cool. She went downstairs without haste, like someone who knows that calm accomplishes more than agitation. Meanwhile Max bundled up Violet's dress and other clothing. He had it all and was about to go.

The ceiling opened suddenly, and something black and heavy dropped through it, destroyed the floor, and vanished. Then from downstairs came an infernal din, a racket of shattered walls, pulverized windows, and cries of pain.

Max rushed downstairs like a madman, leaping four steps at a time. On the ground floor he found chaos: the waiting rooms were havoc—the benches crushed or flipped over onto the rubble, human figures in motion visible through the plaster dust.

"Holy Virgin of Kazan," moaned a rough voice, "my legs have been cut off."

"Help me! Help me!" cried another sad, choking voice.

But from outside someone was calling, "Monsieur Max! Monsieur Max!"

He recognized that precious voice, and began running again. In the darkness on the platform he could vaguely make out a darker mass moving toward the rear lantern of the train—the same red lantern he'd been observing from the window moments earlier. He ran to catch up with the men carrying Violet.

She saw him. "Ah, there you are. My heart almost stopped when that last shell fell on the station."

"And I was afraid for you! What about the duchess?"

"Already aboard, with her luggage and her poor friend."

"Good, good. Let's hurry!"

The wounded woman, still on her mattress, was lifted into a sleeping compartment. Sara went to help Violet settle in. The revolutionaries had gone away—but not before Max, delighted by their help, had warmly shaken them all by the hand.

Suddenly a man leapt into the compartment where Max had taken a seat. It was Sir John, his face incandescent, his red hair rising from his scalp like flames. "May ill-bred people rot in the fires of Hell!" Who was he talking about? And how could he think of good breeding at a time like this? He went on, "Earlier the rebels were saying that the station had been attacked by the same troops who were holding us prisoner, before Miss Musketeer was wounded."

"That's right."

"Well, sometimes I have a good idea. I thought, I'll telephone Lieutenant Colonel Polsky, who set us free."

"Telephone him?"

"Yes, to ask him to send his shells in some other direction."

Max couldn't help laughing at the gentleman's strange notions. Then he forced himself to be serious. "So your device didn't work?"

"I beg your pardon—yes, it did. He said..."

"What?"

"This: 'If you're not an idiot, don't stay a minute longer in the station at Berna, which we're planning to destroy."

"Excellent advice."

"I agree. But why say it with such lack of propriety? 'If you're not an idiot.' He must've known I'm not."

At the risk of strongly displeasing Sir John, Max surrendered to open laughter. But a signal sounded outside. With a slight jolt the train started. Two minutes later it entered a tunnel: the travelers had no more to fear from shelling. They were rolling at top speed toward Odessa, the port they'd been aiming for—and where the Revolution was victorious.

CHAPTER XI
Anxious Days

"Adiessa! Adiessa!" The cry rang out the whole length of the train that had just pulled into the great station at Odessa.

"We're here," said Max, recognizing the name of the commercial port in spite of its very different pronunciation in Russian. Then he added softly, "Our patient needs rest. If she's willing, we'll have her carried to the St. Petersburg Hotel; it's a quiet place, very near the harbor, at the corner of the Boulevard and Ekaterinskaya."

Violet, pale and weak—for the journey had exhausted her—managed a smile to thank him. But then her eyes expressed astonishment: the doors had opened, and common workers were pouring into the compartment. Seeing her lying on her mattress, they cried out in joy and elbowed each other, murmuring, "The *Anglichanka*! The *Anglichanka*!"

What did they want? Four of the strangers grabbed the corners of her mattress and attached them to wooden poles: by God, they were making a stretcher!

When—with the help of his Russian dictionary—Max began laboriously thanking them, they replied, "Lobareff telegraphed from Berna. The *Anglichanka* was hit by the Autocrat's soldiers. The Revolution protects her now; she'll protect the Revolution."

Max understood roughly—but a conversation like that is really too difficult when you don't know the local language. Though he was surprised by what he thought he'd heard, he didn't want them to repeat it. He just named the place to take Violet: "St. Petersburg Hotel, St. Petersburg Hotel," he said over and over, in his desperation opening his mouth very wide, with the instinctive feeling that he could articulate foreign words better that way.

They laughed at his efforts, and replied kindly, "*Nichevo!*"

Violet was carried out to the platform. The volunteer stretcher bearers put the ends of the poles on their shoulders and began to walk in step. Sara, Mona, and Max followed, along with two *moujiks* carrying the chest of luminous tubes. Sir John brought up the rear. He understood absolutely nothing that was going on in front of him—which didn't stop him from scrawling hastily in his notebook, *I observe that in Odessa the railway company takes complete care of the transport of the wounded. The employees' dress leaves much to be desired. It's a shock to British decorum.*

But he stopped there in surprise. They'd reached the courtyard of the great station. Turemnaya Square was crowded with people. A band launched into the British national anthem, *God Save the King*, while hats and caps waved wildly and enthusiastic cries rose the sky. "Hurrah for the *Anglichanka*! Hurrah for the *Anglichanka*!"

148

Sir John finished writing his note: *The people seem to be filled with the greatest affection for the English. The Admiralty should consider whether it might not be desirable to take advantage of this state of mind to annex Odessa to the Crown.*

Max and Sara watched and listened, stunned by this welcome. Of course a pretty young lady hit by an unlucky bullet and lying on a sickbed was an object of interest. But it was a long way from there to hailing her as a sovereign and mobilizing musicians to welcome her as she got off the train! What could this popular excitement mean?

They didn't have time to ask. The stretcher bearers set off walking, led by the band and followed by an immense crowd. The parade ran through streets great and small, past houses grand and humble. And the pedestrians they passed added their voices to the crowd; people came to the windows to cry loudly, "Hurrah for the *Anglichanka!*" Really, the adventure was growing disconcerting.

They reached a fine-looking house. At the door stood a clean-shaven young man wearing a long black frock coat and pearl-gray gloves. He spoke a few words the foreigners couldn't understand. The music and the shouting stopped immediately. The stretcher bearers went into the house, and people gestured to Violet's companions to do the same. When they were inside the doors closed.

"This isn't a hotel," muttered Max.

Sara shrugged slightly. "They probably misunderstood you. I've heard that Russian is very difficult to pronounce."

"But then where are we?"

"Wait. Someone will tell us eventually. Misunderstandings always get cleared up in the end."

And surely she was right to stay calm. Max gave in to the adventure. They followed the makeshift stretcher into a large sitting room—furnished not at all in the Russian style. They could've been in a sumptuous British parlor whose decoration had been done by a well-known firm like Maple or Gillow. In France it wouldn't have been surprising; but in Odessa a taste for the English style seemed odd. Sir John didn't hesitate to find support here for his fantastical theory, and he wrote it down in his notebook.

The mattress was set down on the carpet. Max bent over the patient. It seemed to him that she was even paler, her features more drawn, suggesting painful fatigue. She looked at him affectionately, reading the worry on his face, and murmured, "It's nothing. I'd like to sleep, that's all."

They didn't have time to say more. A door opened softly, and a new person entered: clean-shaven, proper, a little stiff, and wearing a fashionable two-tone gray suit unmistakably tailored in Piccadilly.

The man in the black frock coat bowed and said in excellent English, "The British Consul."

"The British Consul!" exclaimed all the travelers.

The newcomer shook their hands. "Himself. The Head of the Revolutionary Committee didn't let you know?"

In spite of their usual presence of mind, neither Max nor Sara could find a thing to say.

The revolutionary said to them, "You need only listen to understand. Then you'll be escorted to the St. Petersburg Hotel as you wished. I'm sorry to have forced this detour on you, but the future of a people trying to bring down a tyranny is at stake." Then he turned to the Consul. "Sir, on that stretcher you see a fellow countrywoman of yours."

"Really!" said the Consul, suddenly interested.

"Yes, yes," agreed Violet. "I am Violet Musketeer."

"Miss Musketeer the heiress?"

"That's right."

The Consul immediately made a deep bow, showing that he considered wealth to be worthy of the greatest respect.

The revolutionary, noticing the effect produced by the young lady's name, added with a smile, "A countrywoman of... importance."

"Great importance!" agreed the Consul with feeling.

"All right. Now, this young lady, who was traveling for pleasure in Russia—and who must've believed herself to be under the protection of the authorities—was shot by one of those wretches in the pay of the tyranny who dare call themselves soldiers."

"By a soldier?"

"A henchman of the butcher known as the Tsar."

The Consul started. "Mr. Varloff, I represent the commercial interests of a friendly government. I must ask you to refrain from any unseemly reference to the sovereign."

Without displeasure, the revolutionary nodded his agreement. Then he said slowly, "Two facts are still the case. First, here is a British citizen, one who is—as you yourself acknowledged—a person of importance. Second, she was arrested without cause by soldiers and badly wounded."

"Badly?"

"A bullet pierced her shoulder right through. Whoever fired was shooting to kill."

There was an awkward silence.

"Well, what do you want me to do?" asked the Consul softly.

"Inform your government."

"I'd be glad to."

"And make clear to them that they'd be taking up the cause of human civilization by intervening to put an end to the abuses of an army rabble unleashed on the people."

"But that's impossible! It would be an ultimatum, a *casus belli*! We can ask for apologies and damages."

Varloff chuckled, and—with a cutting tone that unwittingly distilled in perfect form the anti-patriotic principles of some Russian revolutionaries—he said, "There can be no *casus belli* in a country as deeply divided as Russia. The Autocrat can't sustain a long war. We're offering Britain a brilliant diplomatic coup. We know that, and we're doing it deliberately, because we believe a defeat suffered by the Russian government would be more than compensated for by the advantage it would give the Revolution."

The shocking morals of the apostles of the Russian Revolution were laid bare by the cynicism of that statement. The Consul understood it was pointless to continue the debate. To rid himself of the zealot before him, he had to appear to give in. "Well, Mr. Varloff, I think you're right. I'll send a cable to that effect."

"I'd be much obliged, and the whole Committee will be grateful to England. But I must point out the importance of acting fast, while Miss Musketeer—brought to the brink of death by the autocracy—is cared for and protected in Odessa by the Revolution. That great contrast should impress your statesmen. The Revolution protects foreigners who've been mistreated by the government that calls itself legitimate."

"Quite right. I'll be sure to emphasize that point."

"I'm happy to hear it. Once the patient has recovered and has left our city, Britain's negotiating position won't be affected—but the Revolution won't draw any advantage from it. It's therefore essential that the business be well under way before she recovers."

"Mr. Varloff, you're a deep political thinker. It's all understood."

At a sign from the Head of the Revolutionary Committee, the stretcher bearers—who'd stood unmoving throughout the interview—picked up the stretcher and headed to the door.

The Consul asked, "I beg your pardon, ladies, gentlemen, where are you planning to stay?"

"The St. Petersburg Hotel," answered Max quickly. He'd caught in the Consul's tone the vague suggestion of a hidden reason for asking.

"Thank you." Then, seeing that Mr. Varloff had paused with a suspicious look, the Consul smiled and said, "When my young countrywoman has gotten the rest she seems to need, I'll go speak with her to learn the details of the adventure to which I owe the honor of her... visit." His courteous tone grew a little firmer as he concluded, "Just like you, dear sir, I wish success for the principles I represent. But I'd be very sorry to aggravate the condition of the patient who'll bring about that success. I'll send the Consulate doctor over right away, so that the poor victim receives all the care her condition calls for."

Twenty minutes later the procession reached the St. Petersburg Hotel, and Violet, completely worn out by fatigue, was installed in a bright room with a view of the boulevard that overlooked the harbor. Through the open windows she could hear the breeze rustling the leaves of the four alleys of trees that bordered the shore; and from her bed she could see the slate-blue waves and the vast horizon of the Black Sea.

But she didn't contemplate the splendid view: the journey by rail, the parade through town, the shouts of the crowd—it had all worn her out. Her flushed cheeks were a sign of another bout of fever. She closed her eyes and fell into a deep sleep, which was shaken by jolts and broken by dreams full of incomprehensible dialogue.

Around four in the afternoon Violet emerged from the feverish torpor that, with good reason, had concerned her friends. They all breathed easier, thinking the danger past. She'd done her best to reassure them, gently teasing Max about his tired face and the look in his eyes, which still expressed suffering, anguish, even a kind of desperation. But her voice when she teased him was so sweet that the irony in her tone became a caress.

Sara and Max sat with her, scolding her affectionately as they forbade her to tire herself by joining their conversation. At the far end of the room sat Mona, with a vacant, absent look, singing an unknown song, the product of her own confused mind—some kind of bleak, sad love song:

"The vengeance of the Gods
Threw Man down to Earth.
Life is an exile from Heaven.
It's pain and misery!
All is dark and all is dread—and tears.
And all ends in unbearable farewells.
Precious family, grown old... farewell.
Love, whose charms men boast—just tears!"

Sir John, tired of being alone in his room, had come to join the group. He couldn't help exclaiming, "By Belphegor's horns, that young lady could make even the desert sands weep!"

Just then a bellboy arrived to ask if the British Consul could come in. Behind him appeared that dignitary, begging their pardon for forcing his way like this into a lady's sickroom, but adding that he felt he had no choice, given his need to speak to all of the travelers together.

No matter how inopportune the Consul's visit seemed, they had to keep up appearances. That was also a way of showing their gratitude to the revolutionaries, who—though of course from motives of self-interest—had saved the fugitives from falling back into the hands of the Tsar's army. Sara therefore indicated a chair, and the Consul settled into it, saying, "I've come chiefly to appeal to Miss Musketeer's patriotism."

"To my patriotism!" Violet repeated, while her friends exchanged a look of surprise.

"Yes. You heard what Mr. Varloff said earlier."

"The Head of the Committee."

152

"And himself a revolutionary from Odessa, yes. He's someone it's important not to displease."

"We have no intention of doing so."

"Oh, as for you, I have no doubt. But I, in light of my responsibilities, I'll have to obey him by disobeying."

"You mean some kind of playacting."

"I'll grant you that. Because I also need your help to get out of the impasse he's put me in." With an anxious expression the Consul paused a while, then lowered his voice. "He wants the British government to reprimand the Russian court for the mistreatment you suffered."

"I remember."

"Now, you're English, and consequently reasonable." His ingenuous Anglo-Saxon arrogance made the French travelers, Sara and Max, smile. The Consul didn't notice. "You'll therefore understand that His Majesty Edward VII cannot take a threatening tone in a diplomatic note. Of course he can ask for justice, punishment for the perpetrators, damages... but international law forbids him to meddle in another country's domestic affairs—to interfere between the legal authorities and the Revolution."

"That seems obvious, sir. But I don't see what I can do about it."

"You? But you can do everything!"

"How so?"

"By not remaining under Varloff's control. He's an awful man, you see, and if the British government doesn't conform to his whims he won't hesitate to stoop to the cruelest means to force its hand."

"Meaning?"

"That clearly your best interests—and Great Britain's—require..."

"Require?"

The Consul lowered his voice still further. "A ship is anchored out on the Quarantine pier: the steamship *Baku* of the Black Sea line. It leaves tonight for India, and ports in China, and Vladivostok. Cabins have been reserved for you and your companions. Have yourself carried aboard, and all is solved."

"Have her carried—now, in her condition!" interrupted Max tensely. "You must mean to kill her."

But he stopped as Violet said softly, "The Consul's right. The greater interests of England are at stake, and I must do as he asks." She went on, tenderly but persuasively, "The fatigue won't last long. Once I'm on the steamer, and during the long crossing, won't I be better off than at a hotel, in the middle of this city, at the mercy of the Revolution?" The Consul began loudly expressing his praise, but she cut him off too. "Your compliments are no more warranted than my friends' fears. As you've established clearly, I'm English and to some degree a prisoner of the Revolutionary Committee of Odessa. Either of those... facts... would be enough to prompt me to leave. So, have done."

153

The Duchess of La Roche-Sonnaille nodded in agreement. The brave Frenchwoman understood the valiant little Anglo-Saxon.

As for the Consul, delighted with the outcome of his visit, he took his leave with these grateful words: "Thanks to you, I'll be able to draw up my report just as the terrible Varloff wants it—and include the usual code meaning *Pay no attention to this message.*"

When the travelers were alone again, Max grumbled, "A plague on the Revolution."

"Shush, shush!" said Violet with a sweet smile. "Don't speak too much ill of it. It brought us to Odessa—the place those we loved before we knew them were trying to reach."

"My sweet dear," murmured Sara.

But Max gestured fiercely. "It's no way to heal a wound. It's as if they were doing it on purpose to worsen your condition."

"Don't worry, Frenchman," said a loud voice, "Miss Musketeer's condition will not worsen, because she won't leave the St. Petersburg Hotel until she's completely recovered."

They all jumped and turned. In the doorway stood the revolutionary Varloff. Without a single muscle on his face revealing whether he was serious, or was just indulging in cold sarcasm, he went on, "The Revolution has no wish to be involved in the crime against beauty proposed by the British Consul. Miss Musketeer will not take passage on the steamer *Baku.*"

Max found his voice. "You'd stop her?"

"Of course. This charming lady has rather rashly given her nation's Consul her promise. I—who have her best interests very much at heart—will make it impossible for her to keep her promise. How? Very simply. All hotels, the St. Petersburg included, are allowed to operate... under the control and supervision of the Committee. I've stationed six men here, with whom I'll be constantly in touch. No one will leave the hotel without a safe conduct from me." He bowed casually. "I'm sorry to displease Miss Musketeer a little, perhaps, as a British citizen. But as a patient I hope she'll be grateful for the measures I've taken to keep her from being disturbed."

He left without waiting for a reply.

"Actually," exclaimed Max, "I'm delighted about this."

Violet shot him a reproachful glance. "You shouldn't be, since it distresses me."

"Bah! Governments always come out all right in the end. Whereas the injured..."

"If it were you, would you be first of all French or injured?"

That direct shot left him speechless. But he soon went on, "Still, here's the thing: I can't think of any way to get you on board the *Baku.*"

That showed at least that he'd completely changed his mind—at a mere word from her. She rewarded him with a look, then said firmly, "Well, let's find one."

But they all put their heads together in vain. Even Sir John, whose loyalty to Britain now brought him closer to his companions, suggested a number of ideas. But they had to be discarded, like all the others, when they were acknowledged to be impractical. The hopeless search for a solution gradually irritated Violet. It worried Max to see her, with her cheeks flushed, resisting his appeals to stay calm and be patient. She loved her country deeply. It pained her to think that she might cause it difficulties. And insidious fever, that silent foe always ready to prey on suffering, rose and rose—speeding her pulse, gradually elevating her temperature. By eight in the evening, when Sara looked at the medical thermometer, it read 39.7° Celsius.[22]

Violet's restlessness grew with the passing time. "The boat sails at midnight: at midnight I need to be aboard." As she got further worked up, almost with tears in her eyes, she begged, "Monsieur Max, you who are so imaginative—please find some way to escape from that stubborn revolutionary!"

But Max's mind was recalcitrant. Painful anxiety paralyzed him. He could think of only one thing, which manifested itself in his tortured nerves by unbearable trembling: "Are they going to take her from me by killing her?"

Nine o'clock! At Max's urging, Sara—who was herself bewildered—checked the thermometer again. The answer was frightening: 41.1°.[23] Violet's sweet face had a worrisome color, a kind of livid red—if such an indescribable color can be described that way—the banner of fever triumphant. Her big blue eyes shone with a disquieting brightness. And through her dry lips her hoarse voice said over and over, "Oh, let's leave, let's leave!"

The days were long at that time of year, and yet night had fallen. The room had grown dark. No one noticed. Outside, through the open windows, could be seen the line of lights along the harbor and the lanterns of the moored ships. Out there, on the Quarantine pier, shone the lights of the *Baku*; a reddish halo glowed over the steam funnels, showing that the ship had reached pressure and was ready to sail. And Max—who'd been so opposed to moving the precious patient—would now have given ten years of his life to get her on board.

He turned. It seemed to him that, from the bed where Violet lay, two phosphorescent eyes stared out, as he did, at the dark expanse of the harbor and the watery horizon. But though his reason told him he must be imagining things, the vision persisted. It grew unbearable. Without quite knowing why, he felt a need for light, which drives away the phantasms of the night. He went to the switch controlling the overhead light, felt for it, found the knob, and turned it. Light abruptly filled the room, causing the other travelers to cry out softly. But before

---

[22] 103.5° Farenheit. Normal body temperature is 37° Celsius.
[23] 106° Fahrenheit.

Max could say anything to explain, Mona had sat up straight. "The light! To the east! To the east!"

And Sara responded, "The light! Who knows? She's already been so helpful to us."

They all looked at each other. Something like hope crossed Violet's face. She'd raised herself on one elbow. Like Max, like Sir John, she was eagerly watching Sara. With a wave of her hand the duchess showed them that now was not the time for explanations: Mona was in the grip of what might be called a luminous crisis. At these times she exhibited a strange and disturbing scientific lucidity. Would it be possible, once again, to make use of her state for the good of all?

Sara went to her. The mad girl, her arms outstretched, her eyes unfocused, said over and over, "The east! Light! Happiness!"

Sara said, "Oh, why do those wretches want to keep us from going east?"

She stopped. Her companions remained silent, holding their breath, stunned at the effect those simple words produced. Mona had suddenly turned to her friend. Her face now shone with intelligence; her eyes were bright and confident. Taking Sara's hand, she asked, "Who's keeping us from going east?"

"The men who are guarding the door."

She led the poor child—a mad girl gone sane—to the window and pointed out the Quarantine pier and the steamer *Baku*. "That ship sails tonight. It's headed east, to India. Cabins have been reserved for us on board."

"Then let's go." The mad girl's entire being seemed to be suffused with the thought of departure.

But Sara answered sadly, "Impossible. Our guards."

"Oh yes, the men at the entrance to the hotel." They were all amazed. The slim, lithe girl bent over with laughter. Finally she said, "Light prevails over the will. Those who stand in its way are shadow beings, beaten in advance." She looked around, then said in a tone of command, "Where are my weapons of light?"

They all understood she wanted the chest of luminous tubes. Could the mad girl do what they in their sanity thought impossible?

"In the next room," said Sara, her voice trembling with hope.

"Then come." Mona took the hand of her companion in suffering, and pulled her along.

As they were leaving, Violet, whose face expressed anxious anticipation, pointed to the door and said, "Go with them, Max, go with them, I beg you."

He didn't object; dashing into the corridor, he went to the room assigned to Mona. The door was open. Mona knelt before the chest of tubes, choosing several out of the compartments numbered from 3 to 12. Then she rose. "This will get us through."

"But we have an injured woman, who'll have to be carried."

"They'll carry her," replied Mona calmly. "And also our chest, the precious gift of light."

Max's heart leapt. Of course, Mona was insane. And yet she spoke with such confidence that he felt persuaded by the confidence she radiated. They'd get through, they'd get aboard the *Baku*, and Violet would be saved.

The chest was closed again. Mona handed one tube to Sara; then, noticing Max, she handed him another. Like an officer issuing orders, she said, "Hide them up your sleeve, with the lens forward, beneath your fingers."[24]

They followed her directions.

"All right, at my signal, press the button."

"And?" asked Max curiously, struck by the oddness of the scene.

"And aim the beam of the orange light..."

"Ah, it's orange light!"

"On your enemies' foreheads."

That didn't satisfy Max: to him, a beam of light—even orange light—didn't seem sufficient to change the minds of people as stubborn as the revolutionaries. He pressed her. "And then what'll happen?"

"A hallucination."

"What hallucination?"

"I don't know. That depends on the individual's mind. But whatever it is, it'll tend to make our enemies act as we want them to."

Seeing Max shake his head dubiously, Sara said, "Let's do it. I believe her. Anytime it's a question of light, she sees and knows and understands things that escape us."

In any case, Mona seemed not to have noticed Max's hesitation. She took Sara's arm. "Where are these fools who block our way?"

"Downstairs, at the front desk and in the hotel vestibule."

"All right. Follow me."

She went out into the corridor. Dominated by the authority she radiated, her companions followed her obediently. She started down the stairs from the second floor to the vestibule; they did the same.

Across from the front desk stood a man armed with a rifle. He raised the bayonet and said, "You can't go by."

The mad girl answered with a tinkling laugh and raised her arm. An orange light seemed to burst from her fingers, and a circle of projected light appeared on the sentry's forehead.

Max, stunned and amazed, watched the strange scene. The revolutionary shouldered his rifle and saluted, with a look of bliss on his face.

---

[24] Apparently d'Ivoi has forgotten that Max, Sara, and Violet already used the light tubes against the three "Orthodox priests" in Kiev—without Mona even being present to coach them.

"Holy Virgin of Kazan," he said softly in a worshipful tone, "thank you for showing yourself to your servant. I'm only a humble carpenter, but I've never ended the day without kneeling before your icon. Give me your orders. Olaf will obey."

"I'll give them when everyone's here. Where are your comrades?"

"In the staff office, with Varloff, the Head of the Revolutionary Committee."

"Show me the way."

As Olaf the carpenter obeyed, the mad girl murmured to Max and Sara, "Do as I've done."

Then she went into the office, followed by the others. There, seated around a table on which stood a china bowl of flaming vodka punch, sat Varloff and his companions, deep in conversation. The arrival of the sentry and the travelers prompted a general cry of surprise. "What's the meaning of this?"

In perfect coordination, the three guests raised their arms, and from their fingertips sprang beams of orange light that produced bright circles on the revolutionaries' foreheads.

"What? What's going on?" stammered Varloff. But soon he stopped speaking, and his face expressed an exhilaration close to madness. "The Republic!" he shouted. "It's the Republic!" And with sudden fervor—the fervor of those Russian revolutionaries for whom the republic is some kind of new religion—he went on, "Yes, yes, as you wish. Victory depends not on Britain, but on us! So be it! We won't set the sovereigns against each other. Your will be done, Republic! We'll coerce no one! Justice alone will guide our actions!"

His companions, working men, listened in dazed surprise. Perhaps for them the orange hallucination—that gave their leader a vision of the Republic incarnate—summoned instead, as for their fellow soldier Olaf, the Cathedral of Our Lady of Kazan or some other Russian church. It didn't matter what they saw; for all of them it led to the same desire: to carry out the wishes of the one who'd granted them the vision.

Ten minutes later, four of the guards, having remade Violet's stretcher, were carrying her out. Two more were bringing the chest of colored tubes.

Violet and Sir John, amazed by the prompt success of the mad girl's plan, had asked for explanations. But Sara—and Max himself—had answered, "We'll have time to tell you everything on board."

And now, swaying in time to the pace of the stretcher bearers, Violet was witnessing a scene that astonished her. Mona, Sara, and Max walked alongside the procession with orange light beaming toward the revolutionaries from their raised hands. They crossed the Boulevard that way, they went down the stairs to the Quarantine Ravine, they passed below the heights on which stood Alexander Park. Then, crossing the tracks of the harbor railroad a little below the station, the little group reached the Quarantine pier, at the far end of which was moored the steamer *Baku*.

At eleven forty-seven—thirteen minutes before sailing time—the travelers climbed the gangway. The Consul hadn't misled them: cabins were reserved for them. And since a Consul doesn't usually trouble himself over people of little account, the captain of the ship hastened to attend on them. Violet was settled in a cabin on the main deck.

Meanwhile Mona said confidentially to Sara, "We have to keep the orange lights on our enemies to the very end, otherwise the hallucination will fade before sailing time."

Once Sara had passed the word to Max, the two of them went on beaming their orange lights, to the great surprise of the captain of the *Baku*, who dared ask, "What's that you're doing?"

To which Max replied calmly, "Medical treatment. We're curing these poor devils of alcoholism."

That only increased the captain's surprise—to the point of rendering him speechless.

Meanwhile Mona ordered the revolutionaries, "Go back down the gangway." They all obeyed, with Varloff leading. "All right, now line up along the pier." While they were doing that, she called over Sara and Max. "We'll stand along the rail and bathe them in orange light until we sail."

The ship's crew watched from a distance, struck by the incomprehensible scene. They listened to the revolutionaries mumbling peculiar prayers, mixed up with exclamations that were rarely heard together:

"Holy Virgin of Kazan!"

"The Republic!"

But then the bosun's piercing whistle rang out, meaning, "To work! Cast off!"

The steamer cast off her moorings. There was a long shudder, as if the ship was expressing her happiness at being free, ready to make her way out onto the liquid road at the end of which she'd reach the marvelous lands of the Far East. The whistled signals continued, became more frequent. The ship's horn added a low, somewhat husky note to the chorus, bellowing into the night and sending up a column of white steam. Then the entire hull shook. The stern moved slightly. They were off.

As if drawn by some overpowering force, the revolutionaries—still bathed in orange light—escorted the steamer all the way to the end of the pier. They stopped at the very tip, calling out fond farewells still interspersed with mentions of Our Lady of Kazan and the Republic. Then they stood still, following the steamer with their eyes as it passed the pier and vanished into the night.

"Saved!" murmured Max.

"Turn off the lights," instructed Mona.

They did so, and handed her the tubes that had made possible their escape from Odessa. She put them back in their compartments, after which she lapsed once again into gentle, contemplative madness—a madness from which she emerged only to amaze her companions by the clarity and precision of her mind as soon as it concerned light. That same thought occurred to all of them. They expressed it to each other in sad looks, but they had no time to put it into words.

In the distance, back at the pier, which was distinguishable now only by its string of lights, rose muted cries that barely reached their ears.

"What's that?" whispered Max.

"No doubt the hallucination coming to an end," Sara whispered back.

"They must be furious."

Indeed, yes, Varloff and his men were foaming at the mouth with rage. Having come to, they stared at each other, stunned. What were they doing there, at the end of the Quarantine pier? A ship's boy—who'd been intrigued by the orange beams and had followed the little procession out here—told them what he'd seen. So... it was clear that the travelers had tricked them. They screamed out orders to the ship to return to port—a pointless effort. The *Baku* was far away, and voices reached it only as a senseless noise.

They'd all left their weapons at the St. Petersburg Hotel, otherwise they would've fired shots at random into the darkness, just to take out their anger on something. Being denied that relief, they traded insults and accusations. The argument grew hotter and more pointed—to the great delight of the ship's boy, and he egged on these men who seemed to him to have gathered purely for his entertainment. It all ended in a Homeric fistfight, whose causes were never satisfactorily explained to the Central Revolutionary Committee of Odessa.

But Max had been wrong about Violet: escaping from Odessa had done nothing to bring down her fever, because its causes were serious. At the start, the luminous cauterization carried out by Mona had prevented the high temperature that normally follows injury and blood loss. And if Violet hadn't gone through the jolting and emotional stress of her repeated moves, it's likely that she would've enjoyed a rapid convalescence. Unfortunately, in her weakened health she'd had been subjected to too many harmful assaults. On board the *Baku* her fever grew worse. With her temperature sometimes rising and sometimes falling, she suffered painfully all through their passage down the Sea of Marmara, across the Archipelago and the Mediterranean, and through the Suez Canal.

Max and Sara took turns at her bedside. The young man was dying a slow death, tortured by anxiety. His hollow cheeks and sunken eyes expressed his despair.

But once they entered the Red Sea—that watery corridor between two deserts—his sadness turned to terror. Anyone who sailed from Europe to the Far East knew that the worst part was crossing the Red Sea. That's where anemic passengers, weakened by life in the colonies, gave up the ghost—just a few days' sail from their home shores, and already thinking they were safe. The heat was stifling. Even the breeze brought no relief, since it had been heated by the desert plains that bordered the sea, and it carried sand so fine that it got everywhere—not even the tightest-woven veils and fabrics could keep it out. So you can imagine the effect it had on the mucous membranes of the mouth and lungs.

Violet had suddenly had a new attack of fever. Her temperature wavered between 41° and 42°[25]—another slight rise would mean death. Adding to the terror, that morning the ship's doctor had looked especially worried while he was rewrapping the patient's bandage.

Max—who never took his eyes off him, and whose anxiety had given him the keen observation that people in love have—had stopped him outside the cabin. "Doctor, are you worried?"

Doctors usually assume they can tell a man the truth, so he replied, "Yes, very."

"What do you fear?"

"I'm still hopeful. If we were out of this damned Red Sea, all would be well. But we still have another twenty-four hours."

"Well, what's the danger?" stammered Max, the doctor's reticence only increasing his anxiety.

The latter lowered his voice. "I'm concerned about gangrene."

Gangrene, that terrible word, that turned a slight injury into a mortal wound! Max gripped the bulkhead to keep from falling. Everything spun around him. It took him a tremendous effort of will to say, "But what about antiseptics?"

"I've done the necessary bandaging. I'll renew it throughout the day—contrary to usual procedures—but…"

"But?"

"But cooler weather would give me greater confidence than all the derivatives of phenol, or sublimates, or formaldehyde." Then—cross at being unable truthfully to ease the despair he saw throbbing before him—the doctor went away.

And Max, distraught, had wept like a child as he passed the doctor's opinion on to Sara. In his distress he was close to blaming poor Mona—who, since she followed Sara everywhere, had witnessed their painful conversation, impassive, uncomprehending, vacant, as always.

He went back on deck. Since standing in full sun could lead to death, the captain had made him squeeze into a shady corner. And then Max had stayed right there, motionless, deep in thought. He didn't come to lunch. His thoughts and his emotions wandered far, losing themselves in impossible, unrealizable hopes: of a cloud that would pass like a screen before the sun, of the freshness a torrential rain would bring. Clouds, rain—chimeras on the Red Sea! Was the sky there not mercilessly blue? Did the sun there not shine down pitilessly?

Suddenly he started at a voice close to him, murmuring, "Monsieur Max, would you please come to Miss Violet's cabin?"

---

[25] Between 106° and 107.5° Fahrenheit.

Sara stood before him. It seemed to him that the duchess's face was more than usually somber. One thought tore across his mind: Violet was calling him to her bedside. She was about to die. The doctor's dark forecast was coming true. Crazed, not hearing the words Sara went on saying to him, Max dashed across the deck, bumping into sailors and into passengers wiped out by the heat, and ran to Violet's cabin. He stopped for a minute at the door. His legs shook under him; he couldn't breathe. And then almost violently—finding courage in the very excess of his despair—he pushed open the door.

He stopped on the sill, stunned, dazed. A wave of fresh air—almost cold— had struck his face. Fresh air in the midst of that accursed Red Sea! The suffering had been too much for him; he was losing his mind.

But he heard soft music. "Monsieur Max," murmured a soft, silvery voice.

Violet was half seated on her bed. Was he just imagining that her face had regained its normal color, that her clear eyes had lost their feverish glitter?

She spoke again. "It's our dear sweet mad girl who saved me."

Her delicate hand gestured toward a corner of the cabin, and Max looked that direction. There, propped on a stool by the porthole, was a metal plate. Across from it, lined up like a battery of tiny artillery guns, an array of tubes bathed the metal plate with emerald green light. He must be dreaming—he thought he could see ice cubes on the metal surface. Ice cubes, when the temperature was $57°$[26] in the shade!

Violet went on, "I needed cool, and Mona gave it to me using the green rays."

It was a revelation. Once again a spell of lucidity in the madness had produced a scientific miracle. The green rays distilled cold, which had cooled both the cabin and a water pitcher. Max was speechless. Reeling, he went over to the bed and dropped to his knees. He took the hand that Violet gave him, and dissolved in tears, murmuring, "Saved! Saved!"

---

[26] 135° Fahrenheit.

162

CHAPTER XII
In Which Max Resumes His Investigation

The following item appeared in the *Bengal Review*, under the heading "Arrivals and Departures":

The multi-millionairess Miss Violet Musketeer and her retinue have arrived in our city. We have learned to our chagrin that, in order to get the rest needed for her convalescence from a wound she received in Russian territory, the charming traveler has declined all interviews. Our readers will understand that in such a case a gentleman reporter—such as we flatter ourselves we are—will not make inappropriate efforts to contradict a wish that is doubly sacred, being that of a lady and a victim of injury.

That brief report was accurate. Violet and her friends had reached Calcutta and had rented a villa, known as Trefald's Cottage, on the heights overlooking the Ganges. There the young woman, who was still weak, could finish recovering her strength in uninterrupted peace, while Max and Sara began the difficult search for the house where the duchess and Mona had said farewell forever to the men they loved.

Sir John had declined to join them in the search, with a ready-made excuse that reeked of Parliamentary cleverness: "Miss Musketeer is wounded; Miss Mona is not in her right mind; I'd be afraid to leave them alone, without a gentleman's protection."

That answer had made Violet shrug, and Max smile. He was now talking with Sara in the deep shade of a ficus, a kind of sacred banyan with dense foliage. "So you believe, Madame, that the sumptuous villa where you—along with your husband and Mademoiselle Mona and Mr. Dodekhan—were taken was northwest of Calcutta."

"About fifty kilometers. When we were being taken there we could observe nothing, because we were all asleep."

"Asleep?"

She nodded. "Our enemies had great powers of enforcing sleep. They're familiar with all the ways known to science of triggering sleep. But that doesn't matter. On the way back, Mona and I were carried in palanquins, or rather in sedan chairs. And the journey from that house to Calcutta lasted four days."

"Four! Indian porters can cover about twenty-five kilometers a day."

"Yes, but they definitely made long detours."

Max sat up with great interest. "You could tell?"

"Only by deduction; the country was and is unfamiliar to me. But we passed through no towns. At night we camped in tents. And to travel so long in Bengal without seeing a town suggests we were avoiding them on purpose."

"Quite right."

"That's why I'm confident that I can ascribe half the distance we covered to needless detours."

"Which leads you to a total of fifty kilometers."

"Exactly."

They fell into thoughtful silence, pondering the challenge of finding that house again. It was like looking for a needle in a haystack.

"And yet we have to find it," muttered Max. "We have to—because it would certainly lead us to the bandits' hideout." Sara looked at him inquiringly, and he went on, "I assume the wireless speaker I took from the Loursinade villa is designed to communicate with a series of stations set up between Marseilles and that mysterious house."

"Yes."

"And so from there we could make contact, uncover some part of the secret, who knows what." Pursuing that idea, he continued, "Another thing. The Amber Masks were afraid of your return to this country. Think about how they tried to stop you going south—south, where you were headed so you could sail to India."

"Sure, but…"

"That means," he went on, using his highly developed powers of deduction, "that from Calcutta, finding the mysterious house must not be as difficult as we think."

"Perhaps."

"Definitely. And what's necessary for that to be the case? That the estate not be located fifty kilometers from Calcutta—which would entail searching an enormous circumference; and that search would draw their attention, and the Amber Masks, with their vast organization, would have time to plan and to act."

"From which you conclude?"

"That it's possible to stumble on the estate, right from the start, so to speak, and that therefore it must be very close to Calcutta."

"All right. Then how do you explain the porters walking for four days?"

"They walked in a big circle, ending very near where they started."

"How did we not notice, while we were held prisoner, the bustle of a great city nearby?"

"It's a question of the landscape contours. Was the horizon obscured?"

Sara sat up straight, and said with deep feeling, "Yes, yes, by wooded hills."

"In which direction?"

"West-southwest, to the extent that I can orient my memories."

Max smiled. "Then I'll go down to the shopping district. At the nearest bookstore I'll get a 1:100,000-scale map of the area, and we'll look for hills to the east-northeast that would conceal Calcutta."

"Why to the northeast?"

"Because from the other side you were seeing the hills to the southwest; from here they'd be the opposite direction."

"Ah!" she exclaimed. "I'm beginning to think that with your help I'll get somewhere. What a detective you'd have made, Monsieur Max!"

He began to laugh. "There's no doubt that if police chiefs could persuade novelists to join the force, the police would be better off; but for now let's remain amateur detectives and summarize our findings." He counted off on his fingers. "The house we're looking for is nine or ten kilometers from the city, separated from it by wooded hills. It's in a valley, which is also wooded, and is far away from major roads, and reached only by insignificant back roads."

"That's true," murmured Sara in surprise. "But how did you know?"

He shrugged. "Easy! Don't forget, you told me you didn't have any sense of the heavy traffic there'd be on the outskirts of a big city."

"All right, but from there to being sure…"

"If there'd been a major artery nearby, you'd have heard traffic, animal flocks, caravans of travelers. Especially at night, sounds carry a long distance."

"Indeed. Why didn't I think of that?"

"Because you wanted to hear me say it," answered Max with a mischievous look. From experience he knew better than anyone that the faculty of deduction is very rare, but that its conclusions are so easy to grasp that people never think they're witnessing the results of superior skills. Nevertheless he said cheerfully, "So, I'm going to town. I'll buy a map. And I'll rent an automobile."

"An automobile?"

"Yes. So we can move faster and get less tired."

"But the driver…"

"Won't trouble us, because it'll be me. For the car rental, it's just a matter of putting down a deposit. Plus which, thanks to the reports in the papers, Miss Musketeer's entourage should have the benefit of popular goodwill."

That made Sara laugh heartily. "Luckily we're considered aristocrats of no importance in that sweet lady's retinue. Imagine if they'd printed my name, or Mona's. There'd be nothing for it but to sail away again as fast as possible, before we fell back into the clutches of those wretches."

Max broke in, "By the way, Madame, may I ask you a question that might be important?"

"Please, go ahead."

"Do you believe that Dodekhan was…" He stopped, reluctant to say the word that would reawaken her pain.

But she gravely finished the sentence for him. "I believe he was murdered, like my beloved Lucien. I saw them both under the assassins' knives."

"Yes, of course. But you also saw their triumphant enemy, Log…"

"Fall, his skull shattered by a pistol shot."

"And it was seeing that on the tele-viewer that caused Mademoiselle Mona to lose her reason."

"My poor dear friend!"

"Yes, it's awful. Still, it seems to me that if you subtract two from the two Masters of the Blue Flag, that leaves zero. So who's taken their place and gone on persecuting you?"

Sara was silent; she'd never asked herself that—though the question, put that way, seemed elementary. She murmured slowly and thoughtfully, "Log was killed. I saw—I clearly saw—his skull shattered, and his body rolling on the ground." Then she added, with a vague look of hope, "What if they spared Dodekhan?"

But Max gently shook his head. "Alas, Madame—Dodekhan wouldn't be your enemy."

She didn't answer, but bowed her face to the ground for a moment. Perhaps deep down she was scolding herself for having once again allowed herself to hope for the impossible. "And yet," she went on, as if eager to show she hadn't given up, "the power struggle was limited to the two of them."

"Strictly?"

"Strictly. Only they had the key to the codes which the secret societies obeyed. Dodekhan above all, since we were allowed to go back to Europe in exchange for his promise to reveal to Log what the latter didn't yet know."

As if to himself, Max said, "Then the current leader is…"

"I don't know."

"I think you do."

She looked at him with undisguised astonishment. "Explain yourself."

"I intend to. One thing struck me about your account. Log shows up like some kind of doubled character, always accompanied by his giant servant."

"San!"

"Exactly. By nature of his job, that San must know a great deal about the structure of that secret society."

"I think Log told him everything."

"Well then, wouldn't he make an obvious leader? Of course an incomplete one, lacking both intelligence and knowledge. But at least a possible leader, compared to all the other followers."

"I believe you're right."

"And that would explain the incoherence of his actions. You and Mademoiselle Mona are locked away in an asylum: a man full of hatred—but at least of level-headed intelligence—would consider you adequately punished, adequately isolated. But no: his agents got orders to bring about your escape and to drive you east. That's the work of a mediocre, second-rate mind. It's complicated and risky, and the proof is that you anticipated him and fled. Without our recklessness—Violet's and mine—they would never have found you again."

"Don't say that."

"Why not? History isn't a novel. That's what happened, and we have to admit it. After all, we did our best to help lose those spies who've now been

166

struck permanently from the rolls of the sane… Coming back to the point, I say San has taken the place of the leaders who are gone." Not wanting to explain further, he stood up and said calmly, "Would you care to go with me, Madame?"

She agreed, still quite stirred by the progress made toward solving the puzzle—in one short conversation with Max. She'd been aware of his great powers of reasoning. Now she could see clearly the chain of logic he'd used to reconstruct what had happened at the Loursinade villa.

Less than half an hour later, having seen Violet and Sir John, and left Mona in their care, Max and Sara left Trefald's Cottage and walked down toward the commercial district along the Ganges. At Broad & Bridd, the principal booksellers and stationers of Calcutta, they easily found an excellent map of the city and surroundings, similar to those put out in France by the Ministry of the Interior. A short stop in an "icer"—an open-sided pavilion in which natives dressed in white robes and Sikh turbans served ice-cold drinks—gave them time to consult the map at leisure. A series of pink patches represented the city spread out along the left bank of the Hooghly River, a branch of the Ganges. They noticed the railroad line, roughly parallel to the river, crossing the city. Perpendicular to the railroad tracks, the Ganges-Brahmaputra Delta Canal, which began in Calcutta, traced a long curve north, then turned east to reach the sacred river.

Almost immediately Max exclaimed quietly, "Here, Madame, see where you were held prisoner." His finger traced a line bisecting the angle formed by the canal and the Hooghly. At a distance that the 1:100,000 scale of the map showed to be about ten kilometers, forming the suggestion of the third side of the triangle—whose other sides were the canal and the river—a line of hatch marks was labeled *Black Hills*; behind that barrier separating it from the city, a plain marked with dots denoting forest cover was labeled *Hunting Reserve*.

"It's in that Hunting Reserve that we have to look," he said. In answer to Sara's questioning glance he went on, "Your enemies certainly took their precautions. Right outside Calcutta they'd set up a safe hideout: an estate deep in a forest, no doubt with possession of the hunting rights. A wooded wilderness in the midst of an area overflowing with people." Then he said suddenly, "When you left your prison, were you free to look around?"

"Of course."

"I mean, neither your guards nor your porters tried in any way to restrict your view?"

"Not at all."

"Would you recognize the route you traveled?"

She hesitated a moment before saying, "I hope so."

"All right, try to remember. At first you went along tree-lined paths, on a forest trail."

"Yes, yes."

"Then the trail, which at first had been flat, began to climb. You seemed to be crossing a pass between hills."

"Not high, but again yes." Sara was filled with admiration, astonished by the clarity with which Max read the map, having already predicted what he'd find there.

"Good," he said calmly, without noticing the reaction he'd caused. "So you crossed that second line of hills, which limit the plain to the north just as the Black Hills do to the south... Did you notice the place where the trail left the woods and ran out onto the plain?"

"Oh, yes. There were cotton fields and a village to the left of the road—a Muslim village, from the minaret above the wooden mosque. After the cotton fields came corrals divided by fences, with grazing herds: horses, humpback cattle, even sheep."

"Yes, an agricultural landscape, with something very unusual in an area that's almost entirely Buddhist or Hindu: a Muslim mosque. Well, Madame, I think we won't have any trouble finding the hideout of the Amber Masks—or the followers of the Blue Flag if you prefer. Let's make arrangements for our vehicle."

Once the barman had been paid, the two travelers went in search of an automobile dealer. In Calcutta—a city of eight hundred thousand people, that the English, with their innate feeling for comfort, had made into a European city—could be found everything relating to the conveniences of life. Fifty paces away down the road an enormous storefront of wood and glass showed them what they were looking for. They entered the shop, where a man dressed in a suit of lightweight white flannel hastened to meet them. "How can I help you?"

"We'd like to rent an automobile for two, to visit the area."

"I have no driver available."

"Just as well, since we don't want one."

The salesman looked first at Max, then at Sara, and smiled warmly. "Well, well, I understand—you're newlyweds." Paying no attention to their startled reaction to his error, he went on, "Well, as soon as we eliminate the need for a driver, it's easy. In fact I have here a perfect automobile for an excursion, a sweet little electric model, very silent, ideal for a lady."

Five minutes later the deal was done. When he found out that his customers were part of the multi-millionairess Miss Violet Musketeer's entourage, the salesman tried to refuse the deposit Max offered him. To change his mind, Max had to insist, even as he thanked him for the trust implied. Clearly the announcement in the papers had produced results, and every worthy merchant in the good city of Calcutta knew by now that Trefald's Cottage was home to the heiress to one of those fortunes that people madly envy and humbly bow down to.

The batteries were fully charged. They were Sheppards, of recent invention, which the Academy of Sciences had praised by calling them "liquefiers of electricity," in light of the fact that, for a given volume, those batteries stored ten times the power of any competing model. "With these," the salesman assured them, "the car can go sixteen hundred kilometers without needing a recharge."

"Off we go!" Max operated the controls like a man for whom driving held no secrets. With his hands on the steering wheel, as they crossed the city at moderate speed, he said to Sara, "Madame, we're going to follow the Hooghly and then head toward the Black Hills. We'll skirt around to the north side of the Hunting Reserve until we find the little Muslim village you noticed."

"And then...?"

"That village will show us the trail by which you left the woods. Then all we'll have to do is follow it to retrace the route your porters took. If you remember it, it'll be easy. If not, we'll poke around a bit, and we'll still get there, since the area to be searched is limited."

Once they'd left the commercial district, they passed through the native city. Then the streets gave way to gardens, and to villas more and more spread out. Here nothing blocked their view of the lazy Hooghly's winding beauty. Pavilions as meticulous as jewel boxes adjoining sumptuous homes, marble staircases descending to the river amid lush foliage—all ran together to form a fairytale landscape.

The travelers were so captivated by the splendid scenery that they forgot the purpose of their excursion—but not for long: a few miles outside Calcutta, a road turned off to the east. Max pointed it out to Sara. She nodded, and the car accelerated and sped that way.

Though at first it was quite flat, the land soon began to climb a series of hills—not steep, but gradual and easy to ascend. Max stopped to ask a fakir mendicant who was crouched by the side of the road, "What are these hills called?"

"The Black Hills," answered the fakir.

"Then we're on the right road," said Max to Sara.

They were still climbing. Finally they reached a plateau from which they could see a great distance. The plateau lay at the top of a hill, in the middle of a line of hills that seemed to be trending east-northeast. On the near side the hills looked bare, and were divided into squares and rectangles by fields. But to the northeast they were covered in a mantle of dark foliage.

"The forest," said Max.

Sara looked but said nothing. She was filled with intense emotion. So it was there, in those woods that concealed the ground, that she'd been held prisoner. It was from there that she'd left trustingly for Europe—a poor unfortunate creature who hadn't understood her husband's tragic devotion to her! He'd saved her, and then died to preserve the honor of Dodekhan, that generous Master of the Blue Flag who'd protected them with all his might. And she'd returned to this accursed land. Some mysterious power had called her back. Yes—she wanted to find her husband's grave. A grave! A void in which human sentimentality insists on seeing something.

Now the car was descending a gentle slope. Below them they could see a large valley divided by fields and pastures. In the distance, lit obliquely by the rays of the sun as it neared the horizon, lay reddish hills, and always, to the east, the dark line of the forest. They crossed the plain, and then passed the second line of hills.

"Now, Madame," said Max, rousing her from her reverie, "we're going to proceed parallel to these hills. Please pay close attention to the landscape, since we're entering the area where your memory can help save us precious time."

She nodded. Bravely driving away her sad reflections, she forced herself to focus entirely on their surroundings. The electric car rolled silently along a side road that closely followed the line of the hills. Soon the slopes were covered with shrubs and isolated clumps of trees—the outposts of the forest's wooded army. Soon the trunks festooned in green grew closer together, and under the dome of foliage a blueish half-light prevailed. They were skirting the forest. From time to time a trail, some shortcut worn by pedestrians, branched off from the road they were following and disappeared into the trees. Then Max down-shifted and slowed the car. But Sara shook her head, and the car sped up again.

That went on a long time; gradually the road moved away from the edge of the woods, tending back toward the north. Now it was lined with high bushes that hid the strip of land between the road and the foot of the hills—so that when a side trail appeared, Max had to turn the car down it and go several hundred meters before turning back when they saw none of the landmarks Sara had named.

And the road increasing turned toward the north. Hesitation tinged Max's face. Had he erred in his deductions? Of course, the trail the porters had followed to leave the forest could join the road far out in the farmland—but then the minaret and the mosque were no longer reliable landmarks, since they wouldn't notice them as they drove by.

Suddenly he started at a hoarse cry beside him. "Stop! Stop!"

He grabbed the lever of the hand brake. "What is it?"

"That! That! I'd forgotten it, but I saw that—I saw it!"

Sara was pointing to a wooden post, painted in red and white spiral stripes, on top of which writhed a grimacing figures of Kali, the sinister goddess of violent death.

"That's a Kali post," said Max.

"Yes, yes. But it struck me, because it stood at the fork where the trail the porters followed met the road."

Max only smiled.

"You don't believe me?" she said in surprise.

"Certainly, I believe you saw a statue like this. There are thousands of them in India. They mark a spot where a murder was committed, like crosses in the French countryside."

"Perhaps so, but I recognize this one."

"You're just suggestible."

"No—I swear that's the post I saw."

"Then how do you explain the forest trail having disappeared?"

Sara turned pale. It was true: she'd said herself that the trail should meet the road at this point, but no matter how hard she stared, she saw nothing that resembled a well-worn path. The entangled branches of bushes formed a green barrier through which it was obvious no sedan chair carried by porters could ever have passed.

"And yet," she said aloud, "my eyes may tell me I'm wrong—but I feel that I'm not wrong."

"My word," laughed Max, "unless the trail was wiped out after you went by..." But then his smile faded. "Well, in fact, why not?" She looked at him curiously, and he went on, "Those people have access to incalculable power."

"Incalculable is the word," she said, her voice shaking.

"And if you're not limited, either by the cost or by the number of workers, nothing could be easier than to wipe out a trail—an ideal way to throw off your scent anyone who wants to find it, and thus keep them from finding you."

He'd jumped out and gone over to the Kali post, where he got down flat on the ground and disappeared halfway into the bushes. But Sara couldn't understand what he did next: he pulled a string out of his pocket and carefully wound it around the base of each of the bushes that formed the hedge, one after another. Then, saying, "I'll be right back," he slipped away through the branches. Sara could no longer see him, and she grew worried. Would he finally agree with her that her feelings weren't mistaken?

The bushes were shaken as if by a cyclone. Max burst back out, his hair tangled, one cheek scratched by a thorn, but looking joyful and triumphant. He cried out, "You were right!" Coming back to the car, he went on more calmly, "Shrubs were planted along the main road. I used my string to find the smallest, youngest stems. The height of the bushes can be made equal, but you can't change the stems."

"And from the other side," murmured Sara eagerly, "did you see the minaret?"

"No. It must be masked by a line of trees. But in the distance I recognized the fenced corrals for animals you mentioned. As for the trail..." He pointed to the Kali post. "At this end it ran the same direction as the road. When they left it the porters must have continued straight north, without turning."

"Yes, yes!"

"It's been moved. It runs across the fields. I assume it rejoins the road a little further on, but meets it at a perpendicular. You can see how that change—from a trail running parallel to the road to a trail crossing it at right angles—is enough to disguise it." Then he added cheerfully, "Onward, onward! I'm beginning to think we're getting warmer!"

He hopped back into the driver's seat and quickly put the car in motion again. Five hundred meters down the road, he stopped at a spot where a trail coming from the right met the road at right angles.

"There it is, Madame: our wandering trail. It's going to lead us to the place where you were carried out of the forest."

The car slowly headed up the poorly maintained trail, littered with bumps and potholes. It took Max's full attention to steer without having a breakdown. This rough trail, looking like some temporary farm track, ran across country, seeming to have no destination other than the fields that backed up against a clump of tall trees. But when they'd passed that small wood, the track made a sharp turn toward the forest, curving this way and that across the plain.

Suddenly they cried out together, "The minaret!" It was true: to their right stood the rustic mosque Sara had described, while to their left were the animal corrals divided by wooden fences. There could be no doubt: it was certainly in that Hunting Reserve that the duchess had said farewell forever to her husband.

Max couldn't stay still any longer. "Madame, I beg you, try to remember. We're about to enter the woods. Do your best to keep me going the right direction."

"Go on. I'll do all I can."

The car slowly entered the woods. A short distance in, they came to a fork. Without hesitating Sara pointed right. That track angled uphill. At the top it ran through thinner woods broken by clearings and grassy stretches. Imperturbably playing her part as guide, the duchess decided their course almost effortlessly. She'd forgotten her suffering, gripped by the anxiety of this pursuit of memory.

The car went downhill again to flat ground. It was now crossing the intermediary valley in the Hunting Reserve, where Lucien's and Dodekhan's killers had carried out their crime in secret. Suddenly, at a crossroads where two tracks met at right angles, Sara pointed one way and murmured in a stifled voice, "There—very close—is the door where I said farewell to him!"

So these two French people, wandering through unfamiliar Bengal, had reached their destination. They were both filled with intense emotion. Perhaps the murderers were still nearby, behind the bushes, unaware that the avengers had come. Avengers! A pretentious word! Were a novelist and a young woman capable of fighting back? The doubt crossed their minds—but it was driven away by anxious curiosity, which Sara almost unwittingly put into words: "Let's hide the car in the thickets, and go have a look."

It was almost two in the morning when the automobile brought the travelers back to the gate of Trefald's Cottage. They'd taken along the keys, so as not to disturb anyone if they came back late. They opened the gate, parked the car in the garage, and went quietly to the front door. There they were met with a surprise: the door was ajar.

"Oh, those servants!" muttered Max. "They're all the same—incapable of conscientious work!"

But inside there was more: all the doors were wide open, and on the floor at the foot of the stairs leading to Violet's room lay a small slipper.

Max grew pale. "What happened here while we were gone?"

Equally anxious, Sara was already headed upstairs. On the second floor as well, all the doors were wide open.

"Mona! Violet!"

"Sir John! Sir John!"

Their calls rose together, but produced no answer. Their hearts pounded with fear. They hurried forward, bursting into the girls' rooms... empty. They ran through the house, calling, shouting, misery making their voices crack. There was no answer. Their traveling companions had disappeared without a trace. The servants seemed to have vanished into smoke.

CHAPTER XIII
The Missing

"Kindly be seated, ladies, and you too, sir." The speaker was a slim young man wearing a white silk turban decorated with five rubies—the emblem of Shiva. He was dressed in a shirt of the same material and color with a whimsical lattice of blue braid, billowing silk trousers that were close-fitting at the ankles, and curving slippers with blue and silver embroidery.

The persons he was addressing, Violet Musketeer and Sir John Lobster, looked around them in astonishment. They were no longer at Trefald's Cottage: how had they come to this great hall, whose large windows, covered by purple blinds, opened onto lush grounds, with emerald green lawns, in the middle of which shivered the moving azure of a body of water, where multicolored ducks and pink flamingos bathed?

And what about the behavior of Mona Labianov, who was with them? Strange behavior: the gentle mad girl had gone to a window and was looking out. Her lips moved, she nodded her head—as if she were greeting familiar sights.

"Would you tell me..." began Violet.

The Indian interrupted her. "I'm here for that very reason, miss. That's why I asked you to be seated: I wouldn't want you to have to stand while you listen to me."

"So it'll take a long time?" she said combatively.

"Long or short, miss—that depends on you."

"Then make it short."

"I sincerely hope so."

She considered him in surprise. What did his words mean? Finally, with a sweeping gesture of impatience, she dropped into a chair. Sir John, ruddier than ever, did the same.

The Indian said, "Miss, the newspapers informed us of your arrival in the capital. All Calcutta is moved at such an honor. But their feelings are nothing compared to ours—we humble country folk, for whom your visit is a blessing!"

"A blessing? You call yourself country folk... Are we outside the city?"

"Outside and far away, yes, miss."

"Far away too. Why? How?"

He bowed and smiled warmly. "I would've asked you to visit me, miss, but you would certainly have declined. So I took the initiative: when a wall blocks your way, you have to go around it."

"I assume you're trying to say that I'm here by force."

"Ah!" cried the courteous stranger, "the voice is too charming for me to take offense at the words. Let's say by force, then. Your native servants at

Trefald's Cottage obeyed me, because everyone obeys me. At my orders they put a sedative in your food."

"A sedative!" exclaimed Violet and Sir John as one.

"Yes. You're aware that India is the traditional land of opium. You understand?"

"But what was the point?"

"Of the opium episode? To abduct you and your friends while you slept, to bring you here, and to negotiate a little bit of very interesting business with you."

Violet shrugged. "If I understand, you're a bandit."

The Indian drew himself up proudly. "The English say so. But the Indians consider me a leader."

"A leader who's probably after a ransom."

"Exactly right. But—and I insist that you know this, miss—a ransom of which I'll keep not even a fraction. Everything will go into the coffers of a great organization for whom I'm no more than a servant."

"I say!" muttered Sir John. "That's a distinction that may perhaps flatter the one who's receiving payment, but which is a matter of indifference to the one who's paying."

"I agree," said Violet. She looked the native in the eye. "Let's get down to it. How much?"

"Two hundred thousand pounds."

"That's plenty!"

"It's in proportion to your fortune, miss."

"Perhaps; I won't debate it. And how would you like to be paid?"

The Indian bowed respectfully. "Ah, miss, allow me to congratulate myself on my plan. It's a pleasure to negotiate with you."

"How?" she repeated coldly.

"Like this. Two members of your party are wandering the countryside. They must now be looking for you in Calcutta." She nodded. "Please write to tell them what's happened to you. Enclose with your letter a check that they'll cash for you. Two hundred thousand pounds—that's nothing surprising, if it's signed Violet Musketeer."

"And they'll hand the money over to you?"

"Exactly, miss."

"No doubt I should advise them not to involve the police in all this?"

The man began to laugh. "No need, miss. The police are powerless against us. An officer who gave signs of looking for us would be dead within the hour."

At those words, spoken so calmly, Violet shivered all over. But she put on a brave face. "Please provide me with writing materials."

"You'll find everything you need on that table," he said, pointing out a kind of side table curiously inlaid with gold and mother-of-pearl, and on which indeed lay an inkstand, a pen, and a blotter filled with paper. He bowed again. "Please call me when you're done, miss. The bell by the door. I'll hurry back."

He went out, leaving the prisoners alone.

Sir John launched into endless recriminations, but Violet cut him off. "Nothing you can say will change matters. The important thing is to quit the company of these rascals as soon as possible. So please keep quiet and let me write in peace."

She sat down at the side table and went straight to work. In only a few lines, her letter to Max Soleil explained the situation and urged him to consider the ransom demand a negligible sum, while on the other hand working urgently to gather the amount. Then she drew up a check, made out to the Asiatic Bank— a correspondent of her own bankers in London, and therefore able to pay out cash with the least delay.

She'd just attached her stylish, decisive signature when Sir John murmured in her ear, "Have a look at Miss Mona."

Violet lifted her head and turned to see. The mad girl had left the window. Now she stood by the wall across from it. And that wall seemed different from the others. Fine paneling went from the floor halfway up the wall; from there to the ceiling the wall was covered in pale gray wallpaper, without any decoration—neither flower nor garland nor figure. At each corner a column half sunk into the wall seemed to hold up the ceiling. Mona was pressing her hands to the columns and to the intricacies of the woodwork, with an intense frowning gaze. She seemed to be looking for something—but what?

Sir John was about to speak again, but Violet put her finger to her lips to silence him. They both stayed still, watching the mad girl's actions.

Mona was speaking softly. "Yes, yes, here it is. The gray wallpaper, the screen, what we saw in Marseilles. Light is magical, but it can't do everything. It showed us this room. Therefore the starting point is here."

Suddenly, as her hand wandered across the paneling in the middle of the wall, there was a soft click. Almost immediately, a kind of white-cupped flower seemed to pop out of the wall beside her.

"Oh! A speaker, like the one the Amber Masks have," murmured Sir John.

"A speaker!" echoed Violet in surprise.

"Yes, except I found out in Russia that you can't always tell who you're connecting to."

Mona had paid no attention to the speaker. She went on with her incomprehensible search, her face clouded, as if she were annoyed at not discovering whatever mysterious thing she hoped to find.

"What if I spoke into the white disc?" said Violet quietly.

Sir John puffed out his cheeks with a dignified air, and didn't answer. But Violet must not have cared much for his opinion, because she went to the wall, bent slowly over the speaker, and pronounced the usual greeting: "Hello?"

Ten seconds went by. Then Violet and Sir John jumped: as softly as a whisper, a clear, gentle voice emerged from the wireless telephone. "Hello?"

For a moment Violet couldn't move. Mona had suddenly stopped her search, as if she'd been upset; her big eyes stared in alarm.

And yet they had to do something. Once again the speaker vibrated: "Hello? Who's calling?"

Violet quickly made up her mind; after all, what harm could come from satisfying her curiosity? She answered clearly, "Miss Violet Musketeer."

"You? You who've taken up the cause of two victims!" Violet started. So that was known, wherever the person who'd answered her was. But she had to listen again. "Press on the third carved rose in the paneling, counting from the left—the third. That'll start the tele-viewer for me, so I can see you."

Mona seemed to be agitated beyond words. Before Violet could act, Mona had already pressed on the rose. She'd barely done so when the voice in the speaker—choked, almost inhuman—cried out, "Mona! Mona! In the house in Bengal!"

The mad girl gave a muffled cry and fell to her knees, hiding her face in her hands with a sob.

The voice went on, "She's a prisoner—once again imprisoned by our enemies!"

Mona seemed not to hear, but Violet leaned close to the vibrating disc. "No—or at least not in her own name."

"What? What do you mean?"

"I was kidnapped, along with my entourage, for a ransom of two hundred thousand pounds. Since you can see, look at my letter and my check on the table. We'll be freed following payment."

She was answered by a long sigh. Then the voice resumed, "Let no one suspect her name. It would mean death for all of you. It would be horrible." More gently, it added, "But I'm forgetting. I want her to see us, so that she understands."

There was a humming sound, and suddenly the gray panel lit up. The neutral shade turned to color, and Violet's and Sir John's astonished eyes beheld a strange scene: some kind of vast cave, whose high roof was marked unevenly by ridges and glittering stalactites. Everywhere, on every wall, on consoles and tripods and assorted shelves, stood instrument panels, like the electronic control boards used in factories and important operations centers—unfamiliar devices of shining copper and blue-tinged steel.

In the midst of all that, bent over speakers identical to the one Violet was using, stood two men. One was tall and slim, and moved with graceful, lively gestures. His olive complexion, his red lips below a thin black mustache, his straight nose and soft, smiling brown eyes, all formed the near ideal of masculine beauty. His companion, though equally tall, offered a vivid contrast. He was blond, with pleasant but slightly hazy features and somewhat vague blue eyes, and he had that indefinable lethargy and careless elegance that mark the tail end of a noble race that's fading away.

But Mona had drawn herself up. She was reaching toward the screen—which they'd all understood to be the display panel of a wireless tele-viewer, like the one mentioned so often in the context of the mystery of the Loursinade villa—and in a passionate, joyful voice, like a jubilant fanfare, she cried, "Dodekhan and the duke! Alive, alive, and escaped from the murderers!"

Violet shivered. So the dead could come to life. These men, whose graves they'd sought, had appeared, conjured up by the marvelous scientific device. They spoke, they moved. And even now Dodekhan was answering. "We were spared, but we're still held prisoner by San, the wretch who's debasing our creation and turning it into an organization for looting. He wanted to draw you here, where we're being held, in the underground temple in the Celestial Mountains—you, Mona, and the duchess."

"Where is Sara?" interrupted Duke Lucien.

"Free, and in Calcutta."

"Thank you, that's all I needed. Go on, Dodekhan, go on."

Dodekhan—Master of the Blue Flag, held captive by his enemies, but eluding the control of his jailers by mean of a scientific instrument—went on, "It's true, we don't have much time. Let's take advantage of the moments we've been given by the miracle that has allowed you to communicate with us. Once you're free, Mona, be sure to tell the duchess to leave India—you'll never reach us from there. Come through China, by way of the Yangtze and Tibet... But it occurs to me that we can guide you. Take along the speaker you're using right now. It's tuned to ours. From no matter where, you can contact us and we can guide you. Every night, attach it to a tree or a roof beam or a post planted in the ground. That's when they're watching us the least. We'll talk to you, we'll tell you..."

"How is that you're still alive?"

"Oh, that was just plain luck—an inspiration on Lucien's part. He'd just killed Log, we'd been overpowered, our murderers were just deciding where to strike first. He cried out, 'At least this way the Blue Flag will be no use to anyone!' You understand—San is a servant, with a servant's soul. Servants can never reconcile themselves to giving up power or wealth. In short, we were spared—in the hope that they'd be able to drag the mysteries of these secret societies out of me." Suddenly Dodekhan grew worried. "Someone's coming. Take the speaker with you. Pull the knob of the tele-viewer. Goodbye, Mona, my beloved, goodbye."

The screen went blank. Those who'd witnessed that astonishing scene now saw before them nothing more than a wall with wood paneling and gray wallpaper. In one quick move, Mona took out the speaker and pulled on the carved wood rose that controlled the wireless cinematographic tele-viewer. She handed the speaker to Violet. "Keep this—I don't trust myself. I feel like I'm coming out of a long sleep. It was night. I dreamt I was far from here, in France, in Marseilles. But I haven't moved—I'm still here, where I must've fallen asleep." Then, with a kind of anxious, almost religious feeling, she added, "I was looking for the light. Oh, what a painful dream! But it's over, I can see, I can see, there's light all around me and in me. Dodekhan, Dodekhan, our souls have united!"

Sir John, who'd witnessed the entire scene in astonishment, shrugged his shoulders and muttered, "She's mad."

But Violet curtly corrected him. "No, she's not anymore, and I'd ask you not to say the word again in front of her. There's no need to disturb a mind that seems to be recovering its reason."

The fat Englishman grimaced in a way he imagined to be a smile. "All right, Violet, I won't mention it again. But before you ring for the bandit who's keeping us here, I'd like to bring up a little matter with you." She looked at him in surprise, and he went on, "Not only are you pretty, but you're very rich—which makes us perfectly matched."

She shrugged. "Oh, you're going to talk about marriage again. Save it for another time."

She reached for the bell to summon the bandit—but Sir John stopped her. "Don't ring. This is a very serious moment. Listen carefully and you'll agree with me."

Sensing something threatening in his tone, she replied with obvious ill humor, "All right, I'm listening."

"You've noticed the Frenchman. You're thinking of marrying him."

"I won't contradict you."

"Thank you for your candor. I, on the other hand, had thought of marrying you myself."

"So you've already told me—several times."

"I'm saying it again. The truth can't be repeated too often—for truth is its own reward and it shines on the flock of man a light as bright as the sun's: Psalm XVII verse 9." Violet was about to burst out laughing, but what Sir John said next froze the smile on her lips. "I thought I was beaten in the hymeneal stakes. But the Lord watches over His own. He stretches out His protecting hand over the brows of the weak. He overthrows the mighty and guides David's stone to bring down Goliath."

Violet could sense some danger hidden under all this Biblical sentiment. She was brave by nature, and faced the coming storm. "Which means in plain English?"

"That the Lord—blessed be His name—has just handed me the weapon that will allow me to bring down the French Philistine." The words were ridiculous, yet they made Violet start. Her heart pounded, as if some calamity loomed. Sir John went on gravely, "I wasn't looking for that weapon, and I did nothing to obtain it. The Lord who watches over England, and its Righteousness, has given me my sword and shield through your own hands."

"What are you trying to say?"

"What I mean is, you're going to swear to marry me as soon as we get back to England."

"Never."

"Hold your tongue, dear Violet, until I'm through. I have complete trust in your oath. And I think you'll do it—because otherwise I can separate you violently from that ridiculous Max Soleil and doom your friends the duchess and Mona."

She stared at him, her eyes wide with alarm. "If you did that, you'd be a contemptible scoundrel."

He shook his head cheerfully. "Don't be childish. Business is business. The business of my heart is marriage. And above all, an Englishman worthy of the name cannot fail at business."

"In short, morality is measured by success?"

"Quite right! Success is everything. I've grasped success and I won't let go. And that doesn't make me a contemptible scoundrel, as you put it, but rather a shrewd and practical man who's giving his fiancée a guarantee that her interests will be in good hands." Delighted with the conclusion to his speech, Sir John rubbed his small red hands together, then went on, "But that's not the point. I'm not debating right and wrong. To my mind, that debate is over. I'm offering you two choices."

"Which are?"

"A formal, sacred promise of marriage once we return to England."

"I'll say it again: never."

"Or to be doomed yourself—separated from Monsieur Max, of course—and to cause the death of Miss Mona and Madame Sara and those two gentlemen who projected their picture on the wall just now."

Glimpsing the awful truth, Violet was silent.

"Ah, you seem as resolved as ever to refuse my hand. But don't decide until you're sure of my plans. I heard the gentleman on the wall. He said the bandits mustn't learn that Miss Mona is Miss Mona, or it'd mean death for her and the duchess. Do you remember his words?"

She bowed her head, unable to answer, feeling the terror rising in her.

"Well, I recognized it as divine protection, a miracle performed in my favor. You'll swear what I'm asking, or when that bandit shows up I'll say, 'Have a look at Miss Mona, old boy. That's Dodekhan's sweetheart. And the Duchess of La Roche-Sonnaille, who lives at Trefald's Cottage in Calcutta, is married to the other prisoner. And Max Soleil knows your secrets and has always been working against you. And I—I whom the Amber Masks chose as their ally—I've been prevented from helping them. They might even have been killed, because I haven't heard from them.'"

He stopped triumphantly. Violet looked at him, indignant and beaten. She understood that at that moment not only her own life and liberty—which she valued little—but those of her friends, and of Max himself, hung at the mercy of one word from Sir John Lobster. For herself, she would've chosen death over a loathsome marriage. But to doom those young women she'd learned to know and to love, to sacrifice that brave writer, that smiling, gallant Frenchman who'd embarked on an act of devoted service, effortlessly and without even seeming to be aware of the magnanimity of what he was doing... Oh, that couldn't happen, it wouldn't happen! Better to submit to the odious marriage. But she wouldn't forget: Max had pulled her out of the boredom into which her vast wealth had plunged her. He'd shown her life. Could she ever erase that from her memory? What a sad fate was hers! To escape boredom only to fall into misery!

"Well, darling Violet?" purred Sir John with a courtesy more cruel than any insult.

In a blank, painful, agonizing voice, she stammered, "I'll swear what you ask for."

"To marry me as soon as we return to England."

"Yes."

"All right! I'm the happiest of men."

She looked him up and down with a hard stare, and with hatred shining in her eyes. "I've sworn it. But you're despicable!"

Sir John was dumbstruck by her whispered insult, but without giving him time to reply she pressed the bell. Almost immediately the Indian with the symbol of the five rubies on his turban appeared. She handed him the letter and the check she'd prepared earlier. When he'd gone, she dissolved in tears. The multimillionairess wept over the cruel wisdom she was gaining: gold was powerless to bring happiness!

CHAPTER XIV
Violet Light

Sara and Max sat together in the flower-filled front garden of Trefald's Cottage.

"That chief of police is cynically indifferent," he muttered.

She shook her head sadly.

"I hurried to him," Max went on, "I reported our friends' disappearance. He said to me with a smile, 'Oh, Miss Musketeer's in no danger. She'll just have to pay a ransom, and since she's very rich the ransom will be high, and that'll gain us a little quiet time.'"

"Really, he dared say that?"

"I'd be as skeptical as you if I hadn't heard it with my own ears. You can imagine, I jumped on that remark, which he'd delivered in the calmest way. I asked him to stop joking..."

"And he answered?"

"'Alas, sir, I don't in the least mean to joke. Strictly speaking my duty would be to assign detectives to the case. But that would be pointless—none of them would follow the trail. For several months now a band of criminals has been operating with impunity in this region. At first the police did their best. Ten detectives in succession fell victim to their fanaticism. And consider the bandits' boldness: each victim was found with a stiletto in his chest, pinned through a sheet of paper on which was written, *Whoever seeks us finds death. Warning to whom it may concern.*'"

"Yes," murmured Sara, "I can imagine that no one's eager to be... the eleventh."

"To the point," concluded Max, "that the... fatherly advice of the pleasant official who received me was, that we just need to wait for a visit from the bandits' business agent, who'll bring us his leader's ultimatum."

He'd stood up, and was pacing feverishly, driving his heels into the ground, furious at being reduced to impotence. "A stupid business," he muttered, "that's cropped up just when things were going so well. We'd found the hideout we were looking for. We were able to spy on our enemies without being noticed. Half a dozen crooks led by a rascal dressed in white, wearing a turban decorated with rubies. We could've driven them off without much trouble. But—bam!—while we doing so well at the Hunting Reserve, some highway robber had to get in our way!"

He broke off suddenly. The bell at the front gate had just rung out, and the figure of an Indian could be seen through the foliage of the trees in whose shade they were talking.

"Well, since we've lost all our servants," cried Max—half serious, half joking—"I'll go answer that myself."

He went to the gate. Outside stood a gray-bearded native, in the humble, petitioning attitude of fakir mendicants. His swarthy, lined face, his downcast eyes, the indifference of his posture—everything suggested a man of that type. And yet when Max came close the Indian said, "Mr. Max Soleil."

"In person," he replied—a little surprised to hear his name on a stranger's lips.

The fakir reached through the gate grille, holding out an envelope. "Read that, man from across the sea. Read it, and give an answer, according to your thoughts, to the servant the Lord of the Ganges has sent to you."

"Lord of the Ganges," muttered Max. "These Indians are certainly imaginative. They award themselves titles of nobility, just like Western businessmen who've made their fortune... Let's see what's in this message."

As he took the letter, he recognized Violet's clear handwriting. He quickly tore open the envelope. Inside he found a fairly long letter and a check. The letter described the kidnapping: the sleep that had rendered all of the prisoners helpless, the abduction she had no memory of, her waking in the room with purple blinds on windows overlooking grounds with a pond full of ducks and flamingos and other brightly colored water birds.

"An odd coincidence," he said to himself. "A lake, flamingos, purple blinds—we saw all of those at the estate in the Hunting Reserve." But then he dismissed the thought. "The wealthy in this area must all show off their money in the same way. Those details are no more distinctive than a rock garden or a ball of mirrored glass would be in little bourgeois gardens in the suburbs of Paris." Returning to the unexpected letter, he read all the way to the signature. "My goodness, two hundred thousand pounds. Ransom enough for two emperors."

The fakir waited motionless, his head lowered meditatively. Max reached through the gate and touched his arm. "I've read it. I'll do what it says."

"Very good, sahib. When do you think you'll have the money?"

"That depends on how fast the bank is. But I don't think the formalities can take more than four or five days."

The visitor looked pleased. "The Lord of the Ganges is in no hurry to get it. When you've gathered the full amount, sahib, just tie a red scarf to this gate."

"A red scarf?"

"Yes. The following night, take the road toward Agaafi, which follows on from the Lime road and the Basketmakers' road... Count five miles from the last house, and you'll come to the edge of the forest that looks out over the Black Hills." At that name, Max couldn't help starting slightly. "Are you afraid, sahib?" asked the fakir, misinterpreting the reason for his movement.

Max realized he needed to reinforce the man's error, and as naturally as possible he said, "My word, at night, carrying so much money!"

"Don't worry. From the moment you put out the red scarf, you'll be under the protection of the Lord of the Ganges. No one would dare attack you."

"That may be. In any case, I have no choice—so I'll go where you tell me to."

"Soon the Lord, or friends of his, will meet you. Trust them and follow them. They'll take you to a delightful place, where the ransom will be counted, and then the prisoners will be turned over to you." Then the fakir winked, and went on with a look of greed. "It's a transaction you won't regret, for the Lord is generous, and rewards royally those who serve him well."

"In that case I'll do my best to please him."

The strange ambassador bowed and brought his hand to his forehead, then went away without looking back.

Max returned to Sara, who'd stayed where she was. Her big black eyes looked at him questioningly. He leaned close to her and whispered, "We're obviously surrounded by spies. So don't cry out or make any gesture that might give away our true thoughts."

"Understood."

"Read that, Madame."

When she'd reached the end of Violet's letter, Max repeated word for word his conversation with the bearer.

She listened with a shrewd light in her eye, and at the end she said, "And you think?..."

"That these bandits are the same group that was harassing you before."

"So their hideout is..."

"The estate in the Hunting Reserve. The location of the rendezvous point I was given leads me to be... almost positive." Then in spite of himself he smiled. "It's becoming farcical. While we were scouting out their headquarters, those rascals were doing the same thing to ours. But they were a little less considerate—they stole our treasures."

"Oh!" she laughed. "Is that how you'd describe Sir John Lobster?"

"Why not? His red complexion would've led the Indian heroes in Fenimore Cooper to dub him Coral Face or Crayfish Eye." Reassured for the moment about the fate of their companions, they both gave way to laughter.

Then Sara pulled herself together. "The crooks don't know they have Mona in their clutches. Presumably the leaders—that bloodthirsty San and his subordinates—have returned to China after killing those we mourn. It's a secondary team that's at work now. But there's the risk that the poor mad girl will say something unfortunate, or see someone who'll recognize her. So we have to act fast."

"I agree, and I'm going straight to the bank named."

"To request the cash?"

"With all supporting documents. It's clear we're being watched. So we need our enemies to think we're being good and obedient."

184

Sara reacted in surprise. "But we're not going to be?"

"You might be, Madame. But I certainly won't."

"What are you planning to do?"

"More like redo. Tonight I'll retrace the route we took yesterday."

"You're going back to the Hunting Reserve? Why?"

"To try to save Miss Violet."

"But with wretches like that, you risk…"

He cut her off. "I can't help it, I'm short-tempered. And I can't bear for her to owe her freedom to her money and not to me."

The duchess's dark eyes moistened with sudden affection. Then she said gently, "I'll go with you. I too want to work for Miss Violet's happiness."

Max began to protest at her putting herself needlessly in danger, but she silenced him. "It's my turn to say I can't help it, I have a woman's temperament. And when a woman can't devote herself to her own love, she dedicates herself to that of her neighbors." Then she added firmly, "Go down to the Asiatic Bank. When you get back, we'll head out in the automobile."

"It'll still be early."

"Yes, but our outing won't attract any attention…"

"Whereas once night falls our impulse to go for a drive would cause surprise. You're right, Madame, and we'll do as you suggest so wisely."

At the bank, Violet Musketeer's signature had an impact that her friends would never have guessed before now, but that the obsequiousness of the heads of the Asiatic Bank made clear. Those gentlemen declared that the funds would be available to the young lady's representative at ten o'clock the next morning. In passing they mentioned a second-hand deal: an ocean-going yacht, a steamer of eight hundred tons, with excellent speed, which a rajah, a friend of theirs, was trying to sell. No doubt the little "commission" they'd been promised made them persuasively eloquent, because Max asked them to have the yacht ready with steam up the next day. They'd take it for a test run, and if it handled well they'd take it on a run of some length, so the hold should be well stocked with coal.

They replied that the yacht was already as he asked. In short, Miss Musketeer's representative withdrew, escorted respectfully by the directors all the way to the outer door of the bank, and followed by the eyes of all the employees—who were astonished at the honor their bosses were showing to a stranger. So the first part of the plan had been carried out without trouble.

Max strolled back toward Trefald's Cottage through streets emptied by the noonday heat. He kept close to walls to stay in their blueish shade. Indeed at that point in its course the sun attacked like an angry beast, and struck down any white man foolish enough to defy its flaming arrows. Max could feel the physical and mental lassitude that rained down on Calcutta at siesta time. It was as hot as an oven. Like the people, the breeze seemed to have fallen asleep. Though he felt sleepy and heavy, he managed to get back to Trefald's Cottage, where Sara awaited him.

"You look tired," she said. "I was watching you carefully yesterday. If I go slowly, I think I could drive. Have a seat, and sleep a little under the shade of the canvas top. You can tell me how it went at the bank when you wake up."

"It went fine."

"That's all I need to hear. Now get in the car."

Max didn't protest. An urgent need to sleep, to forget about life, overpowered him. He settled in comfortably, and his eyes closed.

Sara got into the driver's seat. "This way," she said to herself, "the bandits will have even less reason to be suspicious, since I'm driving."

At barely twelve miles an hour, the automobile carefully followed the city streets, and then the wide avenue that wound along the left bank of the Hooghly.

When Max opened his eyes again, the car had stopped in the shade of thick woods. A fresh smell rose from the ground, and the thin, transparent slate-gray mist under the trees showed him they were almost there. Sara—who'd found it more practical for the journey to dress in the man's smock and loose trousers of "Laroche the student"—was lying on the ground nearby. She seemed very interested in something Max couldn't see, because it was happening on the far side of a tall thicket of bushes covered in white thorns.

He coughed softly to get her attention. She looked his way and put her finger to her lips, then came to him.

"Are we in the Hunting Reserve?" he murmured instinctively, like a soldier when the enemy is near.

"Yes."

"So I slept a long time?"

She smiled. "Even longer than that. I didn't want to take the same track into the forest as yesterday. We might've been seen from the village with the minaret. I don't know if the villagers are working for the bandits, but I thought it wise to act as if they are."

He nodded his approval. "Ah, Madame, what an army scout you'd make!"

"It comes naturally. A city girl from Paris, who's read a lot, and suffered a lot," she added sadly, "can't help but think a little. On the warpath, as Gabriel Ferry[27] observed, thinking will allow you to take the enemy by surprise. Anyway, now that you seem alert enough to listen, I'd like to share the results of my thoughts."

"I'm all ears."

---

[27] The writer Gabriel Ferry the elder (1809-52). The reference is probably to his best-known—and posthumous—novel, *Le Coureur de Bois* (The Woodsman) (1853).

She went on, "We entered the woods along a road parallel to the orientation of the valley of the Hunting Reserve, about equidistant from the Black Hills and the hills that border the valley to the north."

"Perfect! But we might have some trouble locating the bandits' house again..."

"Wrong verb tense."

"You mean?"

"That I already found it."

"You did?"

Max had raised his voice. She grabbed his arm. "Shh! They're right nearby."

"They?"

"Yes. I found their hideout fairly easily. We've approached it from one side, where the boundary line runs through deep woods. The thicket from behind which I was watching just now forms the boundary here. You understand?"

"Of course," he murmured, dazed by how much his brave countrywoman had accomplished while he slept.

"And," she went on, "I've now been... spying for more than an hour, and I've become convinced of something very important in our position." She broke off. "But first, come see for yourself."

He got out, and let her lead him to the place where he'd first noticed her stretched out. She murmured quietly, "Lie down on the ground. Between the branches you'll see the grounds, and the house where our friends are being held prisoner."

He corrected her: "Where we assume they're being held prisoner."

But she shook her head. "I no longer assume it—I'm sure."

"How can you be?"

"I saw them."

"Violet? Mona?"

"Yes."

Max stretched out on the ground and peered through the dense tangle of branches of the thorny hedge. For a moment he could see nothing. Then, glancing around, he spotted a small loophole formed by chance in the crisscrossing branches, a narrow opening through which he could see the grounds: a lawn shaded by big cherry trees, over which palm trees spread their crowns like parasols,[28] and whose green mantle ran up to the façade of a large wooden house—a "palace," as the homes of rajahs, wealthy Parsees, or officials were known in India.

But Max's attention was drawn to the sound of a voice. Around a garden table of white lattice work, four men—Indians by race and dress—sat in a circle

---

[28] It's thanks to the shade cast by palm trees that European fruit trees can be made to thrive in the tropics [*Note from the Author*].

playing *garrat*, an odd game, imported from Nepal, that might've been the ancestor of our pernicious roulette. The equipment consisted of a bowl-like receptacle whose bottom was divided into twenty-seven adjoining cups, each numbered. Only the central cup was decorated; it represented zero. The players held clay marbles of various colors. All the players threw their marbles into the bowl. After rolling around, they all necessarily came to rest in the cups. Whoever landed on the highest number won the stakes. If a marble ended up in the central cup, that player had to double the winner's take and reimburse the other players' stakes.

"Well," murmured Sara, "there are four of them."

"Sure, but is that the whole garrison?"

"No. Two more are standing guard under the windows of the room in which the prisoners are being held."

"You've seen them?" asked Max in surprise.

She shook her lovely brunette head. "No—those windows look out on the opposite side of the house. But I found it out by listening to these men talking. Our friends are being held in the same room where Mona and I were prisoners before, the room we could see from the Loursinade villa using the cinematographic tele-viewer—the room in which we saw our loved ones die." She fell silent a moment from distress, then regained her composure. "Two bandits are watching them, according to what I overheard. So, six men, plus the leader they call the Lord of the Ganges."

"Ah, he was also mentioned by the fakir who brought me Miss Violet's letter at Trefald's Cottage." He went back to his lookout spot. "Well, that rascal is there."

"The fakir?"

"The same. Look, he's just standing up right now."

The emotions of the game had led one of the men to stand up and cry, "Yes! Green, twenty-six! I win!"

Max sat back. "Seven opponents. My revolver will take care of those four gamblers, which leaves three."

He stopped. Sara shook her head.

"I'll go alone..." he began.

But she cut him off. "No—the revolver is too noisy. Do you want the survivors, knowing they're under attack, to kill their prisoners?"

His high spirits fell away suddenly. "Then what can we do?"

"What the poor mad girl taught us to do. Remember that she got us out of worse positions without making a sound or drawing any attention. I thought of that when we were leaving, and in the trunk of the car I put... the chest of luminous tubes."

"Ah, Madame, we're going to owe you our victory!" But then his face darkened. "But... but... there's one problem."

"Which is?"

"Mademoiselle Mona isn't here to direct us, and I'm afraid in our hands the tubes may be useless as weapons. We can't test them."

Sara smiled gently. "You've never examined the chest."

"I admit it."

"You'd have seen some labels that I believe I understood." He looked at her questioningly, and she went on, "Come, you'll decide for yourself."

They went back to the automobile. Sara opened the trunk, and then opened Mona's chest inside it. She pointed to a label glued to the inside of the lid. "Read that."

Max studied the writing:

WARNING
Never aim the beam at yourself.
Exercise particular care when handling
the tubes numbered 3 to 12 and 30 to 35. Their effects are lethal.
For tubes 3 to 12, avoid aiming the beam at wood,
cloth, varnished, or gilded metal surfaces.

The more he read, the more he was filled with a kind of superstitious dread: science had turned colored light, housed in a battery and projected through a glass tube, into a powerful silent weapon that could be controlled by any weakling.

"You're daydreaming," whispered Sara next to him.

He started. "You're right, I beg your pardon. The strangeness of these… weapons had sent me off on a poorly timed train of thought."

"But a philosophical one," she smiled. Then she went on more seriously, "Take two tubes from the series from 3 to 12. I'll take two from the series from 30 to 35." Max did as he was told. "And now," she went on, "you know what the colors are of the beams you control?"

"My word, no."

"Oh, you absentminded knight! They're the color of your lady: violet. You're using violet to fight for Violet."

He couldn't help smiling in admiration at the cheerful courage of his French compatriot. "And you?"

"Oh, I've chosen indigo light."

"Which causes…"

"Lethal effects, according to the instructions. But I want to know exactly what effect. As you can see, since I'm a woman, curiosity plays a part in my decisions."

While she spoke she closed the trunk of the car. Then, with Max following, she returned to the spot from where they'd been watching the bandits earlier. They both handled their tubes with care—not quite trusting them, with their "lethal effects"—and counting above all on making their use a surprise to their enemies.

But when they reached their observation post they stared at each other, barely suppressing a cry. The four gamblers had risen at the approach of an Indian dressed all in white and wearing a turban decorated with rubies that stood out against the cloth like drops of blood. Beside him walked a young peasant. Close behind them, flanked by two bandits holding revolvers, followed Violet, with Mona on her arm, and Sir John—redder and more flabbergasted than ever. What was happening? What had made the bandits bring out their captives?

Max and Sara easily recognized the man in white as the leader, the Lord of the Ganges they'd already unhappily heard about. The deference paid to him by the others was clear. And now, in a loud voice that showed he felt sure no one was eavesdropping, he was speaking, with his hand on the peasant's shoulder. "Adfer here has brought news. Yesterday our friends in the Muslim village notified us that an automobile carrying two passengers had driven into the Hunting Reserve."

They all bowed. "We know, Sahib."

"Well, today Adfer saw a car, which based on his description I think might be the same one. It entered the woods by way of the valley road." All of the bandits reached for the daggers hanging from their belts in the Indian style. "Good! You understand. Two people aren't enough to worry us, but they might be spies—and eyes that have seen must be shut forever."

In their hiding place Max and Sara trembled at his cruel, menacing tone. But still they listened.

The leader was giving orders. "Three of you stay here with me. The rest spread out around the Hunting Reserve and look for that car." They all bowed. "We're also going to minimize the likelihood of surprise. Miss Musketeer's ransom is going to be paid. So only her life has value. Cut the throats of the fat red man and the other girl. Four of us will guard the rich Englishwoman. If we're attacked, at least one of us will have time to strike at her: they'll rescue nothing but a corpse."

He'd barely finished speaking when suddenly he let out a roar of pain, his hands clutched frantically at his chest and his forehead, and he fell back onto the lawn—where in an instant his clothes caught fire, shooting blueish flames into the sky.

"What is it?"

"The Fire of Vishnu!"

"The Wrath of Shiva!"

The bandits all bumped into each other chaotically, shouted in terror, trying in vain to understand what strange accident had befallen their leader. As dusk was now falling, it looked like glowing fires were being lit in the thorn bushes of the hedge surrounding the grounds. Beams of violet or deep indigo light stood out in the twilight, landing in turn on the prisoners' two guards and on the four gamblers. Some of them fell straight to the ground, other caught on fire like their leader. Shouting in terror, the peasant and the three surviving guards tried to escape, but the terrible rays moved faster than the fastest runner. One after another the wretches dropped.

And while Violet, Mona, and Sir John, stunned and filled with fear, stared all around, unable to flee, their feet rooted to the ground by terror, the thickets of the hedge were pushed vigorously apart, and through the opening came two human figures calling out joyfully, "Free! Free!"

Moments later Max was clasping Violet's hands. When she recognized him she began to weep. Sara gathered Mona into her arms. Sir John, standing alone and apart, observed these emotional effusions with concern and mistrust.

An ominous crackling rang out in the night. They all turned, ready to confront new enemies. But Mona pointed to the house. "Fire." She was right: like snakes, flames twisted around the great columns and writhed around the windows.

"The violet rays," murmured Sara.

"Ah! That's what the warning meant when it said to avoid aiming the beam at wood and so forth," cried Max. Then in a different tone he added, "Oh, well—we weren't planning to live here! To the car, ladies, and back to Trefald's Cottage."

Two hours later they were all home. But there, while Sara rejoiced, Max was made miserable. Now that they were all together they both learned of the personal drama that had unfolded along with the kidnapping by the henchmen of the Lord of the Ganges. Max felt overwhelmed by despair. Weeping without constraint, Violet told him she'd become engaged to Sir John, to save the rest of them.

Out of the depths of his pain Max cried, "I'll kill him!"

But she replied with bleak dignity, "I've given my word. Only he can release me from it. He couldn't do it if he were dead."

Staggering, his head spinning, overcome by the gentle voice of the woman who'd sacrificed her fondest hopes to principle, Max withdrew to his room.

Meanwhile Sara, stunned, found out from Mona—Mona, who'd recovered her reason—Mona, who'd found light again in the Orient to which her mad instinct had drawn her—Sara learned that the Duke of La Roche-Sonnaille was alive. The perturbation of her spirits would be impossible to describe.

Max emerged in the morning, pale from a sleepless night. In a dull voice he discussed with Violet—who was as pale as he was—the need to stop by the Asiatic Bank to collect the two hundred thousand pounds he'd requested the day before. He also expressed his fear of another attack by the Lord of the Ganges's men. And he mentioned the bank directors' proposal concerning buying that yacht fitted out for a long voyage. "Mr. Dodekhan and the Duke of La Roche-Sonnaille advised the duchess and Mona to come find them where they're being kept in the Celestial Mountains; that yacht would enable us to reach a Chinese port."

"Yes, you're right, and that'd be safer and faster than taking a commercial liner."

So the same day, toward three in the afternoon, when high tide crested in Calcutta, the *Mabel*, a pretty steam yacht of eight hundred tons, pushed off from the commercial pier, moved out to catch the current in the middle of the Hooghly, and headed to sea.

Mona and Sara stood together on deck, away from the others. They couldn't hide the joy that filled them, but they knew that showing it only deepened Max and Violet's grief. At the stern, alone, stood Sir John. From there he could watch the two young people leaning on the rail some distance away. Fortified by Violet's promise, he smiled.

Perhaps he'd have been less pleased if he could've seen Max's expression just then. The young man's face had suddenly lit up, and his mouth widened in an ironic, resolute smile. "Violet," he said softly, "you promised to marry Sir John as soon as you get back to England?"

"That's right," she said, surprised at both the question and the tone in which it was asked.

"And you believe he alone can release you from your engagement?"

"I believe so, I think so—it's awful, but it's the honorable thing."

"Well, then, smile at me, darling Violet. I think he's going to set you free." She looked surprised, and he added, "Please don't ask me any questions. You have to remain in the dark—otherwise you'd be my accomplice, and we can't allow that, for the sake of principle. But at least say a prayer."

"A prayer," she echoed quietly.

"Yes. Tell me that you're praying for me to succeed."

"Oh, you know very well I am, my dear!"

The *Mabel* increased her speed as she emerged from the sandy delta of the Hooghly. Her slender bow sliced through the waves of the Bay of Bengal.

PART TWO
A SCIENTIFIC HELL

CHAPTER I
Who Is It?

Unease hung over Asia. Anxious dispatches were exchanged between the Western consulates of Europe and America. From Vladivostok, from Yokohama, Peking, Weihaiwei, Canton, Hongkong, Shanghai, Hanoi, Hue, Saigon, Singapore, Bangkok, Calcutta, Bombay, Baghdad, Irkutsk, Tobolsk, Isfahan, Samarkand, the same question was aimed perpetually at the four corners of the Asian continent—a question all the more anxious in tone, all the more worrying to its recipients, because no one could give the answer it begged for.

A revolutionary tremor seemed to be shaking the vast territories of Asia, and no one knew its direction or its goal. Contradictory events defied all logical interpretation. In early December the Western legations—whose fortified compound formed an island within Peking—received a warning: *You will be attacked on the night of the 7th to 8th; be on your guard.*

The military companies assigned by the foreign powers to protect their embassies had taken up arms, and on the night specified—a night dedicated by Chinese rites to the Liberating Dragons—the attack came, furious and appalling. As if by magic, throngs of fanatics had poured out of the alleys, the gardens, the *yamens,*[29] the pagodas of the ancient city of the Son of Heaven and hurled themselves against the European concessions. Deadly fire had greeted the attackers without breaking their momentum. Climbing over the mounds of the dead and dying, the human wave had reached the walls and risen to their tops—their very numbers discouraging any resistance.

"They're too many to kill!" cried one defender, weary of shooting.

All seemed lost! But suddenly an azure fire was kindled on the ramparts of the Chinese citadel. A murmur ran through the mob... and then the besiegers abruptly dispersed, melting away into the night, scorning a victory that their adversaries considered inevitable. In the morning they were stunned to discover that even the bodies of the fallen had vanished. How had they been removed? No one had seen or heard a thing.

On the 15th of the same month, a similar incident took place in the port of Shanghai. Junks, sailing from no one knew where, had entered the harbor by

---

[29] Palaces [*Note from the Author*].

night, and onto the European ships that lay at anchor, asleep in false security, they'd introduced thousands of pirates, who had no trouble overpower the crews taken by surprise. Just when those sailors expected to die, the pirates, at some mysterious signal, had hurriedly abandoned their prizes and regained their junks. At dawn there was no sign of the boats, which seemed to have dissolved into smoke.

The 24th of December, as the British garrison in Lhasa, the capital of Tibet, were celebrating Christmas, fanatics got into the garrison house where the troops had thought they were safe. The soldiers were all massacred—except for two young volunteers who managed to escape and bring news of the disaster. But the government in India didn't have time to retaliate: the very next day, the fort now occupied by the attackers had exploded, hurling men and masonry into the distance—an inexplicable detonation, since the garrison house wasn't yet armed with cannon and contained no gunpowder.

Finally, on the 28th (the 15th according to the Russian calendar), a reconnaissance squadron from Bukhara, encamped on one of the lower plateaus rising toward the Pamir glaciers, had also been surprised in the night by unknown enemies. This time the cavalrymen, bound to their horses, had been led away into the mountains by their attackers. The soldiers despaired, thinking themselves destined for the most cruel tortures—when suddenly the narrow ravine they were passing through was filled with red light; there was an enormous explosion, and the peak of a rocky crag broke off its base and fell so as to block the way, in the process crushing under its weight the vanguard of the column. Panic ensued among their enemies. Crying out with terror, they fled in all directions, abandoning their prisoners, who by helping each other managed to get out of their ropes and take their horses back to camp.

All of those strange, incomprehensible incidents, which no government official had managed to explain logically... what could they mean? So, down the humming wires ran the terse, unnerving dispatches, each reporting a new occurrence, a new anxiety. From north, south, sunrise, sunset, a mysterious wind was blowing across Asia. To the four major incidents already described were added hundreds of smaller disturbances: here a diplomat kidnapped, there two German soldiers in Shandong found tied up and drowned at the bottom of a well. Then the governor of the Shandong concession received a mysterious parcel containing gold bars weighing two kilograms, along with a short note: *To compensate the families of the deceased soldiers.* And so on... It was as if good and evil spirits were at war with each other all over Asia—with the Europeans paying the price, as the clueless authorities put it, crudely but with some justice.

At one point they thought they'd found the key to the enigma. An Indian of the lowly pariah caste, intoxicated on ether given to him by a policeman, had spoken confusedly of some controlling will, originating in the Celestial Mountains, toward which the eyes of all the natives were turned. But presumably that kind of tale displeased those it concerned, because the talkative pariah was found dead in his prison cell, with the red Thuggee noose around his neck. The jailers and the wardens had seen and heard nothing. Idle conjecture led nowhere—but from then on no native seemed to understand the questions, whether subtle or not, asked by those who were trying to solve the mystery.

Meanwhile the incidents continued. Fear gripped the European settlements. One by one, merchants, journalists, industrialists—all those not committed to the country by professional duty—decided to leave those dangerous lands. It was growing into a general exodus that would end in the ruin of all the European concessions.

Taking action was urgent—but what action? How could they engage an enemy who was clearly ubiquitous, but whose intentions and organization and very nature were unknown? The several nations concerned consulted each other—and resolved that, to reassure public opinion, they should at least give the appearance of taking action.

As the powers most deeply committed on the Asian continent, the British and Russian governments were handed the task of defending the civilization at risk. British troops from India and Russian forces from Siberia and Turkestan mustered to form an imposing army, whose objective was the Celestial Mountains mentioned by the dead pariah. Their orders remained a little vague, it was true. The Indian prisoner's death showed that his confused statement contained a germ of truth. There must be something in the Celestial Mountains. What? Nobody knew. Their job was to find that something and destroy it. That way the governments shielded themselves from responsibility; and if the officers assigned to lead this murky expedition failed, they could be blamed for incompetence and suffer loss of promotion and favor. That was how civilization delegated justice.

On April 15th of the following year, the forces of the joint Anglo-Russian expedition were encamped on the marshy shores of Lake Balkhash, the third-largest inland sea in Turkestan. As fast as the eye could see stood ranks of tents made of felt—the only fabric heavy enough to protect the men against the freezing nights. Near the center, on a knoll rising ten meters above the shoreline, stood a *yurt*, a large hut of wood and beaten earth; presumably it had once been used by shepherds on the steppe, but now it bore the grand designation of general headquarters.

English and Russian officers were gathered in the single room on the ground floor. They sat in a semicircle, listening to the supreme commanders of the joint forces, who stood by a map of Central Asia spread out on a table and explained what Europe expected of its sons now assembled here.

The Russian general was named Stanislas Labianov. He was tall and well-built, with high color, and an animated face marked by a hint of sadness. For several months he'd disappeared, then suddenly presented himself again at court in St. Petersburg, refusing to account for his absence. When asked, he always answered, "Some words kill more surely than a sword. I don't want to speak those words." That he was weary of war went without saying; but people noticed that his hair and whiskers, which before had been salt and pepper, had gone completely white during his disappearance.

The British general bore with dignity the honorable title of Lord Aberdeen. He was the consummate example of a distinguished Englishman—tall, slim without being thin, strong-featured. He showed his Russian colleague a marked deference, seeming to pay respect to some grief unknown to others, unknown to himself, no doubt; but his sharp, inquisitive gray eyes had perhaps looked within the closed-off spirit of Stanislas Labianov.

Pointing at the areas on the map to which he was referring, the Russian said, "Gentlemen, bandits wishing to escape reprisals couldn't choose a safer refuge than the Tian Shan Mountains, which we call the Celestial Mountains. As you can see, between Lake Balkhash, the eastern shores of which we now occupy, and those peaks, stretch hundreds of kilometers of labyrinthine mountains and difficult passes, treeless and almost without water. And yet that's the route we're going to take, because it's by far the easiest."

A soft murmur of approval followed his words. Lord Aberdeen nodded to show his agreement with his colleague.

"I said the easiest," went on Labianov. "A glance at the map will show you there can be no doubt about that. To the east, deep in the Chinese Empire, the empty Gobi Desert blocks the passage of any army—more than two hundred kilometers without water. Not to mention the obstacles raised by the Celestial Court, which would most likely be sympathetic to the enemy we're trying to beat." He went on slowly, "To the south and southwest it's even worse. The Pamirs, the Tibetan plateau, and the Himalayan range would foil any attempt to take an army the size of ours across them. Those High Plateaus, with an average elevation of five thousand meters, are frigid deserts where the temperature at night goes down to thirty or forty degrees below zero, and where altitude sickness, from the thinness of the air, overcomes both men and horses."

There was a short silence. The officers looked at each other, wondering where these discouraging observations were leading.

Labianov understood their expressions, and in a firm tone, filled with compelling authority, he went on, "If I'm reminding you of these things, gentlemen, it's to prepare you for the courage, the self-sacrifice, the dedication that I expect from you. Our men will suffer the distress of long marches through a bleak, grueling landscape—long marches at the end of which, when they stop exhausted for the night, they'll find out with a disheartening shock that they've come barely four or five kilometers. We'll constantly have to buoy up the spirits of our men, who are ill-prepared to grasp the unusual aspects of a war in these mountains. You'll have to be not only their commanders, their leaders, their guides, but also their elder brothers. In these conditions, for an officer, failure is tantamount to desertion."

All eyes shone, and hands were raised as if to swear an oath, but before anyone could speak he went on, "I know I can count on you. I want you to know you can count on me. I want your duty—as arduous as it is—to be made easier by the example of your superiors. Lord Aberdeen and I will make do with the same simple felt tents the troops use, and we'll share the men's food. It's not enough for them to obey us out of a sense of discipline; they've got to love us, they've got to trust us blindly. If we ask the impossible of them, we have to prove to them that the impossible is doable. I expect you to follow our example."

English "hurrahs!" and Russian "*uras!*" rang out together.

But Labianov held up his hand, and silence was restored immediately. "We'll break camp tomorrow at dawn," he said slowly. "Once we enter the maze of the mountains, it'll become almost impossible to reconnoiter the road ahead of us—all the more so because the detailed topography of the regions we'll be crossing is completely unknown. So it'll be our aeronauts, going up every afternoon in their tethered balloons, who from their gondolas will chart the next day's course roughly east-southeast." He singled out two officers. "I'll therefore ask you, Captain Follett and Captain Babarin, to carry out an ascension today. Unwind as much cable as possible, and prepare a topographical map of the immediate area."

"A single balloon?" asked Babarin, the Russian.

"No, two. You'll go up from opposite ends of the camp. That way you'll see the elevations from different angles, and together your maps will correct and confirm each other. In future we'll do the same thing whenever the terrain permits. Don't waste any time—go."

The aeronauts saluted and left the meeting, followed soon after by the rest of the officers, who'd stayed to received the instructions appropriate to each division.

General Labianov and Lord Aberdeen remained alone. The Russian had dropped onto a crude stool. With his elbows on the table, and his face hidden in his hands, he seemed to have forgotten his companion. Aberdeen watched him, pity softening his strong features. But then he started. Labianov's shoulders were shaking, betraying a sob. Aberdeen came quickly to him and laid a friendly hand on his arm. "My dear colleague," he said gently, "again this despair whose cause I don't know."

He stopped. Labianov had straightened up, revealing a face twisted with emotion. As if in a dream, he stammered, "I'm killing my daughter, my little Mona." Then he gave a choked cry, "No, no, I'm mad! I don't know what I'm saying. At least don't think…"

Aberdeen calmly interrupted, "Yes, I think you're suffering terribly, my poor friend. If you want, I'll forget the few words that slipped out—I swear it. But they shed a little light, which helps explain your strange behavior since I've had the honor to know you. You're suffering because you're torn between your duty as a soldier and your love as a father."

Labianov shuddered and bowed his head. Aberdeen bent close and said quietly, "I'll forget about it, my friend—unless you decide that the pain is eased by being shared, by confiding in a comrade who's going to tempt death by your side."

As if in spite of himself, drawn by the strong affection radiating from the English commander, Labianov murmured, "If I talk, they'll kill her."

"Who'll know you talked, since I promise you my silence?" Aberdeen went on insistently, "I'm not driven by idle curiosity. I sense in you some enormous sorrow, beyond human power to bear. I think that I—having been sent by my country to share the dangers of the expedition with you—would be doing less than my job if I didn't share all the dangers. Any peril that threatens the head of an army hangs over the entire army. That's why I'm not asking you to tell me your secret, I'm saying I have a right to know it: tell me."

Labianov was visibly struggling within himself, but the other's calm energy had made a strong impression on him. Aberdeen seemed like an indispensable ally, and more than that—a protector. Suddenly, with a gesture of surrender, he said, "You're right. I'll tell you what I've been hiding from everyone. This secret is buried in my heart. I feel like it'll make it burst. Open your heart to receive half of it."

They sat together at the table, with their elbows on the map of Central Asia, which they appeared to be studying. Very quietly, in a murmur that barely reached Aberdeen's ears, Labianov began, "There exists in Asia a mighty and unknown power, the Blue Flag."

"The Blue Flag!" exclaimed Aberdeen, "So it really exists?"

"Alas!"

"I heard mention of it, a few months ago in Europe, at the time of the committal..." The Englishman stopped abruptly, embarrassed.

But the Russian finished his sentence. "At the time of the committal to the Elleviousse Asylum, near Marseilles, of my daughter Mona and her companion, the Duchess of La Roche-Sonnaille."

"Yes," stammered Aberdeen, clearly sorry to have awakened that painful memory.

But his concern quickly changed to surprise when Labianov went on, "They were considered to be insane, especially because they spoke of the unbridled might of the Blue Flag. The concept of powerful Asian organizations is difficult for Westerners to accept, but I myself am sure they were telling the truth."

"You?"

"And you'll soon share my point of view." Labianov let out a long sigh, then went on in a voice trembling with emotion, "You'll remember that at the last Peace Conference held at The Hague I represented the Russian government and Admiral Count Asaki was the Japanese delegate."

"Yes, of course."

"Asaki recently informed me that a message, delivered to him by unknown means, told him of the death of his daughter Lotus Pearl. And I—I!—will be the cause of Mona's death." He brushed a hand across his brow. "But it's not about that. The father is no more. Here there can only be the general responsible for the lives of his men, with an urgent duty to teach you—his colleague, his partner in the most dangerous of adventures—what enemy we're going to face." Then, as if relieved by that stern summons to duty, he went on, "The Blue Flag is not a myth. At the Conference, both Asaki and I were given orders from our respective governments to obey without hesitation any instructions we received under that name."

"What! You had to obey?"

"We had to. At the memorable session in which we both voted against the Anglo-French proposals—which were so humane, so elevated by the conscience of two great nations—a single incident, thought to be trivial, caused our negative votes."

"An incident?" asked Aberdeen curiously.

"Yes. A small balloon floated down from the dome of the conference hall. People thought it was a child's toy. Wrong. At the stern of the gondola of the little balloon flew a blue flag with two golden symbols. Those symbols commanded us to vote no."

"What, that object?..."

"Revealed the astonishing variety of means available to those whose sign is the blue flag. At that very moment, my child and Count Asaki's child were both kidnapped. A message, delivered to our hotel by an unknown driver, informed us of what had happened and ended with this threat:

If you obey my orders, wealth and honors await you. I don't wish to contemplate any other possibility for you. I have hostages, whose lives depend on your submission."

"Wretches!" growled Aberdeen.

"Since that day—and incidentally with the support of our governments—Count Asaki and I have served the pleasure of the Blue Flag. At its orders, we crossed Asia to reach the German concession at Kiautschou Bay, where we were allowed to embrace our children once again. Then we were told to leave by sea. Months went by. No news, nothing. Mona is my only child. She was my light, my life. Neglecting the most pressing business, I wandered across the world, looking, always looking for her.

"One day, in Nagasaki, where I was grieving with Asaki—as defeated and despairing as I was—we happened to see a newspaper from French Tonkin. It reported a bandit attack at the Kilua Pass, and the detonation of underground mines planted in anticipation of such an event. What did that matter to me? One word in the article jumped out at me like a flash: Mona! My daughter Mona was in Haiphong, near death, being nursed by Madame de La Roche-Sonnaille—someone previously unknown to me. Not a word about Miss Asaki.

"Still, the count sailed with me. We reached Tonkin too late: Mona and her companion had disappeared. It was assumed they'd gone back to Europe. New mysteries! New confusions! Then, incredible news: the poor women were in prison in Calcutta, on a charge of banditry."

"Banditry?" echoed Aberdeen, completely stunned.

"Yes—my daughter, a bandit! How? Why? I have no idea. Still with Asaki, I went to India. Again too late. In spite of all the security measures in place, the prisoners had escaped. No trace, nothing. At random, following false leads, fooled by misidentifications and garbled messages, we went as far as Bombay in search of our beloved girls, without finding them. We returned to Calcutta. We went to book passage—and at the shipping agency office we learned that six days earlier Mona and the duchess had sailed on the *Oxus*, a steamer of the Messageries Maritimes line bound for Marseilles."

"So they weren't considered bandits anymore?"

Labianov raised his arms in a gesture of discouragement. "What do I know? Can I understand the incomprehensible? We didn't ask pointless questions. Asaki and I got onto the first steamer going. We'd catch up with them in the end! Oh, that slow passage across the Indian Ocean and the Red Sea! We reached Port Said. There, a slight engine problem meant a thirty-six hour stop. We disembarked. You know Port Said, that English town sprung up on Egyptian soil. We wandered slowly, with the bored stroll of travelers just killing time. A quarrel between some *fellahin* blocked our way. Other *fellahin* surrounded them, egging them on, making a deafening racket. Count Asaki and I got separated. A cloth hood was thrown over my head, blinding me. Twenty hands seized me and pushed me into a sedan chair. Bound, half smothered, I couldn't move. I felt I was being carried. Where? Why? Finally I was removed from my prison and my ropes were taken off.

"I was facing a delightful Egyptian villa, in a pleasant garden. Servants hastened to do my bidding. But they refused to answer my questions. I was a prisoner. Whose? For what reason? Weeks, months went by without my learning anything to solve the mystery. My servant-jailers never let down their guard. I became sadly convinced that I would only regain my freedom if my unknown persecutor felt like it—and I despaired at the thought that he might never want to."

"Astonishing," murmured Aberdeen.

Labianov went on as if he hadn't heard. "One morning my head servant told me I was free—if I agreed to the Master's conditions. I was stunned by this sudden change in my circumstances. I asked, 'What Master?' The man replied, 'Of the Blue Flag.'"

"By the devil!" cried Aberdeen. "That blue dishrag again!"

"Yes, again."

"So it's everywhere—at The Hague, in Asia, in Egypt!"

"It's everywhere," repeated Labianov gloomily. "It hasn't lost sight of me for a second, and it's unknown to me."

A silence followed. Aberdeen asked no further questions. Frowning, his face tense from the effort of thinking, he seemed to be drawing together all the elements of the strange puzzle distilled in those three apparently harmless words: the Blue Flag. Finally, with a gesture of impatience, he said firmly, "And the conditions of your freedom?"

Labianov shrugged. "It was to share them with you that I began this long account. Here's what I was told: 'While you've been held captive here, Miss Mona Labianov was committed for insanity. What her companion, the Duchess of La Roche-Sonnaille, was saying could have harmed the Blue Flag, about which the two women had learned certain details. The Master didn't want you or Count Asaki to be able to confirm some of the duchess's allegations. Now the captives are free, and—without knowing it—have fallen back into the Master's hands. So there's no reason why you shouldn't go free. The Master sets only one condition: you'll go to St. Petersburg, and you'll ask to be given command of an expedition now being organized in Asia. You'll receive it—because the Master wants it that way. Not one word about your captivity here will cross your lips. Once you're in charge of the gathering military force, you'll cause the campaign to fail.'"

"Oh!" cried Aberdeen. "That's a suggestion unworthy of a gentleman, un-worthy of an officer! I assume you refused?"

Labianov shook his head sadly. "Wait. The messenger of the Blue Flag added, 'As of this moment, death hangs over your daughter Mona—a slow, hor-rible death accompanied by unspeakable tortures. Obey and she'll live. Try to shake off our yoke, and you'll condemn her to death.'"

Aberdeen's cheeks trembled. He understood his colleague's terrible moral suffering, but he kept silent. What words could assuage such misery?

Labianov went on, "I accepted. I thought tricking that elusive Master might lead to some chance of unmasking him. I accepted. I refused to explain my ab-sence. And today..." He paused for a moment, then went on with an effort, "To-day I've entrusted the whole truth to your sense of honor. I beg you, my lord, watch over me—keep the father from winning out over the officer." He spoke in a shaking, broken voice, with his hands stretched out in ardent prayer.

Aberdeen took him in his arms. "Dear me! My good friend. We were al-ready allies. Now we're becoming one spirit in two bodies. Yes, I'll watch over you. And if there's some decisive order to give—by Heaven!—even if I have to face all the demons in Hell, I'll arrange to take full responsibility."

"No, no, not that," stammered Labianov.

"Yes indeed, and with pleasure. There's no reason to thank me. I'm just doing my duty as an officer, that's all. I'm risking my life for my country. As for you—you're being drawn and quartered, between military duty and a father's love. If those villains kill your dear child, at least it won't be you who gave the order that led to her death."

Instinctively, in this awful situation, Aberdeen had offered the only relief possible. By God, these men, isolated in the middle of Asia, would stoically do every part of their duty. No doubt the father would lose his daughter—but he wouldn't have to face the monstrous dilemma: to betray his flag or to set in motion Mona's torture.

While they stood there, pale and not yet recovered from the poignant emotions of their conversation, there was a quiet knock at the door.

"Sit down, general," said Aberdeen softly. "Study the map, to hide the look on your face." Once Labianov had done so, Aberdeen called out, "Come in!"

The aeronautic officers entered the room. They'd come to report on the results of their ascensions in the tethered balloons. They'd fully mapped out the route the expedition should follow the next day. They'd seen nothing suspicious from their gondolas. They'd noticed only a small caravan crossing a distant plain—an insignificant group, with a few yaks carrying loads, and half a dozen people.

When they'd finished their report, Lord Aberdeen was about to dismiss them, when the Russian officer, Captain Babarin, turned to Labianov and said, "General, as we were crossing the camp, one of those Buryat merchants who sell victuals to our men asked me to give you a letter he assured me would be 'certain to interest you.' I didn't think I should refuse: out on campaign, any information can come in handy. Here's the letter."

He handed his commander a letter folded inside a silk envelope. Labianov took it and opened it. But no sooner had he glanced at it than he turned terribly pale. Without a word, he handed it to Lord Aberdeen, who read the laconic contents with deep astonishment:

First warning: The travelers observed by the balloonists are escorting Miss Labianov, who is going unwittingly to the place where the Master has decided she will go. It is impossible for you to catch up with her, because the trails are now closed. *Every step forward will take you further from her. Every step forward will bring the black-winged angel of death closer to her.*

That was all. Aberdeen stood dazed for a moment. Urgent questions rushed into his mind. How had the mysterious enemy boldly entered the camp? How could he know what the balloonists had seen? What could it mean that the trails were now closed—words that were underlined in the strange letter? Pulling himself together, he turned to the officers. "Which one of you spotted the caravan in the distance?"

"We both saw it, each from our own vantage point," they answered without hesitating.

"All right. Who was in the balloon with you, Captain Follett?"

"My usual crew."

"No strangers?"

"None. In a situation like this it would be foolish!"

"And you, Babarin?"

"The same. My balloon crew and no one else."

"Let's move on. When you came down, you conferred together."

"In low voices, general, while we headed here, so as not to keep you waiting for your report."

"You didn't notice a spy—or spies—watching you?"

"No."

"What about the man who gave you the letter, Babarin?"

"He approached me before I'd even met up with Captain Follett."

"Oh!" exclaimed Aberdeen involuntarily. He'd assumed that the unknown writer had overheard the two aeronautic officers talking, and now he realized that wasn't it. One last resource remained: to question the Buryat himself. "Would you recognize the man, Babarin?"

"Certainly, general."

"Go find him and bring him here." Before the officers got to the door he added, "Above all, be discreet. We're in the land of spies. The earth, the water, the sky, all have ears."

When the two generals were alone Aberdeen muttered, "By St. George, that rascal will give us the answer to the puzzle or else..."

"Don't threaten him," interrupted Labianov sadly. "A threat you can't carry out is pointless."

"Why's that?"

"Because by now that man is surely out of our reach."

Just as Aberdeen, exasperated by those disheartened words, had launched into an endless explanation to convince his colleague he was wrong, there was an impatient knock on the door. "Devil take it—come in!" he grumbled, beside himself.

Babarin entered, looking sheepish and worried. "General, the Buryat can't be found, he's vanished, nobody saw him leave."

"This is too much!"

The aeronaut mopped the sweat from his brow. Eyes half shut, with the desperate courage of a man falling into an abyss, he said, "What's too much is, at the same spot where I met him..."

"Spit it out, by God!"

"This note was attached to a stick planted in the ground."

Aberdeen stamped his foot. "A note! Another note! But this one's not sealed."

"Right, General, so I was able to read it."

"Go on—since you've sworn to drive me crazy with your unfinished sentences!"

"Here it is, General."

And in a muffled voice Babarin groaned:

"Look for the bird in the highest of skies, look for the fish in the deepest of seas. They'll be easier to find than the messenger of he who must be obeyed."

CHAPTER II
Those Whom the Aeronauts Spotted

"You seem to be sunk in sad thoughts, Monsieur Soleil."

Max gave a melancholy smile. "I am, in fact."

Those brief words rang out like a lament in the great felt tent. Violet, Max, Sara, Mona, and Sir John were gathered around a fire, whose smoke was drawn up a pipe of fireproof canvas and taken outside. After the day's march the little group was encamped in a mountain hollow. Outside it was intensely cold—minus 18 degrees.[30] There was not a sound, not the slightest breeze. The twinkling stars seemed to be shivering in the pitch-black sky. The ground was bare—not a bush, not a blade of grass—just sharp boulders and shattered rocks, their sharp edges harshly lit by the moon, which looked like a plate of ice, a monstrous frozen disc following its infinite course.

A few paces away from the travelers' tent, a smaller tent held four natives: the guides and yak drivers. Those long-haired cattle were the beasts of burden on the High Plateaus, the bearers of supplies and military paraphernalia.

From time to time one of the people in the big tent said a few words, less to express a thought than to throw a spark of life into that mute, sepulchral night.

It was Violet who'd just addressed Max. He passed a hand across his brow as if to drive away a painful thought. Instead of answering the question directly, he looked at Violet with feeling and said firmly, "Let's sleep. Let's conserve our strength, because we don't know what trials we'll face tomorrow."

She shut her eyes obediently. Nothing more could be heard beneath the felt tent but the travelers' breathing, and every now and then the crackling of the fire...

Ish! Evo!... Yashmi! Evo! Evo!

They all woke with a start, sat up, and stretched their sleepy limbs.

The cries of the yak drivers announced the dawn, and the coming start of the march. That was how they addressed the cattle of the High Plateaus while they loaded the animals' sturdy backs with the travelers' luggage.

Fragrant smoke filled the tent: the steaming tea brought by the guide, the tea that would drive away the morning chill. The guide was a tall, lean sharp-featured young fellow with a dark face accented by black eyes.

"What's the weather?" asked Sara.

"Dry, noble lady. Sunny and clear skies."

---

[30] About zero degrees Farenheit.

She smiled. They all sipped their fragrant tea, whose heat filled them and relaxed their muscles. Then they bundled up in their furs, leaving nothing but their eyes and the tips of their noses exposed to the air.

At a curt summons from the guide, the three herdsmen, sturdy mountain peasants, came forward, took down the felt tent, rolled up its walls, and piled them onto the yak assigned to carry them.

"Where's Leddin?"

They all looked at each other. Leddin was the guide. He'd been there a moment earlier; now he'd vanished. But one of the mountain men pointed up the slope above the hollow at the bottom of which they'd made camp. Leddin was standing on the ridge, outlined against the sky. What was he doing? He was staring west, as if enormously interested in some sight invisible to the rest of them. Certainly in any town or populated area his posture would arouse no notice; but here, in the midst of a mountain wilderness, what could possibly have attracted his attention?

With a mix of curiosity and concern, Max set off up the slope, followed by the others. Leddin heard their footsteps on the hard ground. He turned, motioned to them to hurry, and cried, "Sky ship! Sky ship!"

They responded with exclamations of surprise. A sky ship! They all understood. That was what this native called a balloon. He must be dreaming. How could a balloon possibly be aloft in this desolate region? They reached him, looked in the direction he was pointing, and stood silent and stunned. In the distance they could see not one but two balloons standing out against the pale blue of the sky.

"My word—two military balloons... and even tethered. Two reconnaissance balloons." Max turned to the guide. "Are there troops in the area?"

Leddin nodded. "Many soldiers. Their tents cover the shores of Lake Balkhash."

"So, an army?"

"Yes, *Hinglizé* and *Urusk*."[31]

Max gave a start. "You say there are English and Russians there?"

"I say so. You heard right."

"But that's not possible."

The native's face grew serious. "Leddin speaks nothing but truth. He's surprised that you, lord, who have come across the lowlands,[32] didn't hear tell of the expedition mounted by the English and the Russians."

They all listened with their mouths agape. They couldn't explain to their guide that they'd come this far by way of the least busy roads, avoiding towns and major villages, with the aim of eluding the spies of the Blue Flag, whose

---

[31] English and Russian [*Note from the Author*].

[32] The plains of Turkestan [*Note from the Author*].

power they knew well. Expressing the anxiety they all felt, Max asked, "What's the expedition for?"

Leddin gestured vaguely. "I don't know exactly. Some bandits hiding in the Celestial Mountains."

None of them could suppress a start of surprise. Bandits in the Celestial Mountains—it must be their enemies, those from whose clutches they intended to rescue Dodekhan and the Duke of La Roche-Sonnaille. And now an Anglo-Russian army was in the field against those fanatics. They remained suspended, unsure whether to rejoice at or worry about the unexpected competition. Contradictory thoughts collided in their minds. Perhaps this army would draw all of the attention of the followers of the Blue Flag, and make it easier for they themselves to reach their goal. But perhaps instead it would make the vile jailers holding Sara's and Mona's loved ones redouble their precautions.

The travelers' faces cleared and clouded in turn, while—without their noticing—Leddin studied them with his piercing eyes.

Suddenly a gentle voice arose; Mona spoke as if in a dream. "My father is in command there. I see him. Let's go to him. Our reunion will lead to the salvation of all." She stood very straight, as if frozen in a posture of ecstasy. Her big blue eyes stared into space, seeming to read the future beyond the veil formed by the vault of the sky. Again she said gently, "Let's go to him."

They all hesitated, undecided, until Sara, following a sudden impulse, said, "She's right. Up to now our enemies' power has been challenged only by weak, defenseless foes. That power will shatter against a brave, battle-hardened army, led by a father in search of his daughter."

"My word, I agree," said Violet. With a smile she added, "Let's start marching toward them—because I feel the cold creeping into my bones here!"

No one saw the ironic smile that flashed momentarily across the guide's lips—an expression too brief to be noticed.

They all spoke up happily, as hope kindled their spirits. The guide clicked his tongue to give the signal to start, and the yak drivers encouraged their beasts with guttural calls. The young women declined to mount their saddled yaks, preferring to walk. The day's hike would feel easy, because at the end of it they'd find an army of protectors.

But after the little caravan had advanced for quite some time, climbing hill after hill, around them they found high slopes that hid the horizon. The balloons had disappeared, and in no direction could they see any sign of the Anglo-Russian army. Now the guide seemed worried, hesitant. He went right, then left, climbed rocky heights, studied the horizon, then came back to the caravan with an ill-humored look. Occasionally he shot a cunning glance at the Europeans. It was if he were disappointed that no one questioned him about the reasons for his odd behavior. But Sara was chatting with Violet, Mona and Max were both daydreaming, and Sir John chewed on a cigar while cursing the hills and the cold that forced him to wear the heavy furs that were stifling him.

Finally the guide seemed to come to a decision. Putting on a hypocritically sad face, he approached Max. "Lord," he said in a low voice.

"Huh? What is it?" said Max, as he was pulled suddenly out his dreaming.

The native gestured to him make no noise. "Sahib! We mustn't worry the noble ladies."

"Worry them? Why?"

The guide's embarrassment grew more pronounced. "Lord, I have a confession. I no longer know where I'm going." He was whispering.

Max looked at him in surprise. "All right," he said carelessly. "In country like this it could happy to anyone. Look for the trail…"

Leddin interrupted, "I've been looking for it for two hours. The Evil Spirits must've rearranged the mountains, because I recognize nothing. The peaks that surround us are unknown to me." Humbly, bending low before Max, he went on, "Lord, I don't know where we are. Lord, I dare not take it upon myself to lead you in any direction whatsoever."

The guide's voice shook with fear. Max realized that the situation was unusually serious. He grabbed Leddin by the wrist and said through clenched teeth, "A person finds his way again when he wants to." The man shook his head. "Come on, pull yourself together," insisted Max. "I'll call a halt for lunch. While we eat, you go explore the area without sharing your fears with anyone."

"I obey."

And while the travelers and the herdsmen ate, Leddin wandered away. He returned an hour later. Max hastened to meet him, but his anxious question froze on his lips: everything about the guide conveyed utter discouragement. He stretched out his arms and said in a dull voice, "The Evil Spirits are against us." Seeing Max's gesture of impatience, he babbled on, "They've struck me with blindness, lord—or else the landscape has suddenly been changed. Views familiar to me have disappeared and been replaced by others I've never seen. Peaks now rise where I swear there used to be hollows. Further away, the summits have collapsed into valleys."

Max stamped his foot. "You've gone mad!"

But Leddin protested forcefully, "That would be better for you, better for all those who are with us: my madness would affect only me. Alas! My mind is clear. It's not my reason that's vanished, it's the trail that would've led us out of these accursed mountains."

"The trail?" Max began to laugh. "By God, the rascal's drunk too much from his flask of *arak*![33] This proves it beyond doubt! The trail vanished! Why didn't I notice the villain's condition before?"

As he spoke, Max studied the guide's face. What he saw there didn't reassure him. Nothing in Leddin's expression, nothing in his body language, suggested drunkenness. He seemed to be gripped by terror, but his eyes were clear,

---

[33] Local liquor [*Note from the Author*].

and solemnly, reproachfully, he answered, "I drank nothing but tea this morning. My flask is packed in my luggage." Then he went on in a quieter, almost muffled tone, "You're laughing, lord, you're laughing because you don't know the mountains. Those of us born here were taught the dangers by our fathers." He lowered his voice still further. "Every family has lost someone to the Spirits of the Heights. In our poor villages every hut preserves the memory of some ancestor who was never found, because the paths leading to him were erased by the gilds."[34]

Max wasn't a man given to such superstitions. His fingers tightened around the guide's elbow. "Enough of your nonsense," he said harshly. "All right, we're lost. But we know we'll meet the soldiers if we go west. Let's head that way, and we'll get out of the mountains."

"If the gilds allow it. The mountain trails wind. They have many whims. They lead where the slopes wish, and not where the traveler wants to go."

"In any case, we have to try."

"We'll try, lord."

"And keep in mind, Leddin, my revolver is closer to you than the spirits you're worrying about."

That threat only made the guide shrug. "You're unfair, lord. You mistrust a poor man who'd be saved by finding the trail as much as you would."

"Anyway, eat, and then go back to guiding us."

"I'll do my best."

"Above all, keep silent. No need to worry everyone with your imaginary fears."

"I'll be quiet, lord, since you order it."

And Leddin mingled with the other mountain men but took no part in their conversation. He ate somberly, his face calm again. Max, watching him from a distance, gave him a look of encouragement. He couldn't know that at that very moment, behind Leddin's unmoving expression, lay a thought full of menace: "The Master doesn't want you to join the European soldiers. What is your revolver compared to the Master's wishes?"

A few minutes later he came to Max and announced that he was ready to go on. The little caravan soon moved on from its temporary stop. Max walked at the front, next to the guide. Leddin had told the truth: it was impossible to maintain one steady bearing. Piles of boulders, yawning crevasses, ravines that had to be crossed, continually forced the travelers to make confusing detours—after which Max realized with amazement, with annoyance, with growing concern, that they'd advanced not an inch to the west. The mountain truly seemed to be laughing at the struggles of the little group of creatures wandering across its flanks.

---

[34] Genies. This is a common belief among the widely scattered natives of the High Plateaus of Central Asia [*Note from the Author*].

He scolded Leddin, "Search! Search! We have to find the trail to freedom." He criticized the guide's choice of one route or another around an obstacle. He wanted to lead the way himself. Then, when the native submissively, fatalistically followed his orders, he objected that Leddin didn't argue for or defend his own opinions.

The answer he got was always the same: "It doesn't matter which way we go. We'll find death at the end of it, if that's what the *gilds* have decided."

Those words steeped in resignation dug into Max's skull like claws. He tried to make Leddin forget his impatient reproaches. For a few hundred meters he let him go anywhere he wanted. But the calm never lasted.

A few times the ladies had called Max back to them to ask him the banal questions dear to all tourists:

"Will we be there soon?"

"How far are we from the Anglo-Russian troops?"

"Will we reach them before nightfall?"

And then, with an anxious heart, he forced himself to smile while he tossed out some vague answer to keep from worrying them.

Something the duchess said added to his distress. Sara had come to a dead stop in front of three monoliths that stood at the edge of an escarpment like the points of a trident. "Look at that," she said. "I feel like I recognize those rocks. We already passed them earlier."

She had to be right. Max thought he too recognized those granite points. But Leddin told him he was the victim of an illusion. "The landscape of the High Plateaus often looks alike. Rocks of the same kind, exposed to the same climate, erode in the same way, resulting in similar shapes." To Max alone he added in a low voice, "It's one of the many traps in the mountains. Sometimes you think you're returning to a place where in fact you've never been; sometimes you think the reverse. That's how the *gilds* amuse themselves—by disturbing the minds of those they've condemned."

Once his attention had been drawn to the idea, Max soon noticed that indeed the same scenery recurred constantly.[35] As if those highlands—without vegetation, without water, where the air was thin, where frost reigned supreme—weren't barren enough... Nature, in a surfeit of cruelty, wanted hardy explorers of the icy desert to experience the deceptive, discouraging, apparent certainty that they'd marched all day without getting anywhere.

At dawn you set off from some peak. By dint of superhuman effort and unspeakable fatigue, you made your way down into a dark valley and then climbed the opposite slopes. At dusk you reached the summit toward which you'd been working all day. There, your delight in your progress, your triumph at the chal-

---

[35] That phenomenon has been observed by all explorers in the High Plateaus, among them Gabriel Bonvalot and Prince Henri d'Orléans [*Note from the Author*].

lenges overcome—all of it evaporated, vanished, the moment you looked around. You'd think you were in the same place you'd started from: the same ground cracked by frost, the same drab gray colors, the same shapes in the terrain, the same peaks closing off the horizon. You'd walked, climbed, leapt all day long—only to drag along with you the landscape you started with.

The sun sinking into the west still lit up the peaks, but from the valley bottoms twilight rose, like a dark mist, heralding the night. They'd have to stop and put up the tents, because with darkness the cold would intensify to the point of being intolerable. Hearing Leddin explain that, Max found nothing to say. An unshakeable sadness weighed on him. He realized he was in one of those situations where vitality, courage, willpower collided with the impossible. You couldn't fight against emptiness, the void. With a weary gesture he accepted the guide's suggestion.

Leddin pointed out a bowl-shaped hollow below them. "Down there we'll be sheltered from the wind."

Max nodded, and the native started down the slope. Max followed him automatically. Suddenly he was pulled out of his thoughts by hearing exclamations. He looked around. The other travelers and the herdsmen were bent over, examining the ground and calling out to each other with gestures of surprise. He vaguely heard them saying, "Here are yak hoof prints... holes made by tent pegs... ashes from the fire..."

Trying to understand, he went closer. Violet turned to him. With the cheerful manner of someone not at all concerned by the circumstances, she said, "Oh, what a priceless guide you are! We've gone in a circle and come back to the camp we left this morning!" Unaware of any danger, she went on jokingly, "I won't let it annoy me—but I think you'll have to do a splendid job of leading us tomorrow to make us forget about today!" With a smile she shook her finger at him.

Were the mountain men now busy putting up the felt tents filled with memories of the legendary tales of the mountains? Had they been prompted to remember them by some indiscreet word from the guide? Who knows. But suddenly they stopped working and with expressions of terror they threw themselves face down on the ground, mumbling supplications to the *gilds*, the *veneks*, the *tralzhies*—all the mysterious hobgoblins with which the local collective imagination peopled the High Plateaus.

Taken by surprise, Sara, Violet, and Sir John asked what was going on. The truth couldn't be concealed any longer. Summoning all of his willpower, Max explained—but, oh, softening it, hiding his own fears under a lighthearted tone. "Just a little nuisance, a few hours' delay. We'll straighten it all out tomorrow. The natives are terrified by superstitions that are beyond us."

Leddin backed him up. The guide seemed to have recovered his cool, and Max was grateful to him for sparing the other travelers the anxiety he himself felt.

So, once the tents were finally up and the fires were lit, they dined cheerfully. The young women laughed about the adventure. After all, when you traveled from France to the heart of Asia, you couldn't expect it all to go without a hitch! Tomorrow they'd make up the time they'd lost today. The Anglo-Russian army was on the march and getting closer. So they'd have less far to go to meet them. In short, with the help of hot tea, the evening passed pleasantly, and toward eleven they all sank into the deep sleep of people who'd spent all day trekking in the mountains.

In the middle of the night Max sat up. It seemed to him that some unexpected sound had reached his ears while he slept. But he must've been mistaken, because now, thought he listened hard, he heard nothing but the bleak wilderness silence of the plateau. Relieved, he lay back down on his felt mat, scolding himself for his fanciful fears. And, since he was worn out physically and mentally, and overcome by the lethargy that strikes the exhausted, he soon fell back asleep.

An unpleasant feeling woke him again. He was cold. He felt like his limbs were encased in ice. With a violent effort he managed to throw off sleep and sit up. This time he wasn't dreaming: the fire was out, and the breath of his still-sleeping companions fell back down as snow. "Our servants forgot to tend the fire," he grumbled. But then further reflection made him more tolerant. "After all, the poor devils must've been as tired as we were by that pointless march. But the fire's got to be relit, and fast, otherwise we'll turn into ice cubes."

He went to the flap of felt that served as the door. Raising it, he was dazzled for a moment. "Daylight."

Yes, it was broad daylight. A mournful gray light, wearying to the eyes, fell from low clouds that had covered the sky during the night. Why hadn't the mountain men given the signal to awake yet? Max looked around curiously for the answer—and suddenly a new observation sent his thoughts in a different direction. "Snow!"

It had snowed in the night. The peaks and slopes were all white. The landscape had changed completely. No more sharp rocky crags. Delicate snow crystals coated everything, softening angles, rounding points. Hard lines had become strangely blurred.

"The trail!" he said to himself. "How will we find the trail under this blanket of white?" He'd spoken out loud. His own voice sounded muffled, dulled. He shivered. One more enemy had joined the drama: the snow that hid the trail, the snow that trapped the caravan once and for all in the mountains and shattered the lost travelers' last hope. "But where are Leddin, and the herdsmen, and the yaks?" The Europeans' tent stood all by itself at the bottom of the bowl where they'd made camp. The servants' tent and all the animals had disappeared.

Max leapt outside. He looked around. He climbed a slope and got up to the ridge. Nothing—he could see nothing. As far as his eye could reach, all the peaks were covered in the same immaculate shroud. All was frozen, silent, still.

No sign of movement or life. A chill gripped his heart. It was clear now: no doubt driven by their superstitious fears, the natives had fled in the night, abandoning the travelers who—from their ignorant point of view—must've aroused the wrath of the *gilds*. And, being thieves like all of their kind, they'd taken the yaks, the luggage, the provisions. Hunger would add to the cold and doom the unlucky travelers whose noble devotion had led them to this desolate plateau. Max stood there, his feet in the snow, overwhelmed by this trick of fate. Why go back to the tent, since he'd only bring despair with him?

A familiar voice interrupted his thoughts. "What are you up to? Were you going to build a snowman?"

He started violently. It was Violet's voice. The tent flap was lifted partway, and her sweet face was framed in the opening. "It's awfully cold," she went on. "Have them quickly bring us some tea, and come back inside. It makes me shiver to see you out there."

The flap of felt dropped; Violet was gone. And Max stood there, tottering, distraught. Tea! She'd asked for tea! Was there any left? Oh yes, in the tent there was one partly used box. For a few more hours that fragrant beverage would allow them to fight off the freezing temperatures.

Onward: the ultimate struggle had begun! Max owed it to his friends—and to himself—to fight to the very end. He braced himself and got himself under control, and with a firm step he went back to the tent. His arrival caused some surprise—he was so pale, and his eyes were filled with such a desperate resolve that they all stood still where they were. In the anxious silence he said, "My friends, we have only a few hours before us; either we reach the army or we die."

"What are you saying?" they all whispered in fear.

"I'm saying what's unfortunately all too clear. Our guide and our servants abandoned us in the night, taking the animals and the luggage with them."

"The wretches!" shrieked Sir John. "England will avenge this with resounding..."

"England will never know of the death of a few travelers lost on the High Plateaus, their trail hidden under the snow," answered Max sadly. Then he went on firmly, "We have a little firewood, some tea, some biscuits. Let's relight the fire, gather our strength, and form a plan, so as to make the best possible use of the few hours we most likely have left to live."

Sara, who was a little pale but whose movements were firm and decisive, had already relit the fire. Violet set about preparing the tea. While the kettle sang softly over the flickering flames, the unfortunate party lost in a desert of snow held a thoughtful discussion. Max had a small compass, thanks to which he'd do his best to guide his companions west, toward Lake Balkhash. Their salvation lay in reaching the low plains in which the lake rested. Of course, its marshy shores were sparsely settled, but there'd be a few families of fishermen. There they'd find rescue, food, and probably a guide to lead them toward the Anglo-Russian army.

When the tea was poured they all drank some of that strengthening beverage. Then they took down the tent and divided it into its sections, which they distributed among them. Carrying them, the little band set off, led by Max, who checked his compass frequently.

Alas! He soon realized it was impossible to maintain a constant course. It was as if giants had heaped up obstacles in the night. Over and over, piles of loose rock and impassable chasms barred their way, forcing them to make endless detours. With angry despair Max could see that in spite of all his efforts he was constantly being forced east—away from the direction he wanted to go. There was no need for him to express his disappointment aloud: the frown on his face was enough to make the anxiety that filled him clear to his companions.

And that anxiety changed to dejection when, after several hours of walking, they climbed a relatively gently slope and reached a ridge... from which they looked down into the bowl they'd left that morning. Unconsciously, against their will, by detouring around the obstacles placed in their way, they'd made a full circle and come back to their starting point. They stared at each other, stunned, with an almost crazed look in their eyes. Reason faltered before the hostility of things. The same thought ran through their minds, a memory of the bedtime stories common to all of humanity: the mountains held them prisoner, they were trapped inside a ring of cliffs, and they remembered the treacherous magic spells of legend.

The sun was reaching its noonday zenith. Its pale rays warmed the baffled group a little. Finally, in a blank, dull voice, Max said, "One hour's rest. Then we'll try our luck again."

His words sank into the silence. The others took off their loads and let themselves drop to the ground, where they lay motionless. Max walked a little distance away and seemed to be absorbed in studying the surrounding land. Was he looking at the peaks that stretched as far as the eye could see, and between which chasms could be made out? Or by separating himself like this was he just trying to hide his misery and keep from crying out in despair? He'd spoken of trying once more... but even before starting he thought it was pointless.

A few moments later they all set off. Oh, they'd keep going until their courage failed them. It had begun to snow again, and—pressing close together so as not to lose sight of each other—the poor travelers advanced through its fleecy swirls, using up their last strength in a battle against the elements. The struggle wasn't a question of will; it had become automatic, instinctive: like driven game, they frantically tried to outrun death.

And then suddenly a heartrending cry burst from their lips. For the third time, they'd returned to the hollow where they'd camped the night before. Their fate was sealed. They found themselves inexorably brought back here, to the place destiny seemed to have chosen for them to die. After that first involuntary, almost unwitting cry, there was a heavy silence. Crushed by the horror of their fate, the travelers could no longer even think.

Sir John murmured, "Night's coming. It's beginning to grow colder."

Max, dimly reminded of his job as guide, said listlessly, "Let's put up the tent."

No one objected. Instinct—the only thing they had left now—drew the poor wretches to hole up, to keep from seeing the bleak landscape, and to hide themselves from the sight of the invisible enemies they thought they could hear prowling around them. Ground down by fatigue, they were afraid of... whatever it is we sense around us in times of despair.

Soon the felt tent raised its dark cone on the snow, and like ironic onlookers the first stars twinkled in the sky. They sat back to back in a circle around the central pole holding up the fragile structure. With their knees under their chins, and their hands clutching their fur coats around them, they were motionless. Were they asleep? Yes and no. They were aware of a pleasant numbness that slowed their circulation and stilled their minds, replacing pain and anxiety with peaceful indifference.

Suddenly a violent commotion brought them all back to consciousness. As if they'd lost their balance, they all fell onto each other and grabbed hold of each other to regain stability. Voices called out feebly, "What's going on?"

The door flap opened and Max appeared.

"Where've you been?" they asked.

He answered quietly, "Didn't you hear it?" His voice resonated with some extraordinary emotion.

"Hear what?"

"The tiger roaring."

They were all stunned. "A tiger, at this elevation!"

It seemed crazy. That terrible cat lives in jungles as hot as an oven, but snowy peaks and glaciers hold no interest for it.

But Max went on, "I was as surprised as you are. Earlier, while I was fast asleep, I thought I heard a muffled roar. I loaded my revolver and went outside."

"And?"

"It's a clear night, and the snow outside shows the prints of..."

"A tiger!"

"Or some great cat. It circled the tent, then moved away, and pawed the ground at the foot of the slope above us. And there... there..." Max paused.

"Go on!"

"It exposed a stack of firewood and *argol*.[36] We can make a fire."

---

[36] Dried yak dung. The inhabitants of the High Plateaus of Central Asia collect *argol*, which provides almost the only fuel in those barren regions [*Note from the Author*].

"A fire!" They cried out with something close to joy. Hope never dies in the hearts of men, and the thought of crackling flames revived them all. They began impulsively rushing outside, in spite of Max's cautious warning, "Don't wander away. The tiger's certainly still prowling the area."

Oh, the tiger didn't concern them much! Only one idea could interest people who already felt the cold hand of death: making a fire, exposing their stiff limbs to its heat, feasting their eyes on its bright glow. And yet they could see that Max's description had been accurate. Very clear prints, still fresh, wound around the tent, then led toward the eastern slope of the natural bowl that sheltered their camp.

"By the devil," muttered Sir John, "if it isn't a tiger, it's at least a very large cat."

"A panther," said Sara quietly. Her tone of voice surprised her companions, who heard in it something strange and joyful.

"Yes, perhaps a panther; the size would be right. But whether panther or tiger, its presence here in the high mountains is inexplicable."

To their collective amazement, Sara murmured, "No, no, a panther would make more sense." And in response to their questioning looks and gestures she added, "Later. First let's build a fire—I'm freezing. And then... I'm not sure. The fire is more urgent. Then I'll share my thoughts."

With eyes and ears open, fearing the return of the terrible beast at any moment, they all hurried to gather up part of the fuel they'd found so miraculously. Ten minutes later a bright fire blazed and crackled and tossed sparks into the warm air of the tent.

The five travelers huddled around the flames, and Sara said quietly, "I've told you about the painful events that separated me from my husband, and robbed Mona of her reason. But I left four individuals out of my short account: two children and two panthers, four devoted creatures who would've saved us if it had been possible."

"Two children, two panthers?" echoed her listeners with obvious surprise.

"Yes, two abandoned children—of whom there are so many in the Chinese Empire: Tse and Pei, nicknamed by the Europeans Master Merry and Miss Twinkle. A little boy and a little girl, vagabonds without families, taken in by Dodekhan and utterly devoted to him and to everything and everyone dear to him."

"But the panthers?..."

"Were their companions. Two beautiful black panthers, Fred and Zizi, whom they'd tamed and who obeyed them with amazing intelligence. And earlier, the thought crossed my mind that..."

"One of those animals?..."

"Was prowling around us—yes, exactly. If so, their masters, my friends, can't be far away."

"You think?"

"I think nothing. I don't dare think it. But don't you find it strange that this fuel turned up so unexpectedly and conveniently?"

Sir John shook his head. "It could've been forgotten by the rascals who abandoned us."

"Sure, and yet that's not the side on which their tent stood. The yak corral was set up at the foot of the slope to the west."

"True! So you deduce that friends..."

"Are perhaps watching over us."

It would be impossible to express the effect her words had. It was like a distant beacon to travelers wandering blindly in the night. It was hope reborn, the will to live returning to those who'd already resigned themselves to death. Their questions overlapped, driving away sleep."What were those children like? Their looks? Their size?"

With rosy color returning to her cheeks, and a glow returning to her dulled eyes, Sara gently described the Chinese children as thirteen or fourteen years old, small and fragile, yet energetic, with sharp-featured faces and lively black eyes. She described their devotion, their courage, their untiring selflessness... Then she talked about the panthers, who were both messengers and bodyguards, who seemed to understand those Chinese urchins, and who seemed to be—in the words of the philosopher—"an extension of themselves."

The hours passed, and dawn came. The sky was clear of the clouds that had obscured it the day before. Its pale blue dome was gilded by the first light of the sun. And, though their stomachs felt the pinch of hunger, the travelers climbed out of the tent. Their own footprints were clear and sharp. And they hadn't dreamt it: the prints of some animal that walked on its toes were impressed in the snow, its digits and claws perfectly traced.

Max followed the prints, bent forward, his eyes glued to the ground. What was he looking for? Nothing—unless it was some detail to confirm Sara's reassuring theory and turn her hypothesis into certainty. While his companions gathered by the tent watched him, he reached the foot of the slope and climbed it, still following the prints in the snow. He reached the ridge. There he stopped dead, as if frozen in place. Two paces away he could now see a small stick planted in the ground. Its tip had been split with a knife, and a piece of paper had been wedged into that split. The adventure was becoming clearer: a human could now be deduced alongside the panther—which could not reasonably be credited with planting the mysterious stick.

But Max never let surprise delay action for long. With a quick motion he brushed aside his thoughts and bent down to grab the paper. A new surprise— three words had been scrawled on the paper, probably with a piece of charcoal: *Follow the tracks.*

The unknown protector was taking some kind of tangible form. For a moment Max stood there as if stunned, his heart pounding in his chest; then he cast a sharp look around, seeking signs of human presence. Whoever had brought that laconic note to this spot must necessarily have left prints in the snow. But he was disconcerted to see nothing. "Damn! Are the mysteries of the Loursinade villa going to start up again?" Then he scolded himself. "Calm down. It's impossible for the snow not to give away the presence of a person. Whether he used a sled or skis or snowshoes or any other means of traveling, he must've left a trail. That's obvious. So let's look."

But no matter how carefully he examined the ground nearby, he saw nothing that corroborated his reasoning. Unless the stranger had solved the problem of human flight, the mystery remained unsolved. "It's too much," he said to himself with annoyance. "If the duchess's theory is right, then the panther's companion must be some divine child, and that child found a way to hide his tracks! Come on, now. To uphold the honor of novelists, I have to find the answer." He looked back toward his companions, who were busy taking down the felt tent. "All right," he said to himself, "that gives me a few moments' peace..." But the words froze on his lips.

"Well, well!" he went on in a different tone. He'd bent down, and was studying the panther's prints with great care. "The animal stopped here, by the signpost. And beyond it I can see four parallel panther tracks, two coming this direction, two heading away. Why all the coming and going?"

He exclaimed again. "One set of prints going each way is much deeper than the other, as if the animal who made them was considerably heavier." He bent closer. "And yet there was only a single panther. One of the claws on its right front foot is broken. I can see the sign of that break on all four trails. One animal, sometimes lighter, sometimes heavier." He smiled. "I'm getting very warm—let's prove it."

He began to follow one of the trails where the prints were deeper. The panther's tracks went around a knoll. No sooner had Max gone behind it than he rubbed his hands with glee and said only, "Got it!" Over a circular area two feet in diameter, the snow had been cleared and thrown outside to form a ring-shaped bank. Deep prints showed that the panther had stopped there as well.

"Oh ho!" said Max. "Our sign-writer rides on panther-back—a fine sport. The duchess is right: it's one of those kids, Pei or Tse, who are thin and small and light. One of them could've gotten here on the animal's back, which couldn't have borne the weight of someone of average size and bulk. He rode his panther to the place where I found the note. Then he rode back here, got down, and cleared away the snow to hide his footprints—while his black-furred companion went off to surround our tent with tracks that were bound to get our attention. After which the beast came back to pick up its strange rider, and they both went away." He added thoughtfully, "In the middle of the night, at this elevation! That panther is awfully obedient, and the child has an astonishing resistance to cold."

218

With great strides he returned to his traveling companions. The tent was down, and its sections had been divided into loads they'd all already fastened to their backs. "What do you plan to do?" asked Max.

"Follow the tracks of the animal that prowled around us last night," said Sara firmly, "to get to wherever the messenger's gone."

"You think the panther was a messenger?"

"Yes, I do. Past experience helps me explain the present."

Max burst out laughing. "Well, duchess, the present explains itself all by itself!"

"Really?"

"Read the message I just found." He held out the paper for her to see, and said slowly, *"Follow the tracks."* A murmur greeted those words. "Yes," he went on, *"Follow the tracks.* The note says no more, but I think I can add, *and you'll be saved."*

He looked at Violet with infinite tenderness. She blushed a little, then said hesitantly, "We want to be saved. So let's go."

"Let's go," they all agreed.

And the little band, revived by hope, left the hollow where they'd expected to meet their death.

CHAPTER III
One Surprise After Another

"A wall of rock."

"Yes, but a wall with an opening. Here's the entrance to a cave, and the tracks continue inside it."

"Brrr! Go in there? It's pitch black!"

The travelers were holding this conversation before a reddish cliff that hinted at the presence of iron in the rock. For two hours they'd been following the panther's tracks, which had led them on a strange route. They'd had to climb rock falls, to squeeze through narrow breaks in the boulders, to trust themselves to ledges overhanging chasms. And during the tiring journey they'd all understood why they'd been unable to maintain a steady course the day before: they'd chosen the easiest-looking routes, whereas by contrast the animal who was guiding them now seemed to prefer the hardest. And they realized the effectiveness of that perverse choice, because now they were traveling almost directly east.

But now, before the dark hole boring into the cliff, they hesitated. What dangers might be hiding in the shadows of that cave? Only Mona seemed not to share her companions' fears. She stepped forward, plunged into the darkness, and vanished. Their hesitation ended abruptly, and they all hurried after her, bumping into the walls of the cave.

But then a brightness lit up the dark. The always practical Sir John had struck a match. They could all see Mona's figure in motion a few steps ahead of them. Noticing the light, she turned and waved them on. "Come on, come on. There are no obstacles, there's no danger."

From a purely logical point of view that didn't make sense. Yet no one hesitated. They followed her obediently, lighting a series of matches so as to keep from bumping too hard into the walls of the cave. In any case, they didn't have far to go. After barely five hundred meters the tunnel made a sharp turn. Max, walking right behind Mona, cried happily, "Daylight!"

Indeed, some distance ahead of them, but clearly visible, a spot of light stood out in the darkness. The tunnel must've been one of those mysterious passageways by which mountain people stayed connected, crossing the desolate heights with a speed and reliability that amazed explorers in those desolate regions. Outside they'd probably find the same barren, chaotic, snow-covered, ground—but at least they'd be in the always encouraging light. Max put the collective feeling into words with a witticism: "Life depends on light and heat. Since we'll find at least one of the two outside, we'll only be half dead."

So true were his words that his companions—who'd been without food for thirty-six hours in a harsh climate where the cold made substantial nourishment essential—still found the energy to laugh.

The light grew as they got nearer. Streaks of light reaching into the tunnel made the edges of the rocks sparkle. Unconsciously they all picked up their pace. They reached the opening and stood for a moment, blinded by the rays of a sun without warmth, then looked around—and let out a disappointed groan. The tunnel opened onto a rocky ledge, a few meters wide, beneath which the slope fell away abruptly, dropping with dizzying impassable steepness to a sheer-sided ravine whose bottom was hidden under piles of boulders, fragments of the mountain that had broken away over the centuries. They looked at each other. Their way seemed blocked. A great cat might've been able to leap from rock to rock... and even so... If Max and Sir John had been alone, they could've attempted the climb if forced to—but clearly it was out of the question for the ladies.

"Still," muttered Max, "if our invisible guide is a friend, he didn't make us leave our camp just to lead us to a dead end." He turned to his anxious companions, standing in the mouth of the tunnel—and in doing so he caught sight of something on the rocks around the opening that made him jump. "There! There!" He pointed to a rock on which an unknown hand had written in charcoal, *Ladder to reach upper cave.*

They all read the message with happy surprise. Their rescuer anticipated their needs and showed them their route. But before they could put their thoughts into words, a ladder of braided fibers unrolled down the rock slope, so that its bottom end brushed the ledge on which they stood. Their protector must be very close, only a few meters over their heads, since he alone could send them the ladder the message described.

Impulsively Sara called out, "Tse, Pei, Master Merry, Miss Twinkle, is that you?" Her voice echoed in the canyon, rising and dying away in faint reverberations, but no answer came to their ears. "They don't wish to—or can't—let themselves be seen," she murmured regretfully.

But, ignoring her emotion, Max said simply, "We have a way to reach them, so let's climb."

Easier said than done. They had to pull themselves up a sheer cliff overhanging a dreadful abyss. And yet Sara, always brave, volunteered to begin climbing; and Violet—as athletic as any true Englishwoman, and driven on by the notion that an Anglo-Saxon girl had to do what a French girl could do—followed her.

Soon after, both of them set foot in the mouth of another tunnel, about thirty feet above the first one. They called down to their companions to tell them they'd succeeded and to encourage them. So Max led Mona gently to the ladder, and climbing up behind her to support her, he managed without too much trouble to get her safely up to her friends. Then, leaning out of the opening, he called down, "Whenever you're ready, Sir John!"

Ah, he wasn't aware of the bitter irony of that "whenever you're ready," because the corpulent Sir John was by no means ready. While the others had

221

been climbing, his face, usually scarlet, had turned purple. He'd pulled out his handkerchief and mopped the stream of fearful sweat off his brow. No one had noticed. But now that Max had drawn attention to it, they were all aware of the Englishman's predicament.

Sir John called up piteously, "Is the ladder strong enough?"

"Of course."

"It's just that I weigh at least twice as much as the heaviest of you."

"We came up by twos. Come on, hurry, please. Benevolent friends are working to save us; we need to help them a little."

That argument must've struck Sir John, because he approached the ladder and took hold of its vertical ropes. But almost immediately he drew back, calling out in a voice so pitiful that in other circumstances it would've provoked laughter, "I can't!"

"At least try!"

"There's no point. I feel dizzy. I'd fall into the ravine."

Max mumbled an oath. Would that fat gentleman make them stop here? Because it must be acknowledged, to the travelers' credit, that none of them thought to abandon Sir John, though he'd proven himself to be a dangerous impediment. He was now sitting on a rock, whining—near tears—swearing by Satan's horns that he'd die there rather than hang like a spider from a thread.

Max burst out laughing. "A barrel-shaped spider in this case." Put at ease by his own joke, he started back down the ladder. "I'll go get him."

He climbed down to the ledge where Sir John still sat whining. Max shook him and pleaded with him. But in vain: the Englishman wouldn't move. Sprawled across his rock like a human dishrag, fear robbing him of any concern for his dignity, he said over and over in a pitiful voice, "What you're asking of me is impossible. My hands wouldn't have the strength to grip the ropes, nor my legs the strength to climb the rungs."

They couldn't stay in this barren spot forever. On the other hand, since Violet and Max were firmly resolved not to abandon Sir John—no matter what heartache his existence was going to cause them in the future—they somehow had to find a way to make him climb to the upper tunnel.

"Damn it!" growled Max. "This is like getting a hippopotamus down a fire-escape ladder!" Then he shrugged. "No, I'm wrong—the hippopotamus would be more willing!"

From above came voices calling, "Well?"

He looked up. Thirty feet overhead he could see Violet and Sara leaning out over the abyss, trying to find out what was keeping the two men. It made Max shiver to see them hanging over the void, into which the slightest false move would've plunged them. "Back up!" he called, his voice shaking with concern. "I'm going to tie Sir John to the ladder. Then I'll climb up, and together we'll try to haul him up."

But a wild bellow greeted his words. "Tie me! I won't! In the name of England I refuse!" protested Sir John, shaking with emotion at the thought of hanging down the sheer cliff overlooking the abyss.

But his timing was poor. Max's patience had come to an end. Sir John felt something cold against his temple. He opened his terrified eyes and saw that it was the barrel of Max's revolver. "On the ladder, now!"

There's nothing so persuasive as a firearm! Sir John suddenly regained the power to move. Even more, he discovered an unsuspected agility. In two leaps he was at the ladder and seated on the bottom rung with his hands clutching the vertical ropes. Stunned, upset, pitiful, ridiculous, he no longer resisted but obeyed passively.

"Cross your hands on the rung above your head," ordered Max.

Sir John did as he was told. Max used a belt to strap Sir John's wrists to the rung—not without digging into his flesh a little. That way the paunchy fellow was secured to the ladder, and if he couldn't hold on to it, it would hold on to him. Max added a brief warning. "Don't move, or I'll put a bullet in your brain—which'll cure you of vertigo forever."

While Sir John, dazed, pressed himself against the ladder as much as his rotundity allowed, Max climbed over his body. With the agility of a squirrel, he'd soon rejoined the young women, who sighed with relief when they saw him come back.

"And Sir John?' asked Violet.

"Tied to the ladder. And since he's very heavy, I'll have to ask you ladies to be so kind as to help me haul that fat mister up to us."

In spite of the seriousness of the circumstances, his odd request brought a smile to their lips. Together Mona, Sara, and Violet took hold of the ladder—whose top end was securely attached to a projecting rock. But after a vain attempt to pull they stood back, their faces flushed. "Too heavy!"

"A substantial fellow, if not an important one," joked Max. "Allow me to join you, and I think we'll manage to overcome Sir John's reluctance to rise to new heights."

The writer's wit never abandoned him. Once again his friends smiled; then all four of them, working together, hauled on the ladder. It began to rise. A frantic gobbling from below informed them that Sir John had left the ledge and begun his perilous ascent. Again they braced themselves, and little by little, by steady tugs, they drew the rope ladder into their cave.

A cry of pain stopped them. Sir John's bound hands could now be seen above the rim of the ledge. His hands had scraped a little roughly against the rocks, which was why he was complaining.

"Don't slow down," whispered Max. "It doesn't matter if we scratch him up a little, as long as we get him back on solid ground."

Grabbing the nearest rung, he walked off down the tunnel, dragging behind him both the ladder and what was attached to it. As a result Sir John entered the cave mouth with a little spin that rubbed his sides and shoulders somewhat uncomfortably against the rough ground. He was safe, at the cost of a few scrapes and bruises—thanks to which he was able to avoid any expression of gratitude, in favor of complaints at the "brutal, vexatious" treatment, unworthy of civilized people, that had hauled him up a wall like a sack of plaster. He added references to sheriffs, constables, lord mayors, and the royal bench—persons and offices so unlikely to be found on the High Plateaus of Central Asia that his threats worried no one.

Something new had drawn their attention: a letter, with no addressee, left on the ground in plain sight by the little band's mysterious protector. Sara picked it up and read aloud, "*Follow the tunnel. Be careful. The descent is steep in places.*"

"It's like an Automobile Club warning: *Caution, dangerous slope.* Since I still have a few matches—which our friendly guide couldn't have predicted—I'll light them to make sure our route is safer and faster."

The tunnel ran back into the mountain, first in a straight line and then, after about fifty meters, turning sharply so as to follow a line parallel to the exterior cliff face. There began the descent, soon becoming so steep that, in spite of all their care, the travelers slipped and fell often enough to slow their progress.

They kept going that way for over three hours, following the subterranean fault and falling repeatedly. Though they all felt broken by fatigue, the hope of rescue buoyed their courage. Only Sir John went on complaining without end. The fat gentleman, presumably clumsier than his companions, took spill after spill, each of which brought his body into painful contact with the rocks. A dozen times he vowed to give up the "excursion," saying he would go not one step further. But the fear of being left behind in the dark soon forced him back to his feet to catch up to his companions—who didn't give him so much as a thought.

One last difficult, bumpy descent brought them out into the light. They all cried out. They'd reached the bottom of the same ravine they'd earlier considered inaccessible. Ahead of them, winding through the boulder piles, was a narrow snow-covered path, and on its white surface they could see once again the faint paw prints of the panther. They wasted no time wondering where the path led. Exhausted, racked by hunger, they were eager to reach their destination—whatever it might be.

Max, looking around at his companions, said once more, "Let's go."

They all followed him without a word—action being more eloquent than any speech. The narrow path, covered with sharp stones, wound through the fallen boulders. Sometimes the mountain slopes drew in so close that the little band wondered if they'd hit a dead end; but then suddenly it widened again into amphitheaters, ringed by sheer cliffs, whose icy floor was littered with boulders broken off the mountain slopes and now standing ominously upright, giving the landscape the mournful look of a cemetery for giants.

Walking grew harder and harder. Even Violet, in spite of her athletic training, felt at the limit of her strength. Sara and Mona moved slowly, leaning on one another. And Sir John, pale with weariness, moaned at every step. No matter how badly he wanted to reach the shelter the panther's tracks were certainly leading them to, Max realized the moment was near when they'd have to stop. The effort they'd already made exceeded the limits of human strength. The women now advanced mechanically, almost unconsciously. Any moment now their legs would refuse to cooperate. They'd collapse there, at the bottom of that desolate ravine. The deep sleep of the eternally freezing High Plateaus would close their eyes.

Once again Max pulled himself together. He summoned the strength to encourage them, to smile, to promise them shelter was very close. In short, he persuaded his companions to follow him. But that final surge didn't last long. The young women could barely move. Their feet, bruised by the superhuman march, still carried them only at the price of increasingly unbearable suffering.

Suddenly Violet cried out softly and fell to her knees. She'd struck a rock hidden by the snow, and—now too weak to overcome even a slight collision— her legs had collapsed under her.

Max leapt to her, helped her up, supported her in his arms. "I beg you, just a little more courage."

She shook her head, at the limit of her strength, at the end of her hope.

He pointed to a high wall of rock that seemed to bar their way. "Come on, just that far."

"I can't go on," she moaned.

"Yes—you'll lean on me. Who knows, maybe behind that granite cliff we'll find the shelter our mysterious guide wanted to lead us to." He'd said it at random, not really believing in the likelihood of what he was claiming, driven only by the wish to persuade his friends to go a little further.

But such is the power of hope: as vague as it was, that hope galvanized Violet, and Sara, and even Mona. Walking fast, they all followed the path, on which they could still see the panther's prints. They reached the rocky outcrop that forced the path to make a long detour around it. They reached the point of the bend—and there they cried out, stunned, amazed. The ravine widened out into a broad plain surrounded by a granite cliff. At the center lay a small lake, over which hung clouds of white steam.

"A lake that's not frozen at this temperature," murmured Sara.

"Yes," said Max, "it must be fed by hot springs. Explorers in the region mention several like it. But never mind that—look over there, on the shore; what do you see?"

There was a small cottage, whose roof was weighed down with heavy stones to protect it against the winds that swept the High Plateaus. All around it the ground was covered with green grass. Presumably the area right around the warm lake stayed at a mild enough temperature to favor germination. But what drew the travelers' attention above all was a thin column of smoke rising straight into the sky above the cottage. A fire! Which meant heat, and life. The painful journey was over. Safe harbor was only a few hundred meters away.

"One last effort, my friends," cried Max, "and we'll reach the place our unknown protector has guided us to."

"Not unknown!" protested Sara gently. "My heart tells me the one who crossed a wilderness of ice and rock to rescue us is either Master Merry or his little friend Miss Twinkle…" She broke off. "Anyway, let's get to the cottage and find out."

The path along which the panther had preceded them ran straight toward the solitary cottage. Forgetting their weariness, they all set off. Soon the little band reached the narrow strip of flat ground that encircled the lake, and a moment later they were at the cottage. The entrance was merely a door hung on rawhide hinges: no key, no bolt. The owners must've known they didn't have to worry about thieves on the High Plateaus.

They were all filled with curiosity: who lived here, so far from the buzzing of the human swarm? Hunters? Philosophers looking for freedom and solitude? Max knocked with an impatient hand. His rapping echoed, as if amplified by the surrounding silence. But no voice answered his loud summons. "Come on, now!" he muttered. "They must be mutes. The place is occupied—the smoke proves that. No smoke without fire, and fire can't light itself."

Suddenly making up his mind, he pushed open the latchless door and went inside, followed by the others. The same cry of surprise formed on all their lips: they saw no one. But a bright fire blazed on the stone hearth, and over it hung a cooking pot. And on the lid of the pot was a piece of paper, bearing a message in the same handwriting as the previous notes:

Make yourselves at home. Eat, rest, warm your frozen limbs. I've gone to fetch help.

They stood there, speechless, disconcerted by the absence of the mysterious guide they'd hoped to find there. Why had the stranger not waited for them? It wouldn't have mattered if he'd left an hour later. Waiting would've been easy in that cozy cottage. In a corner they could see a plentiful supply of firewood. From the rafters hung smoked venison and dried fish: they had enough food for days. And from the pot simmering on the fire rose a fragrant steam whose odor tickled the nostrils of those famished travelers.

"Bah!" cried Sir John. "The worthy fellow said, eat. That's wise advice, and I think we should follow it."

For once he'd expressed an opinion they could all agree with. Max lifted the pot lid, and a delicious smell soon filled the cottage.

"It's a consommé!" cried Violet.

"A consommé… of smoked fish," replied Max happily.

Sara had already opened a large chest that was set against the wall, and she was pulling out strange utensils that made them all laugh.

"Wooden plates!"

"Chopsticks!"

"A soup ladle!"

Everything was primitive, crude, carved out of solid wood by inexpert hands. But such as they were, those utensils would make it possible for them to eat right away. And there was even a table—a rough plank set on four stakes planted in the dirt floor. When they were all seated, Max plunged the ladle into the pot and served each of them in turn. Once again they exclaimed in delight.

"Vegetables!"

"Yams from Tibet!"

"White carrots from the High Plateaus!"

It was true: the broth was full of vegetables. Happiness is always proportional to the suffering that preceded it. All of them took childish pleasure—which is to say, immense pleasure—in no longer feeling the sharp bite of the icy wind on their skins, and in eating this primitive soup whose heat filled them with a kind of well-being they felt they'd never known before. A few weeks earlier they'd have made faces at a dish prepared with such novice cooking skills; now they cried out at the creaminess of the broth and the flavor of the vegetables. Even the fish was pronounced to be exquisite. Ah, hunger is the best sauce. No condiment, no Vatel,[37] could take its place.

They all ate as if it was a race to see who could finish first. But every craving reaches satiety. Their eyes, once glued to the bottom of the wooden bowls, looked up; they were ready to talk again. Oddly, not one of them felt tired; in filling their stomachs the food had somehow substituted for their lost strength—a temporary effect, familiar to those who take part in vigorous sports. Soon they'd feel the torpor that preceded sleep, their eyelids would grow heavy and begin to close, and they'd give in to unconsciousness.

But for the moment they looked around, taking stock of the furnishings—if that pretentious word could be applied. Even the simplicity of the cottage's construction made them smile: two tree trunks stuck in the ground served as the pillars supporting the entire structure. The posts divided the room unequally into three spaces: the northern section held the firewood, the dish chest, and a large sack full of rice and vegetables all jumbled together; the central section housed the fireplace, the table, and a few blocks of stone that served as seats; and the floor of the last section was hidden under a disorderly mound of furs—red wolves from the Pamirs, coarse-haired yaks, soft-furred spotted foxes, white mouse-deer from the high mountains—suggesting that the unknown proprietors of the rustic cottage intended that area for sleeping.

They were all commenting cheerfully, when Sara suddenly exclaimed, "Hey! Have a look at that post, Monsieur Max." She pointed to the pillar sepa-

---

[37] François Vatel (1631-71), noted chef to powerful patrons in the time of Louis XIV.

rating the dining room from the bedroom—as she had impressively dubbed those ad hoc spaces.

Max looked at it. "Well?"

"You don't see it."

"See what?"

"That bump halfway up."

"Oh yes—I'm sorry—I see it now." He lowered his voice, as if he feared being overheard by invisible listeners. "It could almost be one of those devices, like the one on the column in the Loursinade villa... So, Madame, you think..."

"That with your speaker you might be able to..."

Before the duchess had finished her thought Max was up—but Sir John was even faster than he was: he'd leapt over to the wooden column and was fumbling feverishly in his pocket and mumbling, "A speaker. But I too have a speaker, entrusted to me by those worthy Amber Masks, and I'm going to call them and ask for help. All right!"

Max frowned. The moment he'd been waiting for had arrived: he was going to be able to treat his rival the way he deserved, and without any qualms of conscience, because what was at stake was not merely the thwarting of his own affections but the safely of them all.

But he didn't have time to act. From his pocket Sir John had pulled the little box that held his speaker, and he gave a roar of disappointment. What had happened? The others could see at a glance. What he held was no longer a box—it was a flattened, creased, crumpled thing. Presumably in one of his many falls earlier the heavy gentleman had brought all of his weight to bear on the fragile device, which couldn't resist the pressure and had collapsed, shattered, fallen to bits. The speaker was useless.

To add to his discomfiture, his mishap was met with general laughter. Even Mona—normally so detached from whatever was going on around her—joined in her friends' hilarity. Speechless with anger, Sir John passed through every shade of exasperated red, rolled his eyes, and stamped his foot hard enough to shake the ground.

Meanwhile Max, who'd found his own speaker device in perfect condition, planted it in the wooden column, confirmed by the click of the spring that it was solidly attached, and got ready to send out a call to unknown ears. The strangeness of the moment weighed on all of them. Silence fell. Their hearts beat at the thought of the peculiar conversation Max was about to initiate with strangers. Who would they be? Friends or enemies? No one could predict. It was the paradox of science mixed with its magical results: the possibility of communication across unfathomable distances—but along with that marvel, the frightening impossibility of knowing with whom that communication would take place.

Max too had become solemn. He seemed to hesitate, looking at each of his companions in turn. Then, with a gesture of resolve, he said, "After all, as long as we don't reveal our… location, we're not risking anything." So saying, he bent over the speaker and called out in a clear voice, "Hello? Hello?"

They all waited, anxious to find out who would answer. Perhaps Violet and Sara, if they'd been acting on their own, would've chosen not to use the marvelous device. But since Max had decided to do so, they were sorry to hear no answer. Would the power of the wireless telephone fail them this time?

"It's plain enough," laughed Sir John. "Your speaker may not look broken, like mine, but it works no better."

Max gave him a threatening look that made him retreat several paces—a pointless move, since Max had already forgotten him. He was hunched once again over the device, calling as loud as he could, "Hello?"

A second, a century, went by. Then they all jumped as a distant voice said, "Who is it? The Central Exchange speaks only to the numbers."

"Central Exchange! Numbers!" they all stammered, vexed at this new hurdle.

But then they all fell silent. Mona had come forward into the circle, her face beaming. "It's him—it's Dodekhan. His beloved voice resonates in my heart."

She stopped, but her words had enlightened Max. He bent closer, his lips almost touching the vibrating membrane of the speaker. "Mr. Dodekhan, is that you?" He heard a muffled exclamation—one of those sounds the indiscrete telephone transmits against the will of the person at the other end of the line—and quickly added, "Yes, it's you. Your voice gave you away, but there's no danger. I don't have a number. I'm Max Soleil, a French novelist, and…" He took hold of Mona by the wrist and drew her to him, pointing to the speaker. "Tell him your name."

He didn't have to say it again—she understood. "This is Mona. I can hear you."

"Mona, darling Mona!" The words shook as they emerged from the strange device. "Where are you? I could see you, if I knew."

Mona looked questioningly at Max.

"We don't know exactly. About two days' march east of Lake Balkhash, by the edge of a hot spring feeding a small lake that the cold of the High Plateaus can't freeze over."

Mona was about to repeat his words, when the voice from the speaker said, "I heard that. Wait a moment."

There was a silence. They all stared at each other, unable to put their thoughts into words, so baffled were they by this unbelievable adventure.

The voice from the device said, "I see, you're at Station B."

"Station B?" they echoed uncomprehendingly.

"Who brought you there?"

This time Mona answered on her own. "The panther's paw prints."

"Ah, that's right! Since the death of his master, Log, San has been running the confederation of the Blue Flag, and he took Merry and Twinkle and their animals with him. Obey those children, they can be trusted. No matter what happens, have confidence in them." But then Dodekhan's tone changed. "An Anglo-Russian army also started from Lake Balkhash. You have to join them, so I can protect them as well as you. They're currently… Silence, in God's name!"

Those final words were spoken in a tone of dread. Max instinctively took back the speaker, like a child who fears getting caught. They all turned worried eyes toward the door, as if they expected to see an enemy there. Only Sara kept her cool. "Put the speaker back in position, Monsieur Max. Just like Dodekhan, whoever interrupted our call must be hundreds of leagues from here. Dodekhan will call again when he's alone. He has to tell us how to reach the Anglo-Russian army. He has to, I can feel it. That may be our only hope."

"You're right," said Max, reattaching the speaker to the hollow in the post. "The importance of our meeting up with that army is obvious, just based on how hard they've been working to prevent it—the way we were abandoned on the High Plateaus, the way the trails were erased as if by an evil spirit."

But over-excitement, following the first meal after a long fast, now gave way to a slump. Fatigue took its rightful toll. Their limbs heavy, their brains foggy, one by one the travelers went over and sank onto the furs piled in the southern alcove of the cottage. Max was the last to drop next to his companions, his energy finally sapped by the superhuman weariness he'd endured for hours. For a few minutes more they exchanged scattered words, further and further separated. Then they all fell silent and sank into a deep sleep.

CHAPTER IV
A Strange Duel

"San! We've fallen back into his clutches!" Sara wrung her hands as she cried out in distress.

Her companions, still groggy from long hours of sleep in the pile of furs that had served as their beds, sat up and looked around. She was right: before them a giant with a bestial face stood considering them with cruel eyes. The armed men at his side seemed to be waiting for nothing more than his signal to cut the throats of the Europeans—taken by surprise in the cottage they'd thought of as a refuge. How had their enemies found them?

"Ah," murmured Sara, "the panther's tracks..."

"My idea," chuckled the muscular man. "I wanted to bring you here exhausted, at the limit of your strength, so as to capture you without a struggle. You're not worth spilling the blood of my warriors." Then he sneered. "Let's have a talk, duchess." San gestured, and immediately each of the prisoners was flanked by two of his henchmen. He—who'd once been Log's servant and was now his successor—smiled his approval, then went on slowly, "I'm not telling you anything new, Madame, when I say that my master, Log..." and here his voice shook roughly, "that my master, Log, to whom I belonged as rice belongs in water, was murdered by your husband, that puny son of Europe we were foolish enough to let live."

Sara nodded. Now that the first shock was over, the brave woman had pulled herself together. She was applying her whole mind to understanding the giant, and figuring out what he was thinking behind the veil of his words. It had just occurred to her that San was no fencing partner on a level with his late master. Until recently he'd been a servant, a sidekick, a bandit, who might now hold the magical title of Master of the Blue Flag but had never acquired the subtleties that went with it. He might be giving away his intentions in the very act of thinking he was hiding them.

But soon she had to give up that hope. As San spoke she realized that she would uncover nothing—because he wasn't trying to hide anything. With the instinctive boldness of primitive minds, he made up for the intelligence of those he opposed by the brutality with which he broke their will.

"The Master was dead. What should be done?" he went on calmly. "Honor his remains, summon the entire secret society to his grave. Then what? Throw the seeds of fear into their minds. Cry out to the soldiers, 'The Master, whom you revered as a god, is dead! To reduce him to the inanimate husk in this tomb, all it took was a revolver in the idiotic hands of a puny European—a feeble creature of no account!'" He gave a menacing sigh. "Ah, the Blue Flag! Freedom for Asia! What do I care for that? All I have left is the adoring worship I felt for the

Master. To honor him as he wanted to be honored became the goal of my life. What had he dreamt?" The bandit's voice grew harsh, and his black eyes flashed with red. "He requires blood, a river of blood, and above all, first of all, the blood of the Europeans who caused his death—yours, duchess, and Mona's, and the duke's, and Dodekhan's!"

If he'd thought he was frightening her, he was disappointed. "Well," Sara answered calmly and bravely, "I'm your prisoner. Nothing could be easier than killing me."

San, that Asian Hercules, was certainly as cruel as his old master, Log— maybe even more so—but his mind didn't have the same agility. He could understand and carry out orders; he was incapable of leading. And now the servant, become master by bloody chance, was disconcerted for a moment by his victim's calm courage. The blood rose to his cheeks; his eyes hardened; and finally he growled, "You don't understand. Let me explain. Yes, you'll die—but not now. Not now," he repeated more forcefully, "because the sacrifice wouldn't be complete, because Log's venerated spirit, roaming between heaven and earth, demands other victims, many others, a host of victims."

His teeth were clenched, so that the words seemed barely able to leave his mouth. But then he gradually grew calmer. "Duchess, you don't know what happened in the underground temple of the Prayer Engravers in the Celestial Mountains." He went on mockingly, "I'll tell you—to prove to you that you're here by my will, that my orders were carried out, that they'll be carried out to the very end..." He paused, as if to give what he'd said time to sink into his listeners' minds. Then he went on, speaking with deliberate slowness, "You remember the Loursinade villa, on the road to Aubagne, near Marseilles, in the land of the Franks?"

Sara started violently. But those words had quite a different effect on Mona. She stepped forward and answered firmly, "We remember. On the screen we saw the Duke of La Roche-Sonnaille punishing a bandit." San roared, but Mona paid no attention. "We saw the murderers' daggers raised against the duke, and then against Dodekhan, then nothing more. And yet those we thought were dead are alive. Why are they alive? That's what we want to know. The rest doesn't matter to us."

San's face was transformed, and now he looked stunned. In spite of himself he stammered, "Alive! They know it! How do they know it?"

Max—who up to now had witnessed the scene dispassionately—felt a sudden worry. He remembered that the speaker they'd used to communicate with Dodekhan and the duke had been left stuck into the post holding up the roof. He glanced anxiously toward the post. If that little device were found it would enlighten the enemy. It might even allow them to eavesdrop on the two men who were living, presumably as prisoners, in that unknown cave, from where their voices and their thoughts were able to escape via the elusive vibrations of the wireless telephone… But as hard as he looked, he saw nothing. The speaker had vanished. He was so surprised that he couldn't suppress a muffled exclamation.

San's hard eye rested on him, but only for a moment. The heir to the power of the Blue Flag could spare no thought for this man unknown to him, when his mind was filled with the challenge Mona had just presented to him: how did she know Dodekhan and the duke were alive? The prisoners waited anxiously. They all realized that what Mona had said could betray their secret to their enemy. San said again, "They know it!"

Laughing, Mona replied with unexpected readiness, "Of course I know our friends are alive!"

"How? Who told you?"

She laughed still harder. "You did, Mr. San!" He shook his head vehemently, and she went on, still laughing, "Didn't you say earlier that you intended to kill us?"

"Yes, I said so—and I will," he growled, his eyes flashing.

"I don't doubt it, Mr. San. I'm sure you can be counted on for killing. But from the moment you announced you were going to kill Mr. Dodekhan and the Duke of La Roche-Sonnaille along with us—which is exactly what you said earlier—I could deduce they're alive. After all," she concluded ironically, "you have to admit, if they were already dead you couldn't kill them again."

San's face lit up, and he let out a loud laugh.

"And now," went on Mona, "if I'm not presuming too far, Mr. San, you're going to explain why Duke Lucien and Mr. Dodekhan escaped from death, after we saw them fall under the daggers of your henchmen on Dr. Rodel's screen."

"They didn't escape," San broke in, "I pardoned them."

"Pardon them? You?"

"Oh, only temporarily, that's all, and I've regretted it—right up until the moment I entered this cottage and, finding you asleep, defenseless, utterly in my power, I understood…" He broke off suddenly. "But let's proceed in order. You'll hear later why you drove away my regrets." He cackled. "So, as you say, my servants had your friends on the ground. In another moment their daggers would avenge our Master, Log, treacherously struck down by the accursed duke. Then a thought crossed my mind like a bright light: if they die, there's no more Blue Flag."

"No more Blue Flag!" the prisoners exclaimed as one.

San gave them all a dark look, then shrugged. "I've got you now—no need for secrets. No, no more Blue Flag. Log was a great soul; he'd been Dodekhan's right-hand man, and he'd been able to succeed him without trouble because he knew all the signs and secrets. He possessed the learning that understands all the practical applications of science; he had the eloquence that moves crowds; he was a born leader and Master." With a melancholy they wouldn't have thought him capable of, he went on in a lower voice, "But I'm just a loyal servant, the arm that carries out the Master's will. I lack education and intelligence. Secrets

233

go through my brain like sand through a sieve. The Central Exchange, a system by which complex instruments allow the leader to communicate with all of Asia, to issue orders to the far corners of the continent—all without leaving his chair—that Exchange just seemed like magic to me. I lacked the science to appraise that work of science! What the narrow mind of an ignorant man cannot understand, he considers impossible. But I didn't have that comfort: I'd seen with my own eyes that the incredible, the unbelievable, was possible. I was afraid of the Central Exchange."

San paused for a moment, his eyes half closed, as if he were sunk in his memories. Then he regained his self-control. "I needed those men, whom I would gladly have torn limb from limb. I needed them—but not to carry on the work of the Blue Flag. Bah! I had to avenge Log, I had to spill rivers of blood, so that people everywhere learned from their suffering that the eyes of a Master had been shut against the light. And to strike, to pile up ruins, I had to keep alive the murderers who from then on were the only ones who knew how to operate the vast structure of the Central Exchange in the Celestial Mountains."

He spoke without anger, with the indifference of a barbarian, cruel by atavistic instinct. Clearly, nothing about the bloodstained rituals that once accompanied the funerals of the conquering, annihilating khans would've repelled him. To his horribly simple way of thinking, it seemed logical to immolate countless victims on Log's tomb, since on the death of some mere tribal chieftain the Mongols bathed the tomb in the blood of his wives, his servants, his favorite horse...

He went on slowly, "So I stretched out my hand. The raised daggers didn't come down. I expressed my intentions to Dodekhan and the duke: I'd lead them to the Central Exchange. They'd show me how to operate those diabolical devices I didn't understand—they'd give me the means to wreak havoc across Asia. In exchange I promised them their freedom, and the joy of being reunited with you, duchess, and you, Miss Labianov."

"And they refused?" cried both women impetuously.

San shook his head. "No, they agreed."

"Them, agree? It isn't true!" they cried.

He looked from one to the other of them, with surprise in his eyes. Then he murmured, "Ah, you wouldn't have trusted them to mean it?"

They both shook their heads firmly. "Them, accomplices to crime? Impossible!" Mona spoke with such assurance that San seemed disconcerted.

"They say European women are experts at duplicity," he murmured. "I remembered that Master Log had trusted their word, and they'd betrayed him. But he was asking Dodekhan to hand over the power of the Blue Flag; perhaps he'd aimed too high. I was asking for nothing like that. What did I want? To learn how to use mysterious equipment—not to rule, not to control the world, just to pour rivers of blood over a tomb to honor a leader. They promised. I trusted them. I was wrong."

He stamped his foot. "You're smiling, ladies. Your eyes speak your triumph: San is beaten, fooled. Go ahead and laugh, enjoy the moment. You'll tremble soon." Then suddenly he grew calmer. "On the basis of their promise, I took them to the underground temple of the *Mad*, where the Central Exchange is located. Behind the temple of the *Padme Om*—the center of the Buddhist religion—lies a vast circular cavern whose only access is through the sanctuary itself. There Dodekhan and his father had built the strange machinery that allowed them to see, to speak, to hear at a distance. Someone who knew how to operate it could give orders to fakirs in Singapore, to priests in Peking, to fishermen wandering on the shores of the Arctic Ocean, to pashas in Asia Minor. And then... and then... there's something even more frightening. How—by the mastery of what wonders—is it even possible? I don't know how, but the master of the machines, merely by pressing on a lever, a tiny metal rod, could unleash explosions, devastation, slaughter... a thousand leagues away." He breathed heavily before going on, "it was that power of destruction I wanted."

No one felt like laughing anymore. In San's voice they could hear his stubborn, almost psychotic atavistic cruelty. He was perfectly sincere. The liberating mission of the Blue Flag meant little to him; his dream was that of a barbarian. He wanted destruction for its own sake, to rule over an enormous anarchy, never to tire of ruins. His dizzying goal was to stand atop the rubble, at the center of an Asia covered in pools of blood and littered with razed cities.

"Together we entered the subterranean basilica of the *Mad Padme Om*," he hissed. "We crossed the sanctuary. We went around behind the altar which displays no image of a god, only the invocation *Mad, Lad, Ghad Padme Om* of the Prayer Engravers. We entered the circular cavern containing the equipment. The rock walls were hidden by all the machines: telephote screens, wireless telephone sets, the organization's switchboard—on which two hundred buttons in multiple colors and materials put the Master in touch with the leaders of all the secret societies of Asia. And then there were cast-iron cylinders, copper tubes with curving necks, levers, knobs—who knows what all! A mighty and infernal factory for unleashing death and disaster all across the vast continent of Asia—if that's what you want..."

Once again San breathed heavily, then went on pensively, as if talking to himself. "I said if that's what you want. I was wrong. You also have to have the knowledge. If I'd had the knowledge!" He began to speak faster, as if he was in a hurry to get to the end of his account. "Dodekhan turned to me and said, 'San, stand over by the altar for a moment. The machines haven't been run for a while; I'll test them first. There could be an accident, and since you haven't been trained in how to operate them you might be injured.' I took that as a considerate gesture, and obeyed." His eyes flashed red again. "I retreated to the altar. I murmured very quietly, 'Master, blood will bathe your tomb in profusion and delight your angry spirit.'

"Then I jumped: Dodekhan called out to me mockingly, 'Thanks, worthy San! You've just given me back my power! From now on you'll be helpless to do evil!' What? What could those mocking words mean? I ran to the entrance of the machine cavern. Some invisible force repelled me, threw me to the ground, and Dodekhan said, 'Neither you nor any of your people will cross the threshold. It's guarded by electricity.' It seems that—I can't explain how—the swindler could project electricity; that the ground, the rocks, the air, were saturated with it and formed a barrier as impassable as it was invisible."

"Electrification by conduction," murmured Max with a smile of comprehension.

But San had heard him. "Oh, so you understand…"

He said no more. Mona had stepped forward, her hand outstretched so that her index finger almost touched San's chest, her face glowing with the mystical exaltation that shone from her innocent brow. "Blessed be the Spirits of Good! Dodekhan is once again Master of the Blue Flag!"

The roar of a wounded tiger was nothing next to the terrible cry that burst from San's lips. He raised his mighty fists. For a moment they thought he would crush Mona. But no. Suddenly he grew calm, and a crazy smile appeared on his lined face. He bent down to put his face at the same height as Mona's; then, slowly, in a tone that penetrated the brains of his listeners like the toll of the death knell, he said, "Yes, yes, the Master! But that Master is trapped in the machine cavern. If he comes out I'll tear him to pieces with my own hands!" His face darkened. "I could've let him die of hunger. He didn't let me. He said, 'I want our meals brought every day, without fail. Otherwise I'll destroy the temple.'—'I don't care,' I answered. 'You'll be buried in the ruins.' He began laughing. 'I'll launch attacks against you and your men.'—'If you leave this room I'm not afraid of you.'—'You're wrong: I'll reduce Log's remains to dust, I'll knock down his tomb and eliminate all trace of it.'

"Oh, that touched on the one who'd been my master, my reason for living. Shaking with frenzied anger, I hurled myself at him—but that electrical barrier stopped me and threw me to the ground. Though my strength is that of five ordinary men, I was subdued and flung around by that incomprehensible force, like a straw in a windstorm. And then I grew afraid. Who can predict what those scientists will do! I'd already seen so many marvels that anything seemed possible. I feared for Log's tomb. I gave way. But that night I had the coffin—which had been buried in the temple crypt hollowed out of the rock beneath the altar— taken outside and hidden under a pile of rocks ten *pli*[38] away.

---

[38] A Chinese unit of measure [*Note from the Author*]. D'Ivoi probably meant *li*, also known as the Chinese mile. The *li* has varied considerably over time but was usually about one third of an English mile and now has a standardized length of a half-kilometer (1,640 feet). It is divided into 1,500 *chi* or "Chinese feet."

"Dodekhan's power is terrifying. The next day I went back to the sanctuary—I wanted to confront him. But he greeted me with these words: 'You took all that trouble for nothing, San. I can destroy the grave you dug last night by the Five Red Women.' That was the name of the pile of rocks under which I thought my master's remains would be safe. 'How do you know about that?' I cried—without realizing that I was admitting it. 'I watched you,' he said with an insulting laugh. Watched me? My warriors had been on sentry duty all night in the temple, guarding the only exit. He couldn't have gotten out to spy on me. The next night I had the coffin moved again. In the morning Dodekhan told me where I'd taken it. He'd watched me. How? I don't know. He'd watched me, because he could report circumstances and conversations that he couldn't have known unless he'd been constantly near me."

"The wireless telephote," murmured Max—this time too quietly for San to overhear, because he was fully engrossed in his story and went on, "So I thought of killing him in his sleep. There must be some point when he'd give in to fatigue and fall asleep. A rifle bullet wouldn't be stopped by any electrical barrier. I waited... not long. That evening I hid behind a pillar in the temple and watched Dodekhan and his friend the duke—Buddha confound him!—stretch out on their mats. They closed their eyes. For one long hour I watched them sleep. I suspected a trick, but there was none. They slept peacefully, as if no danger could possibly reach them. My loaded rifle lay next to me. Silently I picked it up, shouldered it, aimed carefully. Finally, when I was sure of my shot, I gently squeezed the trigger. There was a bang and whistle—and I stifled a cry. A miracle had taken place before me: the bullet hadn't crossed the threshold of the machine cavern. It had become incandescent, and was tracing loops around in the air like some great insect on fire.[39]

"At the noise, Dodekhan sat up on his mat. Looking my way, he saw the glowing bullet. He shrugged and called out scornfully, 'Imbecile!' Then he got up, went to one of his damned machines, and pressed some lever. The bullet immediately stopped glowing, fell to the ground, and rolled almost to my feet. Then he moved the lever again, and I heard it click. He strolled over to the threshold—that neither I nor my bullets could cross—and said in a tone that stoked my futile rage, 'You can do nothing to me, San. You're just a common murderer. Give up your pointless attempts, and be satisfied with holding me prisoner.'

"That word brightened my spirits, giving me comfort and consolation. 'Ah—prisoner! At least you admit you don't have the power to get out of here.' He nodded and said, 'Did I need to say so? Could you be stupid enough not to

---

[39] Top-secret experiments carried out by a committee of German engineers in the bunkers at the Essen firing range suggest that this "electromagnetic armor" will soon find defense applications that will render the most powerful bombardment harmless [*Note from the Author*]. Or so d'Ivoi believed.

realize that rather than fall into your clutches again, with no defense against your hordes, I'll stay here under the protection of the machines my father built to bring freedom to Asia?'—'And which now are good for nothing but protecting your own life and that of the damned Frenchman!'—'I'm a willing prisoner, protecting Asia against your criminal enterprises. My father would approve of that.' Then he went calmly back to his mat and lay down as if he'd forgotten all about me."

No one spoke. San's captives watched him, their eyes wide with fear, their minds spinning with the twists and turns of the strange duel that had been described to them by one of the participants.

San continued his story. "Ah, Duchess Sara, young Mona, and the rest of you fools who've yoked your fate to theirs—you're gloating! You're deceiving yourselves with the hope that I've been beaten by your friend Dodekhan's infernal science. Save your rejoicing—save it. I told you earlier that you'd soon tremble. Listen now, and tell me if I was wrong." He paused, then went on. "Dodekhan and the duke will have to leave the machine cavern that protects them from me. The spirit of Master Log has entered me, and has breathed the art of consummate torture into me. Mona's suffering forced Dilevnor's son to promise to hand over the secrets of the confederation of secret societies. Mona's suffering will force him to come out of his refuge."

And now San's voice rose and seemed to beat the cadence of some barbaric victory chant. "That's why, with the help of my followers, I planned your escape from the Elleviousse Asylum. I thought for a moment that you'd slipped from my grasp, because you escaped before the time I'd planned. But what's written in the pages of destiny cannot be prevented. You threw yourselves into the spider's web woven for you. In vain, you struggled. In vain, you thought you'd covered your tracks. In vain, some unknown ally of yours burned down the house outside Calcutta that had once been your prison. Fate brought you to me. Now you're captives, surrounded by my warriors. We'll all travel back to the Central Exchange, and your blood, and the blood of those who've helped you, will delight the spirit of the Master whose servant I was and still am!"

San's voice shook with pitiless menace. But to his captives the horror of their own circumstances almost paled next to the nobility of his devotion to Log. It was the devotion of a torturer, a savage, but it was devotion. Generous hearts admire nobility wherever they find it. This bandit inspired both their fear and their respect. No ambition, no personal motive drove the bloodstained brute who stared down at them. No: he was some kind of madman, spellbound by the memory of the Master whose slave he'd been. He dreamt of slaughter, he strove for some pinnacle of horror—all by some unexpected perversion of that noblest of human feelings: the memory of a lost friend.

Sir John's voice yanked them from their philosophical musings. Bowing politely before San, he said with perfect British phlegm, "Sir, I'm in no position to judge your quarrel with some of those who are here with me. I'd just like to persuade you that all this has nothing to do with me in the slightest. What's more, I've acted as a friend to your agents in Europe."

"Shame on you, Sir John," murmured Violet. "You're despicable for daring to express pride in your contemptible conduct."

"I'm expressing a wish not to see my body chopped into little pieces, dear Violet. And that's a perfectly admirable wish." As he spoke, Sir John drew from his pocket the fragments of his speaker and handed them to San. "You see this thing. Your agents in Europe gave it to me so I could contact them and tell them which way we were going. I can't in fairness be held responsible, one, for their silence for a long time now, and two, for having fallen in the mountains and flattened this fragile device under my weight."

Violet was about to express the anger visible in her lovely face, but San silenced her with a gesture and addressed Sir John with all the cordiality he was capable of. "So you're the Englishman Felly mentioned."

"I am indeed."

"Something must've happened to Felly. Lots of people die these days in revolutionary Russia." San emphasized his sinister little joke with a grating laugh. "But he told me about your goodwill, Englishman. So I'll treat you differently from your companions. You'll go free—after you render me a service that I'll explain in a moment."

"Oh, don't worry, noble San, consider it done. I'd do everything within my power to make you happy."

"Then follow me."

San turned toward the door, but Sir John stopped him. "One moment, sir."

"What is it now?"

"I'd like to ask for someone else's freedom."

San frowned. Stammering in his haste, Sir John went on quickly, "Oh, someone of no great importance to your plans. It's just by chance and her own folly that she got involved in all this business, and since I'm going to marry her, if she were a prisoner and I were free, the wedding wouldn't be possible."

"Which one?" Sir John pointed out Violet. San nodded. "All right. She'll go free when you do. Now, follow me to my tent; I'll tell you what I expect of you."

He'd reached the door. Sir John was hurrying after him, when a delicate hand rested on his arm. He turned quickly. Violet stood close to him. "Sir John." She was no longer angry. He eyes were filled with tears. She was pleading.

"You want to thank me!" he exclaimed with complete self-satisfaction.

"No," she began, but then she caught herself. "I mean, yes, I thank you, even though marrying you... Anyway, I thank you. But it's your duty to ask for someone else's freedom as well."

"Who?"

"Monsieur Soleil." Max was about to protest, but a look from Violet silenced him. "Well?" she said imploringly to Sir John, who puffed out his cheeks and tapped his forehead with one finger. His only answer was to shake his head. "What? You refuse?"

"Completely."

"You must be forgetting that Monsieur Max risked his own life to save you in the mountains, and that without him you'd still be on that ledge outside the tunnel, where you'd have had no choice except dying of hunger or throwing yourself into the canyon."

"I haven't forgotten."

"So you're an ingrate?"

Sir John made a noble gesture. "Not at all—I'm filled with gratitude. If Mr. Soleil found himself in need, I'd offer him a great deal of money out of recognition."

"But?"

"But he's my rival. To give him his freedom wouldn't be convenient. An Englishman doesn't do things that are inconvenient." With that, Sir John neatly pulled himself away from Violet and slipped out the door, which closed behind him.

She gave a despairing gesture, then returned to her friends, exclaiming, "I'll go free only along with you!"

"That's folly," began Sara. "You can be saved..."

"Yes," interrupted Violet firmly, "I could be, but I don't want to be." And she sat back down on the pile of furs—where sleep had delivered them into the clutches of Dodekhan's mortal enemy, and the enemy of the women whose cause she'd taken up.

CHAPTER V
The Veil of Fog

"Never without you!" Violet murmured, her blue eyes fixed on Max. He tried to answer, but she put her delicate hand on his arm to stop him. And that was all. The four people imprisoned in the cottage at Station B were resigned to death. For a long while, Sara, Mona, Violet, and Max all fell silent, wrapped in their own grim thoughts. Through the openings that served as windows—which were covered with ordinary glass, an inexplicable luxury in this wilderness—they could follow the passage of the day. The hours went by one by one. Toward noon, San's warriors brought them a kind of broth made from strips of dried meat and rice. They motioned to the travelers to eat, then withdrew.

Max said slowly, "Let's eat."

"Why?" asked Violet gently.

"To keep up our strength. We have to stay strong to the end. Living means waiting for a dream to come true. Living means hoping against hope. To give up on sustaining life would be surrender."

She nodded her pretty head topped by golden curls, and sat at the table. Presumably Sara agreed with Max, because she'd already come to the table with Mona. Pitiful as it was, the food would sustain them physically. They ate quickly. Then they sat still, once again lost in their thoughts.

Two o'clock. Their jailers returned to take away the dishes, and then left the travelers to their painful solitude. Spurred by an irresistible need to move, Max rose and began to pace from end to end of Station B. Sometimes he stopped by one of the windows and looked outside absently. Twenty large felt tents were set up around the cottage in a double arc, with the edge of the lake forming a chord of the circle. There were also lots of yaks. Then Max gave a cry that made Violet run to him.

"What's wrong?"

He only pointed to an animated, laughing group of men fifteen paces away. She looked at them. "Ah! The guide and the porters who abandoned us in the mountains!"

"Yes, and near them, those yaks..."

"Ours."

"In fact, I recognize our luggage: Mademoiselle Mona's chest, the chest with the tubes of light. Ah, if we still had them!" He didn't go on. The chest that had accompanied Mona since Stittsheim had fallen into the hands of San's henchmen. The slight hope Max had felt at the sight of it soon faded and was replaced by anger. "And there's the one who tricked us," he growled, "the one we thought was our savior."

Out of one of the tents had come a kind of child—thin, scrawny, hollow-cheeked—and at his heels leapt a black panther: the panther whose tracks had led the travelers to the cottage where they were now held prisoner. Before Violet and Max could express their thoughts, another panther appeared. "A second panther," they murmured.

"And a second boy," continued Violet. "No, not a boy—this one's a girl."

It was true: a slim, willowy little Chinese girl with pale amber complexion had run out of the tent to catch up with the boy.

Max called softly, "Duchess?" When Sara had come to them he said, "Have a look, Madame. Do you recognize them?"

She glanced out the window, and her face lit up. "Yes, yes," she stammered. "It's those brave children who were so devoted to us: Master Merry and Miss Twinkle, and their wonderful animals, Fred and Zizi."

"But they're on the best of terms with our jailers." Violet's remark was prompted by the children's behavior. They mingled with the guides, talking animatedly with them. The men seemed to argue, but finally gave way. It wasn't hard to deduce the subject of that exchange: the luggage taken from the travelers was carried to the tent the children had come out of. Then the guide and the porters returned to the yaks, and patted them possessively.

"Hell," muttered Max, "those little bandits may once have shown their devotion; now I think they're acting entirely out of self-interest."

"What do you mean?" asked Sara, a little displeased.

"What we just saw is clear, Madame. Those worthy bandits have divided up our spoils. The children, and those they represent, took our luggage. The traitors who got us lost took our yaks."

But Sara shook her head. "Don't jump to conclusions yet."

Max said nothing; no need to tell the duchess he didn't share her hope. Instead he stayed thoughtfully at the window, idly watching the bandits' comings and goings in the camp. That was how he caught sight of San, followed closely by Sir John, who was more scarlet than ever. They came out of San's tent—identifiable by the blue flag flying from its peak—went into Merry and Twinkle's tent, came back out carrying a bulky package, and returned to San's tent.

The daylight began to dim, as if a grayish haze were hanging over the surrounding heights and gradually sinking into the valley nestled between the rocky cliffs and the shores of the little lake. Then they all heard Mona's voice. "The fog, the fog," she murmured. "Our Slavic folk tales say the spirits of hot springs take on that mobile form. Spirits! Which of them will come to our rescue?"

The others heard her words with concern. Was the madness from which she'd recovered taking hold of her wits again? But she smiled at them reassuringly. "I'm just dreaming out loud," she said gently. "I'm recalling the bedtime stories of my childhood. And do you know why? I won't make you guess. I have a premonition—a feeling, if you prefer a less pretentious word—that the fog thickening on the lake and spreading onto the shore will be our salvation." She noticed their skeptical smiles. "You're silently making fun of me, I understand that. But many times, some hidden instinct has warned me of things to come. When I've had that kind of... foresight, I've never been wrong about what followed. I like this fog, and I welcome it happily."

For a moment her voice had rung with an oracular tone that struck Violet and Sara. Women are more sensitive than men, and more willing to believe in inexplicable phenomena like telepathy and precognition. Perhaps—as a giant of modern physics has nicely put it—women are simply "better conductors" of the unidentified fluids that support the mystery of life on our planet. In any case, slowly and almost reluctantly, the brunette duchess and the blonde Englishwoman moved closer to Mona, and together all three of them looked out at the lake. Mona was right: the curtain of steam that always hung over the warm water was spreading visibly. Curls of white fog rolled over each other like a series of waves crashing on a beach. They began to hide the shore and spread across the narrow band of ground warm enough to support vegetation. It was as if the lake were growing, overflowing its banks, advancing slowly but surely toward the cottage and the tents.

It was now completely dark. Fires had been lit in front of the warriors' tents. The cottage was now the center of a semicircle of glowing lights that threw dancing flames and reddish smoke into the sky. Still the fog spread. It reached the cottage, and passed it. The prisoners watched as the fires were shrouded, lost their clarity, became reddish halos harder and harder to distinguish, until they seemed to be no more than vague reflections in the almost opaque whiteness of the fog.

The same jailers who'd come at noon returned to set their dinner—a primitive stew—on the rustic table. At around nine they came back to clear away the dishes. One of them spoke a single word, that sounded like a command: "Sleep!"

Intense curiosity led the prisoners back to the window. They watched their jailers walk away, become vague shapes, and vanish into the dense fog. All around the cottage the fog formed a moving wall. It was like a natural manifestation of a fairy tale in which, as a result of a magic spell, persecuted mortals are locked away in castles of fog, cut off from the world by impassable ramparts of mist. An oppressive sense of isolation weighed on the prisoners. They could see nothing, but reason reminded them with cruel clarity that, even within that foggy night, the deep water of the lake before them and the line of tents behind them blocked any attempt at flight.

With a gesture of irritation, Max said, "Let's sleep!" And, setting the example, he stretched out on the pile of furs—an unwitting reminder of the cruel awakening that had begun this dismal day. Silence and darkness filled the cottage.

How long did that sleep, or seeming sleep, go on? None of them could've said exactly. But suddenly they all started, and looked toward the door, where they'd heard a quiet creak. Strange: the door had swung open, and against the dark of the doorway they saw the silhouette of someone slipping inside. The door closed again, bringing total darkness. The prisoners could see nothing. But if their eyes were useless, their ears still worked. They heard a sliding sound, like someone crawling carefully toward them across the floor. Then came an almost imperceptible whistle.

"Who's there?" asked Max cautiously. Why the caution? It was instinctive, and not at all rational. Caution is the instinct for self-preservation. So, unconsciously, he kept his voice down.

A muffled voice, almost a whisper, replied, "Is Madame de La Roche-Sonnaille awake?"

"Who's that?" stammered Sara in the dark.

"Don't call out. They're on guard. I'm Merry."

"Merry! Oh, little one, I knew that if you were around we hadn't been abandoned." A firm shush reminded her of the danger, and she went on more quietly, "What do you want, child?"

"To lead you to safety."

"Can you really?"

"Yes. Fog covers the land and the water. No one will see us reach the lake. The boat will take you where the Master has decided you should go."

For ten seconds no one said a word. An inexpressible emotion closed their mouths. The fog was helping their escape—wasn't that what Mona had predicted earlier?

Then Max pulled himself together and said firmly, though still quietly, "To take us to safety, sure, that's a good idea. But it would've been better not to deliver us into that beast San's hands in the first place."

Sara broke in, "No doubt that was necessary, wasn't it, Merry? Our friend doesn't know you. Otherwise he wouldn't be suspicious."

The voice in the darkness whispered, "Yes, it was necessary. The Master wanted it that way for two reasons: first, the wireless telephote showed him that the only trail allowing you to meet the Anglo-Russian army would force you to run into San and his men."

"Ah!" said Max.

"Then, I was supposed to appear to lead to you San, so as to make him trust me—and allow me to carry out fully the orders of the one I serve."

"You have orders. So Dodekhan is fighting against San? And what about Duke Lucien?" asked Sara, her voice shaking.

Merry answered quietly, "Duke Lucien is with the Master, whom he calls his brother. He too is fighting San." Then his tone changed. "But Sahib Dodekhan's orders for now are that I lead you to the army."

"Through the middle of...? Can you really do it?"

"The fog on the lake that never freezes has blinded your enemies. Are you all ready?"

244

"Yes," they murmured.

"Put on furs, because once we're out of the fog the cold will be terrible." Rustling noises showed they were following the boy's advice. "Now follow me in single file, and without a sound. Noises carry better in fog than in clear air. If our enemies have the slightest suspicion, we're done for. The Master himself couldn't save us."

The Master himself! They all trembled as those words reminded them of the danger they were in, which they'd forgotten for a moment: their prison lay at the center of a ring of fires, around which sentries waited with their eyes fastened on the cottage wrapped in fog. Escape seemed like a fantasy, and they might've wasted more precious time questioning Merry—but the boy had already slipped outside, and the cold wind coming through the open door invited them to follow him.

Max took Violet's hand, and Sara and Mona linked their arms. They stepped outside. In the fog that struck their faces like warm steam they could vaguely make out a thin figure in motion. It was their guide, advancing with silent steps as if he were crossing a lawn. His outline, blurred by the fog, looked eerie, almost inhuman. They followed him, though with the troubling sensation that a goblin of the night was leading them somewhere unknown. They set their feet down slowly, shivering at the sounds that reminded them of the proximity of the enemy camp: murmurs of conversation, the calls of the sentries, the crackling of firewood.

But now their guide stopped, and made the little group come to a halt. Why? Because they'd reached the edge of the lake. The deceiving water lapped at their feet, barely visible in the veiling fog. But what was that darker patch there, a meter offshore? As if in answer to their unspoken question, Merry gestured strangely, and the dark patch drew nearer and ran up onto the shore. Now they understood the boy had been hauling on the bow of a boat. Without even whispering, and keeping them from speaking, he gestured for them to get into the boat. He helped the women. His fear of making any noise was so clear from his actions that unconsciously they all followed his example. They crawled and slid to the stern of the rough-hewn craft.

Merry cast off, and pushed the boat out into the lake. The shore vanished in the fog. They now moved through mist so heavy they could barely see him standing in the bow, manipulating a pole. Where was he taking them, across the black water, through the cloud that made it impossible to find their way? Slowly, at regular intervals, he pushed the pole into the water. The boat began to pick up speed. Ah, the boy knew what he was doing. He knew his way through the fog. They followed the shore. There, in the midst of the fog, they could see the reddish glow of the last fires of their enemies, still guarding the now-empty cottage. Then those lights were gone, and black night was everywhere. Not a single landmark. The boat advanced through a tunnel of endless darkness.

Though the journey lasted barely half an hour, they all thought several hours had gone by since they started. With a slight bump, the boat ran aground on a sandy bottom. Merry leapt ashore, moored the boat, and said softly, "Get out, we're here!"

"Where?"

"At the start of the trail that'll lead you to the English and Russian camp." Exclamation of thanks filled the air, but he interrupted them. "Time is short. The path runs between those two boulders. Five hundred meters from here the fog ends. You can easily follow the track up the slopes. At the top you'll find some caves, and a fire already lit. Wait there for your companion, the one San took to his tent."

"Sir John Lobster!" cried Violet.

"That's what he calls himself. He'll be escorted there, but he'll stay there alone. So then grab him. He's got the safe-conduct with the Master's seal. Without that you'll never get through the lines of spies that surround the European camp." After a pause that no one thought to interrupt, Merry droned on like a schoolboy reciting a lesson, "One you're with your countrymen, you'll see the leader. You'll tell him to stay there with his troops, where they're encamped."

"He won't listen to us!" exclaimed Max. "Can you imagine a general taking our advice!"

"He'll follow your advice," insisted the boy with feeling.

Max was surprised by his confidence. "Why would he?"

"I don't know."

"So how can you be sure?"

"I'm sure, because the Master told me that to be obeyed all you need is to say, 'If you scorn this warning, you'll paralyze the goodwill of those trying to protect you, and you'll condemn yourselves and everyone around you to death.'"

"You think that'll do it?" joked Max.

"I'm sure it will," replied Merry curtly. "The Master said it will, so it will."

In spite of everything, the boy's assurance made an impression on them. And after all, why doubt him? Hadn't inexplicable adventures been assailing them from all sides for weeks? And from what they'd already seen of the irresistible power of the Blue Flag, why wouldn't that mysterious emblem also have influence on the commander-in-chief of an Anglo-Russian army? So Max took an accepting tone as he asked, "From those caves, is it far to the army camp?"

"Four hours' trek, on an easy trail."

"All right. Once we reach the camp, we deliver the message we've been charged with. Then what?"

"Then you wait for the Master's orders."

"Orders... We'll receive his orders in the middle of the camp. Is that what you're saying, Master Merry?"

"Exactly."

246

"But how? How?"

"By the same means he's already used to talk to you."

"Ah!" cried Max, smacking his forehead. "How stupid not to have thought of it! My speaker, the speaker I took from the Loursinade villa."

"Yes, yes," his companions agreed.

But then his face darkened. "But there's a slight problem. I no longer have that speaker."

"Here it is." Merry held out his hand, with the device held gently between the fingers of his fur-lined glove. "I collected it when San and his men surprised you. On the Master's orders, I'm returning it to you. You'll call every day, and the Master will answer." Then the boy cut short the conversation and leapt back into his boat.

"Merry! Merry!" called out Sara and Mona.

With one push of his pole, he moved the boat away from shore. As he slipped away into the fog, he answered, "I've said all I was supposed to say. Now I have to be present for the departure of the one you'll wait for in the caves. And then I'll erase all sign of your escape."

The fog had closed over him. Now the fugitives standing on shore could see no sign of their little savior. And yet through the billows of fog his voice still reached them: "I can't let San suspect me, because the Master still needs me."

What could that mean? No further explanation was possible, as the boy was now definitely gone.

Alone in his boat, gliding over the inky water, poling his way through the fragile cotton of fog, he was happy, as was proved by the quiet tune on his lips—oh, a cautious sound that was to whistling as whispering is to ordinary speech. Then he stopped whistling and said to himself, "Now to find out if Twinkle succeeded too." He shrugged. "I'm an idiot. She succeeded, because the Master telephoned. He knows all about it. Those strange tubes manufactured in Stittsheim, in Miss Mona's luggage that I took as my share of the loot. Who'd believe it? I certainly believe it, if the Master says so. But if anyone else told me, I wouldn't believe it."

The pole still moved the boat along steadily. But soon it began to slow down. "What a terrible fog," thought Merry. "I hope I don't miss the agreed-upon spot."

His concern was well justified: the fog had grown increasingly opaque, and it was almost impossible to set a course. Eyesight was useless in the midst of that cloud covering the water. Again and again the boy aimed the boat toward where he knew the land lay. Each time he reached shore almost without seeing it, he tried to steer parallel to the bank.

Then he stopped cold. The brief call of the skylark of the High Plateaus had rung out a short distance ahead. He put the tips of his fingers between his lips and replied with a similar call. From out of the fog the call came again. "It's

Twinkle," he said to himself happily. "Whew! All went well, as the Master promised."

Then he turned the boat and poled straight for shore. At this spot the action of the water had eroded the bank, leaving under it a kind of hollow large enough for the boat to disappear into. He felt his way in the dark until he touched a ring to which he fastened the boat line. Then he stepped out onto a narrow rocky ledge and followed it up a steep slope to the top of the bank.

"Is that you, Merry?" came an anxious whisper in his ear.

"Yes, dear Twinkle."

"I was worried; you're late. I was afraid the Spirits of the Night had dragged you to the bottom of the lake."

"Well, it isn't easy to steer a course through this fog."

The girl named Twinkle was as thin and delicate as her young companion. Together they'd known the same misery, the same privations. They both showed the lasting effects of the suffering common to abandoned children. But they weren't thinking about the painful past now, nor about the biting cold of the night.

"And the Master's orders?" asked Merry anxiously.

"Done."

"Just like that?"

"Yes. I opened the chest from Stittsheim. I took out a blue tube. Then I left the tent and went to the fire where Dag-Nin was on guard."

"Oh, yeah, the big Prayer Engraver who calls us rats because we're so small."

"That's him. I was very tense—though he didn't see it—very tense, you understand? If the tube hadn't worked, you couldn't have hidden the boat, nor gotten back to camp without being seen."

"And did it work?" he asked with great curiosity.

"Yes, it worked."

"The Master was right."

"He's always right. While Dag-Nin was looking away, I aimed the little blue light at his head." She paused.

"Go on, go on," he growled impatiently.

"Well, he sank gently to the ground. He's been asleep ever since. But let's get back to camp without wasting any time. When he wakes up he needs to find me sitting alone by his fire."

The two children held hands and ran through the heavy fog. Soon they could see a reddish glow flickering ahead of them. They began to move more carefully, but soon they could see there was no need for caution: a large body lay on the ground by the fire.

"Dag-Nin," whispered Twinkle.

The warrior was fast asleep. He'd let go of his rifle, which lay next to him on the grass.

The girl sat down next to the fire and pretended to be asleep. "Go," she murmured.

Merry didn't need to be told twice. Like a shadow, he ran across the area lit by fires, and vanished into the mantle of fog covering the camp. He'd crossed the line of sentries without being spotted. Two minutes later he slipped into the felt tent assigned to the children. Two black panthers—slim, lithe, and affectionate—leapt up to greet him. He petted them gently. "Hello, Fred, hello Zizi. No loud purring, my darlings. We have to be careful. The hardest part's done, but it's not over yet."

The animals seemed to understand him. They arched and pressed themselves against his caresses, but they made none of the satisfied growls that their kind would normally make. That went on for several minutes. The boy was about to stretch out on the mats piled in the middle of the tent when the felt flap that served as the door opened and Twinkle came in.

"You!" cried Merry.

She laughed silently. "Yes, Dag-Nin woke up. He shook me, he scolded me, he told me it was silly for a rat like me to sleep outdoors when I could be inside a good felt tent."

"He suspected nothing?"

"No, no. Those big warriors are more trusting than rats. He thinks I didn't notice he was asleep on duty. He won't betray us, don't worry." Then her tone changed. "On my way back I noticed they were harnessing the yaks."

Merry sat up. "The yaks! Then San's envoy and his escort will be leaving soon."

"I believe so."

"It's true—they have to reach the European army before they strike camp." He stood up. "In that case, we've got to keep watch. When they've gone, Station B has to disappear. All right—I'll sleep some other night."

Twinkle was right: muffled noises could be heard in camp. Men were moving around in the yak pen, setting either pack loads or saddles for riders onto the backs of those animals—the only beasts of burden on the High Plateaus.

Inside the leader's spacious tent two people were ending a conversation that had gone on for a while, as indicated by the flasks of rice wine and the tumblers laid out on a small folding table, a gem of Chinese cabinetmaking out of place in this wilderness.

"So," said San, "do you understand?"

"Perfectly," replied Sir John. "I present myself as a casual traveler. Two days' march away, I ran across a Chinese army sent out by the Son of Heaven to join the European forces and help them capture the bandits of the Blue Flag. I provide the position of the Chinese, so that the army heads that way to meet them."

"That's right. Once they head that way, not one of them will ever see Europe again. That'll discourage those whites who are so eager to meddle in our business!" Those last words were spoken so quietly that they must not have been intended for Sir John to overhear. But then San raised his voice again. "What I want is for the Chinese troops to lead the Anglo-Russian forces away from my Central Exchange." He smiled. "One favor deserves another, Sir John. You're sending my enemies on a false trail. In return I'll give you the prisoner you asked for."

"Miss Violet."

"Exactly. As for my other captives…"

Sir John shrugged. "I don't need to know what happens to them. If you don't bring it up with me, worthy Master San, I won't bring it up with you."

That made San burst out laughing. When he'd calmed down, he said, "Bundle up, Sir John. It's an awfully cold night. The time has come for you to set off."

Sir John must've been waiting impatiently for this moment, because he quickly put on his furs, saying cheerfully, "I'll leave right now. The sooner I go, the sooner I'll be back."

"Oh, little Miss Violet will be waiting for you."

"I'm sure of it. The wise thing is not to run so fast that you get out of breath. But wisdom and the desire to enter into matrimony don't always go together. You understand that, old boy, I'm sure."

San listened, squinting, his face expressing boundless scorn. But if that was his reaction, he felt no need share it with Sir John, who went right on calmly explaining his ideas.

"Yes, that damned Frenchman has thrown himself in the way of my nuptials. I didn't ask him to do that. You can imagine, old boy, I didn't ask him to do that. A sensible man doesn't put obstacles in his own path. And I am sensible: I'm even known for it, since the voters in the constituency of Beggingbridge have chosen me to sit in the House of Commons. You might answer that the voters don't always know what they're doing. Yes, very true for many of my colleagues, but in my case they know very well what they're doing. I'm a perfect gentleman, and I've got a head full of solid, practical ideas."

The speech by the Member for Beggingbridge might've gone on a while longer—but San, seeing that he'd finished dressing, interrupted to say, "Are you ready?"

"Quite, Master San," said Sir John with all the composure a Parliamentary orator can muster when confronted by a premeditated interruption.

"Your escort must be waiting for you." San gave a piercing whistle, and instantly a man appeared at the door of the tent.

Sir John exclaimed in surprise: he recognized the guide who'd abandoned him and his companions in the mountains.

"He's loyal to me," said San, as if in response to his thoughts. Then he went on quickly, "They'll escort you to the caves at the top of the ridge, after which the trail is easy. And then you've got the gold plaque I gave you."

"The plaque engraved with the sign of the Blue Flag."

"Show that image to anyone who tries to keep you from passing, and you'll get through."

"So everyone in the mountains obeys you?"

"Everyone here, yes—and plenty more elsewhere," growled Log's successor arrogantly. Then in a different tone he said, "Enough talking. It's getting late. We cannot allow the European troops to begin moving in a direction I don't want them to go. Come!"

The guide had withdrawn, and Sir John and his host left the tent. A dozen yaks carrying a dozen warriors were waiting outside. One of the men held the reins of a yak without a rider. San pointed it out to Sir John. "For you."

Not without some difficulty, the corpulent English gentleman heaved himself into the saddle.

"Go!" said the leader of the Prayer Engravers once again. "Go, succeed, and return to claim the woman you consider the payment for your services." There was a tone of bitter irony in San's voice.

Before Sir John could answer, the guide gave a guttural cry, and at his signal the whole group set off. Surrounded by his escort, Sir John plunged into the still-dense fog.

Other than those escorting the Englishman, not one of San's henchmen had moved, nor come out of their tents to see what the racket was that had disturbed their rest. When San had gone back into his tent and dropped the felt flap of the door, silence and darkness fell once again.

Then Merry and Twinkle slipped out of their own tent; without being seen, they'd watched the group leave. What would they do now? They whispered together animatedly in a hurried, trembling back and forth.

"I'm going with you," said Twinkle.

"No," answered Merry. "What's the point of doubling the chances of getting caught?"

"To share the danger equally."

"There is none."

"Yes, there is. Earlier, I let you go alone. Everyone was sleeping. Now lots of the camp is awake. If they catch you, you're dead. Why would I go on living?" Ah, words in which sweet, profound affection blossomed between those two rejects of society, those two foundlings! In her cry of utter devotion, of shared misery, something as infinite as the universe burst forth from that small child's soul.

Merry couldn't resist. "Come along, my poor Twinkle. In fact you're right. Whichever of us stayed behind would be too miserable."

And, holding hands, tiny shadows amid the immense shadows of the night, the children crept toward the cottage Dodekhan had called Station B. They moved stealthily, pausing to listen at the slightest sound, then hurrying to stop a little further on. When they reached the cottage they pushed open the door and went in. A red glow lit the middle of the room: the embers of the dying fire lit for the now-escaped prisoners. They went to it, chose the brightest embers, and carried them over to the pile of furs left behind by the fugitives. They slipped some between the rafters, and between the timbers in the walls. Then they blew frantically to revive the dying flames. Within a few minutes they'd started ten fires—still invisible for now, but that would soon incinerate the cottage in a sheet of flame.

"Quick, back to our tent," said Merry joyfully. "The Master's last order has been carried out: burn Station B so as to leave some doubt in San's mind about the fate of the prisoners."

Together they leapt outside. They could already see the glow of those fires through the windows. The critical thing was to reach their tent before the guards posted around the cottage noticed the flames. They hurried.

Suddenly a great cry rang out in the night, like the scream of an eagle. It was the terrifying cry of the Yakuts warning of fire. Now shouts could be heard on all sides. But the two children had reached their tent. They dove inside, then came back out almost immediately, calling out in sleepy voices, "What's going on? What's going on?"

Dark shapes answered as they ran by, "Fire! The prisoners! Station B!"

Ah, the fire had done its work: through the fog they could see an immense sheet of flames lighting up the night. San appeared—hideous, frightful, furious, and roaring in a voice like thunder, "Get the prisoners out!"

He ran on. The children exchanged a sly look, then ran after him with shrill cries. They ran back toward the cottage. All the warriors were there, trying in vain to overcome the flames. A pointless effort! The fire had been set with too much care. Everything was burning at once.

Within two hours it was all consumed. Holding a spear, San searched angrily through the blackened, smoking ruins for any sign of the prisoners he thought had perished in the blaze. Of course, he found nothing—not the slightest charred skeleton. The children right behind him were highly entertained by his soliloquy: "But they were here. They couldn't have escaped. My soldiers on one side, the lake on the other side. So they were here. They're still here. So why can't I find them?"

CHAPTER VI
An Envoy's Misadventures

"By the devil's cloven hoof, this is really a tiring climb!" That was how Sir John Lobster, Member of Parliament for Beggingbridge, expressed his opinion of the night journey that had brought him to the mouth of the caves at the top of the ridge, south of the hot springs lake.

The leader of the escort came to him. "Your lordship, here's where we must leave you. We've lit a fire, by which you can wait for the three servants who've been notified and who'll escort you to the European army."

Sir John bowed with dignity. His current role suited him perfectly—he was the Envoy of the Blue Flag! He might've reminded himself that he was preparing to deceive his countrymen. San's explanations had left him in no doubt about that, though the Master hadn't told him everything. But Sir John was too intent on ensuring his own personal well-being to be inconvenienced by reasoning that would just trouble his conscience.

The fire had been lit in the shelter of overhanging rocks. Sir John sat down next to it, after having tethered his yak next to three others, intended, he'd been told, for the servants who would join him here. Lost in his own thoughts, he hadn't noticed the tone of surprise in the voice of the guide who explained that to him. Too bad for him: if he'd noticed it, he could've inquired. The guide would've admitted his surprise at not finding those servants already waiting at the rendezvous. That kind of lack of punctuality was not the norm among the followers of the Blue Flag. And then Sir John would've worried, and would probably have kept his escort with him until the tardy servants showed up. But he hadn't done so.

The warriors had bowed to him, as it's proper to bow to a great chief's guest, and then returned along the trail by which they'd come.

So now Sir John sat alone, facing the fire and enveloped in its red glow. Bundled deep in his furs against the cold, with only the tip of his nose exposed, he leaned toward the fire, saying to himself that it was cold as Hell, and that he'd give those servants who were making him wait a sharp talking to... when he had the feeling that something had moved at the edge of the circle of light around the fire. What kind of thing? Perhaps an animal. What kind of animal could be prowling around in the freezing night in the midst of these desolate mountains? He answered promptly, "A bear." Why a bear—an animal that's almost unknown in the Pamirs? Sir John had once traveled in the Pyrenees, where you sometimes met bears, and since then he'd considered bears to be an indispensable feature of every self-respecting mountain range. Many of our conclusions rest on equally shaky logic.

He turned his head and gave a stifled cry. A fur-covered mass met his eyes. It was the bear, with a doubt—the bear up on its hind legs. What was worse, he could see three other equally frightening shapes behind it. The proximity of danger lent him an agility he'd thought himself no longer capable of: he leapt to his feet to elude the first bear's embrace.

But oh—stupefaction! The first bear bowed respectfully to the Member of Parliament, and in a voice that sounded nothing like a carnivorous beast he said, "A landslide forced us to make a long detour. That's why we're late. We should get started on our walk toward the European army, as Master San ordered."

Those bears just had bear skins! It was the servants he'd been waiting for. Sir John was filled with unspeakable joy. They were here to serve him, and not to serve out among themselves, to his cost, the choicest morsels of his being. His strength returned as if by magic. He stood squarely on his legs, and in a firm voice he ordered, "Saddle up, fellows!"

And he was delighted to see them hastening to obey. They hurried to the yaks and untethered them. But then a thought crossed Sir John's mind. There were four yaks: one for him, and one for each of the three servants he'd been told about. Yet he counted four servants. "Why four?" he asked.

"The Master's orders."

"So he made a mistake?"

"The Master never makes a mistake."

"Still…"

"No doubt the mistake is yours, man of the West."

Sir John shrugged: what was the point of debating with fanatics? So he went on carelessly, "It's nothing to me. I only mentioned it because of the number of yaks."

"What's wrong with the number?"

"It's less than the number of riders. Four yaks, five riders. One of the five will have to go on foot."

"That one will be you."

At that, Sir John couldn't help giving a start. "Walk!—Me!—The Envoy!—The chief!"

"That's how the Prayer Engravers honor their rulers."

The Englishman found nothing to say. He let them fasten silk ribbons to his arms; the four servants each held one of the ribbons by its other end. And he didn't resist when two of the servants, riding on yaks, positioned him between them. On their signal, he began to walk. Only then did he find means to express his thoughts, and he grumbled, "San didn't warn me about this. Of course I'm grateful to him for having wanted to honor me like this, but if he'd consulted me I'd have asked for some less pedestrian honor."

After that he calmed down. The trail was easy, winding its way across a fairly smooth plain. Occasionally armed warriors seemed to emerge from the ground to block the way of the little caravan. Then, with a noble gesture, Sir

John showed them the gold plaque of the Blue Flag. The captain of the sentries took it, touched it to his forehead with respect, and handed it back to the Envoy. And then with a guttural call, the men vanished, dissolving into the night. Ah, at least on that point San hadn't misled his guest. Without that metal safe-conduct, it would've been impossible to get through the dense ring of scouts spread around the Anglo-Russian encampment.

Two hours, three hours had gone by since they set off. A pale light heralding the dawn spread in the sky and across the landscape. Darkness retreated, and the slopes and ridges, though still unclear, at least grew visible. Suddenly the riders tugged on their reins, and the yaks stopped. Sir John stopped as well, and gave a cry of satisfaction. "The army!"

Yes, the Anglo-Russian encampment was there, straight ahead. He and his servants had climbed a slight rise in the terrain, and the other side sloped gently down toward a circular valley, at the center of which, on a small hill, stood the expedition leaders' tents, marked by the flags of the United Kingdom and the Russian Empire.

Presumably that basin was the filled-in crater of some ancient extinct volcano. It had the regular rounded form of the volcanic craters in the Auvergne region—but, oh, vastly greater in size! It was bigger across than the sixty Auvergne craters put together. The plutonic forces that raised Central Asia to colossal heights, that pushed the Pamir Plateau to five thousand meters above sea level and the Himalayan summits to over eight thousand, would only smile at the little volcanic hiccups in the Auvergne, which labored to raise the very tip of the volcanic cone of the Puy de Dôme to twenty-seven hundred meters. But the action of Nature is one in all its manifestations. Whether weak or strong, its results are the same. Their dimensions vary, but their forms remain identical.

And on the floor of that crater were arrayed the tents of the encampment. The quarters of the various service functions could be distinguished, and the line of battle flags, and the calvary guard, and the outer line of sentries. And at that outer line, in fact, there was some movement: the sentries were gathering, talking and pointing toward where the little group had just come into view. They'd been spotted. The best thing now would be to walk straight toward the camp; so obvious was that, that without a word the five travelers urged their yaks forward.

But there'd been a slight change: the party no longer had a foot soldier. One of the servants had climbed up behind one of his companions, and Sir John had been invited to ride the yak now available. "The Europeans don't know how to honor their dignitaries the way we do," explained the one who seemed to be the spokesman for all. "Forgive us, Your Lordship, for making you ride."

I do believe Sir John forgave them; he would've forgiven such a "dishonor" quite a while back. But they were reaching their destination—why harp on bygone exhaustion? The yaks themselves seemed to sense the end of the trail was near, because they sped up as they descended the inner slope of the crater.

Thanks to Sir John's nationality, when the travelers were stopped by the sentries they were directed from guard post to guard post all the way to command headquarters—the spacious tent where the generals leading the expedition met with their staff officers. Word of their arrival had preceded them. Lord Aberdeen and General Labianov awaited the Member of Parliament traveling for his own pleasure—that was how Sir John was presenting himself—and who claimed to have information of the greatest importance to share with them.

Sir John and the servants accompanying him got down from their yaks in front of the generals' tent. The soldiers on guard had their orders, and they stepped aside and gestured for the travelers to pass. Proudly, with his head held high and walking on the balls of his feet, the gentleman Envoy entered the tent, followed respectfully by his servants.

It would be difficult to say exactly what effect the sight of the generals had on Sir John's escort—but one of them cried out slightly, and the other three hastened around him. It was as quick as it was brief. By the time Sir John, feeling vaguely that something curious was going on being him, had turned around, all of his companions had recovered their correct, unemotional demeanor.

Meanwhile Lord Aberdeen had begun to address him, so he had no time for reflection. "You've asked to meet with the high command," said Aberdeen.

"Yes," replied Sir John, "and particularly with my fellow countryman, Lord Aberdeen."

"You haven't appealed to English blood in vain. I am he, and I'm listening."

Sir John bowed ceremoniously, and then, with all the dignity his portly self could muster, he went on, "My lord, you've been informed that my name is Sir John Lobster, and my position is Member of Parliament for Beggingbridge."

"I have indeed been informed."

"Allow me to supplement and corroborate that information by means of my card as Member, which bears my photograph. I feel it to be judicious and useful to back up my words with the most mathematical proof."

He held out his card to Aberdeen, who glanced at it and passed it to his Russian colleague before returning it to Sir John. "Quite right, Sir John. We know each other now—we've been properly introduced. I'm therefore ready to hear what you have to say."

The bright fire burning in the portable field hearth—a device with heat-reflecting tiles that could be dismantled—spread a gentle warmth through the tent. Sir John felt the need to loosen the furs that, while excellent for the outdoors, now felt a little oppressive. While he pushed back his hood and undid the ties at his collar, he took his eyes off the generals for a moment. When he glanced back at them, his mouth dropped open.

The two officers were no longer looking at him. Labianov, who'd suddenly gone quite pale, held a sheet of paper folded in the form of a letter, and he was pointing out the handwriting to Aberdeen. What had just happened? A simple thing: that sheet of paper had just fallen onto the table. Where had it come from? No one present could've said for sure. Labianov had automatically picked it up—and the writing on the outside had stunned and almost paralyzed him.

The letter was addressed:

To His Excellency General Labianov.

To my father. Read this without saying a word, and follow the directions. That way we'll be saved.

Labianov leaned over and murmured so that only Aberdeen could hear him, "It's my Mona's handwriting."

You can imagine the two generals' emotions. Not for a moment did they guess at the truth: that Mona and her friends had taken the place of San's servants—who now lay securely tied up in the caves where Sir John had been so afraid of bears—and that Mona, unrecognizable wrapped in furs, was here and eager to see her father alone.

Labianov unfolded the letter. Together he and Aberdeen read the contents anxiously:

Sir John Lobster is a simpleton who is unwittingly acting as an agent of the bandits you came to punish. His directions will lead you into disaster. Pretend to believe him. Send him back where he came from, while keeping his companions as hostages. Your Mona will immediately be in your arms. She'll tell you how she escaped from her terrible enemies, and how they can be beaten.

Sir John—increasingly annoyed by the inexplicable way the commanders of the Anglo-Russian army were ignoring him—saw them exchange a glance. Aberdeen looked doubtful, but Labianov answered with a vigorous positive gesture. Then Aberdeen shrugged in resignation, as if to say, "Do what you think is right."

Labianov seemed to expect that agreement, because he straightened up and, turning to San's Envoy, he said quietly, "Go ahead, Sir John. You have our full attention."

Finally these officers were focusing! The Envoy puffed himself up. "I'm going to speak as clearly as possible." Then he took a step forward and—in fulsome rhetorical periods, even chancing a few orator's gestures—he explained that while doing some "yakking" through Central Asia "for his own personal pleasure," he'd encountered, "two days prior to the present," a Chinese army that he could attest was sizable. What size exactly, was "not within the realm of possibility" for him to determine, given that he'd not had time to make a precise enumeration. The "coral flower" in command of that military force, on learning that he was headed toward Lake Balkhash on his way back to Europe and his seat in Parliament, had thought immediately that his path would cross that of the Anglo-Russian army, and had asked him, "in the most honorable fashion," to be so kind as to be his messenger to the commanders of the aforesaid army. Then followed the instructions San had planted in Sir John's arrogant mind: The Chinese were pursuing the same goal as the Europeans—to capture and exterminate the bandits of the Blue Flag. It would be advantageous for the two armies to join forces. The troops of the Celestial Empire knew the area better, while the Europeans had superior military skills.

To his great surprise, Sir John was heard in complete silence—no interruptions, no expressions of agreement. Then Labianov bowed to him politely. "My colleague and I are grateful to you for the worthy sentiments that led you to interrupt your pleasure trip to bring us information. We'd like to offer you the provisions and ammunition you'll need as you pursue your journey."

"Pursue my journey?" stammered Sir John, taken aback at the outcome of his mission.

"I beg your pardon," went on the general still more politely. "Outsiders are not permitted to stay in camp."

"I'm not an outsider—I'm English!"

"English, yes, but an outsider to the army."

"I'll grant you that."

"We must therefore banish you from the camp, since a civilian can remain here in only one capacity."

The Envoy's face cleared. "Only one capacity... I'm sure I qualify."

"I doubt it would suit you," replied Labianov with irony. "The capacity in question is that of a prisoner or a hostage."

This time Sir John didn't insist. With great dignity, standing on tiptoe to lend a little majesty to his figure—which was somewhat broader than it was tall—he turned and gestured at his servants with a commanding air. "About face, fellows. We'll set up our tents outside the encampment, since military caution had denied us here within its confines the rest we've so amply earned after our long nighttime walk!"

But the worthy Member of Parliament was clearly having a bad day. Dignity did him no more good than eloquence had. Labianov said, "One moment."

"Are you changing your mind?" asked Sir John, already anticipating a lavish dinner followed by deep sleep.

"How do you mean, changing my mind?"

"I mean you're going to extend your hospitality to me."

Labianov shook his head. "No, no. The orders from our governments are explicit."

"Then why impede my departure?"

"I'm not impeding your departure, dear sir."

"But..."

"Only, you seem to want to take with you the persons in your party."

"Of course—they're as much outsiders to the army as I am."

"You're mistaken."

"Mistaken in what way?"

"In the following way: I now see that they qualify for the capacity you declined earlier, and I'm going to keep them as hostages."

Sir John's mouth formed an O. His eyebrows took on the shape of circumflex accents—which, as is well known, expresses the greatest possible astonishment. But he was given no time to put into words the feelings provoked in him by the sudden end to the interview. At a sign from Lord Aberdeen, two captains flanked Sir John, took hold of him politely by the arms, and firmly—though without violence—ushered him out of the tent.

Once outside, Sir John tried to explain. His handlers let him talk, let him swear by "Satan's big toe" and "John Bull's pipe" and "St. George's lance"... but they didn't say a word in reply. But if their tongues were still, their legs made up for it. Borne along irresistibly by those "legs without ears," as he called them, Sir John was hustled across the camp, followed by a soldier leading his yak. He went back through the cavalry lines, and through the various sentry lines. Finally he crossed the last outer line of guards. There his escort saluted him, still without a word. After which, turning on their heels, they headed back to camp, leaving the dazed Sir John to himself.

"By the horns of Beelzebub," he sighed. "I'm sorry to say so about an army that includes lots of Englishmen—but I believe they're all mad!"

As if to plant that idea deeper in the poor man's brain, the nearest sentry cocked his rifle and called out menacingly, "Move on, or I'll fire!"

"Another madman!" sighed Sir John. Notwithstanding, he took hold of the bridle of his yak—which was standing next to him, looking just as shamefaced as its rider—and went away, heading back toward San's camp... with hopes of a warmer welcome there. As he rode slowly along, Sir John said to himself, "This is a complete overturning of my beliefs. People call Asians savages and Westerners civilized. But the natives welcomed me as a gentleman, while the white men treated me like a beggar. So which side is more civilized? Which side is more reasonable?"

While San's Envoy was undergoing that expulsion, Aberdeen, at Labianov's request, invited the staff officers to "dismiss"—military-speak for, "Friends, you're free to go."

Only Sir John's former servants remained with the generals. Then, in a single movement, all four of them dropped the furs in which they were bundled, and revealed their faces for the first time.

His voice breaking, Stanislas Labianov cried out, "Mona!" His beloved daughter, whom he'd given up hope of ever seeing again, stood before him. She leapt into his arms. For a few seconds the tent was filled with the sound of kisses and soft words of endearment.

"Father! My dear father!"

"My darling little Mona!"

Aberdeen looked on, overcome by emotion, his thin face shaken by waves of some inner turbulence. He—who'd heard his colleague's painful secret—understood what boundless joy now filled the father's heart. But then his insistent curiosity returned: How had Mona arrived at the camp like that, disguised as the servant of a man supposedly sent there by the Blue Flag? What chain of events had brought her to the terrible wastes of the High Plateaus? Who were her companions? Aberdeen wanted to know all that, and was driven to inquire—motivated not by idle curiosity but by a clear, specific feeling that the girl's arrival was closely connected to the larger task that he and Labianov, as representatives of European civilization under threat, had come to the wastes of Central Asia to carry out. He asked abruptly, "What does all this mean?"

He'd spoken quietly, reluctant to break into his colleague's emotional outpourings. But those words were enough to help Labianov regain control of himself. He loosened his embrace and moved Mona gently away; and then in a voice still shaking with intense emotion, he said in turn, "Yes, yes, it's like a dream. Here you are, my sweet child, and I don't dare believe in the reality of what I see. I would've considered mad anyone who told me, 'It's amid the sharp peaks of the Pamirs that you'll see the one you weep for once again.' Child! Darling Mona! Why and how has this come to be?"

The brave girl had pulled herself together. She understood that before thinking of the sweetness of the reunion, they had to ensure the safety of the army encamped around them. She grew serious, and her face betrayed no trace of her filial feelings. Labianov and Aberdeen, surprised at the change in her, observed her with great attention as she went on slowly, "Father, forget for a moment that I'm your child, and see in me only the messenger of the Blue Flag."

"What! You too!"

"The girl too!" cried Aberdeen, losing his customary cool.

"Yes, but not of the same one."

To describe the generals' astonishment would be impossible. They both murmured, "Not the same one! Well! Then there must be several Blue Flags!"

Mona shook her head sadly. "There's only one, but two different factions are contending for it. One that tortured me, and that seeks your doom, which I hate. The other good, and trustworthy, which I love."

That last word emerged from her mouth borne on the wings of a sigh. It had cost her enormously to confess the feeling that filled her soul—in the presence of the English general so recently a stranger to her—but she'd willed herself to do it, because that confession seemed essential to lend weight to what she was about to say.

As if to distract her listeners, she went on quickly, "I see that I've neglected something very important: to introduce my friends to you—my companions in suffering." She pointed out each of them in turn. "The Duchess of La Roche-Sonnaille..."

"You!" cried Labianov impulsively. "You, Madame, who in my heart I also considered my daughter, you who were for Mona the dearest of sisters!"

But Mona went on, "Monsieur Max Soleil, a French writer. Miss Violet Musketeer, the Australian heiress. Two devoted souls: just from reading a newspaper, they resolved to help two victims—Sara and me, whom they didn't know. They faced a thousand perils for two strangers—and it may be that misery will be the only reward for their goodness." She shook her head as if to drive away an unwelcome thought. "But why predict unhappiness? I'm wrong! We have to hope—always hope!"

Then in a different tone she said, "You, the generals responsible for the lives of the soldiers entrusted to your leadership by your governments, now know who's standing here before you. That was essential—because all of us can only be saved if you feel the same confidence we do. So listen to what I have to say on behalf of the Blue Flag." She paused a moment to think, then went on, "No, not like this. First you have to know how our faith in Dodekhan—the Master of the Blue Flag whose messenger I am—originated and grew."

They listened in silence as she explained. She summarized the strange adventure that had thrust her and Sara into the vast plot that shook all of Asia. She spoke of their brutal separation from their loved ones and their return to France, while Dodekhan and Lucien de La Roche-Sonnaille remained in the hands of the usurper Log; and of what happened at the Loursinade villa, and at the Elleviousse Asylum; and their escape to Stittsheim, and the relentless pursuit by the Amber Masks; and their return to Calcutta, to the palace where they'd been held prisoner before. And there—inexpressible joy—the telephote screen brought proof that the men whose graves they were looking for were still alive. Finally she described the circumstances that had brought them to these labyrinthine mountains, and their betrayal by their guides, and then the black panther that led them to Station B, and their escape.

Labianov and Aberdeen listened without interrupting her. Though they were both well educated, they were men of the little world of Europe, with its preoccupation with petty controversies, where people are oblivious to the great current of ideas that stirs the rest of the globe. The revelation of that ferment left them deeply astonished. They felt like they'd been sucked into a giant whirlpool in a dream. Their European rationality refused to credit it. They wanted it all to be a fairy tale, and yet they couldn't refute the truth being reported by these people, who'd been buffeted by the intense convulsions triggered by the confederation of the secret societies of Asia.

Mona had fallen silent.

"And now?" asked the generals in spite of themselves.

She seemed to return from some train of thought with an effort. She said hesitantly, "Now, I'm afraid."

"Afraid?"

"Afraid that you'll refuse to obey."

The generals drew themselves up. "Obey?"

"Yes, obey the Blue Flag—the good one, the legitimate one."

They wanted to object: they, submit themselves to the orders of the organization they'd come here to fight?

But before they could do so, Mona clasped her hands and said, "Father, father, believe me. You must obey. You hear me? You must! Otherwise all of us—your troops, you, I—will perish." Then, with an effort visible in the tension on her face, she calmed herself and went on slowly, "San—that soul full of hatred, in whose name Sir John Lobster spoke—San wants you to move your camp two days' march to the east. His bait is the news of a Chinese army. It doesn't exist, I'm sure of that. Why does he want you to go that way? I don't know. And yet I sense that he's planning some treachery, preparing some ambush there."

"A military commander can't base his actions on such vague suppositions. Our orders are to proceed east, to find the hideout where..."

Mona fell to her knees.

"What are you doing, child?" stammered Labianov, interrupting his discourse on duty.

"I'm begging you to listen to the advice Dodekhan directed us to pass on to you. Trust him, general. He's the noblest man who ever lived." Then, more quietly, her voice shaking at the violation of all modest reticence, she went on, "Remember, he's the one who saved you on Sakhalin Island, the one who risked his life a hundred times to protect me, the one my soul has chosen over all others. Father, listen to the one who, by right of affection, is your own son."

Her pleading tone made a deep impression on the two generals. They hesitated, exchanging a glance. Finally Aberdeen made a vague gesture and said, "And what does he advise?"

Mona cried out with joy. She spoke breathlessly, her voice shaking with the beating of her heart. "He asks that you remain encamped here."

"Why?"

"I don't know. But the very fact that San is trying to get you to move your army to the east shows that Dodekhan means to thwart his plans. He understands his enemy's intentions. He'll defeat him."

"I'm sure you're right, Mademoiselle," replied Aberdeen. "But consider for a moment the responsibilities we bear. What would our governments say to commanders who came back and reported, 'I sat still and did nothing, because a gentleman who seemed well intentioned advised me to do so'?"

She closed her eyes, struck to the heart by the indisputable logic of what he said.

"You have no answer, Mademoiselle," said Aberdeen, "no doubt because you can see, as we do, that to such a report our governments would reply, 'We entrusted you with troops, because we had faith in your initiative and your military skills. By obeying the word of some stranger, you've betrayed our trust, you've betrayed the hope of the entire nation.'"

"And therefore?" asked Mona, trembling, unable to say more.

"And therefore," concluded Aberdeen, "we must follow our orders and proceed east. If we're going to our death, we'll go to it in accordance with our orders. Russia and Britain will crown our names with honor."

"Father," begged Mona, reaching out to Labianov.

But he looked away, and said firmly, "Lord Aberdeen is exactly right."

Mona frantically passed her hands across her face, as if to drive away a fog obscuring her thoughts. She felt like she was about to fall, like the ground had dropped away beneath her. She'd gone from the pinnacle of hope to the depths of despair. She thought she'd succeeded in putting her father and his troops under Dodekhan's protection—but all of her efforts had run aground against the generals' valiant but narrow-minded conscientiousness. She shivered.

Then Max spoke up. "These gentlemen are entirely in the right. They're in no position to give way without complete information." Mona gestured miserably in disagreement, but Max went on, "I'm sure Monsieur Dodekhan would agree. So, with these gentlemen's permission, we'll get in touch with him. He'll certainly agree to expand on our explanations, which I grant were somewhat cursory."

Mona looked reassured. As for the two generals, they listened in astonishment. Get in touch with the Blue Flag? What could this Frenchman be saying? And Mona seemed to understand him! She'd stood up, and was laughing through her tears and stammering, "Yes, yes, good idea. The speaker, right? Where can we attach it?"

Max looked around the tent, then pointed to the central pole that held it up. "This pole."

"Try it."

"Yes, try it, try it," murmured Violet and Sara.

Witnessing this incomprehensible scene, Labianov could no longer contain himself. Going over to Max, he asked, "What are you planning to do?" while Aberdeen expressed the same question by his looks and gestures.

Max smiled as he unfolded the speaker little Merry had given back to him. He stuck the point into the pole, then beckoned Mona over to the device. "You call, Mademoiselle. Your voice will be more pleasing to our friend's ears."

The baffled generals watched Mona lean down. "Hello? Hello?"

A moment later, there a was slight crackle, followed by a distant but still perfectly clear voice: "Mona, it's you! Your voice is unmistakable. What do you need?"

"I need you to convince my father."

"Your father? So you're with him?"

"Yes, in his tent. He's here, listening. Can you inspire in him the blind trust I have in you?"

The peculiar conversation filled the tent. Aberdeen was leaning forward, as if to seize in midair the words coming out of the speaker. Labianov held his head in his hands. Both generals were as white as sheets. Of course they were brave; both of them had demonstrated the staunchest courage in their careers. But for a soldier, facing death is a familiar thing—whereas this conversation, by means of some device, with a person in some unknown location, had a fantastical aspect that stunned them.

"Well, will you do it?" implored Mona again.

"I'll do whatever you wish, Mona," said the distant voice gently. "I was silent because I was starting up my telephote. I can see you now. I see His Excellency General Labianov. Tell him to put his mind at ease. Science shouldn't be so upsetting. Let him come closer and question me. I'll answer him just as I would you, the best part of my soul."

At Mona's request, and Aberdeen's urging, Labianov found himself at the speaker before he knew it. He was dumbfounded to the point of freezing up, with not a single clear thought in his head.

But far away, deep in the Central Exchange where he was at the same time San's prisoner and the master of the indescribable scientific power assembled by his father, Dodekhan could presumably see every detail of what was happening. He called out cheerfully, "Your Excellency, I'm at your disposal."

That acted like a bugle call on Labianov. His face cleared instantly and shone with a soldier's pride. Dodekhan was watching him and had heard him earlier: it was important now to keep his misgivings to himself. Overcoming his emotions and steadying his voice, the general said firmly, "Why does San want us to move two days' march east? Why do you, on the contrary, wish us to stay put?"

"Two questions, two answers," came the voice from the speaker. "First: San wants to lead you to a place called the Valley of the *Gilds*, for the simple reason that the ground is covered in mines whose explosions can be heard far away."

"Mines, out here?"

"It only seems uninhabited, don't forget. Hundred of eyes are watching your camp. Hundred of ears are listening for the slightest sound. Right now Sir John Lobster, whom you expelled, has already been picked up by one of San's patrols. They're rushing him to where San waits for news of the outcome of his treacherous plotting."

"How do you know that?" blurted Labianov involuntarily.

"I can see him. But to continue: San will learn that you've kept as hostages the people Sir John still thinks were his servants—and he'll be surprised to hear that the real servants were found tied up in the caves, where they were caught and overpowered by the people now with you, so they could take their places and reach you."

The generals looked questioningly at the travelers for confirmation, and they nodded. That detail did more than anything else to convince the commanders, since the man whose voice they could hear had scientific means of seeing from afar what was going on in the camp, and around it, and miles away from it. They grasped the enormous benefits of an alliance with him. And when

Labianov spoke again, it was in a tone of noticeably greater respect. "So now what will San think?"

"That his prisoners, and not his bandits, reached your headquarters. He'll realize that rather than break camp to move, you're going to stay where you are."

"I haven't said so."

"But you're going to say it, general. I can see it on your face. You trust me."

Labianov turned to his colleague as if to deny it, but Aberdeen murmured, "It's perfectly understandable. I too feel a growing confidence in this gentleman."

Dodekhan went on, "So now San and his forces will attack you where you are—and he'll settle on that plan once he's sure you mean to stay there."

"Attack us? But then we need to occupy the surrounding ridges."

"Do no such thing."

"It would be too risky just to stay at the bottom of this extinct crater."

"Good point! I promise that no one will come any closer than a hundred paces from your outer lines."

"Hurrah," muttered Aberdeen. "But what if they attack us without coming any closer?"

"They'll be driven back. A terrible panic will scatter them to the four corners of the horizon. I'll make sure of that."

"You?"

"Myself. But to spare you solving riddles, I'll explain. You're aware that the ground near electrical machinery can become charged, just like a battery.[40] Well, thanks to the use of various lines of electrical conductivity, I've managed to charge certain places. The entire outer slope of the crater you're in is one of those places. An impassable zone separates you from your enemies—and mine. That's why I'm asking you not to move elsewhere." There was a long silence. Finally Dodekhan spoke again. "Will you stay, general?"

"Yes!" cried Aberdeen, who was quicker to make up his mind than his colleague.

Labianov smiled. He gave his daughter a long look, then quietly confirmed, "We'll stay."

---

[40] Recent accidents at a number of electrical power plants have drawn the attention of the scientific world to this phenomenon [*Note from the Author*]. Earth can conduct telluric electricity, but not as well as wires. Its resistance depends on the type of the ground, the moisture, how far is one point from the other where one measures the resistance, and other factors.

CHAPTER VII
The Prisoners in the Central Exchange

"As you're aware, my friend, here's the dilemma: On the one hand, we're trapped here, and we can only get out if someone comes to free us. On the other hand, I don't want the instruments to which my father devoted his life to fall into the hands of any government."

"Damn! Damn! Then we'll never get out!"

That exchange between Dodekhan and Lucien, Duke of La Roche-Sonnaille, clearly laid out their complicated, troubling position. They were sitting in the Central Exchange as described by San to Mona at Station B: a circular hall, whose stone walls were only partly visible, their lower half hidden behind strange machines bristling with handles, levers, gears, and buttons of all kinds. That enormous laboratory of sorts had only one exit, and through that arched passageway could be seen, in a purplish gloom, the sanctuary of the underground temple, with its lines of staggered columns rising toward the vaulted ceiling like the trunks of a stone forest.

Facing that single doorway, the gray canvas of a telephote screen, framed by copper rods, covered the wall. But that screen could pivot on hinges. Wheels, levers, and a whole clockwork apparatus attached to the copper frame showed how the screen was moved.

"Anyway," said Lucien with a show of cheerfulness, "thank you, my dear Dodekhan, for presenting the situation so clearly. You want to prepare me for a long lease on this apartment—which wouldn't be bad at all, if we were allowed to go out."

"We'll get out."

"You think?"

"You don't take my word for it," murmured Dodekhan.

"Forgive me for having doubts. Believe me, it's not intended as a slight against you. But these past few days I've watched you: First you worked to guide my wife and Mona and their friends to Station B to meet that rascal San. Then you worked to get them to the Anglo-Russian army camp."

"Do you think I did wrong?"

"You know I don't. Now you're doing everything you can to protect that army against an attack by the forces San has spread out in the mountains. That too seems admirable, but... it also seems to have very little connection to our own freedom."

Dodekhan smiled. "And yet," he said confidently, "reuniting Mona with her father, and saving those brave British and Russian troops, are essential steps toward bringing about our own release."

Lucien looked surprised.

"For you to understand," continued Dodekhan, "I'll have share with you some details you're not aware of." He looked down before going on. "Neither my father nor I considered the possibility of betrayal, and as a result our work remains unfinished."

"Unfinished?"

"Decide for yourself. From here we can strike at enemies two thousand leagues away. What does it take? By pressing a lever or pulling on a handle, we unleash our speedy silent servant, electrical current. We can do that—and yet our power stops at the threshold of that temple. A few steps from here, I become powerless. I repeat, neither my father nor I imagined that betrayal would surround us, that we'd have to defend ourselves against those who were our friends the day before, yesterday's soldiers now become our worst enemies." Lucien nodded in understanding. "That's why those guarding us have eluded my wrath," went on Dodekhan slowly. "Sure, I can follow everything they do on the telephote screen, but I can't strike them or punish them. Right outside the Central Exchange, I'm merely a man, who'd be shattered against the immovable obstacle of hundreds of guards."

He stopped. Lucien watched him with friendly sympathy. He wanted to say something to comfort and relieve him, but no words came to mind. The peculiar situation they were in lay outside all the normal terms of human relations.

The Master of the Blue Flag broke the silence once again. "To fall in some final battle would be nothing, my dear duke; but it would be disastrous to fall while leaving this vast enterprise—a structure meant to emancipate a whole race—in the hands of either these bloodstained brutes or the European powers, any of whom would turn it into an instrument of oppression." With a deep sigh, Dodekhan concluded, "The means for destroying the only access to the temple are a kilometer away from here, in a bunker we named Station A. Barely a thousand meters of tunnel separate us from it—but I can't get there, because so many of our jailers are guarding the route. That's what keeps me here, and leads me to take actions at a distance that you mock. Ah, duke, don't mock me: I'm searching for someone who might save us, who'll reach Station A from the outside. I hope my heart doesn't break in the search!"

His head sank to his chest, and his face filled with deep discouragement. Impulsively, Lucien took him in his arms; he was touched by his friend's suffering. For him, Dodekhan had become a brother by choice. The dangers and challenges they'd faced together had in some way bonded the two men.

But before he could express his affection and devotion, hoarse voices rang out under the temple vault. It was those Prayer Engravers, those without respect for the man whose dream it was to liberate Asia. Why? Because Asians are no more clairvoyant than Europeans: they curse their benefactors and praise those who take advantage of their folly. San had told them, "Dodekhan wanted to be nice to the Europeans who stole our lands. I want to spill their blood, because we'd betray our fathers by not avenging them!"

267

His hollow words rang in those thick skulls. Barbaric atavism did the rest. Every single one of them would happily have slain Dodekhan. Since the impassable electrical barrier blocking the entrance to the Central Exchange wouldn't let them, since it repelled attackers the way it had repelled San's bullet, those idiots stayed safely in the sanctuary while they howled out their hatred of the man they should've loved—the man who represented the second generation dedicated to the freedom of Asia. "Death to Dodekhan, that flunky of the Europeans!" they roared. "Death to the traitor!" Insults filled the air and rose to the vaulted ceiling.

Irritated, Lucien felt a mounting anger against the injustice, the idiocy of those loudmouths, those spokesmen for the madness of crowds. He'd learned to love his friend for his steadfastness and his fairness. He could imagine what he must be suffering as he listened to that frenzy of ingratitude. Turning to Dodekhan, he was struck by how sad he looked. Taking him by the hand, he cried, "Never mind the howling of those fools! Your own conscience testifies to your devotion and self-sacrifice!"

He stopped as Dodekhan smiled sadly. "That's not what bothers me."

"What—you don't mind it?"

"Yes and no. It doesn't bother me personally, but it's terribly painful as it relates to the plans I inherited from my father."

"I don't follow."

Dodekhan gestured toward the fanatics. "You see those men."

"And I hear them," said Lucien lightly.

"Do you think they're ready for independence?"

"Certainly not."

"And yet those Prayer Engravers are an elite among Asians."

"That doesn't speak well for the rest."

"And it fills me with despair—because they force me to acknowledge that my father and I believed too soon in their capacity for emancipation. Our call for freedom will become a call for butchery. And it pains me to think I won't be the one who'll have the supreme joy of leading Asia to independence."

For a moment the two friends sat in silence, their eyes locked. Then Dodekhan passed a hand across his brow, as if to drive away a veil of thought. He went on in a firm voice, "That means I have to husband the inheritance my father passed on to me. At the hour of destiny—the hour that'll lead Asia to freedom—the powers gathered by Dilevnor's genius must be found intact." He gestured at the machinery around them. "This is the arsenal of liberty. It has to be saved from both Asians and the even greedier Europeans."

The shouting in the sanctuary had ended. Presumably the mob, without knowing why, had realized that the prisoners didn't care; nothing discourages insults or teasing like the indifference of its target. So they'd decided to leave the temple and take the proof of their loud ineptitude elsewhere.

Noticing the silence in the temple, Dodekhan went to the entrance of the Central Exchange—without stepping through it. He looked carefully to make sure that none of the Prayer Engravers had stayed by the altar, or around the columns, or near the incense-burning niches carved into the rock walls. Coming back to Lucien, he said, "The little daily demonstration is over. No one will come bother us. Let's use the telephote to make a tour of our friends and enemies."

He approached the gray screen. A soft metallic click rang out in the silence: he'd just activated the mechanism attached to the copper frame. The telephote screen brightened, and a mountainous landscape appeared. Then a steady vibration of the image created the sensation of moving rapidly by locomotive. They appeared to be rushing toward the landscape: ridges gave way to higher ridges, valleys to ravines, rounded hills to bare peaks. The awful desolation of the High Plateaus was spread out before Dodekhan's eyes.

He reached out and made a small ratchet drop between the teeth of a gear. The screen froze, holding the image that was currently on it. It was the shore of a lake, from which rose lazy curls of steam. A few steps away, a pile of ruins charred by fire formed a patch of black on the pale green grass. "Station B," he murmured. "San has broken camp. There's the trail his troops followed. Of course it leads toward the Anglo-Russian camp. He's decided to attack— perfect! Let's see what that traitor has planned..."

He flicked the ratchet up and gave a steel handle a quarter turn, and the screen pivoted about forty-five degrees on its hinges. Once again the image vibrated. Once again the scenery of the High Plateaus rolled by. At first it was empty, but then people appeared. Groups of men on barely visible trails were in motion, all converging in the same direction. They were natives, bundled in furs, with cruel, sinister faces.

"They're all on the way," murmured Dodekhan. "The attack is near."

The image on the screen still rushed forward. Now the groups of men were larger and more numerous. Then, through a break in the mountains, they could see a wild valley surrounded by sheer cliffs, and that valley was filled with an indescribable bustle of men, animals, and felt tents. At the center of all that ferment and rising above it stood San's conical tent; the blue flag flying over it snapped in the wind that howled through the valley.

"How far away is the Anglo-Russian camp?" wondered Dodekhan, his voice betraying no emotion.

The image rushed onward. The valley filled with San's forces vanished, and now the screen showed nothing but empty wasteland. Suddenly two sentries appeared, one British and one Russian. Dodekhan quickly dropped the ratchet again, and the scenery froze. He consulted a dial attached to the bottom of the screen, on which a pivoting needle trembled. "Fifty-five seconds," he said. "The two armies are six kilometers apart. San will order the attack for tonight." He turned to his companion, who'd gone to check the exit to the temple. "Lucien," he called, and the duke turned. "Without a doubt, our friends will be attacked tonight."

Lucien gave a start. "Tonight?" he echoed in a choked voice.

"Yes. San has massed his forces barely six kilometers from the outer Anglo-Russian lines. That suggests the attack is imminent. You know my plans as well as I do. You can explain them to your brave wife, when they call us on the wireless speaker."

"Ah! Thank you for that kind thought, Dodekhan."

"Don't thank me—you who sacrificed yourself for me." Seeing Lucien about to protest, Dodekhan went on, "Take my place here. See what your beloved is doing right now. The sight of her will be sweet to you, while you wait until you can talk to her."

He gently led the duke to the screen. Lucien didn't resist. He released the locked gear, but lowered the speed of the moving image on the screen. They passed the outer sentries, then the several defense lines. Now they could see the European camp on the floor of the crater. They climbed the small hill, revealing the headquarters of the generals and their staff officers. Beyond it stood a large tent.

Lucien froze the image. He knew that tent was home to Sara, Mona, and Violet, since for a week now he'd been directing the telephote there every time the temple sanctuary was unoccupied. Oh, he knew everything about the life of those whom Dodekhan had guided to the European encampment. He knew that Max was sharing a nearby tent with the chief of staff, that the writer spent all day with the young women, that he made them go for walks around camp, that every day exactly at noon he attached his speaker to the central tent post and sent out a loud hello, which he tried again every hour if for some reason—such as guards being in the sanctuary, those fanatics praying before the altar to no god—Dodekhan was unable to answer. For a week now, Lucien's imprisonment had grown more painful to him. He could see Sara! But she couldn't see him. And he reflected bitterly that she'd never see him again, that he'd never escape past all those guards. But earlier, Dodekhan had said something that gave him hope: "The protection of the Anglo-Russian army is one step toward the liberation of the captives in the underground temple."

Of course Lucien hadn't understood the connection between the two, but he had total confidence in his friend. The vague promise implied in those words had comforted him. And today seeing Sara on the screen would give him unalloyed pleasure. He loosened the screws on two threaded coils, and suddenly the tent walls seemed to dissolve and vanish, allowing him to see what was going on inside.

Sara was seated on a camp cot, hugging Mona, whose face was pressed against Sara's elbow. Max and Violet stood before them in animated conversation—at least based on their gestures and their moving mouths. Fear, surprise, and irritation were visible on all their faces.

"What can have stirred them up like this?" Without meaning to, Lucien had spoken aloud. Thanks to the telephote he could see—but he couldn't hear: only the speaker device could transmit sounds. So it gave him intense anxiety to be able to guess, purely by sight, that Sara and her friends were upset—and yet be unable to know exactly what was upsetting them. Now he saw Max take out his pocket watch—and Lucien unconsciously did the same. "Five minutes till twelve." To him it meant that in five minutes the speaker would ring, in five minutes he'd be able to question Sara, and find out why her normally sparkling eyes now looked so worried.

"What's wrong?" asked Dodekhan in surprise.

"I can see they're upset. I'm waiting to find out why."

"You won't have long to wait. Monsieur Max is setting up the speaker now."

He was right: Max was attaching his speaker to the central tent pole, to bring together across a vast distance all of San's victims. The silence lasted another second; then a large membrane at right angles to the screen vibrated: "Hello?"

"I'm here," replied Lucien, his voice shaking.

Sara leapt up and came to the speaker. "It's Lucien—let me speak to him." Max stepped aside. She leaned close to the speaker, and in an indecipherable tone she said, "Reassure me, Lucien. I'm frightened."

"Frightened?"

"I've been waiting anxiously for noon. For a week everything was fine. Then last night, inexplicable things began happening again."

"What do you mean?"

"The reconnaissance balloons—though they were well guarded—have been sliced to bits; they're useless."

"That means San's about to attack," replied Lucien with a sigh of relief. "The balloons would've detected his army's movements. Is that what was upsetting you earlier?"

The membrane vibrated with an exclamation of surprise. "How did you know we were upset?"

"By means of the telephote. I was watching you, darling, and I was going mad because I couldn't tell what was bothering you."

Dodekhan broke in, "Hurry, my dear Lucien. We could be interrupted at any moment. We have to pass on our instructions."

"You're right." And Lucien went on quickly, "Dodekhan believes the camp will be attacked tonight. Have Generals Labianov and Aberdeen give strict orders that no soldier take action. Have all the electric lights ready to use as soon as the attack starts, but let no one take action. The troops will be treated to a fine show—but they should remain spectators, otherwise they'll share their enemies' fate."

"Get to the part about them," said Dodekhan. "Our jailers haven't been by in quite a while."

Lucien went on, "Without telling anyone—you understand?—once the battle's over, you and Miss Mona will go out to the sentry lines. If anyone asks, say you're curious. Stay calm; no one will be surprised. Head toward the little red peak that overlooks the crater on the southeast, and which is lit up by the sun around four o'clock."

"I know the place."

"Merry and Twinkle will be waiting for you there. Follow them. They'll tell you what you have to do to be reunited with us for good."

Mona had come to stand with Sara, and together they said, "We'll go."

"And so will I!" cried Max cheerfully.

Lucien glanced at Dodekhan, who nodded, after which the duke said, "If you'd like, Monsieur Soleil—though it involves some danger."

"That settles it!" said Max.

"We know you're brave. We're only pointing out the danger because if Miss Musketeer stays in camp alone…"

Violet cut him off. "I'm going with my friends. Monsieur Max and I started this journey to help two strangers. They're our friends now, and this is no time to abandon them."

Dodekhan signaled to him again, and Lucien hurried to wrap up the call. "As you wish. Don't try to contact us again today. You'll call again only when you're on the way. It'd be awful if some mishap thwarted all our plans. Goodbye, Sara, goodbye."

"Goodbye!" That was all. Max, struck by Lucien's warning, had taken down the speaker and was putting it carefully back in his pocket.

"Someone's coming," said Dodekhan. "The telephote!"

Gears and levers turned, the screen went gray and was pushed back against the wall, and by the time half a dozen fanatics entered the temple sanctuary howling for the death of the prisoners protected in the Central Exchange by the electric barrier, no trace remained of the "interview."

The morning's violent demonstration was repeated: in their impotent fury, the men hurled insults and curses at their unreachable adversaries. Then, when they'd shouted themselves hoarse, they withdrew.

Apparently Dodekhan hadn't even noticed them. When silence was restored, he said only, "Everything's ready now. Let's eat, then sleep until the evening meal. We'll be up all night."

He flipped the switch that controlled the protective electric curtain—against which all of San's efforts had failed—then stepped through the doorway. A basket had been left at the foot of the marble cube of the altar. He picked it up, returned to the room, and reset the switch.

The fanatics who'd been insulting them were also the guards assigned to bring them food. The two prisoners willingly ate the coarse fare they'd been given. Then they stretched out on their mats and went to sleep. At a moment when they were getting ready to risk their lives and their happiness, they fell into a calm, dreamless sleep... two heroes preparing for battle.

"Nine o'clock," said Lucien.

Dodekhan nodded. "The vigil begins. Activate the electro-telluric devices that'll protect the Anglo-Russian camp from surprise attack."

Overcome by emotion, the two men shook hands. The ultimate battle—at least so they hoped—was about to begin. They powered up the telephote. The screen must already have been aimed correctly, because right away in the nighttime landscape they were looking at the floor of the extinct crater, and the sleeping camp of the armies sent from Europe.

But soon they heard noises: footsteps, still distant, were advancing down the passages leading to the underground sanctuary. What could it mean? Who'd be coming there so late? Usually their jailers left them alone after the evening meal. Why had their routine changed? With a turn of the gears, the image vanished from the screen.

Just in time: a group of Prayer Engravers, of Amber Masks, burst into the temple, escorting a portly red-faced man with fiery hair, who was panting and struggling and resisting—squeezed into a suit of European cut. This time the men didn't shout insults at the prisoners. They gathered respectfully around the stranger while they showed him the altar, and the Central Exchange, and the passage between them. Then, on his signal, they withdrew in orderly fashion, leaving him standing there alone, lit by a heavy bronze lamp carved in the form of a dragon.

Dodekhan and Lucien exchanged a glance in silence. Clearly they were wondering what this stranger wanted, and if he meant to stay there, and if his unexpected presence was going to hinder them in carrying out their plans.

They were soon answered. Once the stranger was sure he was alone in the sanctuary, he approached the entrance to the Central Exchange—cautiously, like a man who'd been warned not to get too close—and in a strong English accent he said, "Good evening to you, gentlemen. I'm to spend my time in your company for a few days. To keep our relations correct, I'll introduce myself." He struck a buffoonish attitude that he must've thought impressive, and went on, "Sir John Lobster, Member of Parliament for Beggingbridge, currently Envoy and friend of the distinguished San, Master of the Blue Flag."

Dodekhan and Lucien started. Lobster! In the past few days, via Max's speaker, they'd learned about Sir John and what role he'd played.

"I'm charged," went on Sir John, "with conveying to your ears a verbal message from the great San; and my pleasure in passing it on will be the greater because, when you separated San from the two ladies who interest him, you also separated me from my fiancée." He paused. Since his listeners made no answer, he went on, "The two ladies and my sweetheart have escaped. San is sure your tricks played a part in that. As he's very busy with some small matter, he's dispatched me to you: *primo*, to warn you that he'll soon be back to finish you off, and *secundo*, he said, addressing my honorable self, 'Sir John, you're English, you understand machinery, all Englishmen understand machinery. You'll keep a close eye on my prisoners, and you'll find out how to work the diabolical instruments thanks to which they're keeping me in check.'" Puffing out his checks with satisfaction, he concluded, "I assume my explanation is clear to you, as well as candid. Now you know a pair of English eyes are watching you."

Upon which, Sir John went back to his earlier spot. From a basket the prisoners hadn't noticed when he arrived, he drew a flask, a glass, a pitcher, and a spirit lamp, and directed his attention to the expert mixing of a hot toddy. No doubt that's what he meant by keeping a pair of English eyes on them.

They—alas—felt in no mood for comical reflections. With him here, they could do nothing. And even if they resolved to act anyway, and to reveal to him the secret of the telephote, they had no way to warn Sara and Mona and their friends of the unexpected complication—that San was returning. So the women would leave camp, guided by Merry and Twinkle, and suddenly run into San on their way. Why had they told their friends not to use the speaker again before they carried out their instructions?

They stood there for a while, appalled. Then Dodekhan whispered, so quietly that Lucien could barely hear him, "Our first priority is to make sure the Anglo-Russian army has the protection it's rightly counting on."

Switches and levers clicked, and then a humming noise, like a waterfall, filled the room and reached the sanctuary. Sir John raised his eyes from his hot toddy and looked anxiously right, then left. Seeing nothing, he muttered, "What's going on?"

"It's a waterfall I've just located, which is pouring into the temple galleries," replied Dodekhan with impressive calm.

"A waterfall, quite so. I thought I recognized the sound."

"In half an hour the water will fill the sanctuary to the ceiling."

"To the ceiling!" cried Sir John in a panic. "I won't be able to breathe!" But then, thinking it over, he added, "And you'll be drowned too!"

"No, we won't."

"How not?"

"The electrical barrier that keeps people out will stop the water, just as it stopped the bullet San fired at me. He must've told you about that."

"Yes, yes," stammered the apoplectic Sir John, whose terror was rising by the minute. "In that case, I'm running away. San didn't foresee a waterfall." He hastily stuffed the spirit lamp, the glass, the flask, and the pitcher back into the wicker basket, picked it up, and ran toward the passageway by which he'd entered the sanctuary earlier.

But Dodekhan's voice stopped him cold. "That's useless! By now the tunnels are impassable. They're flooded. In ten minutes the surging water will reach the hall you're in."

Sir John wheezed with terror. His legs shook under him. In his distress he dropped the basket, which rolled across the floor with a sound of breaking glass. "How can I escape? How?" cried the poor man in a choked voice.

"Take refuge in here with us. I wanted to show you that I don't wish for your death."

"But what about the electric curtain?"

"I'll interrupt it for a moment."

Dodekhan flipped the switch, came down the passage, and stepped through the opening without incident. But, seeing him approach, Sir John was seized by a new suspicion. He drew his revolver and roared, "One more step and I'll fire!"

"Don't bother," said Dodekhan, as he spun around and returned the way he came. "I don't try to save people against their will." He went back inside and made a few careful adjustments to the electro-telluric instruments, and the noise grew louder, until it sounded like a torrent roaring right nearby.

A climax of fear now blinded Sir John. He'd passed from terror to panic. Unthinkingly he rushed to the entrance to the Central Exchange, and crossed the threshold. Once he was inside there was a loud click. He turned, revolver in hand. "Don't come any closer!"

"Fear has confused you, sir," said Dodekhan cooly. "I just switched back on the current that'll protect us from the water."

Embarrassed, Sir John lowered his gun and let his arm hang loose by his side. But then Dodekhan activated a set of miniature interlocked gears... Sir John cried out in astonishment—an irresistible force had torn his revolver from his hand. He spun around: his pistol was stuck to the two poles of an electromagnet that Dodekhan had just switched on. In a frenzy Sir John rushed over to reclaim his gun—but he succeeded only in getting a shock that threw him three paces back and left him rolling across the floor.

Though wrenched and bruised, he tried to get up. Impossible: understanding what he was trying to do, Dodekhan and Lucien had leapt on the fat man. They tied him up, gagged him, and blindfolded him with a strip of cloth. They carried him to one of the mats and laid him down with his face to the wall.

Then, with a sigh of relief, Dodekhan cried, "Now he's blind and deaf, and nothing more will stop us from seeing what's going on over there in the crater!" But then he lowered his voice and said sadly, "My dear duke, take this man's revolver. It might come in handy later."

Lucien switched off the electromagnet and collected the pistol, while Dodekhan started up the telephote again. On the screen they could see the crater floor, and the tents. It was a dark night. Heavy clouds crossed the sky, pushed along by storm winds. There was no light. A few campfires were burning out. There must've been braziers inside the tents to keep them warm, but all the openings were sealed tight. The generals had faithfully followed the directions Sara had passed on to them.

Ten o'clock. They two men stood facing the screen, waiting for the arrival of the enemy through the dark landscape. Dodekhan reflected bitterly that he— the advocate of Asian liberation—was a prisoner, alone against all the sons of Asia. How ironic! His only friends now were that little group of Europeans: thanks to them, he might perhaps defeat San.

CHAPTER VIII
In Which Neither the Russians, Nor the English,
Nor the Prayer Engravers, Nor Even San Himself
Can Understand a Thing

Using the telephote in the Central Exchange, Dodekhan and Duke Lucien could see the interior of the tent in which Sara and her friends still waited together. After their conversation on the speaker, they'd passed his instructions on to the generals... of course leaving out the part that applied to them. Then, filled with emotions—partly the anxiety of waiting and partly the uncertainly about what they'd have to do once they left the camp—they'd wandered around among the tents, trying in vain to take an interest in all the little details of camp life. They needed relief from their obsessive thoughts, escape from the endless alternatives their imaginations conjured. Alas! They'd all been made cruelly aware that when the inner monologue had free rein, nothing could stop the mind spinning wildly. At nightfall, as dark and cold began to descend, they made their way to command headquarters, where the generals expected them for dinner.

In the week they'd been staying in camp, the travelers and their hosts had come to think alike. By now—long conversations having brought them up to date on all of the duchess's adventures—Labianov and Lord Aberdeen had come to believe in Dodekhan as fervently as Sara did. So now Labianov greeted them with the words, "All of the arrangements asked for by the Blue Flag have been taken care of."

"Wonderful," exclaimed Mona, delighted by the new alliance between her father and the man she privately called her fiancé.

"We've pulled our line of sentries back to the inner slope of the crater."

"Well done, again."

"But, since we need to be prepared for anything, all of the troops will be armed and ready. We've concentrated the artillery on the hill around command headquarters, so that if need be their fire can be aimed in any direction. But strict orders have been given that the troops take no action, and don't fire a single bullet, until they see a red flare fired from this hill."

"What about the electric lights?"

"They've been arrayed along the battlefront, and can be switched on instantly." The two generals laughed, and Labianov said, "It'll be as bright as day on that plateau. I expect the attackers will be unpleasantly surprised."

During dinner the generals were in a cheerful mood. Nothing makes leaders of men happier than the thought that they've made their subordinates safe and discomfited their enemies. If they'd been less focused on approaching events, they'd have noticed a certain constraint in Mona and Sara. The two women seemed to be making an effort to hide their thoughts. In fact they were reflecting that once the battle was won, sadness would strike General Labianov in his hour of joy: his daughter would secretly leave the camp, to head for a destination chosen by the Master of the Blue Flag and known only to him.

Finally dinner came to an end. The generals went out around the camp, to make sure one last time that their orders had been carried out exactly. The travelers returned together to their own tent.

Sara, who was always attentive to her friend's sadness, asked her quietly, "Mona, why not leave word for your father?"

"Why not?" Mona's eyes brightened. But after a short pause she said, "Still, can I? Wouldn't that go against the wishes of..."

"Of Dodekhan. I don't think so. It all depends on what's in your note." Sara went on gently, "Come on, think it over, dear. What pain is it that you wish to spare your wonderful father? That of learning of your disappearance without knowing its cause, right?"

"Of course."

"Then wouldn't it be enough to let him know you left camp voluntarily, to do your part in the final destruction of the enemies of European civilization? Ask him to keep your secret—by order of Dodekhan. You won't have given away anything Dodekhan told us in confidence, and yet you'll have given your father hope."

Mona's only answer was to hug Sara. Then she wrote out a short letter along the lines her friend had suggested. Once that was done, they all felt at a loose end—the natural emotion of anyone waiting for an event over which they have no control. But they also felt a vague anxiety: would the scientific effect Dodekhan had predicted work? Of course the four travelers gathered in the tent had now spent months living in a scientific wonderland; still, they had yet to witness a phenomenon as powerful as this one: a single man, using an unknown device, from a distance, stopping the furious charge of a barbarian horde. Doubt—that subtle torturer in times of waiting—seeped into them, nibbled at their minds, planted in their spirits the seeds of discouragement.

The whole camp had fallen silent. The lines of tents could barely be seen by the dim light of the stars. On the high ground around the generals' headquarters, the cannons—freed from their protective wrappings—stretched their steel throats toward the dark horizon that hid the movements of the enemy they all waited for.

From time to time, one or another of the travelers lifted the tent flap, glanced outside, then came back with a shake of the head. No one considered that, at that same hour, deep in their prison in the Central Exchange, Dodekhan and Lucien, facing the telephote screen, were watching the same landscape with the same attention to the mysteries of that tense night.

Midnight, then one in the morning.

Early in their vigil, Max had tried a few times to lead his companions into meandering conversations, whose main point was to distract all of them from

278

their thoughts. But gradually he'd met with more and more resistance; and perhaps he himself had grown tired of trying. Silence now prevailed.

The troops, the officers, the generals, must've found that night's vigil interminable. Danger itself wasn't hard to face; what was painful, what sapped courage, was the proximity of danger without knowing when it would strike. Everyone's brave in the heat of battle; almost everyone trembles when waiting, armed and ready, for the order that'll hurl them into the inferno. Indeed, San seemed to be taking mischievous pleasure in prolonging the army's uncertainty.

After another long silence, Violet said, "Two o'clock."

At that very moment, Max was looking out through the tent flap. He turned. "Shh!"

The young women stood up and came toward him. "Do you hear something?"

He whispered, "Listen."

They stood still, listening. That night the biting cold seemed to claw the earth with icy talons. The ground crackled, and occasionally gave off a short loud bang. It was cold enough to shatter rock. The temperature dropped so low that boulders fell gradually to dust, which the next summer's thaw would carry down to the plains, toward the sea, to be deposited as alluvial silt in river deltas.

"Well?" asked Sara after a moment.

Max cut her off with a gesture. "I feel like out there, beyond the ring of darkness around us, I can hear noises other than the sounds of Nature."

The others listened more carefully. By now their ears were used to the sound of shattering rocks, and they thought they could hear other noises in the distance.

Suddenly Violet pointed. "Someone's marching over there."

It was true! They could make out the careful footsteps of an army—not the steady rhythm of a disciplined detachment, but the confused rumble of a band of irregulars, each man advancing at will, without concern for the pace of the rest.

"From that side too," murmured Mona, pointing in the opposite direction. She too was right. The same confused tramping filled the darkness. Yes, it was the enemy—finally! A quiet hum rose in the camp, along with movement: men were coming out of their tents; they went to their assigned stations; regiments drew themselves up in battle lines.

Now the sound of the troops advancing in the darkness could be heard on all sides. An enormous cordon of natives was steadily tightening around the crater that sheltered the little European army. It sounded like a numberless horde converging on the spoils. Where had San recruited so many fighters? How had he brought them all here? No European could've said. The secret of their routes and resupply on the High Plateaus had been well guarded. And yet, in those wastes where a man could die of hunger, San had found means to feed his warriors and keep them strong and healthy.

The noise grew, became an uproar. Dark figures could be seen moving in the night. Then a terrifying howl rose to the sky—a menacing war cry encircling the camp. The feet of a great host shook the ground: it was the attack.

And then suddenly the darkness fled. Brilliant white light flooded the edges of the camp. All the spotlights had been switched on at once. The sudden brightness astonished the attackers. The now-exposed mass of men wavered, but only for a moment. The crowd came on again. It was now barely two hundred meters from the rim of the crater, and still advancing. It reached a hundred and fifty, a hundred and twenty-five meters. Had Dodekhan been wrong about the power of his electro-telluric apparatus? Was the barrier he hoped to set in the path of the opposing army an illusion? The enemy kept coming.

The generals watching from their quarters felt the same doubts as the travelers. A red flare rose whistling above the hill. At that signal, the crater floor swarmed like an anthill. Battalions converged, commands rang out. Around the generals' tent, artillerymen readied and aimed the cannons.

But all those preparation ended before they were complete. A kind of crackling rippled around the crater, and a great shout—of terror on the outside, of elation on the inside—shook the air. An invisible enemy had neatly cut down the front ranks of the attackers. Hundreds of natives had been flung to the ground, where they writhed with the howls of the damned. Those behind them tried to retreat—impossible: the rear ranks pushed relentlessly forward, forcing the van to step out onto the electrified ground.

With their weapons at ease, the Russians watched and the British joked. A tremendous, feverish delight seized the troops—and overflowed when electric sparks like spears of fire filled the no man's land. It lasted just a few minutes. Of the great host San had sent to attack, only two or three hundred men remained, scattered in the circle around the camp—stunned, driven mad, fleeing in all directions, howling in terror. All the rest had been struck down by the prodigious electrical display.

The survivors' panic intoxicated the defending soldiers. Though their officers tried in vain to stop them, they made an instinctive, irresistible rush forward. They didn't get far: the first ones to reach the rim of the crater were flung back and rolled at the feet of their comrades. That was all it took to break the fighting momentum. Clearly, if they'd persisted in trying to cross the electrified zone, the Europeans would've suffered the same fate as the natives. The men who'd been knocked down were picked up. They were fine, just a little bruised.

From the top of the hill at the center of the crater, Labianov and Aberdeen had watched the whole thing. The artillerymen ready to fire their cannons had paused their maneuvers: this battle—in which the earth itself had shattered and destroyed an army—seemed like a dream to them.

Articulating the lesson he himself had drawn from the incident, Lord Aberdeen said, "The Blue Flag! If he felt like it, not one of you would leave here alive." Serious words, coming from the mouth of one the commanders of the expedition! They implied the futility of the army sent from Europe, and the impossibility of defeating an adversary who was not only protected by the almost impassable wastes of the High Plateaus but in addition had at his disposal the most terrifying scientific power ever known to man!

Labianov didn't answer. What would be the use? It was clear he agreed with his colleague. At that moment they both understood that thrones and crowns were irreversibly doomed by the logic of progress itself. What was imperial or royal power in comparison? Merely an accepted social convention, that the people's will could overturn at any time. Whereas science was a tangible reality—whether awful or pleasant—whose grip no one could slip out of. They both felt the need to escape the looks of the officers and artillerymen around them. They had to be in private, without witnesses, to express their great shock. Their sudden victory had left their spirits shattered, broken, as if they were in a nightmare.

They surveyed the field of battle one last time. The electrification of the ground had clearly ended: in the area that had previously crackled with lightning, soldiers now strolled, calling to one other as they harvested the exotic weapons, the outlandish headgear, the peculiar equipment that the men slain in that electric hecatomb had been brandishing an hour earlier. The generals shivered at the sight. Taking each other by the arm, in silence, their legs tottering, leaning on each other, they went slowly back toward their headquarters tent.

On the way, they looked into the tent belonging to their guests—Mona, Sara, Violet, and Max—those friends who'd brought them an alliance with Dodekhan, whose power they'd now witnessed. The tent was empty. Labianov gestured into the distance. "They're probably out there—they wanted to have a look." He went on, more quietly, "They've grown accustomed to these marvels. Courage consists partly in familiarity."

Aberdeen nodded silently, and together they went on to their own tent, where the sentry, a Russian infantryman, cried out in delight, "Oh, little father, what a lovely battle!" That simple man expressed the feelings of all the soldiers celebrating in camp.

As soon as the battle had begun, Mona had left the letter of farewell she'd written to her father fastened in plain sight to the tent pole. Then she turned to her companions. "Let's go down into the camp. When the opportunity comes, we need to get as quickly as we can to the red boulder where we're to meet Master Merry and Miss Twinkle."

"Quite right," said Sara. "I was going to suggest the same thing." And Max and Violet showed their agreement by going straight to the tent door.

Oh, they didn't need to worry about taking any care to conceal their movements! At that moment the entire army was as if mesmerized by the scene unfolding before them. Mona and her friends reached the crater floor without trouble. They made their way through the rows of empty tents—because even the sick had dragged themselves to the battlefront to see better. As the travelers approached the front lines, they had to stop—their way was blocked by gawkers. But that obstacle soon dissipated: once a few soldiers, bolder than their peers, had made sure the ground was no longer electrified, the troops pulled along their officers and scattered like a flock of birds across the battlefield.

"Let's keep going," murmured Max. "The time is right. They're all busy picking up weapons and equipment. They won't even notice us."

And in fact he was quite right. The little group crossed the field of carnage without arousing the least attention. And yet for the young women the experience was dominated by awful feelings. Bodies lay everywhere—scattered here, piled up there. Under the harsh glare of the spotlights, the dead were hideous, grotesque, their limbs frozen in unbelievable contortions. Some showed signs of terrible burns. It was the dreadful site of a mass electrocution.

Max went from one of his companions to the next, leading them through the bodies. Several times he had to help them scale veritable ramparts of cadavers. Without him, the young women would certainly have abandoned that sinister procession. But Max gave them courage. Meanwhile around them the Russians and the English laughed and made macabre jokes, each in his native language, with the soldier's indifference to death, that constant companion in war, which strikes down this man today and another man tomorrow.

Finally they reached the end of the field of death. A hundred paces away stood the red boulder Dodekhan had chosen—a goal all the more welcome now to the young women whose eyes were still filled with the horrors they'd seen. They hastened toward it. They were almost there when suddenly darkness fell: the spotlights had all been switched off, and bugles and fifes rang out to summon the troops back to camp. Blinded by the sudden dark, Violet and Sara stopped where they were. Mona whispered shakily, "Where are you?"

Max, who'd already reached the boulder, called back softly, "This way. I'm at the red boulder." But then he broke off and cried, "What's that?"

A hand had just grabbed his hand. But then the answer to his question came. "Merry."

"Ah!" Max had no time to say more—the boy had already left him. He could just make out one, then two slim figures bounding toward where his companions had stopped. He said to himself, "Merry and his little friend Twinkle."

But now what? More shadows went by, following the children with the slim, lithe shape of big cats. Max scolded himself, "All right, it's their black panthers. I followed the tracks of one of them long enough not to be surprised by the sight of them!"

Now, led by the children, his companions approached, with the panthers fawning on them affectionately. Sara and Mona petted the animals without the least fear.

"Hello, you pretty Zizi."

"Hello, you good Fred."

Violet, who'd been a little taken aback at first by the arrival of the panthers, was relieved by her friends' calm. She too petted the animals, who seemed to feel honored by a stranger's attention.

They were all speaking at once, asking questions. Merry said seriously, "Later, when we're out of sight of the camp."

Twinkle added, "We have a camp in the mountains. A good fire. Yaks. Venison. Tea!"

They all understood: If their absence was noticed, the spotlights would rake the landscape with their bright beams. They'd be spotted, pursued, brought back to camp. General Labianov would never agree to let his daughter wander off once again into the icy wastes of the High Plateaus. They remembered the farewell letter Mona had left. Though it might be found any moment now, none of them would've had the courage to stop her from writing it. So now the fear of being caught spurred them on. They hurried after the two children, who'd taken Sara and Mona by the hand to guide them and point out rough spots in the trail. Fred and Zizi bounded happily around the group, playing, chasing each other, vanishing into the dark only to leap back out of it. The local people would've taken them for *gilds*, those goblins of the High Plateaus.

Meanwhile they climbed, they descended, they climbed again. Suddenly they saw a dim reddish glow in the distance. Sara stopped Merry, who was leading her.

"What is it?" the boy asked.

"A fire, over there."

"Yes, ours. That's where we're going."

The trek resumed. They detoured around a pile of enormous boulders that looked like they'd been heaped up by giants. In a kind of enclosed "room" in the middle of the boulder field, a cooking pot simmered over a bright fire.

"Well, Merry, this is quite the establishment!" cried Sara in delight. "But aren't you afraid the fire will attract prowlers?"

The boy laughed silently. "San's troops?" he said with irony.

"Exactly."

"Don't worry, duchess. They're far away. They'll run until they drop. They thought the mountain spirits had struck their spears with fire. San will never get them back again."

The boy briefly explained the panic that had scattered the survivors of San's army. With their belief in magic, and their total ignorance of science, the warriors encircling the European camp had attributed all of the electrical phenomena that lay beyond their own intellects to the spirits of the night. It was those genies who'd beaten them, scattered them, decimated them. Clearly the genies disapproved of San's plans—they'd protected the Europeans San wanted to destroy. So the mountain people had turned against the giant Prayer Engraver and refused to obey him. They'd abandoned him. And now, far away, in every direction, they were carrying the news of San's defeat by supernatural forces. They would spread their disobedience and discouragement everywhere.

Merry and Twinkle described all that in such a comical way that the travelers joined in their infectious joy. They gathered around the fire, which spread a soft heat throughout the "room" in the boulders. They felt good: the warmth, the simmering of the pot whose monotonous song promised a hot meal, comforted them with the physical pleasures of the moment.

But Merry didn't forget the instructions he'd been given by Dodekhan—the only master he'd ever met who'd been good to him in his weakness. And anyway their days of misery had toughened both Merry and Twinkle. "While Twinkle tends the pot," said the boy, "I'll explain to Miss Mona and the duchess what my master expects of them."

His words dispelled the little group's sybaritic mood and brought back the reality of their situation. They all turned to the boy, whose thin face and bright eyes, shining strangely in the firelight, made him resemble one of those mountain gremlins. He explained first how Dodekhan and the duke—though from their Central Exchange they could devastate points in Asia two or three thousand kilometers away—were powerless in the single kilometer that separated their prison from Station A. They were all struck by that discrepancy: Dodekhan had destroyed San's warriors by means of the electrical force they'd all witnessed. And yet right next to him, almost within arm's reach, he couldn't overcome a few jailers.

Then Merry described Dodekhan's sad realization that his brethren were still far from prepared for the peaceful liberation that Dilevnor had planned and his son had attempted. The hour of freedom had to be postponed. But Dodekhan wanted to preserve the admirable, irresistible power his father had collected in the bowels of the mountain. He wanted that power to be put out of reach of others. He wanted it to wait, unknown but intact, for the time when Asia could conceive the union of freedom and goodness. To do that, he'd have to hide the room full of electro-telluric equipment, and close the only entrance to the temple. The secret would be kept by Dodekhan and his descendants, passed from generation to generation, until the predestined one arrived who'd have the joy of accomplishing the great task. The explosions and landslides that would bury the sacred trail and cut off access to the temple and the Central Exchange could be controlled only from Station A. But Dodekhan, trapped in the Central Exchange, couldn't get to Station A.

They all listened without a word, motionless, riveted by the vision of the enormous dream—a vision summoned, with outlandish gestures, by this boy, this urchin. They all shivered. Mona asked hesitantly, "What does the Master of the Blue Flag want us to do?"

"He wants us to open the passage between Station A and the Central Exchange. He wants us to remove all opposition from the thousand meters of tunnels that connect those two points."

"Us? How could we do it?"

"We could do it," the boy replied calmly, "if Miss Mona understands *the value of the colored glass.*"

Those cryptic words left them all openmouthed.

"What are you trying to say, Merry?"

"What colored glass?"

"The glass that was in your luggage, in the chest from Stittsheim."

"Yes, I know very well how to use the glass tubes."

"Then, Miss Mona, can you say which of those tubes killed San's people in Calcutta?"

"The violet ones."

"Are they the only ones that kill?"

"No. The indigo or blue-black tubes are also fatal. The violets burn, incinerating flammable matter; the blue-black tubes stop the circulation without leaving any sign."

"That's better. So we'll take the violet and indigo tubes."

"We'll take them?" they all protested. "Didn't they stay in San's hands?"

The children laughed. "He didn't even suspect he had them. So we asked for that chest as our share of the loot. It's over there, hidden in the rocks."

They turned to look at the hollow he pointed to. Indeed, in the gap between two of the boulders that formed the natural "room" they were sheltering in, the travelers could see the oak chest that held the array of tubes of colored light. Though they hadn't shared their thoughts aloud, they'd all repeatedly regretted the loss of that "arsenal of light." Seeing it there, within reach, filled them with intense joy.

But they were startled to hear Merry say, "We'll bury the chest under rocks so we can retrieve it later."

"Why bury it?"

"Because we have nothing but yaks, and we can't carry that much weight." They lowered their heads: the boy was right. "But since the violet and indigo tubes are fatal," he went on, "we'll divide them up. Those weapons are too unusual for our adversaries to suspect anything. There are maybe two hundred of them; there are eight of us, counting the panthers—each of whom can take on twenty or more of San's men. But then what?"

He laid out the situation with total calm. It was unthinkable for this small, thin boy to propose launching an attack against the Prayer Engravers—vastly superior in numbers—under those conditions. "Therefore," he went on imperturbably, "we have to use guile. They say children and women are good at guile. Twinkle and I know that from experience." The girl nodded mischievously. "So guile will serve us. We'll head to Station A. We'll present ourselves there." They all listened, stunned by the simplicity of the boy's plan. "They'll welcome us with open arms, of course. We'll wait for the right moment, and then, using the tubes of light..."

He broke off to laugh, showing a mouthful of white teeth, which sent Miss Twinkle into such a fit of laughter that she couldn't put the lid back on the pot after she'd lifted it to check the progress of the stew.

No matter how much they hated San and his minions, the young women had gone pale. They all asked, "What are you trying to say, Merry?"

He looked at them for a moment, as if in surprise that they hadn't understood him. Then he answered very matter-of-factly, "Two hundred rascals are spread out between the Central Exchange and Station A, blocking the Master's way. The violet or indigo tubes will kill them, with or without burns. That's all." The prospect of that massacre didn't bother him. Inspired by devotion, as others are inspired by vengeance, he unconsciously applied his calm and reasonable logic.

No one spoke. The urchin's words had struck them like a lightning bolt. Suddenly they understood the moral anguish that had driven Dodekhan to say, "Asia isn't ready for freedom!"

And in the silence of the night, with the pot simmering over the campfire amid the moaning gusts of wind, they thought of the wall of corpses they'd have to pile up to free Dodekhan, that poet of science who'd dreamt of liberating Asia without sacrificing human lives.

CHAPTER IX
The Final Meeting of the Masters of the Blue Flag

"By the devil! God bless me! I want to get out of this electrical dungeon!" roared Sir John Lobster, who was scarlet, sweating, stamping, and foaming at the mouth. After they'd used the telephote to watch the destruction of San's hordes, and the departure of Mona and her friends from the Anglo-Russian camp, and their reunion with the children and their panthers, Dodekhan and the duke had shut down the electro-telluric apparatus and put away the viewing screen.

When all evidence of their strange work had been cleared away, they turned their attention to the portly gentleman. They untied his bonds, took off his blindfold, and helped him sit up. So upset was the Member of Parliament by his recent treatment that it took him almost an hour to regain the use of his senses. Finally his blood pressure came down and his pulse returned to normal. He rubbed his legs, his torso, his arms, and especially his wrists, on which the tightly wound ropes had left red marks. When he recovered his voice he used it to claim the status of martyr. "Poor me! Look what they've done to me!" Then, with his legislator's instincts returning, he decided it was time to give his persecutors a thorough dressing down. "These people don't have the least notion of civilized, parliamentary behavior!"

Since neither Dodekhan nor Lucien bothered to reply, Sir John concluded they were sorry. How could they possibly not regret mistreating one of the leading lights of the House of Commons, the staunch and dignified defender of the interests of the voters of Beggingbridge? In short, the gentleman rose onto his massive legs and, planting himself in front of the two men whose involuntary companion he'd become, he declared solemnly, "Gentlemen, I presume that as people of good breeding you regret actions for which in fact there's no excuse. I'm willing to let it go, given your remorse. But on one condition: I want to get out of here."

They stared at him. In spite of the gravity of the circumstances, a certain twitching of their face muscles and a certain twinkle in their eyes suggested that only with great effort were they controlling a desire to laugh.

Blinded by his natural self-importance, Sir John noticed nothing—not even the note of irony in the duke's voice as he asked, "You wish to leave us?"

"Would you dare try to stop me?" cried the Englishman majestically.

"I? Heaven forbid! If you'd like to leave, sir, well then, leave."

"It's about time!"

Privately Sir John reflected that with some people all you had to do was speak loudly and clearly. Pleased with his psychological acuity, he hurried to the doorway leading to the temple. But just as he thought he was through it, a violent jolt knocked him down and spun him across the floor, and he remembered too late the electric barrier that he'd been so wary of when he'd arrived.

His companions ran to help him, and pulled him to his feet. But then Lucien made him howl with rage by observing, with infuriating cool, "Since I thought you were in a hurry to leave, I hadn't expected that little gymnastic interlude—such a delightful entertainment for us poor prisoners."

Sir John thought he might choke with fury. For a moment he stammered, he shook, he writhed, without managing to articulate the eloquent words that were trying to get out of his mouth. Finally he found his voice: he thundered, he threatened his listeners with all the lightning bolts in England. He was vehement, petulant, pathetic…

They didn't interrupt him even once, but very politely let him express all of his complaints and opinions. They waited for him to run out of breath. Only then did Dodekhan reply, with gentle insolence, "Mr. Lobster, as you've mentioned, you represent the voters of Beggingbridge."

"I'm proud to do so," he interjected.

"Everyone's entitled to feel proud. Be proud, but be logical. You've been entrusted with the interests of Beggingbridge. Why didn't you stay in England, to carry out the mandate given to you by the voters?"

"But that has nothing to do with it!" grumbled Sir John, though he was taken aback by the direction of the conversation.

"I beg your pardon. You're betraying Beggingbridge, just so you can act as the police for a local potentate."

"Police? I'm no policeman."

"Pardon me again. You told us you were here to keep us under surveillance."

"Surveillance and police are two different things."

"Two kinds of police, sir. One is honest and honorable, making his rounds in broad daylight in a respectable uniform. The other… I won't go on—since the political police, to which you belong, would rather not be described."

Sir John clutched at his red hair. For a moment they feared he would tear it out, but presumably he realized that damaging that flaming crown would lessen his physical attractions, because he dropped his arms by his sides and bleated in despair, "What do you want from me, anyway?"

"Patience."

"Patience, when I'm locked up!"

"Just as we are."

"Oh you!—You!"

He didn't complete the thought, but Dodekhan took care of that for him. "I see what you're thinking. You think captivity is easier for us than it is for you."

"Well, look at it from my point of view!"

"No, Mr. Lobster, I won't. But I'll give you some good advice. Stay calm. Because you'll be a prisoner just as long as we will."

"Alas, that'll be the death of me! I'll die a prisoner!"

"No, you won't, Mr. Lobster."

"Why not?" he asked, with the faint hope that the possibility of his death would bring Dodekhan to make terms.

"You won't, because it wouldn't be seemly."

"Seemly?"

"Of course! It's unseemly to play at dying in public."

This time Sir John got it: they were mocking him. His anger rekindled, louder and more turbulent than ever. But all he accomplished was to tire himself out, because his listeners just impassively watched all of his varied displays of rage. Nothing could upset their calm—in fact, Sir John's insults and threats just seemed to entertain them.

And when their fanatical jailers brought their meal and launched into their usual chorus of insults against Dodekhan, he seemed delighted to hear Sir John contribute a solo in the same style. The Asians and the Anglo-Saxon howled away impressively; surely that underground temple had never hosted virtuosi like them. But all good things come to an end. The jailers soon withdrew, in accordance with their orders, so that the prisoners could come out to take their food back into the Central Exchange.

Meanwhile Sir John—held in check by Lucien, who pointed the Englishman's own revolver at him—felt his annoyance rising to delirium. Without being allowed to follow him, he watched Dodekhan go out into the temple, pick up the basket containing their dinner, come back inside, and switch back on the electric barrier. Sir John shouted until he could shout no more. He'd grown hoarse, and his painful, rasping, piteous cries just left him depressed. He quieted down, and accepted his share of the food. Then he stretched out on a mat, turned his back on his companions, and fell asleep.

For forty-eight hours now, Sir John had shared the Central Exchange with Dodekhan and Lucien. To say that he'd resigned himself to the adventure would be too much, but he'd finally stopped complaining, and he'd given up the insults and accusations whose pointlessness had become clear. Oh, not that he'd become friendly. His tense, sullen, menacing expression made him strangely resemble a bulldog. Still, since he didn't bark, his fellow prisoners didn't worry about it.

They had other concerns. For two days now, they'd heard nothing from their friends over the speaker. They knew Mona, Sara, Violet, and Max had left the Anglo-Russian camp and rendezvoused with the children sent to guide them. Thanks to the telephote, the prisoners had observed every detail of their departure. So why the silence now? Following the route Dodekhan had carefully explained to Merry, they should've reached safety at Station R the day before. That shelter had plenty of posts and beams ideal for attaching the speaker. Max should've called that evening. Why hadn't he done so? The prisoners' unhappiness at that question was only augmented by the answers supplied by their imagination.

Oh, why had Sir John come? If they'd been alone, the two men would've switched on the telephote, and traced the route the children were to follow, and the images on the screen would've explained the silence that so concerned them. But the Englishman was there, sullenly and suspiciously watching their every movement. Why should they let a spy find out that—though they were trapped underground here—their eyes were free to roam across the surrounding landscape, free to participate in the lives of those who stood under open skies?

Still, their anxiety grew by the hour. Toward evening, lowering his voice so that Sir John couldn't overhear, Lucien said to Dodekhan, "I've been thinking. What would we do if the speaker transmitted a call from our friends?"

Dodekhan looked uncomfortable.

"We'd answer, wouldn't we?" pressed the duke.

"Of course."

"And to keep that fatso from following our conversation, I think we'd do well to tie him up and blindfold and gag him again, leaving him as blind and deaf as when we first had the misfortune to make his acquaintance."

"So you suggest…"

"We've eaten. That pest seems to be staying awake deliberately. I'm impatient to use the screen to solve the mystery that's gnawing at us. You can act calm, Dodekhan, but you're as anxious as I am."

"I'll admit it."

"Then why hesitate? Wrap some rope around the fat man, put a blanket over his head, and we'll be free to use the telephote to find out why Sara and Mona haven't called. It might be nothing, or almost nothing: some minor trouble on the journey. It's absurd to let ourselves be consumed by worry."

"Then let's do as you say, my dear Lucien—I'm as eager as you are."

Sir John was watching them suspiciously. As they came toward him he prepared to defend himself, taking up the classic posture of an English boxer. But it was pointless: Lucien raised the revolver that the electromagnet had robbed the Englishman of earlier, and said pleasantly, "Don't get excited, Mr. Lobster. My intentions are friendly. I'll only pull the trigger if you put up a struggle against my friend Dodekhan."

Of course that warning was no comfort to Sir John. "What do you want with me now?"

"Almost nothing—just to keep you from learning a dangerous secret."

"I don't care about your secrets!" grumbled Sir John haughtily.

Lucien said, even more politely, "We're aware of your discretion, sir. So we're only trying to prevent some unlucky accident that would force us to eliminate you."

"To eliminate…"

"You heard me. So behave, and let yourself be tied up."

Sir John was tempted to fight back. But as Dodekhan came at him with the same rope they'd already used on him, Lucien brandished the revolver so convincingly that the fat man held out his wrists, though he grumbled, "You've got the power, and I have to submit to your whims."

To which Lucien replied amiably, "I knew I could count on your graciousness."

Two minutes later Sir John—bound, blindfolded, deafened by a felt blanket wrapped around his head—lay on his mat, unable to move or hear a sound or see a sliver of light. The prisoners, now free to use the telephote, wasted no time. In their haste, perhaps they dumped Sir John a little roughly on his mat—but since he couldn't make a sound he didn't complain.

Dodekhan switched on the device. On the screen they could see the Anglo-Russian camp, the crater rim, and the red boulder where the Chinese children and their panthers had met the travelers. Then, slowly, the landscape on the screen began to move. Now they could see the group's first camp, the shelter amid the boulders where Merry had explained the mission. The movement continued. Mountains gave way to other mountains, all arid, gloomy, somber.

Suddenly Dodekhan paused the machine with a cry of surprise.

"What is it?" asked Lucien.

"Station R has disappeared."

"Where should it be?"

"It stood right there, in that ravine."

"Are you sure?"

"Absolutely. Plus, near that scree, you can see the marks of the posts that held it up. Look at where they were planted in the ground."

Dodekhan was right. At the spot he pointed to, square holes were visible in the soil. There was no doubt that wooden posts had stood in those holes. But what had become of the posts? As Dodekhan made adjustments to the telephote controls he murmured, "The hut and all of its timbers have vanished. Who destroyed the station? And why?" He shrugged. "And first of all, what did they do with the timbers? On the High Plateaus you don't haul around heavy, awkward objects for fun. Whoever knocked the hut down must've abandoned the lumber nearby."

He used the telephote to inspect the scree, the gullies, the ravines. Finally at the bottom of a gully they saw planks and posts and rafters—already burned down to cinders. "The remains of Station R," he said slowly.

"But why destroy it?" asked Lucien. "Why carry the timbers there? Why the fire? What's the point of all that effort and time?"

"I don't know. But at least now we understand our friends' silence on their first day's travel."

After a pause, Lucien said, "Yet we still don't know why the station was destroyed?"

"Let's look a little further," murmured Dodekhan. With a worried expression he reoriented the telephote. "We'll follow the route our friends should be taking."

Starting from where Station R had been, once again the screen displayed a landscape of mountains, undulating plateaus, sheer drops into rocky ravines, frozen ponds on whose shores the salt left behind by evaporation glittered in the moonlight, then iced-over rivers and streams whose rushing currents were frozen in mid-motion. The screen paused again, on a view of a craggy peak, whose slopes were so smooth and whose ridges were so sharp that it looked as if it had been carved artificially.

"Antenna 25 has been torn down," whistled Dodekhan. In response to Lucien's questioning look he went on, "There was a wireless antenna there. Merry was to camp at the foot of that peak on the second night—tonight. Without an antenna, they can't call us."

"But did they at least reach camp?"

"We'll see."

The peak slowly grew larger until it filled the screen, revealing to their eager eyes its red and gray and yellow slopes, with patches of snow remaining in places where it was less steep. They saw smoke, and with another move of the screen they saw a crackling fire. The two men shook hands with joy in their eyes. "It's them!"

Them—yes—them! There they all were, gathered around the fire, huddled beneath a rocky overhang. Dodekhan and the duke could recognize Mona, Sara, Violet, and Max, with the very tame black panthers stretched out at their feet. Then two other figures appeared on screen: Merry and Twinkle. The children were explaining something—which, alas, the prisoners couldn't hear. They were gesturing as they spoke, pointing to the top of the peak.

"What are they saying?"

Then Merry handed Max a small object, and Dodekhan and Lucien both cried, "The speaker!" Now they knew what the children were saying. They'd climbed the peak, carrying the speaker, meaning to attach it to the antenna and call the prisoners in the Central Exchange. They'd come back down without doing so—because the antenna was gone, just like Station R. They could see the looks of surprise and concern on the travelers' faces. They were all talking animatedly. Forgetting their own problems, Dodekhan and Lucien examined the faces of their beloved, trying to guess at what was being said.

How long did that go on? For how long had they been absorbed in that observation? They couldn't have said. But a sinister chuckle brought them back to reality. What was that? They turned to look. Out in the temple, at the mouth of the connecting passageway, stood a tall figure—a man who was staring eagerly at the screen, a man who'd discovered the secret of the telephote. Dodekhan hastily flipped the levers, and the screen went blank.

Another chuckle greeted his action. "Too late! I saw it."

The two prisoners reeled. It was the voice of their mortal enemy. They moaned, "San!"

"Yes, San!" replied the mighty Prayer Engraver. "San, beaten by your deviltry, Dodekhan. San, whose powers died with his warriors. San, who has no men left except the two hundred guards in the temple. San, who's come back for revenge." He smashed the ground with a stamp of his foot that echoed dismally through the tunnels. "Ah, I hadn't hoped for so complete a vengeance!"

He smiled hideously. "Listen carefully, Dodekhan, because your death throes begin now!" He took a deep breath, as if his lungs were short of air. "I came intending to tell you this: Dodekhan, the empire of the Blue Flag is lost. My men have been mown down by some unknown thunderbolt hidden in the ground. I no longer want to be the Master. I no longer care about the secrets you held that have protected your life. I only want to avenge Log—to get revenge on that accursed Frenchman who serves you." The fury boiling within him made his voice shake. "You'll never leave this hole in which you thought you could defy me forever. I don't know how to get in. Your diabolical electricity blocks my bullets. But I want you dead, and there's one enemy you can't keep out: hunger!"

The sinister word rang through the passageway: hunger!

"That's what I meant to tell you when I came here. But sentiment—idiotic sentiment, as my master Log called it—had a sweet surprise for me. Haha! Your machines allow you to see at a distance. Perhaps you've been following the stages of my defeat, perhaps you've been cheering at my catastrophic ruin. Well, it's my turn to laugh now!" Shaking his fists at them, with bloodshot eyes and spittle on his lips, he went on, "You were so happy to see those women who've put your hearts in chains, you didn't hear me come into the temple—though I wasn't especially quiet. But blind sentiment robs a man of the power to reason. And I glimpsed an even greater, more delightful vengeance. All those responsible for Log's death will perish. They'll all die—all of them!" He paced like a caged beast, filled with demented exhilaration, his clenched fists striking at the air, his heavy feet pounding the earth. "So! The women are at Antenna 25! They're headed here, because you summoned them, right?"

But then he stopped shouting, and froze. In a flash, Dodekhan understood that, at all costs, he had to drive that thought from his enemy's mind. If the young women responded to his summons, their guides Merry and Twinkle must therefore be traitors to San. When they arrived, they'd be seized and put to death. The rescue plan would turn into a trap for those children who were loyal to him, and for those accompanying them, for everything in the world that was precious to Dodekhan and Lucien. So he called out, "You're wrong about that, San. I thought I'd see them in the Anglo-Russian camp. Not finding them anywhere there, I looked around. I saw signs that they'd left camp, heading for Station R."

"Did you see Station R?" cackled San.

293

"No. It had been destroyed, and the ruins are still smoldering at the bottom of a ravine."

"Ah!" murmured San. "So you saw that." He wiped his brow. Clearly, Dodekhan's candid admission had confused his dull mind. But he tried to hide it. "It was I who destroyed the station. Just like Antenna 25. The Blue Flag is dead—what good are those stations?" Then he circled back to what Dodekhan had said. "So if you didn't summon them, why did they leave the army camp?"

Dodekhan gestured sadly. "Wasn't it you who summoned them, San?"

He shook his head. "No, it wasn't me." Then, dismissing what he couldn't understand, he went on, "Anyway, what does it matter? Let them come! All of my dear master Log's enemies will be in my hands! His spirit will rejoice to see their suffering! For you, starvation. For the others, torture!"

He gave a piercing whistle, with a strange timbre. Almost immediately, footsteps rang out in the tunnels leading from the temple out to the surface, and a dozen warriors burst into the sanctuary.

"From now on you'll bivouac in the temple," ordered San. "No food for the prisoners. If they try to escape—death!"

A howl of approval greeted his words. He began to leave, but Dodekhan called him back.

"We captured one of your followers... Sir John Lobster. We took him by surprise. You wouldn't want him to die. If you agree to withdraw, with your men, to the far side of the sanctuary, we'll let him out."

San hesitated briefly, but mistrust outweighed reason. Himself incapable of generosity, he was unable to recognize it in his enemy. He answered brutally, "Too bad for him. If you're stupid enough to let yourself get caught, you have to suffer the consequences."

And he left the temple without further debate. As a result, when Sir John had been released from his ropes and from the blanket over his head, he learned with somewhat... lukewarm... pleasure that all of the diplomatic missions he'd undertaken for San had led to the less than satisfying result that he was likely to die of hunger.

CHAPTER X
The Talking Spring

The prisoners hadn't eaten for three days. They lay motionless on their mats. They'd passed through the first phase of hunger—the one in which you suffered, and were conscious of the workings of an empty stomach. In the second phase, now beginning, the gastric secretions slowed down. The weakening of all the organs in the absence of food was marked by a slowing of the blood circulation, by general fatigue, and by a slight lowering of body temperature. Normal was no longer 37°—it fell to 36°, then 35°, and finally 34°.[41] That heralded the approach of death. The prisoners were only at the beginning of that descent, but already their energy was flagging, leaving them reluctant to make any movement. From time to time Sir John moaned pitifully. Neither Dodekhan nor Lucien said a word.

From the temple came the loud sounds of a dozen Prayer Engravers eating, and drinking rice wine cut with water, to add the tortures of Tantalus to the prisoners' suffering. Delighted to be able to give vent to their hatred of those they were guarding, they shouted out brutal jokes, threats, vulgar insults.

But the prisoners appeared to hear nothing. They lay silent, still, lost in their nagging thoughts: San had discovered their contact with the outside by means of the telephote. The screen had given away the secret of the Master of the Blue Flag. San now realized that Mona, Sara, and their devoted friends were there on the High Plateaus. Knowing how far they were from any help, what would he do? Would his plans follow the one hinted at by Dodekhan? Or would he still have his suspicions about the children, Tse and Pei?

Hours passed. Suddenly Lucien and Dodekhan started, and their hearts leapt. They'd heard a quiet whisper in the silence: "Hello?" They both looked anxiously toward the noisy torchlit group of guards they could see through the arched passageway to the temple. The guards too had heard—conversation had suddenly ceased, and they looked around inquisitively.

"Hello?" sighed the vibrating membrane attached to the telephote screen once again.

Dodekhan got up, and pulled Lucien to his feet. In a low, hurried voice, he said, "It's *them*. We must—we must!—speak to them."

"But how?"

For a moment Dodekhan looked undecided. Then his face cleared. "I'll drive away the spies who're watching us. Hand me Lobster's revolver."

Though he didn't understand, Lucien passed him the weapon.

---

[41] In Fahrenheit, a drop from 98.6° to about 93°.

"All right," said Dodekhan. "Go to the controls for the electric barrier. On my signal, switch off the current just long enough for me to fire."

"Hello?" The membrane vibrated again. "Hello?"

As if spurred on by that renewed call, the two men hastened, Lucien to the controls, Dodekhan to the arched opening. "Go ahead," he said.

The levers clicked. San's henchmen watched from the sanctuary, surprised by the prisoners' sudden activity. Dodekhan aimed at the group. A shot rang out. One man dropped with a cry of pain. The others leapt to their feet. But more shots followed. Dodekhan fired six times, emptying the cylinder. Each shot found a target. Six guards lay writhing in their final agonies on the flagstone floor. Terror and panic followed. The survivors rushed madly for the exit tunnel.

Lucien was about to switch the current back on, but Dodekhan signaled him to wait. Then he ran out into the temple, grabbed the provisions the bandits had left behind, ran back inside, and set the food down inside the Central Exchange. Going finally to the vibrating speaker—his voice tense with fear that the long silence had worn out the patience of whoever had called—he cried out, "Hello? Who is it?"

A moment went by, that seemed to the prisoners to last a hundred years. Finally a voice said weakly, "It's me, Max Soleil. Can you hear me clearly?"

"It's weak, but it's still enough. Let's waste no time. I want to warn you, San is here, at the underground temple. He destroyed Station R and Antenna 25. What's worse, he saw us while we were looking for you on the telephote."

A muffled cry came in response, but Dodekhan went on, "He might come out to meet you. Merry and Twinkle should choose their route with that in mind. And they should be ready with an answer to any challenge. The safety of the whole group depends entirely on their skill and their keeping their heads." Then he added curiously, "Where are you?"

Before any answer could come, heavy footsteps rang out in the tunnels leading to the temple. Someone was coming—perhaps San bringing new jailers. They must not let him suspect they'd been using the speaker. Therefore, though he was disappointed not to learn where their friends were, Dodekhan said quickly into the vibrating membrane, "Don't call anymore—we're being closely watched. You've been warned. Farewell."

Sir John Lobster, sitting up on his mat, had followed all of their comings and goings with astonishment. Dodekhan said severely, "Not a word about what you've seen. Otherwise…" He had no need to go on. The fat gentleman understood, and quickly lay back down with a whimper of fear.

So when San and a mob of armed men burst into the sanctuary, the prisoners were once again stretched out on their mats. The report by the bandits who'd escaped from Dodekhan's shots had shaken all of their comrades, and they'll all rushed to follow San back. San examined the doorway leading to the Central Exchange. What was he looking for? An explanation of a phenomenon his thick head couldn't make sense of: bullets fired from the sanctuary into the Central

Exchange had been stopped at the threshold, but Dodekhan had been able to fire in the opposite direction—the bodies now stiffening on the flagstone floor were abundant proof of that.

San frowned anxiously. Though of immense physical strength, he trembled before a scientific power whose source escaped him. For a moment he seemed about to charge the opening to the inner room. Then he changed his mind: he remembered the hard shock of touching the invisible barrier. Affecting a composure very far from his actual mood, he positioned his guards, using the temple columns for cover. Then he had the bodies removed, and withdrew majestically.

Dodekhan leaned close to Lucien. "Let's eat. I took all the food those rascals left behind."

"What's the point of eating?"

He smiled sadly. "Eating means buying time. Who knows!"

A large flat boulder, tilted forward and held up by two granite pillars, with the whole primitive structure propped up against a sheer basalt cliff; a thread of water, dropping from the top of the cliff, passing through a notch carved into the lip of the stone roof, foaming into a tiny bowl hollowed out by its perpetual fall, then running off in a thin stream of warm water that soon cooled and froze. The rare caravans crossing those desert regions knew that little warm spring very well. They called it "Summer Crystal": since it never froze, it was renowned as a source of drinking water in that wasteland of rock and ice.

That's where Merry and Twinkle had brought the travelers at the end of the third day's march. "Tomorrow we'll reach Station A," announced the boy.

They needed to camp, and sleep, because the last stage would be difficult: they'd be crossing rough terrain, littered with obstacles. Mona, Sara, and Violet sat sadly on the ground under the stone shelter. Since they'd quit the Anglo-Russian camp three days earlier, persistent bad luck had left them unable to make contact with the prisoners in the Central Exchange. They were afraid—of what, they couldn't quite say, but the scientific oddities they'd experienced had taught them to see as plausible things they would previously have dismissed as impossible.

The disappearance of Station R and Antenna 25, reported by their young guides, had become a menacing question mark in their minds. Why had they vanished? Whose interests did that serve? Without hesitating, each of them said to herself, "A hostile will." Whose will? They couldn't name him, but still that will existed, and still its purpose was clear: to keep the travelers from communicating with Dodekhan and Lucien... As we know, the young women were wrong. In his fury at being beaten, San had destroyed those places for his own pleasure, without yet knowing that the travelers had left the protection of the Anglo-Russian army.

Max, who'd been away, now appeared at the entrance to the shelter. He seemed out of breath.

"What's going on?" asked Violet.

"I just climbed the cliff."

"To enjoy the view," she joked.

"Exactly. I'd noticed that the waterfall drops from the top of the cliff against which our shelter is built."

"We all noticed it," she agreed, "but that's no reason to take on such a difficult climb..."

He interrupted, "Excuse me. You'll soon understand. So I climbed up, and found a plateau as flat as a table, across which a steaming brook runs for fifty meters from its source to the top of the waterfall. And that source is a small geyser that throws a column of water fifteen feet into the air."

"Well?"

"Well! Together the falls, the brook, and the geyser form an antenna."

"An antenna?"

"Thanks to which I might be able to telephone."

The young women were now fully engaged, no longer laughing. Their faces expressed a mix of hope and skepticism. "You really think so?" they murmured.

"Absolutely. What do I need? A post, a downspout, a lightning rod, anything pointing upward. A column of water should do the same job."

"But how will you attach the speaker?"

"It won't be attached, that's all. I'll hold it in my fingers, I'll immerse the point carefully in the warm water falling from the cliff, and I'll say, 'Hello?'"

As he spoke he carried out, step by step, the operation he was describing. Complete silence had fallen in the stone shelter. All of them watched with great attention, their faces serious. A few seconds passed.

"Hello?" said Max, leaning close to the speaker, as if to give his call more force.

Again they waited.

"No, this method doesn't work," sighed Sara. "It's too bad, because the idea seemed appealing."

Max seemed about to back away from the waterfall, but Mona begged him to wait. What feeling inspired her? If anyone had asked, she'd certainly have said she had no idea. It was one of those sudden, irrational impulses which are all the more irresistible because they defy any logic.

Violet's soft blue eyes supported Mona's plea. Max stayed still, keeping the point of the speaker in the column of water. His somewhat ironic expression showed that only to be agreeable was he obeying a request he considered childish. So his startlement was even greater than that of his companions when suddenly a voice could be heard from the speaker. It wasn't as clear as usual; the voice seemed hazy. Presumably the liquid antenna carried the signal less efficiently. Even so, Dodekhan's voice was clear enough.

And when the call ended they all looked at each other, and then the young women's eyes searched the darkness around them. San's name alone had terrified them. They'd expected to surprise him, but now he knew they were nearby. He could appear at any moment, and force Merry and Twinkle to explain why the travelers were with them, far from the European army camp. Would he fall for their explanation?

Once they were informed, the children seemed unconcerned. "The thing is," said Merry, "tomorrow, when we're close to Station A, I'd already planned to give the impression of prisoners and guards. So I'll ask you to play along with that bit of theater starting this evening, so that if San shows up he'll have to acknowledge that Twinkle and I have taken all the measures necessary to keep our captives from escaping."

"That'd be wise, indeed," agreed the young women. "What are you planning to do, child?"

"Oh, it's very simple. I'll bind Mr. Max's wrists with a rope which I'll then wrap around his ankles. If it's done right, you can walk and use your hands, but you can't make any sudden violent motions. As for you, ladies, I'll ask you to allow me to deprive you of the use of one arm only. I'll tie your right arm behind your back, and the other end of the rope will go around your left wrist, so that it can't reach the bound hand. That way all four of you will be left powerless; and Twinkle and I, with Fred and Zizi's help, can realistically control you, and lead you where we want."

They all nodded their approval. They were surprised to see how easily these children, accustomed to a constant struggle against men and the elements, found a response to every setback. San himself would certainly be taken in by the illusion created by his frail enemies. Already, with the gentle touch and comforting murmur of a nurse caring for her patients, Twinkle was following Merry's instructions, while the boy tied up Max.

"You know," said Max, "it's all very well to tie us up—all very well in a manner of speaking—but by what miracle can you account for our having let you do it? Because, after all, if I wanted to resist…"

"You couldn't," said the boy solemnly.

Max started, which undid his partly tied ropes. "I couldn't! My word, if you can prove that, a visit from San will worry me no more than my first day of school."

It was Twinkle who answered, "Merry thought of it long ago. Back when we were lurking near the European army camp, waiting for you to join us, he already knew how he'd explain it all to San."

"Really!"

"He had to. You have to know before, because after is usually too late."

Meanwhile Merry had finished tying up Max. He stepped back a couple of paces to study with obvious satisfaction the travelers who'd now become his "prisoners." Then, lowering his voice—as if he feared being overheard—he said, "You, Mr. Max, and you, duchess, you submitted to our orders out of fear, one for Miss Musketeer, the other for Miss Mona…"

"Fear? Fear of what?"

"Of seeing them eaten by Fred and Zizi."

"But, damn it," grumbled Max, "why would the beasts eat our friends?"

"On my orders, sahib."

"On your orders?"

"Of course, on my orders. After the battle, you left the camp, just like the soldiers. You crossed the area where San's warriors lay, struck down by the earth that had risen against them. We were nearby, hiding in the rocks, half paralyzed by fear of the 'terrifying display of the power of the mountain spirits' we'd just witnessed. You understand, we had to believe, just like the warriors, that if the earth threw lightning bolts, it could only be because the spirits were angry."

He smiled mischievously. "So, from our hiding place, we spotted you. I said to my little sister in misery, 'Twinkle, do you recognize them?' And she said, 'Yes, they're Dodekhan's and Duke Lucien's sweethearts.' I said, 'But what about the other two?'—meaning you, Mr. Max and Miss Violet. 'The blonde girl is certainly the young man's sweetheart. Their eyes say so.' Then I said, 'Good! If we could take them to Master San, I'm sure he'd be happy with his servants.' And she said, 'Take them to him… that seems hard to manage.'

"Meanwhile you'd moved away from the other people. You were picking up weapons. I nudged Twinkle. 'Hey, if they come a few more steps toward us, they'll be hidden from the camp by that knoll. We could take them prisoner. We… and our panthers…' And then you came those few more steps. We showed ourselves suddenly, siccing Fred on Miss Mona and Zizi on Miss Violet. Out of fear that those dear beasts would pounce on their designated victims, you, Mr. Max, let me tie you up, while the duchess surrendered to Twinkle's attentions." The boy planted himself in front of his listeners, who were stunned by the plausibility of his story. "Do you think that's a good enough explanation?"

With a chorus of praise, they all agreed it could've have happened that way. Neither Max nor Sara would've put up a struggle if Mona and Violet were being threatened by black panthers. No part of the story needed to be changed.

But the time had come to take nourishment. The panthers were positioned as sentries some distance away, and—once they were sure not to be surprised by the unexpected arrival of the enemy—the children unbound their captives so they could eat more easily. The meal passed without incident. Then, with their ropes tightened again, in spite of the cares that weighed on them, they all gave way to the fatigue of the day and fell fast asleep…

No alarms troubled their sleep. Dawn came, throwing misty light on the heights. The warm spring water served for their morning ablutions. Then the stirred-up fire licked the sides of the metal pot in which travelers on the High Plateaus boil their tea. They were a little surprised at their peaceful awakening.

They couldn't understand San's absence. Putting her friends' thoughts into words, Sara declared that if she'd known, she wouldn't have slept with one arm behind her back, an unnatural position that had left her a little sore now. But in spite of those perfectly understandable complaints, they all drank their portion of hot tea, and then the little caravan made ready to set off.

Merry now connected all the captives with a rope tied to the ones they already wore. When that was done, he fell in behind the line of "prisoners," with the end of the rope in his hand. Twinkle placed herself at the head of the column. The panthers gamboled alongside. Once again Max and his companions admired their guides' ingenuity. The staging of the pseudo-convoy of prisoners seemed exceptionally well managed.

Merry, modestly triumphant, was about to give the signal to start—when Fred and Zizi suddenly flattened themselves on the ground.

"What is it?" cried Mona and Sara.

A muffled growl from the panthers made them all shiver. Twinkle looked ahead, then turned and whispered, "Look out! Warriors…yaks… It's Master San!"

San! They'd all been expecting him since the night before. Still, the news that he was here gave them goose bumps. Their ruthless enemy approached. The final round was about to begin. All of their lives were at stake.

CHAPTER XI
An Innovative Torture

"I don't want you to arrive tired out, ladies. Yaks will be put at your disposal. Don't thank me: my aim is to conserve your strength—so that you can devote all of it to suffering." San was exultant. He said those cruel things with a jovial insulting smile. His victory would clearly be brutal. His congratulations to the children—whose fantastical tale he'd accepted without the slightest suspicion—had turned his prisoners' joy to anxiety. "Merry, Twinkle, you're rejoicing at having served me well. You'll see that on my side I've thought up a fairly interesting little ordeal." What barbaric invention had germinated in that strange mind?

When the captives had been lifted up and bound onto yaks, the band of twenty or so warriors set off, heading east from the hot springs. But soon it became impossible for the Europeans to orient themselves with certainty. The caravan followed an established trail, but one whose creators had been unbelievably bold: narrow ledges along the sides of sheer cliffs; passes so tight that only one rider at a time could slip through the gaps in the rocks that seemed to have been cut with an ax; abysses they crossed on boulders that seemed to have been tossed there like gargantuan bridges over yawning precipices so deep that daylight couldn't reach the bottom veiled in eternal night. Endless detours—inexplicable, because they turned aside from one obstacle only to climb another that seemed equally difficult—made it impossible to keep track of their course.

They'd left at six in the morning. Around noon they stopped to let the yaks catch their breath, and so the men could prepare a much-needed meal. The menu—slices of dried meat, rice seasoned with curry powder, plain black tea, rice wine—counted as lavish on the High Plateaus, and in spite of their worries the travelers did it justice.

San seemed to enjoy watching them eat. Toward the end of the meal he even said cheerfully, "I notice with pleasure that you don't seem to share the scorn some of your compatriots feel for our simple mountain fare. I congratulate you. Anyway, you'll soon find out that others would give years of their lives for an invitation to a feast like this."

What could he mean? The captives could only speculate. San didn't feel like explaining, any more than he had in the morning.

Seeing the harnesses being taken off the yaks, Max asked, "Is it going to be a long stop?"

"Two hours," replied San laconically, and he moved away almost immediately, leaving the prisoners to their own thoughts. They looked at each other questioningly.

"That man terrifies me," murmured Mona finally. "I feel like he's nursing some sinister plan. What? I have no idea. And yet I feel sure that calamity is upon us."

"Bah!" said Max lightly, wishing to reassure his companions. "That good Monsieur San plans to chop us into little pieces while Dodekhan and the duke watch. That would explain his sly manner." Seeing Mona shake her head, he went on, "If our young panther tamers were with us, they'd surely say the same thing. But ever since that big nincompoop San showed up, they act like they don't know us." He lowered his voice. "Come now, Miss Mona, have you lost faith in the power of the violet and indigo tubes we shared out among ourselves earlier?"

"Oh, of course not," she said softly. "But there are so many of *them*."

"We'll wipe them all out by stages."

"I myself am feeling fairly hopeful," said Violet.

"Of course," agreed Max. "We're armed—with weapons our enemies don't even suspect. We can see San's cards, and he can't see ours. Really, the deck is stacked. I almost feel guilty for winning like this—it's like we're taking advantage of them!"

"We're about to leave!" called Sara, who'd wandered away. "San just gave the signal. Look, the bandits are rounding up the yaks. The same awful procession as this morning is about to begin again."

Indeed, the bandits were moving around. Max whispered in Violet's ear, "For now, let's concentrate on the struggle against San. Later, I'll be thinking about nothing but freeing you from the promise that binds you. Will it mean happiness? I can't say for sure. In any case, it'll mean a chance to suffer in freedom rather than slavery."

Her sweet blue eyes gazed at him, but she made no answer.

Warriors ordered the prisoners to saddle back up on the yaks that had carried them in the morning. The convoy formed up again. Merry and Twinkle and their panthers surrounded San, as if they were his bodyguards. They paid no attention to their former traveling companions—not a look, not a sign. If Max and his friends hadn't been warned, they would no doubt have wondered whether the children had deceived them: whether they weren't in fact loyal to San.

With a long, shrill whistle, the caravan set off. Soon a rocky ridge hid the lunch camp from view. Once again the winding, difficult trail led through harsh, rocky terrain—one landscape after another like a vision of Hell... A long journey, long hours punctuated by the sound of the yaks' hooves. The sun sank lower, then set... Night fell. The warriors lit torches and held them up, giving the caravan a fantastical look. By those smoky lights they crossed chasms, slipped through narrow gorges, climbed steep slopes. Would the day's journey never end? Like the "possessed" in the Rhenish ballad, the travelers felt themselves being carried along through the night by powers beyond their control.

Now they entered a narrow passage whose rocky sides were as smooth and regular as man-made walls. The corridor turned back on itself, followed sharp bends—and then suddenly the walls widened out to form a funnel whose long open side, facing them, was the lip of a sheer drop-off into an abyss. On the other side of the precipice, a vertical cliff rose fifty meters higher than the flat ground on which the caravan stood. The prisoners could see that the drop-off barred the way: the trail therefore ended in a cul-de-sac. Why had they been brought here? They didn't ask, since no one seemed disposed to answer.

San dismounted, and at his sign the warriors helped the Europeans off their yaks. The Prayer Engraver chuckled. "We'll camp here for a few days."

He whistled, which brought the children and their panthers running. He greeted them with a smile and patted their heads with a heavy hand, the caress of a satisfied tyrant. "I promised you some fun, my dears. The time has come to tell you more."

He motioned to the prisoners, who'd begun to move away. "Stay, duchess. Stay, charming Miss Mona—and you others too, amiable fools who, for no reason, wanted to pry into the mysteries of Asia. I have no secrets from those who must die." He turned to the children and pointed to the cliff that formed the opposite side of the crevasse. "Do you know what that granite wall is, children? No, of course not. Well, that's Station A, which guards the secret entrance to the underground temple and the Central Exchange."

The prisoners shivered like leaves stirred by the wind. San noticed, and said mockingly, "Ha, ha! Mona, Sara—your women's hearts beat harder at the thought of how close you are to your beloved! But a crevasse blocks the way, Station A is a rampart of rock, without a single opening. How can you cross? How can you get in?" He laughed harder. His face folded into a thousand wrinkles. His hatred made him hideous, his treacherous cruelty made him terrifying. "Well, I won't keep you in suspense. There are ways of leaping across the chasm, of making the cliff open up. Just like in the Arab legend, all you need is to know the 'Open Sesame!'"

Then, with affected consideration that was more threatening than anger, he went on, "That 'Sesame' will be spoken, you'll get into the underground temple, you'll see again those whose memory haunts you... But it'll take patience, lots of patience. We have to wait for the right moment."

Standing stock still, as if their feet were nailed to the ground, the prisoners waited in silence. What could they have said? All of them felt that the moment Mona had predicted had arrived, in which the Prayer Engraver would reveal some unexpected torture.

Still laughing, San put his hand on Merry's shoulder. "You see, my boy, after my warriors were wiped out, I came back here, howling with fury. The power of the Blue Flag was crumbling away. The only thing left was to avenge the dead."

"Master Log?" asked the boy with well-feigned emotion.

"Yes, Master Log. Ah, you miss him too. Well, you're right to. He had the intelligence to control the apparatus of science. I—we—we're only followers, servants, without initiative, weak now that his closed lips can never command again." He shook his head, and waved away the unwelcome thought. "The Blue Flag will no longer exterminate the people of Europe," he muttered. "He who could've led us in conquest is gone. His servants are good for nothing more than avenging the Master. That's why I came back." Casting his eye on the prisoners, he said with cold irony, "For... let's see... four days now, by my order, they've been suffering the pangs of hunger."

A heartrending cry interrupted him. Mona reached out to him in supplication. "Mercy! Mercy!"

"You ask for mercy, girl? Have you forgotten the past? Would you have shown mercy to the Master, any of you? The dead cry out that they're not yet avenged." San's voice grew harsher. "They'll be avenged. Dodekhan and Duke Lucien will fade away slowly. You'll suffer cruelly. We'll camp here. Every day I'll report to you on the progress of their decline. At mealtime you'll remember they're hungry. In idle hours your love will magnify your distress. Every suffering they experience will cause your hearts pain."

Clenching his teeth and bending down to put his face on a level with theirs, he went on, "When I calculate that they have only a few hours left to live, I'll take you to the temple, and in their presence—when they're too weak to help you, when they're almost out of their minds from starvation—ingenious executioners will slowly torture you to death. I'll bring about your reunion in death. In the spirit world, you'll all be the slaves of the Master you killed."

The prisoners were stunned. The whole elaborate construction of their plans crumbled before San's intentions. They'd counted on reaching the temple, and getting into it. There, the colored tubes would've overcome the garrison. In any case, they could've provoked a battle in the hope of freeing Dodekhan and the duke. Now they were left powerless. Kept outside the sanctuary, separated from their friends by a crevasse and a wall of granite—impassable to anyone who didn't know the secret of gaining access—what could they do? With their tubes, they could strike down San and destroy his warriors here. But then, would they be any better off? Alas, no! Reason made it clear: they'd still be here, at the edge of the precipice, across from the sheer cliff, behind which those they loved would still be dying.

Log's successor relished their despondency. In him slept a merciless torturer. The sufferings of others constituted perhaps his greatest joy. So you can imagine his state of mind.

Merry tugged on his sleeve. "Master, I'm so happy! You've prepared such wonderful entertainment for your servants! But..."

"Now what? Have you thought of something better?"

"Impossible, Master—in your wisdom you've thought of everything. I just have one request to share with you."

305

"Speak without fear. I'm too well satisfied with your service to deny you anything."

The boy bowed, with joy written on his pallid face. "Master," he said, lowering his eyes as if frightened by what he was about to ask for, "this morning you told Twinkle and me that we'd earned your favor. Well... Would you like us not just to consider ourselves fully repaid—but even more, to be in your debt again?"

"Keep talking."

"Grant us the pleasure of being the means of communication between you and the Central Exchange."

San looked him up and down in surprise, but the boy went on with total confidence, "We worshiped Log. It would be sweet for us to witness the final agonies of his murderers, to call out to them, 'Those you love are right outside, waiting for you to draw even closer to death before they're handed over to the torturers.' And then we'd come back here and tell them, 'In there they haven't eaten in five days, six days, a week; they're dragging themselves painfully around their prison; they can barely walk; they have to lie down because their legs refuse to support them.'"

The boy's face was transformed: his eyes, his curled lips, suggested horrifying savagery. And, as if the two children shared one mind, one will, Twinkle's face too wore the same look. The prisoners couldn't tear their eyes away from those two faces. Fear tightened their chests: could the art of acting reach such a height of perfection? Were the children playing a role, or—by some sudden about-face—had they genuinely gone over to the enemy?

Merry and Twinkle didn't even glance at the Europeans. Their eyes were on San, pleading with him as hard as they could. He smiled at them affectionately. "Yes, yes—the mosquito alighting on the open wound! Its bite is nothing compared to the pain of torn flesh... and yet it seems more unbearable, more maddening. It'll be exactly as you ask, children. Through my mouth Master Log thanks you for knowing how to hate. You'll begin your duties tonight."

He turned away from his captives and called to the warriors nearby, "Set up the tents. Put the accursed Europeans in one of them and have it guarded." Then he laid his hands on the children's heads. "These two can go anywhere, anytime, without restriction. They're my eyes, my heart!"

CHAPTER XII
The City of the Prayer Engravers

Four people sat in a roomy tent: Max, Mona, Sara, and Violet. A week had passed since the camp was set up on the narrow plateau bounded by the precipice, the gargantuan moat protecting the subterranean stronghold of the Prayer Engravers. For a week, they'd suffered the most harrowing mental agony. Every evening Merry and Twinkle and their panthers came into their tent, and San followed them. Then, for the benefit of San—shaking with awful laughter—and for the benefit of the prisoners, overwhelmed by the horror of their situation, Merry reported on how the day had gone inside the sanctuary.

He described bizarre and terrifying things that sounded like hallucinatory ramblings. One slope of the mountain had turned on some invisible pivot, forming a bridge over the chasm and revealing a dark, narrow opening in the cliff. Then, beyond that entrance, a black tunnel fifty meters long pierced the thickness of the rock wall. Further on, under an overhang, lay a small courtyard open to the sky, onto which looked the irregularly shaped windows of Station A.

Inside Station A itself an enormous instrument panel filled one wall, a blue panel on which stood row upon row of copper levers, colored yellow and red and silver. Next to the panel, drawn on a blackboard, was a diagram—a diagram no one could make out, composed of nothing but blue dots of various shapes and sizes, each labeled with a number. What did it mean? None of the temple guards knew. When the children question them, they answered angrily, "Only Dodekhan knows the hidden meaning of these things. Even Master San doesn't know. He told us to touch none of the levers, because he thinks they might be booby traps for inquisitive visitors, set by the traitor in the Central Exchange."

Ten men had been posted in Station A, to guard the opening to the secret passage that gave access to the interior. At the rear of the little courtyard stood the entrance to the maze of tunnels leading to the sanctuary. "Tunnels" was not exactly the right word: they were streets, intersections, plazas—the metropolis of the *Lad*, the *Mad*, and the *Ghad*, the three great tribes that carved the *Padme Om*, the supreme prayer, on the schist and porphyry and basalt of the enormous range of the Celestial Mountains.

From Station A to the Central Exchange was a kilometer. Twenty sentry posts, each of five to ten warriors, were spread out along the route, making any thought of escape impossible. Merry seemed to wallow in those descriptions; and San considered them dispiriting enough for the prisoners that he let him talk, sometimes even emphasizing what the boy said with some coarse joke.

From an account of the place, Merry moved on to the men. He described the sanctuary, hollowed out of solid granite, with its squat columns, and then the Central Exchange itself, and inside it three captives: two traitors, Dodekhan and the Duke of La Roche-Sonnaille, and one simpleton, Sir John Lobster. He depicted them, hungrier every day, their weakness increasing until they were indifferent to the news San's little messengers brought. And it made the giant laugh to hear the boy cry out in his treble voice, "They know you're here, ladies. They don't act like they're in any hurry to see you. I think if we offered them food they'd eat, even if it meant postponing indefinitely their reunion with you!"

"By Confucius!" gasped San in the throes of hilarity, "Log would've made you his right-hand man, boy! Where'd you learn to talk like that?"

To which Merry replied with great feeling, "I guess I'm inspired by the wish to serve you well, master."

The prisoners certainly grasped that, under the guise of taunting them, the brave children were doing their best to inform them about the terrain they'd have to embark upon some day soon—but that didn't help lessen their discouragement. The subterranean city, the abundance of precautions and guards and sentry posts linked together and backing each other up—all of that made them feel they ought to give up any attempt to help their captive friends.

Ah, those tubes of colored light seemed like paltry weapons now. To be victorious they'd have to strike everywhere at once, and the impossibility of carrying out such a rapid, instantaneous action left them in despair. Every night, alone in their tent, they gave way to dismal thoughts. Their disappointment was all the greater, all the more painful, because they'd all expected an easy victory.

On the seventh day all four of them were in the tent. Night had come, a gloomy, starless night, with an icy wind howling mournfully.

"How they must be suffering from hunger," said Mona almost to herself.

"Alas!" came Sara's plaintive reply.

They were sitting on the ground, side by side, instinctively huddling close together from being long accustomed to shared misery.

Violet stood at the tent opening, through which could be seen the campfires of San's warriors. She turned suddenly. "Have courage."

"Courage!" echoed Sara in a heartrending voice. "I've got none left. In a little while Merry will come, like every evening. Maybe this time they'll decide the men beneath those accursed boulders have suffered enough—and they'll take us to them." She wrung her hands. "Ah, our luminous tubes will at least save us from torture... but them? They'll die just like we will. Death is our last hope! Why do we have to wait so long for it?"

"Yes, why?" sighed Mona, throwing her arms around the neck of her partner in martyrdom.

It was Max who answered. Since that morning he'd presumably been caught up in an absorbing train of thought, because all day he'd seemed distant from his companions' concerns. Though he usually exhorted them, encouraged them, did his best to inspire them with a little of the carefree courage typical of him... today he'd remained quiet. It took the young women's despairing question to pull him out of his thoughts. To their great amazement, after first making sure no spies were prowling around outside the tent, he said, "Are you sure they're as hungry as all that?"

Sara, Mona, and even Violet studied him with concern. Had he by chance gone mad? What could his absurd question mean? If they were counting right, Dodekhan and Lucien had been without food for eleven days. Eleven days of total starvation. It seemed almost cruel to question the awfulness of their suffering.

But Max went on calmly, "I haven't made myself clear. I just wanted to say, I'm not at all sure they've been deprived of food as completely as San thinks."

Mona straightened up. "What makes you think that?"

Max went on slowly, "We've been camped for a week at this horrible spot. And for a week, Merry and his inseparable Twinkle and their panthers have vanished at dawn and not returned until evening. Meaning that every day our former guides spend twelve to fourteen hours in the subterranean city of the Prayer Engravers."

"All right, but what do you conclude from that?"

"Wait, let's not move too fast. They spend twelve hours away. But when they get back, what they report doing—to the loud delight of our thickheaded jailer—would fill at most two of those twelve hours. A kilometer of tunnels on the way there... call that ten or twenty minutes... and the same on the way back. That leaves an hour and twenty minutes to look at and taunt the prisoners. That's enough, isn't it? The clever little fellow can bring us up to date in a quarter of an hour. No doubt he does the same to Messrs Dodekhan and Lucien."

"Of course, of course," agreed his listeners, drawn in by the unexpected way Max was presenting the problem.

"Well, my friends, did you never wonder how those two excellent little devils—who are neither dumb, nor blundering, nor lazy—spend the other ten hours?"

"And what do you imagine?"

After a broad, vague gesture, Max leaned toward them and murmured, "I don't imagine, I reason; and I believe I've figured it out. Think back: last night, when Merry came back and described the prostration of the captives in the temple, when he warned us that the end of the drama was coming... didn't you notice his shining eyes and exaggerated gestures?"

"Yes, yes, indeed."

"It was as if his entire frail being was trying to tell us what San's presence kept him from saying aloud. I took his performance to mean, 'The final battle is about to begin—be ready.'"

They all nodded in agreement.

"And when San took them back outside, remember: little Twinkle turned around and rubbed her hands together—the universal sign for 'all's well.' And that gesture wasn't addressed to San, since she was behind him and he couldn't see her. It was addressed only to us. What could that mean—all's well—unless it meant, 'Keep your eyes open, and be ready to take advantage of any opportunity that arises.'"

"It's true, it's true!" they all cried.

"But what could they have planned?" wondered Sara.

"Don't ask me for answers I don't have," Max answered cheerfully. "Instead, focus your attention on the least details, and above all rest assured that our valiant little guides, those matchless actors—as you've witnessed—haven't been wasting their time."

Holding up his hand for silence, he hurried to the tent opening. Then he returned, saying, "San's coming this way. They're with him. We're reaching the moment of truth. Be careful and alert."

He'd barely finished when the massive form of the Prayer Engraver appeared at the tent opening. "No lights?" he grumbled.

"The darkness is the color of our thoughts," replied Max quickly. "It's precious to us."

"Well! A little light won't hurt anything. I want to see written on your faces the joy you'll feel at the interesting news I bring."

San whistled softly. Almost immediately a warrior appeared, carrying a heavy iron candlestick that held one of those torches made of brown wax that are the primitive homemade candles of China. The smoky reddish flames threw a flickering light on their faces.

"All right," said San. "Now, let's talk." With ironic kindliness he went on, "I'm quite sure this long stay in a rather dull spot must bore you. You'll be happy to hear that it ends tonight."

They all shivered. Each of the young women could still hear Max saying, "We're reaching the moment of truth. Be careful and alert."

San noticed their excitement without understanding its cause. He cackled. "At midnight you'll enter the subterranean metropolis. When the sun come up over the horizon, you'll be dead."

For several seconds he let his eyes rest on his prisoners. Perhaps he hoped for some sign of fear, some cry for mercy. But none of them moved. With a discontented gesture he left, pushing Merry and Twinkle—who'd stood still, as if frozen, by his side—out ahead of him.

The prisoners were alone again. The crude wax candle illuminated them. They looked at each other as if they were waking from a dream. San's sudden appearance, following so closely on the explanation of Max's deductions, made them feel like they were inside a fairy tale. For a week they'd been living a recurring nightmare, until they'd entered a state of mental fog that felt like they were in a dream, where real action had no place. And now suddenly, without preparation, the time for action rose urgent and inexorable before them. They were going to have to act. In what way? On what signal? They had the dismaying certainty that one false move would doom them without recourse.

"Bah!" said Violet finally, addressing their common concern. "You chart your course as well as you can, and then you hope it'll be enough."

"That's fatalism!" protested Sara.

"Oh, my poor dear friend," said Violet in her softest voice. "I offer what I have on me. If I had more, you can be sure I'd contribute it."

"And you're right, Violet. With the logic of your pure heart, you've expressed the wisdom of humanity: do the best you can, and let events have the last word."

Any resolve, no matter how vague, is beneficial: the prisoners felt comforted. Yes, at the critical juncture they'd now reached, they'd act for the best, with the hope of being helped by... the unknown forces that guide or stymie the plans of men.

For starters, they readied their weapons. The violet and indigo tubes they'd kept carefully hidden were now placed in combat position—namely, slid up their sleeves. That way they'd only have to extend their arms, press one finger on the button that switched on the light, and aim the beam at the enemies barring their path.

But now the camp was stirring: the warriors were gathering the yaks and taking down the tents. They had to dress, and put on their furs. They'd barely done so when several warriors arrived to take down their felt tent.

The prisoners went out, with Max in the lead. Already nothing was left of the camp. The yaks were loaded up, and San's escort—as always, including the two children and their panthers—was gathered around him. In another five minutes the captives' tent had been loaded onto the yaks assigned to carry it.

San must've been waiting for this moment, because now he approached the prisoners. "All four of you will walk behind me," he said harshly. "My young servants and their animals will keep you in line."

Merry, Twinkle, and the two great cats surrounded the little group, and they all set off behind San. The warriors, with the yaks, brought up the rear. The Prayer Engraver led the way along the edge of the precipice until he was blocked by the rock wall that enclosed the plateau in its triangular ramparts. There, stopping and facing the abyss, he picked up a few stones and tossed them one by one, at irregular intervals, into the chasm. No sound returned to suggest the stones had reached the bottom—and yet the garrison of the underground metropolis certainly understood the signal, because a strange, unbelievable phenomenon stunned the prisoners: the cliff across the precipice seemed to come to life. One rock face pivoted on an enormous hinge, extending its mass across the yawning chasm like a swing drawbridge—at the far end of which a dark opening now appeared, as if suddenly carved out of the granite wall.

San pointed to it, and started across the bridge. Max followed him bravely, and behind him came the ladies, and then the children and the animals. The travelers had suspended thought: they didn't want to reflect on the dark abyss into which one step to the right or the left would've plunged them. They moved forward, in some sense pulled along by fate, in the vigorous words of the great Persian poet Rumi.

They'd crossed the bridge. They all followed San into the tunnel Merry had described before, which ran from the secret entrance through the cliff to the courtyard outside Station A.

But no sooner had they started down it than something happened—something terrible, astounding, unexpected. A click rang out inside the mountain, followed by a metallic hum, like the sound of anchor chains running out on a man-o-war. Shouts of fear greeted those noises. San and the prisoners and the children all stood still, shivering. They looked back, and—just before the opening by which they'd entered the tunnel closed once again—they saw the stone bridge tipping toward the abyss, into which it spilled all the warriors and all the yaks that were then crossing it.

With a dull roar, San tried to turn back. Impossible: a block of granite, presumably the counterweight to the bridge, had risen and sealed off the opening with an impassable rampart.[42] He tried in vain to push the barrier aside; he did nothing but scrape his hands. His great strength was worth no more here than that of a weak child. You can't move part of a mountain. Ominously, filled with sudden anxiety, still shaking at the agonized cry of the men thrown into the abyss, he stammered, "What is this? With my bare hands I'll tear apart whoever did this!"

Merry murmured, "Maybe it was a mistake by the guards at Station A. Maybe they didn't understand your signal to open up."

They set off again. Soon they were out of the tunnel, in the open-air courtyard whose irregular walls conformed to the shape of Station A.

"Hey in there!" called San as loud as he could. His cry rang out, reverberating in ever-diminishing echoes, and was followed by a dismal silence. He wiped a hand across his brow.

"They got scared after their blunder," suggested Merry. "They're probably hiding in the tunnels."

San looked at the boy gratefully for doing his best to ease his rising anxiety. And anyway, that might be the right explanation. San knew he wasn't gentle

---

[42] That isn't an architectural whimsy, like the ones from the *Thousand and One Nights*. It's just possible that those storytellers were remembering traditions passed down orally, reporting secrets learned by travelers who'd met the Prayer Engravers. In their never-ending struggle against the roc, those tribes achieved marvels. The theory of equilibrium and counterweights was well known to them. And here also we could cite a mountain on the edge of the Gobi Desert, Kung Chu, elevation nine hundred meters, which pivots on its base at the push of a man's hand—as a result of underground work by those tireless diggers in granite known as the Prayer Engravers [*Note from the Author*].

when he was angry. The guards at Station A had been afraid of the sharp leading edge of his rage.

He went into the station. No one! Merry had been right—they'd all fled before him. And at the idea that he could inspire such terror, he broke into an arrogant smile. After all, what did the dead men matter, what did the runaway cowards matter? Wasn't he going to reward Log's restless spirit with complete revenge? That thought alone was worth hanging onto.

Behind him stood the prisoners, eyeing the instrument panel on the wall, with its yellow and red and silver-colored copper levers, and the strange diagram next to it, with its blue dots and mysterious numbers. The silence weighed on them, smothered them. Something inexplicable was happening: they'd sworn to act, and yet their plan seemed so paltry, so unnecessary—compared to the work of men who fought using sections of a mountain—that now they felt something like a paralysis of willpower. They were Lilliputians lost in a world of Titans.

They moved aside to let San pass. Not waiting for his invitation, they followed him toward the dark opening that led into the maze of streets of the subterranean metropolis. San pulled on a bronze handle, and electric lights came on, illuminating the tunnel entrance. They followed the tunnel, and reached a crossroads.

"There was a sentry post here," said San in a dull voice.

"Yes," agreed Merry, his expression unreadable. "There used to be ten men stationed at this intersection."

"Where are they? Where are they?" roared San, his features tense with anxiety.

He kept going, through tunnel after tunnel. Lateral galleries ran deep into the mountain. At every junction, the children stopped and called in their shrill voices. But no human voice replied—just the echoes, like cackling. He began to panic. He walked faster and faster, no longer stopping at the places where he should've found warriors, and where now there were none. He ordered Merry and Twinkle to stop calling: in those silent tunnels their cries filled him with superstitious fear. It was no longer the city of the Prayer Engravers he was passing through—it was a necropolis.

"Ah, at last! The temple!" he cried, unaware that he was expressing his thoughts aloud. Yes, it was the sanctuary with its squat columns and its marble altar on which appeared the image of no god—because the features of the god of the *Lad*, the *Mad*, and the *Ghad* couldn't be traced, nor could its name be engraved. Just like Station A and the tunnels and the crossroads, the temple was empty. The inexplicable disappearance of two hundred warriors—who'd been warned that the Master would arrive that night, bringing captives to torture—was enough to drive San mad.

Merry went to the arched opening leading to the Central Exchange. Before San had time to call out to warn him about the terrible electric barrier—whose effects he himself had suffered earlier—the boy walked through without any trouble. What? Was the current no longer on? San hurried over, crossed the threshold... and stood there stunned, floored: the Central Exchange was empty, the prisoners were gone.

Now he was filled with wild fury. He'd been betrayed! Only treason could've emptied out the subterranean city! Dodekhan was free! The duke was free! Well, at least they wouldn't rejoice in their triumph! They'd weep tears of blood. He'd make corpses of those women, their beloved!

San pulled his revolver from his belt and aimed at Mona—but the girl stretched out her arm, and a beam of violet light seemed to flow from her slender fingers. San stopped as if he were rooted to the ground. He reached instinctively for his forehead, where a red dot, like a burn mark, had appeared. He gave a muffled cry, then fell to the ground with the thud of dead flesh.

And as they all stood there watching, amazed at this unexpected turn of events, a voice that made them shiver uncontrollably rang out under the vault of the temple. "Mona! Mona! Dear Mona, thank you for saving Asia!"

And now Dodekhan and Lucien were standing there.

Two hoarse, barely human cries filled the air. Sara had thrown herself into her husband's arms, while Mona was held up by those of Dodekhan, and for several minutes they wept the wonderful tears of love finally victorious.

"Lucien! We'll go straight back to France—no more travels. I never want to leave the Paris city limits again!"

"My darling Sara, your wish is mine."

And Mona, blushing, her face pressed to Dodekhan's shoulder, murmured, "Now will you agree to join my life to yours?"

He gazed at her tenderly, and his eyes expressed both transcendent joy and unspeakable sadness. "My life will be peaceful, Mona. The spirit of Asia is not yet ready to make my dream a reality. We have to wait. Perhaps our descendants will see that happy day."

Then he pushed Merry and Twinkle into the young women's arms. "From now on these children must have a family. During the past week they destroyed the sentry posts guarding us, one by one. The fallen warriors were thrown into the abyss."

"But who manipulated the bridge earlier?" asked Max, as curious as ever.

"We did," said Lucien. "We were hidden inside Station A, where San couldn't see us, and we followed you here at a distance."

"Well then," murmured Violet with a glance at Max, "we've helped bring about everybody's happiness... but we've destroyed our own."

Dodekhan left Mona's side to go to Violet. "You're mistaken, miss. We've thought to make you as happy as you deserve. Follow me."

They all followed Dodekhan back up the same way they'd recently come down. When they reached Station A, they were greeted by a bizarre spectacle: Sir John Lobster, carefully bound, lay on a mat stretched between four iron posts. From each of those posts a copper wire ran toward the big blue instrument panel, where it was wound around one of the levers.

"Sir John," said the duke soberly, "You will release Miss Musketeer from the promise of marriage that you extracted from her by force."

"Oh, then I'd be giving way to force as well."

"If you wish. But in your place I'd prefer to think I was giving way to reason. If you refuse, of course, I'll flip the levers you see over there on the instrument panel, and the current will run through the wires leading to your cot and electrocute you like any ordinary American convict."

"There's no need for that," whimpered the fat man. "I prefer bachelorhood." Then, red-faced, furious, beaten, he added, "Miss Musketeer, I release you from your promise. You are no longer engaged to me."

Max had already seized her delicate—and now free—hands and was squeezing them in his, where they seemed happy to be.

But now Dodekhan spoke again, and his sad and serious voice drew the attention of all of them. "Friends, my father and I wished too soon for the emancipation of Asia. Time alone will give the continent some understanding of liberty. I want the scientific marvels gathered together here by Dilevnor to pass intact to whichever of our descendants will have the honor to lead Asia to freedom. This temple and this underground chamber will be inaccessible from now on. The tunnels that lead here will vanish, destroyed by explosives laid long ago. Only my fiancée Mona and I will know how the chosen one will be able to enter the metropolis of the Prayer Engravers. The secret will be passed on, from generation to generation, to the eldest of the descendants of Dilevnor."

While Dodekhan was speaking, Lucien had untied Sir John, who shook himself off with all the grace of a duck climbing out of water. Dodekhan went to the blue instrument panel. His index finger touched each of the points marked on the nearby diagram, and then his hands ran across the row of levers, stopping in a predetermined order on the copper and silver handles.

Suddenly the earth seemed to shiver. Rumbling filled the air, the mountain shook to its very base, and the booming went on, getting fainter as it grew more distant, ending finally in oppressive silence. Then Dodekhan wiped away a tear that hung from his eyelashes. To his friends he looked pale and stooped under the weight of a destiny more powerful than human will. In a shaking voice he said, "The secret entrance to the temple no longer exists. May the genius of Dilevnor's science sleep here until the coming of the one chosen to regenerate Asia."

Five days later, General Stanislas Labianov watched as his daughter and her friends entered his staff headquarters. They all looked exhausted. Dodekhan had led them out through the temple tunnels. There they'd begun an almost unbelievable journey—the memory of which made their heads spin—with rock walls opening at the release of mysterious springs to let them through, then closing again behind them. Finally they'd emerged in a ravine, but without being able to see how they'd gotten out. Four more days of walking, full of detours and obstacles of all sorts, had brought them to the Anglo-Russian camp.

To all of Labianov's and Lord Aberdeen's questions, the Master of the Blue Flag replied only, "It's beyond anyone's power to find the hideout of the bandits you're after. In any case, as of now they've been wiped out. The few survivors are scattered, and even they wouldn't know how to find their way back to their headquarters."

"Oh!" cried Mona's father, "believe me, as far as I'm concerned, I ask for nothing more. But I'm afraid my government may be more inquisitive, and may inflict on you an involuntary stay in some Russian city."

Smiling at Mona, Dodekhan answered, "My heart is already a captive in Russia."

No doubt to give the young woman a chance to blush unnoticed, the Duke of La Roche-Sonnaille said cheerfully, "By the way, Sir John, you've complained on several occasions of having been compelled by force to renounce Miss Violet's hand."

"Yes—and I'll go on complaining."

"Did that wound you so deeply?"

"Indeed! I consider force to be a tactic resorted to by people of low intelligence."

"In that case," said Lucien impassively, "you should know that we just used our wits. There was no current at Station A capable of electrocuting you."

And that triggered a collective burst of laughter.

SOME OTHER FRENCH SCIENCE FICTION
& ROMAN SCIENTIFIQUE TITLES
AVAILABLE FROM BLACK COAT PRESS

1834 - Félix Bodin - *The Novel of the Future*
1856 - Alfred Driou - *The Adventures Of A Parisian Aeronaut In The Unknown Worlds*
1865 - Hippolyte Mettais - *The Year 5865*
1865 - Achille Eyraud - *Voyage to Venus*
1869 – Dr. Tony Moilin - *Paris in the Year 2000*
1878 - Georges Pellerin - *The World In 2000 Years*
1879 - Albert Robida - *The Adventures of Saturnin Farandoul*
1880 - Alphonse Brown - *The Conquerors of the Air*
1883 - Didier de Chousy - *Ignis*
1884 - Emile Calvet - *In A Thousand Years*
1886 - Louise Michel - *The Human Microbes; The New World*
1888 - Louis Boussenard - *Mr. Synthesis*
1888 - Georges Le Faure & Henri de Graffigny - *The Extraordinay Adventures of a Russian Scientist* (2 volumes)
1890 - Alain Le Drimeur - *The Future City*
1891 - Alphonse Brown - *City Of Glass*
1892 - Albert Robida - *Electric Life*
1892 - Jules Lermina - *The Battle of Strasbourg*
1900 - Gustave Le Rouge & Gustave Guitton - *The Dominion of the World* (4 volumes)
1905 - Jules Lermina - *Mysteryville*
1906 - Arnould Galopin - *Doctor Omega*
1907 - Charles Derennes - *The People of the Pole*
1908 - Henri Gayar - *The Wondrous Adventures Of Serge Myrandhal On The Planet Mars*
1908 - Jean de La Hire - *The Fiery Wheel*
1908 - Gustave Le Rouge - *The Vampires of Mars*
1908 - Maurice Renard - *A Man Among the Microbes*
1909 - André Couvreur - *The Exploits of Professor Tornada* (3 volumes)
1910 - Jules Lermina - *Panic in Paris*
1910 - Jules Perrin & Henri Lanos - *The World Above the World*
1911 - Jean de La Hire - *The Nyctalope on Mars*
1911 - Maurice Renard - *The Blue Peril*
1911 - Jean Richepin - *The Wing*
1913 - André Mas - *The Germans on Venus*

1913 - J.H. Rosny Aîné - *The Mysterious Force*
1921 - Maurice Renard - *The Doctored Man*
1922 - Henri Allorge - *The Great Cataclysm*
1922 - Henri Falk -*The Age of Lead*
1922 - Octave Joncquel & Théo Varlet - *The Martian Epic*
1923 - Théo Varlet - *Timeslip Troopers*
1925 - José Moselli - *The End of Illa*
1925 - Ernest Pérochon - *The Frenetic People*
1925 - Albert Robida - *Chalet in the Sky*
1925- J.H. Rosny Aîné - *The Navigatorsd of Space*
1926 - Jean Petithuguenin - *An International Mission on the Moon*
1927 - Henri Allorge - *The Great Cataclysm*
1928 - Guy d'Armen – *Doc Ardan: The City of Gold and Lepers*
1929 - Paul Féval, Fils - *Felifax*
1929 - Han Ryner - *Les Surhommes*
1930 - Eugène Thébault -*Radio Terror*
1930 - Théo Varlet - *The Xenobiotic Invasion*
1931 - Michel Coudray - *The Eternal Flame*